D0426985

The House on Honeysuckle Lane

Books by Mary McDonough

LESSONS FROM THE MOUNTAIN: *What I Learned from Erin Walton*

ONE YEAR

THE HOUSE ON HONEYSUCKLE LANE

Published by Kensington Publishing Corporation

The House on Honeysuckle Lane

Mary McDonough

KENSINGTON BOOKS
http://www.kensingtonbooks.com

KENSINGTON BOOKS are published by

Kensington Publishing Corp.
119 West 40th Street
New York, NY 10018

All Kensington titles, imprints and distributed lines are available at special quantity discounts for bulk purchases for sales promotion, premiums, fund-raising, educational or institutional use.

Special book excerpts or customized printings can also be created to fit specific needs. For details, write or phone the office of the Kensington Special Sales Manager: Kensington Publishing Corp., 119 West 40th Street, New York, NY, 10018, Attn. Special Sales Department. Phone: 1-800-221-2647.

Library of Congress Card Catalogue Number: 2016945052

ISBN-13: 978-0-7582-9351-0
ISBN-10: 0-7582-9351-8
First Kensington Hardcover Edition: October 2016

eISBN-13: 978-0-7582-9352-7
eISBN-10: 0-7582-9352-6
First Kensington Electronic Edition: October 2016

10 9 8 7 6 5 4 3 2 1

Printed in the United States of America

To all the "Orphans" out there.

Introduction

My mother used to say a person was an "orphan" when they lost the second of their two parents, no matter how old the person was. I have been an orphan for a while now. I lost my father when I was sixteen, my mother twenty-seven years later.

Maybe because of this, I have "adopted" siblings and families over the years. I often say that family is really what you make it. Bloodlines may make us feel related, but it's truly love, compassion and sometimes tears that bring us together. Tears of laughter, tears of joy.

I have been lucky to have many "families." My McDonough and Walton families molded me into who I am. My adopted families have made a huge difference in my life.

Losing one's parents is never easy. Going through their possessions can be daunting. What they leave behind isn't just *their* things. I found the mementos of other deceased family members when I sorted through what my parents left behind. Each one's life was reduced to a mere suitcase or trunk. How can a life fit in a suitcase? Sorting through the remnants of what my parents left behind was illuminating, frustrating, horribly sad, difficult and oddly uplifting. One can truly honor and contemplate someone's life by examining what they leave behind. It forced me to ponder for my own life; what is important, what are my own attachments and the meaning of the items I'll leave behind.

So what does it all mean? How do we ever let go of our loved ones? I don't know if we ever do. I know I haven't. They are with me forever like scars on my heart. They remind me of who I am and encourage me to create my own legacy... one that isn't summed up in a box of old check stubs, old glasses, a watch, cards, drawings, mildewed bibles, photos with no names, love letters and farm notes.

The House on Honeysuckle Lane is for anyone who has had to go through a parent or loved one's *life*. It's about attachment. The "stuff," traditions, people, beliefs, and the objects we get attached to. It's about what we hold on to, and, what we let go of. It's understanding the connection between material things and important memories. Family is made up as much of memories, love, compassion and choices as it is DNA. Sometimes, through loss, we find the greatest treasures inside our memories.

Acknowledgments

Thanks to my parents. From beginning to end, all roads lead back to you. So much gratitude for my brothers; we have been in this together. My appreciation of you grew as we traveled through our own attachments. I am forever attached to you, from this life to the next.

My related family who make my life complete: John, Michael, Sydnee, Aunt Ellen, Jackson and Christopher and all my cousins, Irish and American!

More thanks than I can ever say to the insightful John Scognamiglio. You make it all possible. Thanks for listening and giving my stories a voice and life. Your guidance, help, care and trust in me are appreciated more than I can say.

To Kevin for your support and encouragement in everything! To Elise for always understanding me, family and the importance of sharing thoughts and words. You GET it! My Maria, my wordsmith queen, I adore you! To my personal Buddhas Jeanne Russell and Pete Lee, whose practices inspire me. Thanks for reminding me who I am. To my writing sisters, Jane Porter and Mary Alice Monroe, thanks for the inspiration and for taking me under your wing. To my girls, Kylie and Robyn, thanks for choosing me to be your family.

Hugs of thanks to all my chosen "family": Kate, Caren, June, Kari, Mary G, Mo, Ann, Tom, Mellie, Sylvane, Dave, Karen, Pam, Earl, Jane, Claire, Rod, Will, Ellen, Leslie, Eric, Cindy, Jon, Marion, Judy, Bob, Kami, Kim, David, Richard, Georgie, Ralph, Michael, John, Mama Marlene, Papa Kruger, Sister Shatto, Jake, Ray, Tim, Carol, Don, Bethie and Nancy.

To my Reynolds family, my childhood siblings, parents and grandparents. To Granny and Gramps and Mary Beth, you taught me what a big, sharing family is. To all the Walton fans and my online Facebook family, your support is so appreciated!

To my Don, without you, there is no sunrise. I am forever grateful for your encouragement and loving me through each step I take. My books would not be possible without you. You amaze me daily with your care and love of me and our family. You are my hero.

A family is a place where minds come in contact with one another. If these minds love one another the home will be as beautiful as a flower garden.

The Buddha

PROLOGUE

It was a beautiful day in late October; the sky was a brilliant blue and there was a slightly spicy smell of wood smoke in the clear, cool air. It was the perfect day for a funeral—if there ever was such a thing—and Daniel Reynolds was weary after the emotional service to say farewell to his mother.

The turnout at the Unitarian Universalist Church had been large, so large that at least ten or fifteen people had been forced to stand for the duration of the service. Caroline Reynolds had been a popular resident of Oliver's Well, Virginia, since she had moved to the little town over forty years ago with her new husband, Clifford. His funeral, only a few years earlier, had also been well attended. Cliff had grown up in Oliver's Well and had returned after college to build a successful accounting and tax preparation practice. He had been highly regarded as an utterly trustworthy man, discrete, dedicated, and loyal to his clients. That both of the senior members of the Reynolds family had passed at such a young age—each still in their sixties—was seen as a tragedy in the town's close-knit community.

In spite of the healthy turnout at Caro's funeral, the Reynolds siblings had invited only a few close friends to the luncheon afterward at the Angry Squire, Oliver's Well's most popular restaurant. Daniel, the youngest child and the only son, as well as the only one of the Reynolds siblings to have made a life in Oliver's Well after completing his education, had compiled the guest list. In fact, he had organized the funeral as well, working with Reverend Fox to create a personalized service for each of his parents. This dedication was nothing unusual; ever since Cliff Reynolds's passing, Daniel had acted as his mother's caretaker and as the official trustee of his parents' estate.

Daniel, too, felt that his parents' deaths warranted the description of tragedy. When he had chosen the menu for the luncheon, he had taken care to select what had been his father's favorite entrée and his mother's favorite wine as a small tribute to them. He had wondered if either of his sisters, Andie or Emma, would recognize the significance of the London broil and the French Chablis; neither had commented, so Daniel had sadly concluded that the significance of his selections were lost on all but himself.

Joe Herbert, once Cliff's protégé and then his successor in the firm of Reynolds and Herbert, and his wife, Jenna, a doctor with a thriving practice in family medicine, were two of the last to leave the restaurant. Joe shook Daniel's hand. "I'll call you tomorrow," he said, "to discuss those questions you had about the estate." Jenna kissed Daniel on the cheek and wished him well. "Let me know if there's anything I can do," she offered. "If you and Anna Maria need a night out on your own I can bring your kids to my house for a few hours. My kids would love it." Daniel thanked her and, not for the first time, felt grateful for the Herberts' friendship.

The very last to leave the Angry Squire was Maureen Kline, Emma's friend from childhood. Maureen, too, offered a final word of condolence to Daniel, then shook his hand and went on her way.

When Maureen was gone and only the family remained, Daniel realized that he felt a profound sense of let down. It was over, his mother's life, and with it, an entire chapter of the Reynolds family's history; with both parents gone, Cliff and now Caro, it was time for what remained of the family to move on with the rest of their lives. Watching his sisters talking quietly with his wife and their two children, seeing Bob Dolman, Andie's ex-husband, with his arm around their daughter, Rumi, Daniel felt the poignancy of the moment. The surviving family was poised on the brink between the past and the future. It was said by men far wiser than Daniel that the threshold was the place where one should pause. And then, the wise men said, one should continue on.

Problem was, Daniel wasn't quite sure how continuing on was going to play out. He wanted the family to thrive as a strong unit. And he believed that he was the one to make a future happen for the Reynoldses. But as for a plan . . .

Ian Hayes, Emma's long-time boyfriend, came back into the dining room; he had gone to bring his car around from the municipal lot. Now, Emma, Ian, and Andie came over to where Daniel stood on his own, hands in the pockets of his suit pants.

"Ian and I are heading back to Annapolis now, Danny," Emma said, her eyes still a little red from crying.

"And I'm off to the airport," Andie told him in her famously melodious voice.

Daniel nodded. "All right," he said. "But don't forget, there's the contents of the house to go through and a decision about what if anything to sell outright or put up for auction. And we'll need to sell the house itself before long. It shouldn't be left standing empty. And Mom wanted us all here together to make those decisions."

"I've got commitments through July," Andie said. "My publisher has arranged a series of readings from New York to California. I should be free to make a plan when the book tour is done." She reached for and hugged her brother; he took his hands from his pockets and briefly patted her back.

"Six months is too—" he began, but his sister cut him off.

"Don't worry, Danny," Andie said quietly but firmly. "There's no real rush, is there? And thanks for handling everything so beautifully."

"Thank you, Danny," Emma said, reaching out to take his hands in hers. "You did a great job with everything. Mom would have been proud. So would Dad."

Ian put out his hand for Daniel to shake. "Keep in touch,

Danny," he said. And then, taking Emma's hand, they left for their life back in Annapolis, Andie following a few steps behind on the first leg of her journey back to her home in upstate New York.

Daniel watched his sisters leave the Angry Squire, once the scene of so many pleasant evenings with their parents, the whole family gathered together to share a meal and conversation and laughter. Suddenly, Daniel felt a surge of frustration rise up in him. Getting Andie and Emma back to Oliver's Well any time soon to sort through the house and make the important decisions together as a family, as their mother had wanted, would not be easy. And of course, it would be up to him to orchestrate the visit, not only because he was the trustee of their mother's estate but also because over the years he had become—for better or worse he sometimes didn't know—the acknowledged head of the family.

Daniel's wife, Anna Maria, joined him and slipped her arm through his. He noted the simple gold wedding band on her slim finger and felt enormously thankful she had agreed to marry him thirteen years earlier.

"You okay?" she asked.

Daniel put his hand over hers. "I'm fine. I was just wondering when we'll see my sisters again."

Anna Maria smiled reassuringly. "Don't worry about that now. It's been a long day for everyone, especially the kids. Sophia is a little bit weepy again, and Marco is falling asleep on his feet. Let's go home."

"Yes," Daniel said, suddenly feeling as exhausted as his son. "Home."

CHAPTER 1

It was an easy drive from Emma's home in Annapolis to Oliver's Well. Emma enjoyed driving and took meticulous care of her car, a 2015 Lexus RX 350 in deep sea mica with a light gray interior. It had only recently been to the mechanic for a checkup; Ollie had been servicing Emma's cars for close to eight years and swore that not one of his clients had ever taken better care of her vehicle.

Emma Reynolds had turned forty-two in April. Her once bright blond hair had darkened in the past few years, and now there were natural streaks of white and silver threaded throughout. She glanced in the mirror over the dashboard and smiled. Her hair stylist had told her that plenty of women paid for the effect that in Emma's case had taken place all on its own.

Emma suppressed a yawn and sat up straighter. It wouldn't do to fall asleep behind the wheel. Still, she thought, opening her window and the moon roof to let the fresh late December air flow through the car, a nap once she arrived at number 32 Honeysuckle Lane would probably be a good idea. She had been at the office until ten the night before, and two nights before that she had been at her desk until almost midnight. Emma was proud of her career as a personal financial advisor and money manager, but time had stripped the bloom off the rose and there were days when she found it a serious chore to get out of bed, shower and dress, and leave her condo on Franklin Street, knowing what was in store for her once she got to her office near the corner of West Street and Church Circle.

A quick glance at her iPhone in its charger revealed that Ian had sent her a text. It would have to wait. For one, she didn't make it a habit of using her phone while driving. For another, Ian Hayes was no longer a priority. Just the day before, she had finally ended their relationship. It had not gone well. She had gotten the feeling that Ian hadn't really *heard* her. He hadn't shown any anger or even puzzlement; he hadn't tried to argue her out of her decision. Instead, he had been remarkably calm and collected. She had seen that behavior countless times before, his escaping (that's how Emma saw it) into a deeply reasonable state of mind, almost emotionless but not cold.

With some effort Emma shook off the uncomfortable memory. She had more important and immediate things to think about, like what was waiting for her in Oliver's Well. She felt slightly apprehensive about this gathering of siblings. She didn't foresee any arguing over the sale or distribution of what was left of their parents' estate; none of the siblings badly needed money. But Daniel had been so adamant about their all being together for this Christmas, as if their coming together was of life or death importance. Maybe that was overdoing it a bit. Still, her brother had made it clear he would not be happy taking no for an answer.

Not that Emma would have said no. She loved her brother and his family and hadn't seen them since Rumi's birthday back in June. And she hadn't seen Andie since Caro's funeral fourteen months ago; Andie had been on an extended book signing tour at the time of Rumi's celebration. Emma and her sister kept in touch as best they could. Though Andie had a presence online, it was for her professional self, not for sharing intimacies with her younger sister. And Andie frequently traveled to places where cell phone service was spotty or simply not available. Besides, the last thing Emma wanted was to interrupt a visit to an ashram for study and meditation with relatively trivial concerns like the latest antics of the annoying president of her condo board.

If Emma remembered correctly she would soon be passing Holinshed Nursery; it was where her mother had bought most of her garden supplies through the years. Caro had kept a lovely garden, and Emma knew that Daniel had been doing his best to care for it since her passing, though he hadn't much time to spare for watering, pruning, and planting.

Time. Emma found it hard to believe that her mother had been gone for over a year. Last Thanksgiving she and Ian had stayed in Annapolis rather than travel to Oliver's Well; they had been back only the month before to attend Caro's funeral. And Christmas, too, they had spent at home, and while Emma sipped a classic whiskey sour and nibbled on spicy roasted almonds, she had given barely a thought to either of her parents. Thinking back on those two holidays, Emma realized the fact that her mother was no longer in this world hadn't entirely registered with her until now. Now, in these final weeks before the second Christmas since Caro's death, Emma felt her mother's absence keenly. That they hadn't been close for years didn't diminish the fact that they had been mother and daughter, and that primary relationship could never be ignored.

It was odd, Emma thought, how something small or mundane could trigger a wave of strong emotion and nostalgia. Just the other day she had been walking along a street close to her home, and the sight of a Christmas wreath decorated with a velvety blue ribbon on a storefront had literally stopped her in her tracks. Her mother had decorated her Christmas wreaths with the same velvety blue ribbon. It was a moment before Emma could move on, tears in her eyes.

While Andie was probably expertly handling her mourning—she had the skills and the training to do so—Emma wasn't quite so sure about Daniel. If his adamant invitation that his sisters gather for Christmas was any indication of his emotional state, he might still be feeling pretty raw. In fact, when she had last seen Daniel, at Rumi's twentieth birthday celebration at the Angry

Squire, he had seemed tense. Even Ian had noticed the change. Ian had gone to the party with Emma, of course. He had always enjoyed visiting the Reynoldses in Oliver's Well, and they had always enjoyed being with him.

Emma closed her window and wondered how her brother and his wife would take the news of the demise of her relationship. Anna Maria would be supportive, and while Daniel wouldn't want to see his sister stick around in an unfulfilling relationship, he could be awfully . . . What was the word? Old-fashioned? Whatever the word, the fact was that Daniel had married his first and only love and sometimes seemed to have difficulty understanding that not everyone was quite so lucky.

And Andie? Well, she would respond with her native gifts of sympathy and empathy. Emma deeply admired her sister; she believed that Andie deserved what success she had achieved as a writer and speaker, not that fame or money mattered to Andie Reynolds. She had always been of a self-effacing and generous nature, even as a child. Emma remembered Andie routinely giving half her lunch money to a boy whose family was known to be struggling, and she never failed to rush to the aid of an older person having trouble reaching a can from a high shelf in the grocery store or to open doors for mothers juggling a stroller laden with diaper bags, plush toys, and an antsy toddler. Emma smiled to herself. Her sister simply couldn't help helping people.

Happily, Emma saw some of that generous nature in Andie's daughter, Rumi, who from the first had been very loving with her younger cousins. Sophia was a sweetheart; at twelve she was already taller than her mother. Marco, a charmer and now ten, looked to have inherited his mother's small stature, but you never knew what changes adolescence might bring.

Emma smiled. There, up ahead, just past Holinshed Nursery, was the town line. Oliver's Well at last. Emma needed a big dose of small town charm after the year she'd had; she had been too swamped with work even to take a brief vacation. And the breakup with Ian, and before that, the long and difficult process of coming to terms with the fact that the break had to be made had taken its toll.

Instead of going directly to the house on Honeysuckle Lane, Emma decided to make a detour and visit one of her favorite places in Oliver's Well, an old gristmill. Nettles Mill had been beautifully restored by the Oliver's Well Historical Association, but back when she was young the buildings were still largely dilapidated. Emma used to ride her bicycle to the site, prop it against the remains of an old stone wall, and explore the property, losing herself in thoughts of what life must have been like for the people who had operated the huge stone grinding mechanism and who had lived in a few rough rooms attached to the mill building. Caro would have forbidden Emma to visit the old mill on her own; knowing this, Emma simply never told her mother where she was going.

Emma pulled her car into the visitors' parking lot and climbed out. A volunteer member of the OWHA, bright red Santa hat on her head, was leading a group of visitors out of one building and toward a structure Emma remembered from her childhood as a pile of rubble. As she stood gazing up at the water wheel by the building that housed the original millstones, she thought about the last time all three Reynolds siblings had gathered for Christmas, five years earlier. Ian had danced attendance on Caro for the two days of their visit, and had spent far more time with Daniel than Emma had. *At least I had time to talk with Dad,* Emma thought. And even if their conversation had been mostly about business, at least it was conversation.

Emma felt an involuntary shiver run through her. That was all ancient history. Her mother and father were gone now. The slate was wiped clean. Strange that she would see their passing as events that finally allowed for a fresh start, but that *was* how it felt to Emma, like a release of sorts. In fact, since shortly after Caro's death Emma had been feeling a stirring inside, a yearning for some essential change in her life. And she had been experiencing an emptiness that bothered her, a longing.

A longing for home? But what did that mean? Was home really

an ideal to achieve, or was it only a place to which you could return for short periods of time before your heart told you to move on? A longing for love? That's why she had finally ended the relationship with Ian. It hadn't been *love*, not the kind that could sustain and nourish a marriage over the years.

Emma sighed and looked at her watch. With a silent good-bye to Nettles Mill, she got back into her car and continued on to the house on Honeysuckle Lane where, she knew, her brother would be anxiously awaiting her arrival.

CHAPTER 2

Andie Reynolds had picked up a rental car at Dulles airport for the final leg of her journey to Oliver's Well. Andie didn't enjoy driving. In fact, she had delayed getting her license until she was nineteen, in spite of living in a town with no public transportation. She had been perfectly happy until her father sat her down and explained that getting a driver's license was an important milestone for every young person to achieve. "Andie," he had said, "you've let it go too long already." So, obliging person that she was, she had gotten her license. And she was a good driver, careful, attentive, and when necessary defensive. She just didn't enjoy being behind the wheel.

Andie, born Andrea Jane, was forty-four years old. She had always been "a bit on the heavy side"—those were her mother's words—built more like her father than her siblings were, both of whom tended to be tall and slim like Caro Reynolds. Her hair was dark and unruly, also like Cliff's, and rather than struggle with blow dryers and straightening products, she simply tied it back in a ponytail or stuck it up with a big plastic clip. What jewelry she wore had meaning for her—a beaded necklace given to her by an elderly woman she had befriended on her first trip to Mexico, a silver cuff she had bought from a street vendor in India, the tiny gold and moonstone ring she had found half buried in the dirt close by the rim of the Grand Canyon. As for her clothes, Andie liked them to be colorful and, above all, comfortable. There were far more important things to be concerned with than tight waist-bands and restricting tops.

Andie glanced down at her paisley ankle length skirt and pink and purple striped top and couldn't help but smile. No, her mother, always impeccably and conservatively dressed, would find her daughter's outfit sloppy and bohemian and she would say as much. But Caro Carlyle Reynolds was no longer here to approve or disapprove of her children, and that, Andie had realized with surprise, was still taking some getting used to. Just before she had left her home in Woodville Junction Andie had spent a fair amount of time meditating on the fact of her mother's death and wondering about the answer to an important question she had never ventured to ask. Had her mother feared death or had she welcomed it? In her ill and weakened state had she longed for this life to be over and for whatever was to come to come quickly? "Without health life is not life; it is only a state of languor and suffering—an image of death." Had Caro Reynolds agreed with the Buddha on this matter?

"Welcome to Oliver's Well," Andie read aloud. "Founded 1632." Not far up the first turn off to the right was the Unitarian Univer-salist Church, where she had married Bob Dolman when she was just out of college. Andie was looking forward to seeing Bob; she thought they might be the only divorced couple in the country to consider each other dearest friends.

Still, Andie felt her stomach flutter with the proverbial butter-flies. No matter how much time had passed and how much seren-ity she had achieved, going home to Oliver's Well always caused a degree of unease. She wondered how Emma felt when she vis-ited. Was she, too, haunted by the ghosts? Daniel was the only Reynolds sibling who had chosen to make a life in Oliver's Well, and from what Andie could tell, he had chosen wisely for him-self. If he was troubled by the past and its habit of lingering in the present, he hadn't shared that trouble with his oldest sister.

We three siblings are so different in some ways, Andie thought. *United by DNA, but at times, not much more.*

There, Andie noted, coming up on the left was the rambling old house in which Dr. Burton had lived and practiced family medicine until well into his eighties. Andie remembered as if it were yesterday the big jar of hard candies and lollipops on his desk. And she remembered how she had loved old Dr. Burton as if he were her grandfather. Who knew who occupied the house now? *So much change,* Andie thought as the house receded into the distance. *So much we need to learn how to let go of.*

The last time Andie had been back to Oliver's Well was for her mother's funeral. The compelling reason for *this* visit was her brother's insistence on the whole family being together for Christmas. The butterflies took flight again in Andie's stomach, a manifestation of her well-honed instinct for unhappiness, her own or someone else's. She almost smiled as she wondered what people would think if they knew that Andie Reynolds—she had reverted to her birth name after her divorce—self-help author/speaker/respected guru and lifestyle coach (call her what you will), was momentarily overcome with good old-fashioned fear.

"Just as a snake sheds its skin, we must shed our past over and over again." Andie firmly believed this process of shedding was necessary; problem was that too often the past dug in its claws and refused to be thrown off without almost superhuman effort. And here was a good example, Andie thought. Six months earlier she had missed Rumi's twentieth birthday celebration due to a long-standing commitment to her publisher. Since then she had sensed from Rumi a slight coldness. Well, maybe coldness was too strong a word. It might be more accurate to say that the usual easy way they had with one another seemed a bit forced; instead of being her warm and bubbly self, Rumi seemed reserved. Hopefully, coming face to face would allow them to regain their happy intimacy. Andie knew she wasn't the most conventional mother in the world; she also knew that she truly loved her child.

"Here we are," Andie murmured as she turned onto Honeysuckle Lane. She had spent most of the first twenty some odd years of her life on this street. It was all so terribly familiar. There was the Burrowses' house on the left, a thorn in the side of the more "respectable" homeowners, who didn't approve of the family's lackadaisical ways or their less than diligent upkeep of house and property. And then, a bit further on and across the way, was the perfectly kept home of the Fitzgibbon family, well-known and respected in Oliver's Well, and once, friends of a sort to Cliff and Caro Reynolds.

And then, just up ahead, number 32 Honeysuckle Lane. Like most of the other houses on the block, it was a handsome, mid-nineteenth-century white clapboard two-story structure with black shutters and a large central chimney. Andie pulled into the drive in front of the house in which her mother had breathed her last. And there was her brother, standing at the window, waiting. Daniel Reynolds. The Keeper of the Flame. With a silent prayer for strength, Andie got out of the car and, grabbing her bag from the backseat, walked briskly up to the front door.

CHAPTER 3

Daniel and his son, Marco, stood at the living room window keeping an eye out for Daniel's sisters.

"What time is it, Dad?" Marco asked.

"Ten minutes after ten," Daniel told his son, looking at his watch. It had once belonged to his father and had come to him after Cliff's passing. Daniel only took it off when he showered.

Marco frowned. "Why don't I have a watch?"

"You can have my old one if you want."

"Nah," Marco said after a moment's consideration. "I like to ask you what time it is."

Daniel smiled and ruffled his son's thick dark hair. Daniel had turned forty at the end of August, though sometimes lately he felt as if he were half again as old. Maybe that was the result of the long hours he put into the business. Maybe it was also due to the stress that resulted from trying to be the best husband and parent and, once, son he could be. His medium brown hair was beginning to thin, and there were lines around his mouth caused as much by frowning as by smiling. He was still as slim as he had been in college, and that was entirely due to the Carlyle genetics. Life as a professional chef wasn't exactly conducive to, as his mother might have said, "maintaining one's figure."

Anna Maria, Daniel's wife, had also inherited the "slim gene." At five feet one inch tall she was a whopping ninety pounds, with exuberant dark curls and bright brown eyes. Though she complained about her hair being impossible to manage and about not being tall enough to reach the uppermost cabinets in their kitchen, Daniel knew she didn't care one whit about her appearance. Anna Maria focused on the important things in life, like her family. For example, just the day before she had asked Daniel what he expected from his sisters' visit; she was concerned he was gearing up for a showdown of sorts.

"Why should I be expecting a showdown?" Daniel had asked.

"Because," she said, "you seem unhappy. I know you, Daniel. I can tell when you're feeling stressed."

He had roundly denied feeling stressed, certainly not about his sisters. "I think it'll be great, all three of us together at Christmas for the first time in years."

"Visions of a Norman Rockwell holiday dancing in your head?" She hadn't said it mockingly.

Daniel had shrugged. "Yeah, why not?"

But the truth was that he *had* been unhappy for the past months. The house and all it contained, both tangible and intangible, had become a drain on Daniel. Caro had left the property to all three of her children equally, but Daniel, as the local one and the trustee of the estate, had been the person keeping it in perfect order, paying bills and seeing to essential repairs. He glanced over his shoulder to the painting above the mantel of the fireplace. It was an oil portrait of his parents, done years ago by an artist in Westminster. Cliff and Caro were dressed formally, Caro seated in a high-backed armchair, Cliff standing a bit to the side, his hand resting on his wife's shoulder. Both looked properly dignified. Daniel knew that his parents had paid dearly for the portrait, and to be fair it was a good likeness, but for some reason he couldn't name, the painting had never appealed to him.

With a small sigh Daniel turned back to the window. If one of his sisters wanted the painting—and that would probably be Emma—she was welcome to it. It was high time for the siblings

to make a decision on the future of the house and its contents—
and, as Daniel saw it, the future of the family.

"Dad, when are Aunt Andie and Aunt Emma getting here?"
Sophia asked. Daniel hadn't heard her come into the room. Unlike her brother, Sophia moved with grace.

Daniel smiled at his daughter. "When they get here."

"Dad!" she protested. "That's not a real answer."

"They said they'd be here sometime this morning. Travel is
unpredictable, Sophia. Flights can be delayed and cars can break
down."

Sophia sighed. "I wish they'd show up so the Christmas season can start. You know I'm impatient."

Daniel laughed. "You don't get that from me."

"Oh, yes," she said, very seriously, "I do."

Daniel watched as his daughter ran off toward the kitchen
where Anna Maria was monitoring the cookies that had gone into
the oven about ten minutes earlier. From the wonderful aroma in
the air, the cookies were doing just fine.

Marco now had his nose pressed to the glass. "You'll steam up
the window," Daniel said.

Marco moved back an inch or two and with his forefinger drew
a heart on the glass where his nose and mouth had been. "But
now I've got a heart," he said.

And in his son's simple reply Daniel saw an affirmation that he
had chosen wisely for his life. After college in Arlington Daniel
had gone to California to earn an associate degree with a major in
culinary arts from the CIA. While there he had also taken a certificate program in wine and beverage studies. Why not? The
campus was in the glorious Napa Valley. His plan had been to go
home to Oliver's Well after completion of his studies and pursue
a career in cooking. And then he had met Anna Maria Spinelli in
the lobby of the old-fashioned movie house in Westminster; they
had both gone to see a screening of *Casablanca*.

To say it was love at first sight wouldn't be far off. There was
an immediate physical attraction followed by the discovery of a
shared love of food and family and the realization that they truly

enjoyed being together, whether it be watching movies on Netflix or sitting quietly side by side on a bench in Oliver's Grove, the town's park, or experimenting with recipes. Anna Maria was close to her large family, still living in her hometown of Nicholsborough, and wanted her children—those she hoped to have—to benefit from the presence of grandparents and aunts and uncles and cousins. Daniel thought that a wise idea. A life in Oliver's Well would suit him just fine.

They were married eight months after their first date and moved into a charming little house on the outskirts of town that had been gifted to them by Anna Maria's great-aunt and great-uncle. There was a small but manageable mortgage, and if over time the house proved to be a bit tight for a family of four, they were happy there and in the end that was everything.

Together Daniel and Anna Maria had started a small catering business called Savories and Seasonings. For a time they struggled, but they never wavered in their dedication and desire for success. They borrowed money from parents and the bank, worked hard, spent ridiculously little on extras, paid back the loans as soon as possible, and learned as they went along. Bonnie Eckman, a resident of Oliver's Well who had once worked as a personal chef as well as a caterer, generously gave Daniel and Anna Maria advice and encouragement. It was a while before they had enough money to convert their garage into a licensed commercial kitchen, but once they did, the business really took off. Now, a year after Caro Reynolds's death, Savories and Seasonings was firmly in the black with a roster of regular clients to which several new ones were added each season.

"Dad!" Marco's still high-pitched voice cried, making Daniel flinch. "Here comes Aunt Emma!"

Daniel watched as his sister pulled into the driveway in the car she kept spotlessly clean and perfectly maintained. Anna Maria appeared at his side and put a hand on her husband's shoulder.

"You okay?" she asked.

Daniel turned away from the window and smiled. "Yeah," he said. But inside he felt not so certain.

CHAPTER 4

His eyes are tired, Andie thought. He's troubled.

This was Andie's first impression of the brother she had not seen since their mother's funeral. She reached out to hug him, and while Daniel didn't pull away, she thought she sensed, as she had after the funeral, a slight hesitation in his manner.

"Emma's already here," Daniel told her as they went inside the house that had been their parents' for so many years. He closed the front door, on which someone—maybe Anna Maria, Andie thought—had hung a large pine wreath decorated with the same velvety blue ribbon Caro had favored, in honor of the Christmas season. "She's upstairs getting settled."

Andie smiled. "The shiny Lexus in the driveway was a hint."

"Right. Well, I'm glad you're here. How was the trip?" he asked.

Andie glanced at the tall and stately grandfather clock that had stood in the living room at number 32 Honeysuckle Lane for as far back as she could remember. "Long but uneventful," she said, noting the time.

Andie headed for the den, located at the rear of the first floor; its windows overlooked the backyard and patio, once the scene of Caro's famous Labor Day cocktail party, at which she would serve her guests dainty canapés and frosty gin and tonics.

"Where are you going?" Daniel asked.

"I'm staying in the den," she told him.

Daniel looked confused. "But I made up the bed in your old room," he said. "I thought you'd want to stay there."

Andie smiled. "Thanks, Danny, but I prefer the den. I'll find some sheets and make up the couch."

Andie continued on her way. Obviously, she thought, dropping her slouchy bag onto the carpeted floor of the den, Daniel didn't know that whenever she visited her parents' home she bunked down here. She simply couldn't bear to stay in her childhood bedroom. The room that she had shared with baby Rumi after her divorce. The room that had witnessed her suffering through the final months of a cruel and debilitating postpartum depression.

At times Andie still felt embarrassed by what she initially had considered the flaws of character that had manifested at that point in her life, even though the flaws—not flaws at all, she had come to see—had to some degree been brought about by her misguided attempt to live a life someone else had planned for her. A life that she, Andie Reynolds, was not meant to live.

And Andie's authentic life did not include marriage or full time, hands-on parenthood. Rather, it meant a life of study and prayer, of meditation and writing, of trying to help as many people as she could to achieve a degree of spiritual awareness and inner peace. She hadn't intended on becoming a popular and fairly famous spiritual advisor and teacher, but that was exactly what she had become. With courage and determination Andie had learned to humbly embrace her gifts; to share those gifts with others was her greatest joy.

For the past ten years or so, Andie had considered herself a Buddhist, though not exclusively so. She admired and tried to live by the Eightfold Path and to follow what practices she had found personally meaningful and helpful in her work with others, such as regular meditation and the following of ethical practices. She held to the Three Marks of Existence—impermanence, suffering or disquietude, and the not-self. She believed in the wisdom of avoiding the extremes of permanence and nihilism, of inherent existence and nothingness. And these were only some of the ideas she tried to share with those who wanted to listen.

Once Andie had found sheets in the downstairs linen closet and hastily put them on the couch, she left the den and went to find the family. They were, of course, gathered in the kitchen. The hearth, Andie thought, was always where people gathered, no matter how small or primitive it might be.

"Emma," Andie said, going to her sister. "It's been too long, and yes, I know, it's been my fault."

"Not your fault, Andie," Emma said, returning her sister's hug. "Just life getting in the way of itself."

"That's a creative way of putting it!" Next Andie turned to her sister-in-law. "It's so good to see you, Anna Maria. You look wonderful. Positively glowing."

Anna Maria laughed and wiped her forehead with the back of her hand. "That's because I've been standing over a hot stove for most of the day!"

"Oof!" Andie tottered under the assault from her niece and nephew.

"Hi, Aunt Andie!" Sophia cried, hugging her fiercely. Marco tugged on her arm. "Come see what we're doing!"

What Daniel's children were doing was decorating cookies at a small table set up near the rear of the kitchen. There were at least eight or nine tubes of icing and plastic containers of colored sugar and sprinkles piled on the tabletop. "Did you help bake them?" Andie asked, suddenly remembering as if it were only yesterday the many times she and Emma had helped their mother bake Christmas cookies and pans of spicy gingerbread. She felt a wave of sadness, the intensity of which surprised her.

"Yup," Marco said. "I stirred the batter."

"And I added some of the ingredients," Sophia said. "You have to measure really exactly when you're baking. That's what Dad says."

Andie smiled. "Your father's a smart man." She joined the other adults, sitting at the main table. Anna Maria was pouring coffee from a press pot, and Andie gratefully accepted a cup. "So, Danny, what do you need from us?" she asked.

Andie had phrased her question carefully. Since Daniel had first pressed his sisters to come home to Oliver's Well for the Christmas holiday, it had been clear that he needed something more than help sorting through the credenza and taking old clothing to the charity shop, though what that something was Andie still didn't know.

Daniel didn't answer his sister's question. Instead he took a few sheets of paper from a glossy folder and distributed them around the table. "I've made a list of suggestions for what we might do together as a family this holiday season."

Emma smiled as she looked down at her paper. "A snowman-building contest? In this neck of the woods? How exactly does that work?"

"It's artificial snow," Daniel explained. "It's created with one of those machines used at ski resorts when Mother Nature doesn't come through. The kids love it."

"It's so much fun, Aunt Emma!" Marco called out.

"I'm sure it is," Emma replied. "Hey, when are you guys going to be done with those cookies?"

"Don't be impatient, Aunt Emma," Marco told her. "Mom always says good things come to those who wait. Right, Mom?"

Andie smiled at her sister-in-law. "Children listen more carefully than we give them credit for!" She looked at her own copy of Daniel's suggestions. A concert at the Catholic Church. The children's school pageant. The Christmas Parade and Festival. The butterflies took flight again in Andie's stomach. She was still a bit shy among the people of Oliver's Well who might not have approved of her decision to leave Rumi with her father when Rumi was eight years old in order to forge a meaningful life on her own. Wasn't being a mother meaningful enough, some might ask? Wasn't being present to watch your child grow and learn and become a full person the most important thing a parent could do? Natural enough questions, but ones Andie didn't want to answer for a merely curious stranger.

"I just thought that now we're all here together, we should have some fun," Daniel said. "We might not get to do everything, but we can't miss the kids' school pageant and the Christmas Festival, especially the lighting of the tree at the end. That's one of the most important local events of the year. Remember all the times we went when we were children? We always had so much fun."

"I remember getting my first kiss at the festival when I was thirteen," Emma said.

Sophia squealed from the other end of the kitchen. "Really? What was it like?"

"Don't go putting ideas into my daughter's head," Daniel warned. "I told her no boys whatsoever until she's sixteen."

Emma patted her brother's arm. "It was only a little kiss, Danny. Nothing to get worked up about." Emma turned to Sophia. "And your dad's right," she said. "There's no rush where boys are concerned."

Sophia shrugged and went back to sprinkling pink sugar on a cookie.

"How is Rumi?" Andie asked, wondering if Daniel or Anna Maria knew if her daughter was romantically involved. Andie had recently asked via e-mail, but Rumi hadn't replied to the question. "It would be nice if she's able to join us for some of these festivities."

"Haven't you two been in touch?" Daniel asked with a frown.

"Of course we have. But I don't always know what her daily schedule entails. Young people are so busy, especially in this plugged-in age. It's hard to keep up with them."

"Rumi will be here for dinner tomorrow," Anna Maria said. "She's been working as a waitress at the Angry Squire between semesters, and she's been helping us at Savories and Seasonings, so her schedule has been pretty tight. Still, I know she wouldn't miss the kids' pageant at the very least."

"And she's doing really well at school," Daniel said. "She'll have finished her degree in dental hygiene by the end of next semester."

That her daughter had chosen to work in the medical profes-

sion rather than in a creative field was still a bit of a surprise to
Andie, though not a disappointment. All that mattered was that
Rumi live the life she freely chose. But before Andie could say as
much, her brother was going on.

"Money matters," Daniel said firmly. "Rumi is a smart young
woman. She's got a good steady head on her shoulders."

"Yes," said Andie. "I know she does." Daniel's implication
was perfectly clear; he had never quite accepted his sister's work
as something "good" or "steady."

"I don't mean to pry, but are things okay with you and Ian?"
Anna Maria asked Emma. "I was surprised when you said you'd
be coming for Christmas on your own."

"Well, actually . . ." Emma said quietly. "The thing is, I ended
the relationship."

Andie briefly took her sister's hand; Emma smiled her thanks.

"For good this time?" Daniel asked, eyes wide.

"Yes, Danny," Emma replied. "For good this time."

"You know Mom hoped you two would get married. Dad, too."

"And you?" Emma asked her brother.

"Well," he said, "you *were* together for almost a decade, leaving aside your brief split."

"Thanks for the reminder," Emma said dryly. "Again."

"What finally went wrong?"

"It's too complicated to explain," Emma said quietly. "But it
was the right thing to do."

Andie nodded. "Ian is a good man, Danny, but that doesn't
mean he was the right man for Emma."

"Seriously, Emma, what was it?" Daniel pressed. "Did he suddenly start to drink? Did he take up gambling?"

"No, no, nothing like that," Emma laughed. "Don't be so dramatic, Danny!"

"Ian's been part of the family since Marco was born." Daniel
shot a glance at his children. "The kids consider him an uncle."

Anna Maria put her hand on her husband's arm. "Daniel thinks
everyone should be married," she said softly. "He's a big fan of
marriage, and believe me, I'm grateful for that. But he doesn't

understand that not every couple is meant to live happily ever after."

Like Bob and me, Andie thought. *Dearest friends but not husband and wife. Something Mom and Dad as well as Danny could never understand.*

Marco and Sophia came over to the table where the adults sat; they were each holding out a plate of heavily decorated cookies. "We're all done!" Marco announced.

"And about time!" Andie said. In spite of the fact she thought she might drop into a sugar coma—the icing on each cookie had to be a quarter of an inch thick—she reached for a cookie in the shape of a Christmas tree.

"Don't want to eat the reindeer?" Daniel asked with a grin. "It's not real meat, you know."

"I know," Andie said. "But I try always to be consistent in my behavior and beliefs."

Daniel reached for the reindeer cookie on his daughter's plate. "As do I," he said, biting off the animal's iced head.

"The fact that we're all unique," Andie said, refusing to be riled and speaking in the famed voice she knew so many people found soothing, "is one of the things that makes life so interesting."

To that, her brother had nothing to say.

CHAPTER 5

Emma and Andie were in the den while Sophia and Marco were playing in the backyard, which Emma could see was in immaculate condition, the lawn mowed and the patio swept clear of leaves and other debris. Daniel and Anna Maria were in the kitchen preparing dinner.

Andie was sitting comfortably in the large brown leather armchair that had been in the den for as long as Emma could remember. "Remember how Dad used to fall asleep in this chair reading the Sunday paper?" Andie said from its depths. "And how when one of us would find him he'd swear he was just 'resting his eyes'? I always wondered why he felt he had to make an excuse for taking a nap in the middle of the day."

"An overdeveloped sense of responsibility?" Emma guessed. She was roaming the room as they talked, noting things she hadn't noted for some time, like the small oil painting depicting a brilliant sunset, and the framed embroidered sampler her mother's great-aunt Abigail had sewn as a small girl. "And a good work ethic. He probably felt he should be doing something productive rather than nodding off."

"I love a good nap when I can catch one," Andie admitted. "It helps my productivity. The lucid dreaming can get in the way of real rest at times, but I guess that's just one of my crosses to bear!"

"Better you than me," Emma laughed. "I rarely even remember my dreams, and when I do I'm either horrified or embarrassed."

"That's why dreams are private and most times not for public consumption."

Emma turned to her sister and leaned against their father's writing desk. "Danny was pretty nosy about why I left Ian, wasn't he?"

"He's probably just concerned. You know, playing big brother, which is what he seems to have become for us over the past few years."

"Yeah. There's no one else, by the way. I mean, I didn't leave Ian for another man." Emma sighed. "Sometimes I seriously doubt I'll ever find 'the right one.' "

"In the words of Rumi, my beloved poet and prophet: 'Your task is not to seek for love, but merely to seek and find all barriers within yourself that you have built against it.' "

"Well," Emma said, "that certainly gives me a lot to think about. Internal barriers to love. Who knew?"

"Dinner is served!" Daniel called from the kitchen.

"Gosh, he's got a pair of lungs!" Emma laughed. She held out a hand to help Andie out of the armchair, and linking arms with her sister, they left the den. "Danny doesn't have to wait on us like we're his clients," Emma whispered. "But when I suggested we order in from the Chinese place downtown or even go out to the Angry Squire, he was pretty adamant about cooking dinner for us all."

"Maybe we should contribute some money to his holiday budget, especially if he continues to treat us like guests and not like plain ole family."

"Good idea," Emma said. "But I wonder if he'll take it."

Sophia and Marco came running into the kitchen through the back door just as their aunts came in through the door off the living room.

"Wash your hands," Anna Maria instructed. Obediently, Sophia and Marco made a beeline for the sink.

Daniel was putting platters of food on the table. "I made chicken with caramelized onions and cardamom rice," he announced. "It's a Middle Eastern recipe. There's also brussels sprouts with pancetta, and green beans made with chicken stock."

Andie smiled and glanced over to the counter on which the chopping board sat. "Anything vegetarian on the menu, Danny?"

Daniel shrugged. "I brought in some tofu and there are some raw veggies. They're in the fridge. And there's always some jarred tomato sauce if you want some pasta."

Emma felt the blood rush to her cheeks. It was unlike Daniel to be so rude to his sister. She remembered his earlier totally unnecessary comment about the reindeer cookie and repressed a sharp retort after the fact; the children were in the room and they didn't need to be dragged into a dispute. She tried to catch Anna Maria's eye, but her sister-in-law looked as discomfited as she felt. As for Andie . . .

"We vegetarians do eat dairy products, Danny," Andie said lightly, seemingly unoffended. "Didn't the CIA teach you that much?"

"We concentrated on serious food," he countered, "and that includes the flesh of fish, fowl, and creatures on the hoof."

"Since when did you get to be so narrow minded?" Emma asked her brother as she took a seat at the table.

Anna Maria laughed, but to Emma it sounded forced. "He's a grumpy old man before his time," she said. "That's all."

"Why are you a vegetarian, Aunt Andie?" Sophia asked.

Andie smiled at her niece. "Let's just say vegetarianism is one way for me to keep my vow of nurturing a wholesome attitude toward all living beings." Sophia nodded and Andie went on, her tone still neutral. "I'll make some pasta and salad," she said. "Go ahead and eat. I'll run out to the store after dinner."

Dinner was a fairly tense affair, Emma thought, her brother not saying much, her sister-in-law making small talk of the kind that could interest and offend no one, and Andie being determinedly pleasant over her dish of pasta and tomato sauce. Emma was glad when dinner was over. Andie went off to the grocery store, and the children retreated to the den with their handheld devices, leaving Emma with Daniel and Anna Maria in the living room. Daniel sat in what had been Cliff's favorite chair. Anna Maria sat at one end of the couch. Emma sat at the other, leaving what had been Caro's favorite chair unoccupied. From their exalted place above the fireplace, Cliff and Caro, forever captured in oil paint, kept watch. Emma, never a fan of the painting, made certain not to look in its direction.

"Did you like the chicken?" Daniel asked.

Emma refrained from rolling her eyes. "You asked me that at least twice already and the answer is still the same. Yes, it was delicious."

"He tried it out at a private dinner party about a month ago," Anna Maria explained. "Everybody loved it, but he's been perfecting the recipe ever since."

"Andie should have been here for Rumi's birthday," Daniel said suddenly.

"What brought that up?" Emma asked.

Daniel tapped his fingers against the arm of the chair, as if, Emma thought, he were full of nervous energy. "It's been on my mind. Rumi's had a tough time since Mom died. She was so close to her grandmother. She's really suffering."

So that was what was behind Daniel's rude treatment of his sister, Emma thought. He was sitting in self-appointed judgment. "Rumi's not a child anymore, Danny," she said. "She'll have to learn how to recover from loss as we've all learned."

"But—" he began.

Emma leaned forward. "Danny," she said, "Andie would have been here for the party if she could have been. But that was six months ago, so let's move on."

"Emma," Anna Maria said brightly, "I've been meaning to ask you where you got that scarf. It's so pretty."

Emma turned to her sister-in-law, grateful for the change of subject. "Thanks," she said. "It was on sale at Talbots."

"What was Andie going on about at dinner?" Daniel asked suddenly. "Something about a podcast?"

"She wasn't going on about it, Danny," Emma said a bit sharply.

"I told her I'd listened to her latest podcast and really enjoyed it." She turned to Anna Maria. "She took as her theme the idea of being able to let go gracefully of things and people not meant for you."

"That sounds interesting. I'll try to listen," Anna Maria promised.

Daniel laughed. "Well, I'll give it a pass. I have other, more important things demanding my attention."

Emma refrained from a reply. Instead, she asked: "How's Bob?" When Andie and Bob had married, Daniel was only a teen and Bob had quickly become a sort of big brother to him. Over the years, and in spite of the divorce, Daniel and Bob's relationship had continued to grow. Bob, Emma thought, was a truly good man. He was someone no one would want to let go of, gracefully or not.

"He's fine," Daniel said. "He's been helping us out on a few catering gigs, circulating with trays, loading and unloading the car."

"But what about his bad knee?"

Daniel shrugged. "Times are tough. He takes what work he can find. I pay him off the books, of course."

"That's not a great idea, Danny. Speaking as a professional, I'm obliged to tell you that."

"Maybe not," Daniel said. "But he's my brother-in-law, and my friend. I do what I can for him. Unlike some people."

Emma suddenly felt exhausted by her brother's strange mood. "I'm going to bed," she announced. "You guys don't have to leave now. . . ."

Anna Maria got briskly to her feet. "No, we should be getting home. The kids have school tomorrow and we've got yet another holiday office party to plan for."

"I'll see you tomorrow morning, as soon as I can get here," Daniel told his sister, getting up from their father's chair.

Emma went to the door and watched as Daniel's family climbed into his car and pulled away. When they were out of sight she closed the door and locked it. She stood for a moment looking around the living room, at all the familiar bits and pieces, the antiques her mother had inherited and treasured as well as the art and furniture she had purchased through the years. It was all so well remembered, so comforting in its way, certainly innocuous but . . .

A wave of disorientation swept over Emma. For the life of her she couldn't remember the last time she had been completely alone in this house. *I'm a stranger here in some ways*, she thought. *And I'm not sure that I like that.*

Emma shook herself in an attempt to shift the sadness and, leaving a small light on for her sister, retreated to her bed.

CHAPTER 6

Daniel and his family were safely home in their house on Little Rock Lane. The children were in bed, though whether either was asleep was anyone's guess. Sophia was a bookworm, not something either of her parents wanted to discourage; when she brought a flashlight with her to bed and snuck a book along with it, they turned a blind eye. And Marco had always been a "bad sleeper," ever since infancy. The poor kid was always tired, but when it came to actually falling asleep and staying asleep, well, there he had trouble. That he managed not to nod off during school hours—not usually, anyway—was, Daniel thought, a bit of a miracle.

Daniel was also in bed, pillows propped up against the headboard. He wasn't sure how he felt about his sisters' visit so far. He was glad they had come home and yet, since their arrival, he had felt increasingly . . . irritated.

Anna Maria came into the bedroom and closed the door behind her. "Marco's actually asleep," she said, climbing into bed next to Daniel. "Even after all the sugar he ate earlier."

"A Christmas miracle."

"I'm surprised you didn't talk about the estate with your sisters this evening," Anna Maria said, tucking the covers around her. "You've been so eager to finalize things."

"Don't worry. Estate business is on the agenda for first thing tomorrow morning."

Anna Maria shifted so that she was looking at Daniel. Her expression, he saw, was serious. "You know," she said, "you shouldn't have teased Andie about being a vegetarian. And what were you thinking, not making her a decent meal? Vegetarianism is important to your sister, and it's not exactly weird or exotic."

Daniel had half expected his wife to scold him; he hoped he looked as sheepish as he felt. "Sorry," he said. And he was. Still, he just didn't understand why Andie had to set herself up to be so different. It was especially annoying now that Cliff and Caro were gone and all that remained of the family were his sisters and himself. The three of them should be united.

"And if you're going to be as harsh with Andie for the rest of the visit as you were today," Anna Maria went on, "the holiday season is going to be miserable."

"Sorry," Daniel said again. "Really."

"Keep in mind the children. If not for anyone else's sake, try to keep a civil tongue."

"I will. I promise."

"Good." Anna Maria finally smiled. "I'm holding you to that promise."

Daniel knew that she would. "Anna Maria," he said, "you did more for my mother during the last years of her life than either of my sisters. Didn't you ever feel taken advantage of?"

"There were a few times in Caro's final months when I could have used another pair of hands. But in the end it was no big deal. And now," Anna Maria said, putting her hand on her husband's, "now it's over and we have the satisfaction of knowing that we helped make your mother's last years as good as they could be. She didn't suffer neglect or abuse. She was rarely alone in the last months of her life, what with Rumi helping out as well as the visiting nurse. What does it matter who did the caretaking? As long as it was done, and done well."

"Still—"

"Let it go, Daniel," Anna Maria said, her voice low but urgent.

Daniel laughed, though there was nothing funny about what he had been feeling these past months. "I can't."

"Why?"

"I don't know," he admitted. "I do know that my sisters could have offered to help when Mom suffered those bouts of depression, like at the first anniversary of Dad's death. And there was the time when Mom had the flu and you spent almost two weeks living with her when the kids and I needed you at home—and on the job."

Anna Maria sighed. "Daniel, how often did you ask your sisters for their help? People aren't mind readers. They can't know what you need unless you tell them."

"In this case, 'people' are Caro's daughters," Daniel argued. "They should have known their presence would have been welcome."

"Would it have been?" Anna Maria wondered. "I'm not so sure about that. Your mother was never as comfortable with her daughters as she was with you, Daniel. At least, that's the way I saw it. I think she might have felt, I don't know, a certain loss of dignity if Andie and Emma—especially Emma, I think—were around to see her at the last. Weak. Unnerved."

"She didn't mind Rumi and Sophia being around," Daniel said. "Or you."

"Yes, but we weren't her children," Anna Maria pointed out. "You know how Caro was so keen on keeping up appearances with her daughters. Just the way she was raised, I suppose. Not to show weakness. Not to admit defeat. Remember how she insisted on using that face powder she was fond of no matter how awful she felt, no matter that she wasn't going to see anyone that day but us! And lipstick. Do you know I once found Sophia putting Caro's lipstick on for her?" Anna Maria laughed. "Caro was directing the entire thing, of course, which made it that much more difficult for the poor girl to get the lipstick on Caro's lips and not across her cheeks. But it was clear they were having a good time."

Daniel smiled. "Mom *was* always particular about her appearance."

"And now she's gone, and I don't think she'd welcome the idea of your clinging to old grievances. Caro always had your happiness uppermost in her mind, especially after she lost Cliff. Frankly, you were such the apple of her eye I don't know how you didn't turn out to be insufferable."

"My sisters might very well call me insufferable."

"Maybe," his wife agreed, "but they're not the ones who count. I am. You are. Sophia and Marco. *Our* family counts. The present counts, and the future."

Daniel squeezed his wife's hand. "Were you always so smart?" he asked.

Anna Maria yawned. "Yes. And now I'm also tired, so let's go to sleep."

This Christmas counts, Daniel thought, kissing his wife's cheek and turning out the light. *What happens this Christmas matters for all of us. It matters for the future of the Reynolds family. It matters for me.*

CHAPTER 7

It was well after midnight and still Emma couldn't fall asleep. She wondered how her sister was faring in the den, enjoying a deep and restful sleep or staring at the darkened ceiling like she was, her mind active and alert.

With a sigh of frustration Emma reached over and turned on the bedside lamp. She had chosen to say in her parents' room and not her childhood bedroom where she and Ian had regularly bunked down when they visited the senior Reynoldses. It was the first time she had ever slept—or tried to—in her parents' bed, and it had seemed an important thing for her to do, though she couldn't quite say why. On a different note entirely, she *did* know that she hadn't wanted to be forcibly reminded of Ian by the presence of his slippers by her old bed, and the extra razor he kept in the top drawer of her old dresser.

Now, with the light casting a soft glow across the room, Emma could see her parents' wedding portrait standing on her mother's long, low dresser. Her father, proud in a classic black tuxedo, a white rose in his lapel. Her mother, taller than her husband, looking elegant in a candlelight ivory *peau de soie* gown that had been handmade by a seamstress in Boston, the same woman who had made Martha Carlyle's dress forty years before. Caro's bouquet was a cascade of white lilies and white roses. On her head was delicately perched a small pearl crown, from which a veil of tulle netting sprung.

It truly had been love at first sight for her parents, Emma reflected. Caroline Carlyle, recently graduated from a women's academy on the outskirts of Boston and spending a few months with her aunt and uncle in an old-money area of DC, had been on her way to hear a talk on the Impressionists at the National Gallery. It was spring and she was wearing her favorite lightweight coat in rose pink; she wore pinned to her right lapel a small pearl brooch that had belonged to her maternal grandmother.

Two stops before her destination a young man got on the bus, dressed neatly but in a navy suit that had seen a lot of wear. He took the only vacant seat, diagonally across from Caroline. Caro noticed him. He noticed her. She smiled at him. "I simply couldn't help myself," she would later tell her children. "And he smiled back."

When the bus arrived at her stop, Caroline once again met the man's eyes, stood, and got off. The doors of the bus had barely closed behind her when a voice said, "My name is Clifford Reynolds." Caro had turned around to find the man in the navy suit. He was a few inches shorter than her in her low-heeled pumps, but his affect was that of a much larger man, and his smile was the most perfect smile she had ever seen.

"This isn't your stop," she said. "Is it?"

"No," the man replied. "Well, it wasn't. But I think it is now."

"I never dreamed he would follow me off the bus," Caro would later say, with the sort of expression that belied her words.

Cliff had accompanied Caroline to the museum, where they had coffee in the café instead of attending the lecture. After they had spent an hour talking nonstop about everything and nothing, Cliff had risen reluctantly. "I've got a meeting with a new client," he told Caro. "Well, to be honest, he's my only client so far. But look, can I take you to dinner sometime? Tomorrow night perhaps? I'm afraid it won't be anything five star."

To which Caroline had replied, "It will be perfect."

Both of Emma's parents had loved to tell the story of their fateful meeting, and for a long time Emma had loved to hear it— until at some point in her early thirties, having failed to find the sort of love her parents had enjoyed, she began to feel a tiny bit resentful of their romantic happiness. She would never admit aloud that she felt jealous of her parents' marital bliss. But she did, especially now, alone, at the age of forty-two.

Emma sat up in the bed and plumped the pillows to better support her back. She had very much wanted to come home for Christmas, partly to be with her family, partly to get away from Ian's near proximity, partly to explore her growing feelings of dis- satisfaction with her life in Annapolis, but . . . But she was afraid. She was aware that something was about to change. She was aware that she couldn't continue to live her life in the way that she had been living it, not if she was ever to be truly happy. But the idea of change scared Emma. For so long her life had been ordered and unexciting. Predictable. Safe. She had liked it that way. Maybe, she thought, that was why it had taken her so long to leave Ian for good.

Emma thought again about what Andie had said to her earlier, that her task now was to seek, find, and tear down the barriers she had erected against true love. Far easier said than done, and Andie, of course, knew that. Andie's natural empathy was one of the things that made her such a successful healer of troubled souls. *You could fake a lot of emotions*, Emma thought, *but not empathy*.

And speaking of empathy or the lack thereof . . . Emma frowned. It had been mean of Daniel to tease Andie about being a vegetarian, to dismiss her latest podcast as unimportant, to crit- icize her for not having been around for Rumi's birthday in June. For that matter, there had been no need for him to mention the fact that Emma had left Ian once before; it was a memory that embarrassed her.

It had been a spur of the moment thing. One of Ian's friends from architecture school had invited them to his wedding, an event that took place over a weekend in Savannah. From the moment Emma was introduced to Ted and Maggie she was struck by just how much in love they were; their feelings for each other radiated in waves of happiness and goodwill. She had been so reminded of her parents' relationship and had found it almost unbearable to witness Ted and Maggie's joy in each other's company. They were in such stark contrast to her and Ian, who were moving along the road of life with little if any real passion, their souls never quite touching. As soon as they were back in Annapolis Emma had told Ian she was leaving him. "Things don't feel right," she'd said, and he was understandably puzzled, but as with this last time, he hadn't seemed much affected. And less than two weeks later, Emma found herself asking him to meet for lunch and they had picked up right where they left off. The loneliness she had felt without Ian around had surprised her, and she had asked herself if something wasn't better than nothing. In short, she hadn't been ready to walk away. Not like now.

Anyway, Emma thought, that wasn't the Daniel she knew, kind, good natured, ready for a laugh, willing to be teased by his older sisters. Still, time and tragedy changed people, and while she had been battling her own demons since their mother had died, who knew what Daniel had been going through—and if he had been going through it alone or if he was sharing the experience with his wife.

Emma hoped it was the latter; she admired her sister-in-law. From the start Anna Maria had held her own with the strong-willed Caro, and it couldn't have been easy. Her brother had always been their mother's favorite, and Caro could be vocal about how she felt he should be treated. Maybe having grown up in a "big, noisy, passionate" family—Anna Maria's description—had prepared her not to be cowed by a doting mother-in-law too often tempted to point out what she saw as mistakes or omissions in her daughter-in-law's housekeeping or the attention she paid to her husband.

And Daniel could be a bit full of himself, Emma thought, and that was partially her fault, and Andie's. Along with Caro they had spoiled him as a child, the adorable baby brother. Emma often wondered how Anna Maria handled Daniel when he was in a difficult mood. Probably with grace, patience, and a well-turned phrase.

In a way, Emma thought, settling more comfortably against the pillows, Daniel and Anna Maria reminded her of Cliff and Caro Reynolds; they were a good, solid team built on love, respect, and friendship. But Daniel and Anna Maria lacked the glamour that seemed to hang around Cliff and Caro like a shimmering cloak. For so many years Emma had felt in awe of her parents. Cliff and Caro Reynolds had been so good-looking, so personable and charismatic, so intelligent. In short, they had been overwhelming.

That was why when her father had approached her at the start of her last semester in graduate school with his remarkably generous offer, Emma had momentarily panicked. It would be an honor, he said, for his daughter to join him in his practice. He hoped to offer her the benefit of his years of experience. "And eventually," he said, "when I retire, the business will be yours. And don't worry about finding a place to live," Cliff had gone on. "Your mother and I are more than happy to have you back home with us until you've saved enough money to buy a home of your own in Oliver's Well."

Emma had been speechless. The idea of moving back to Oliver's Well—specifically, to the house on Honeysuckle Lane— was appalling. She wanted a life of her own. She *needed* a life of her own. And to leave Oliver's Well and the immediate sphere of her parents' influence was, Emma believed, the only way to achieve full independence. She had seen what had happened with Andie and viewed her sister's predicament—an early mistaken marriage—as a warning of what might come to pass if she stayed around. Unhappiness, dissatisfaction, and an unintentional dependence on her parents, those powerful, commanding personalities.

Finally, after almost a full minute of silence, Emma admitted she simply didn't know what to say. "Think about it," her father had said, putting a hand on her shoulder. "You're bound to have questions." Cliff had chuckled. "I pride myself on keeping accurate accounts, but after all, you're the one getting the MBA."

It was several days before Emma told her father that while she was grateful for his generous offer of a partnership, she intended to pursue other plans. His immediate reaction had almost made her change her mind; he was so very disappointed that Emma's heart almost broke. Really, what was so wrong with staying in Oliver's Well and working alongside her father, a man she loved and respected? But deep down she knew she couldn't let guilt and a sense of duty override her intentions for a life of her own making. She knew that it would be a grave mistake to live out her adulthood in Oliver's Well, with her parents ever present and exuding such a powerful influence.

In spite of his disappointment, Cliff Reynolds had been gracious about his daughter's refusal to join him in his business and had wished her success in her ventures. "Just know," he'd said, "that if you change your mind the offer is always open."

But she hadn't changed her mind, and within eighteen months Joe Herbert, the young man who had once interned with her father, was firmly installed as a junior partner. She didn't feel any regret when she heard this news. She liked Joe and she knew that with her father's heart condition, it was only wise for him to share the burden of his work.

Her mother, however, had not been as gracious as her father. "It's a slap in your father's face is what it is," she had told Emma angrily. "After all he's done for you." Caro simply hadn't understood her daughter's need to forge her own life elsewhere. "Oliver's Well has always been good enough for your father and me," she had said. "I don't see why it's not good enough for you."

Their relationship had changed after that, though given the fact that neither Caro nor Emma enjoyed altercations and were not the type to provoke just for the fun of it, things had fairly quickly settled into a state of only slightly uneasy détente.

A huge yawn half convinced Emma that if she tried once again to fall asleep she would meet with success. But before she turned out the light, she picked up her iPhone from where it sat charging on the nightstand, ringer turned off for the night, and saw that Ian had left a message. She did not listen to it. And suddenly, she felt angry. That it should all have come to this . . . Emma didn't entirely regret the relationship with Ian, but she did regret all the years she had put into something that had never quite felt joyful. And joy was important.

They had met almost eleven years earlier at a party given by mutual friends. They hit it off and by the end of the evening had agreed to meet for drinks the following week. On that first date they discovered a mutual interest in history. Ian hadn't yawned when she described her career as a financial advisor. Emma had enjoyed Ian's stories about his time in architecture school. At dinner the following week they discovered a mutual passion for sushi. They took a day trip to Williamsburg. They binge-watched the first British version of *House of Cards*. They went to bed, and it was good if not great. Emma found the relationship comfortable and unchallenging, and that, she thought, was fine. She was challenged enough in her career; what she needed from Ian—from any man—was an uncomplicated companionship.

A few months after they first met, Ian had suggested they spend a weekend in Paris. He had found a cheap flight, and a friend who lived in the fourth arrondissement had offered them his apartment while he paid a visit to his sister in Amsterdam. And while a tiny part of her had wondered if going to Paris with Ian was such a wise idea—she wasn't in love with him, and Paris was the fabled city of romance; might her agreeing to go with Ian give him the wrong idea?—she accepted his suggestion. They had a fantastic time. While they strolled the Champs-Élysées one evening, Ian told Emma he was in no rush to get married. Still, he made it clear that he felt committed to her. Emma told him that she wasn't sure—and never had been—that marriage was the right thing for her. "But you're committed to me?" Ian had asked. What was there to say but yes? After all, it wasn't a lie, not really. She wasn't interested in seeing anyone else. She wasn't a cheater. It was all very civilized.

Andie was right—Ian Hayes was a good man. On paper he was

a real catch, partner in a successful architecture firm, in excellent health, an active contributor to the maintenance of the local homeless shelter, and unencumbered by bitter former wives or unhappy grasping children. But he was not the right man for Emma.

In the end the relationship had proved too much work, and for what? A degree of comfort? A companion with whom she could attend dinner parties and go on summer vacations? No, there had to be more to a relationship than convenience. There had to be love, plain and simple. The kind of love that made a man follow a woman off a bus; the kind of love that made that woman happily agree to marry him only months later.

With a sigh, Emma turned off the light and lay down once again. And this time, she quickly entered sleep.

CHAPTER 8

Andie couldn't sleep. She had repeated a prayer that most often helped her mind settle into a state of receptivity. She had dipped into one of the several books she carried with her whenever she traveled. A few of the titles explored Buddhist practice and others focused on the spiritual teachings of Rumi, the thirteenth-century Sufi mystic, poet, and prophet.

But it was all no good. She shifted on the leather couch and sighed. She couldn't get the memories of Daniel's behavior out of her mind. Was it always going to be this way, her brother, as had her parents, not understanding—refusing to understand?—the choices she had made for her life? The Buddha had said: "Your work is to discover your work, and then with all your heart to give yourself to it." That's exactly what Andie had done.

Well, Andie thought, if Daniel was determined to be aggressive with her this holiday, there was nothing she could do about it. In a few weeks she would be home in Woodville Junction, a little haven ten miles from the closest large town, ensconced in her three-room apartment in a residential building on property communally owned by Andie and her fellow spiritual explorers. While the ten or twelve people living there at any given time spent much of the day in each other's company, there was also ample provision for privacy and for essential prayer and meditation. The arrangement in upstate New York—so far from Oliver's Well—suited Andie perfectly.

"Do not dwell in the past, do not dream of the future, concentrate the mind on the present moment." No matter how wise, Andie thought, the Buddha's teachings were never easy to put into practice. She reached behind her and pulled the cord on the table lamp. If she was going to be awake, she might as well have light as her companion. She blinked at the sudden illumination and then found herself looking directly at her father's armchair, over the back of which was draped a gorgeous tweed throw her parents had bought on their trip to Ireland one summer. Cliff and Caro had often traveled alone together. In fact, only once had the Reynoldses gone abroad as a family, and that was to Italy when Andie was sixteen, Emma fourteen, and Daniel twelve. Andie remembered it as a magical two weeks, replete with new sights and sounds, new tastes and smells. It was a trip that had first opened her eyes to the possibilities of travel, a trip that had allowed her to catch a glimpse of a future that might truly suit her. But only a glimpse. At that tender age Andie hadn't been equipped to envision much else besides what her mother had already decided for her older daughter's future—marriage and children, membership in a respectable women's club, and if she were tenacious, the presidency of the PTA.

Andie's eyes shifted to a photograph of her father in a highly polished silver frame. *Danny must be in this house every week to keep everything so shipshape and sparkling*, she thought. In the photo Cliff looked downright robust, a broad smile on his face, his thick dark hair waving back off his forehead, his fists on his hips. Nothing in the image betrayed the fact that Cliff Reynolds had a congenital heart condition that would eventually take his life. The Reynolds children had known about their father's heart condition from an early age, but for them it was just a fact, like their father's brown eyes or the round-faced watch he always wore. The knowledge carried no threat to their safety as a family, and that was because Cliff had never let the heart defect get in the way of a zest for life. If Daniel wanted a "horseyback ride" around the living room, he got one. If Andie wanted a tent pitched in the backyard for a sleepover with her friends, the tent was pitched. If Emma wanted to show her father a new move she had learned in dance class, Cliff Reynolds was always a willing partner, even if he just stood there as a support when his middle child got up on her toes and attempted a pirouette.

Caro, on the other hand, had often used Cliff's condition to guilt her children into behaving. "Don't fight," she would say. "You know your father has a weak heart." Or "Make sure your homework is done before dinner. You don't want to upset your father." If Cliff was in earshot he would turn to the kids and wink. It was amusing, Andie thought, how her mother used her husband's heart trouble to justify all sorts of things, like trips to London or Japan or Hawaii. "Your father needs a nice long holiday," she would say, though Andie had never understood how the sheer physical strain of busy airports and long plane rides would be helpful to a man with a weak heart. Still, she smiled at the memory. And then Andie's smile faded when she remembered how her mother had told her that her divorcing Bob would kill her father. "His death will be on your head," Caro had warned. "If you still want to go ahead with this ridiculous idea, then you'll have to accept the consequences."

But the divorce had not been a ridiculous idea and it hadn't killed her father, Andie reminded herself. Cliff and Caro had gone on having dinner at the Angry Squire and attending dances at the Lower Waterville Country Club and hosting cocktail parties for the members of the Women's Institute and their husbands. And, of course, traveling.

Andie shifted again on the couch, remembering when she had been alone in the house for weeks at a time when her parents took off for foreign climes, a young and unhappy woman with a small child. Though part of her welcomed the chance to live without what she sometimes thought of as her parents' surveillance, she remembered all too well how the silence of the house would soon begin to prey on her nerves. She liked it when Daniel would come by for a few days between semesters at college. Emma rarely returned to Oliver's Well in those years, busy as she was with getting an education and later, starting her own business in Annapolis. Even Bob, never neglectful of those he loved, had been overworked, trying to grow and improve the plumbing business his father had started, and his visits to Honeysuckle Lane were often short and distracted.

Andie crossed her arms over her chest in a consciously self-protective gesture, as if the depression and anxiety of the past could somehow still hurt her. The nights, she recalled, had been the worst. Alone in the house with Rumi, she would become overwhelmed by feelings of inadequacy, certain that she would do something stupid or careless and accidentally put her child in harm's way. She imagined all sorts of disastrous scenarios. She would forget to turn off one of the gas burners and they would suffocate in their beds. She would spill scalding water from the teakettle over her daughter as she sat innocently in her high chair. She would trip while carrying Rumi down the stairs and the child would land on her head, killed instantly. Once or twice, when the panic was riding high, she had asked Bob to stay with her and he had obliged, until he began to date someone who, understandably, didn't want her boyfriend sleeping in the room next to his ex-wife. After that she considered seeing a doctor for an antianxiety prescription, but then felt afraid that she would accidentally overdose, leaving Rumi alone and helpless until someone finally came to find her, cold, dirty, and hungry.

When her parents finally returned from their travels, Andie would greet their arrival with mixed emotion, glad of their company and yet aware of their displeasure. For a few days they would be overly solicitous, as if they felt guilty for having left their troubled daughter and their innocent, helpless granddaughter alone. And then they would resume their usual behavior toward her, pleasant enough but always with an edge of disappointment.

And of course Caro always had something critical to say about how Andie had cared for the house in her absence. Well, Caro had been a perfectionist. Every picture frame in exact alignment, the house vacuumed every other day, sheets and towels neatly folded and stacked in a linen closet that would have made the most exacting housekeeper proud. *Not like me*, Andie thought with a rueful smile for no one. "I don't know where you came from," Caro would say, shaking her head at her oldest child's messy habits.

Sometimes Andie still asked herself the same question. Where indeed had she come from? From the very beginning she had been a disappointment. Her parents had fully expected their first child to be a boy; he was to be named after Cliff's father, Andrew. But a girl had come along instead, and "Andrew" became "Andrea." *I've never been what was expected of me*, she thought. *A miniature of my mother, a girl who excelled at the expected.*

Expectation. It could be a terrible thing when the expectations you attempted to fulfill were not of your own choosing. The expected would have been for Andie to give her daughter a more mainstream name. The expected would have been for Andie to stay in Oliver's Well with her husband and child, rather than for her to travel the world on her own. Sometimes, in very dark moments, Andie thought she would gladly give up all that she had achieved if she could turn back the clock and be a "normal" wife and mother. But only in very dark moments.

Andie scooted to a sitting position and reached for one of her books. It was Rumi's *The Spiritual Couplets*, a six-volume mystical poem regarded by some Sufis as the Persian language's Koran. Simply holding the book for a moment could bring Andie comfort. "Life is a beautiful gift from God," she whispered to the room.

And then she smiled, remembering the text that Bob—her anchor—had sent her earlier that evening. **Happy yr here**, it said. **Hugs, B**. Texting might be inadequate for what Andie thought of as true communication, but there was no denying it was quick and efficient. **Happy yr here, 2**, she had replied. **Kisses, A**.

Andie returned the book to the little table by the couch, turned off the light, and snuggled down under the old but immaculately clean blanket she had found in the linen closet that afternoon. Gratefully she welcomed the gift of sleep as it approached.

CHAPTER 9

At nine A.M. sharp, Daniel pulled into the drive in front of the house on Honeysuckle Lane. He got out of his car—a Honda CRV that doubled as his work vehicle—and jogged up the steps to the front door. He didn't bother to knock or to ring the bell. Why should he when he had a key and was the caretaker of the house? He was the one who had had the boiler repaired that February, the one who knew where all the cleaning supplies lived. He was the one who religiously and ever so carefully polished his mother's most prized possession, a desk of pollard oak designed and crafted by the famous British Regency cabinetmaker George Bullock.

Daniel opened the door, went inside, and closed the door behind him.

"Who's there?" Emma emerged from the direction of the kitchen, a dish towel in hand. "Oh, Danny, it's you. Why didn't you knock? I know there's not a lot of crime in Oliver's Well, but you startled me."

"But I have a key," he said. And then he added, "I'm used to coming and going as I please. Sorry if I frightened you."

Emma shrugged. "No big deal. Come on in. We're in the kitchen."

Daniel followed his sister. "Still eating breakfast?" he said, noting the slice of half-eaten toast at Emma's place, a bowl of yogurt and fruit in front of Andie, the half-empty press pot of coffee in the center of the table.

"We both slept late," Emma said. "Bad night for me, at least."

Andie was on her phone and taking notes in a small spiral notebook in front of her.

"Someone from her publisher," Emma explained, nodding toward her sister.

"I suppose you've checked into your office already?" Daniel asked Emma.

"Of course. I might be having trouble waking up, but I can't let my clients down."

Andie ended her call then and greeted her brother. "Good morning, Danny. You're out and about early."

"What's early about nine A.M.? Bad night for you, too?" he asked.

"Dreams. Exhausting dreams," Andie said. And then she yawned widely and reached for the coffeepot. "Being a lucid dreamer is not all it's cracked up to be."

Emma nodded toward the brown leather satchel slung across Daniel's chest. "Business?"

"Yes," he said. "Family business." Daniel took a seat across from his sisters and opened the satchel. "Here," he said, handing a stack of brochures to Emma. "These are from the top local real estate agents. Will you meet with each of them as soon as possible and decide on one who can best handle the sale of the house? I'm assuming we want to sell, right?"

Emma nodded.

"I think it's probably for the best if we sell as soon as we can," Andie said. "It's sort of awful to know the house is just sitting empty, when a family might be very happy living here. There was good energy here. There can be again."

A blob of yogurt fell from her spoon onto the table. Daniel reached for a napkin and wiped it up. "Good or bad energy, let's try to keep the place intact," he said, trying to keep a note of annoyance from his voice. "If we're going to auction off the furniture it's got to be in good condition. I've been keeping every-thing in pristine shape and I don't want it getting ruined now."

"Sorry, Danny," Andie said.

"Speaking of all you've been doing around here," Emma said, "Andie and I would like to give you some money to repay what you've obviously put out stocking the kitchen for our stay. Would—"

"No." Daniel knew that his tone had been harsh, but he hadn't been able to help it. "I'm not taking money from my sisters," he went on. "I don't need it." Daniel cleared his throat and removed a sheaf of papers from the satchel. He handed one set to each of his sisters. "I've made an inventory of the contents of the house. I need you both to go through it carefully and note anything I might have missed."

Emma flipped through her set of stapled pages. "This must have taken you ages," she said. "It looks very thorough."

Andie put her copy on the table. "Most of this is just stuff, Danny. I really don't care what happens to the bric-a-brac. You and Emma can decide what to do with it."

Daniel felt his frustration mounting. "We *all* have to make the decisions about the contents of the house," he said firmly. "What to sell, what to keep, how to sell. It's what Mom wanted. Anna Maria can help you if you really feel overwhelmed. But remem-ber, she's already stretched pretty thin."

"Don't worry, Danny," Emma said. "Andie and I will handle this on our own. Do you want some coffee?"

"No," Daniel said. "Thanks. Oh, Emma. I talked to Joe Her-bert this morning. He suggested I might want to reconsider the way Anna Maria and I have been putting away in the kids' col-lege savings plan. He said because college is still some time away, we might want to be a bit less conservative than we've been."

"I think Joe's probably right," Emma said. "But as I don't have access to your accounts, I can't be certain. If you'd like me to take a look at anything, I'd be happy to, though I totally trust Joe. He hasn't steered us wrong yet."

"Dad would be glad to see you taking an interest," Daniel said.

"Why wouldn't I be?" Emma asked, shaking her head. "Sophia and Marco are my family."

Daniel turned to Andie. "Well, we all know that Dad intended Emma to be his successor, but our Emma had other ideas. She wasn't interested in inheriting the family business."

"What made you bring that up?' Emma asked. "It's ancient history and hardly news."

Daniel shrugged. "No reason. Oh, and you should know that Mary Bernadette Fitzgibbon has been pestering me about our giving the Oliver's Well Historical Association the George Bullock desk. She reminded me the other day—as if I could forget—that in 1805 the British government ordered a suite of furniture from George Bullock for Emperor Napoleon when he was exiled on Saint Helena." Daniel laughed. "Anyway, I wouldn't put it past her to approach either one of you if she runs into you around town."

"Is she still chairperson?" Emma asked. "The estimable Mrs. Fitzgibbon."

"No, she retired from that position about six months ago," Daniel said. "Leonard De Witt took over. But she still plays a vital if unofficial role. Mary Bernadette Fitzgibbon *is* the OWHA."

"Mom cherished that desk, didn't she?" Andie commented. "Passed down through the generations of her family like it was."

"Maybe we should find out its financial worth," Emma suggested. "If it's valuable, and I'd guess it is, we could sell it and split the proceeds. I'd be happy to give my share to Sophia and Marco," she added. "Something else to stash away toward college."

"Why not just let the OWHA have the desk?" Andie asked. "That way everyone can enjoy it, not just a single owner. It's a very beautiful piece."

Daniel shook his head. "But it doesn't belong to everyone. It belongs to us, the Reynoldses via the Carlyles. By the way, Rumi agrees with me one hundred percent. She absolutely doesn't want the desk to leave the family. It's what Mom wanted."

Andie smiled. "Do you remember the time when you were about five or six, Danny, and Mom caught you using crayons at the desk?"

Daniel frowned. "I had a coloring book. The desk wasn't at risk."

"That's not what Mom thought."

"She wouldn't even let Dad use the desk," Emma added. "I'm surprised she didn't keep it tucked away somewhere under lock and key instead of in the living room where it was vulnerable."

"She liked to see it every day," Daniel said.

Andie nodded. "And she wanted other people to see it, too. It always elicited comment."

"She was proud of it," Daniel said firmly, "and rightly so."

"Okay, so the desk stays here, at least for now." Emma poured more coffee into her cup; Daniel hoped that she knew how to properly clean the filter in a press pot. If it wasn't properly cleaned the resulting coffee could be negatively affected.

"I've got to go," he said, rising from the table. At the door to the kitchen he turned. "One more thing. I just had the baseboards in the living room painted, so try not to damage them. And don't dust Mom's desk. I use a special-formula polish." Daniel loved his sisters, but he wasn't entirely sure they fully realized the preciousness of this house and all that it contained. In fact, he was pretty certain they didn't understand the half of it.

"Okay, Danny," Emma said. Andie just nodded.

CHAPTER 10

"This could take us forever!" Andie waved her copy of Daniel's inventory.

Emma laughed. She held her own copy of their brother's inventory in one hand and a pencil in the other. "We'd better get cracking," she said. "I'll start at this end of the room, by Dad's writing table. Why don't you start on the bookshelves?"

While her sister began to check the tightly stocked shelves against the inventory Daniel had compiled, Emma began, half-absentmindedly, to check off the vases and candlesticks and small statuettes her brother had so meticulously listed. When she turned her attention to the room's alcove, home to a plaster column on top of which sat a bronze bust of Shakespeare, she smiled. She had always loved this house, with its clean layout, relatively spacious rooms, and its various unique touches not found in the other houses on Honeysuckle Lane—and over the years Emma had been inside most of them. The alcove in the den was one such touch; the archway separating the dining from the living room was another; the bow window in the master bedroom yet another. Whoever had built number 32 had succeeded in balancing function with charm.

Though Emma had never regretted leaving Oliver's Well, she had always missed the house itself and had often thought of how small changes here and there might make it even more pleasant. Of course, she would have to own the house outright to make any changes.

Emma was so forcibly struck by the thought the pencil fell from her hand and onto her father's writing table. Since when had she ever even *vaguely* considered being the sole owner of her parents' house? But it wasn't so outrageous an idea, was it? She was discontent with her life as it was and she no longer had Ian to use as an excuse for not making whatever changes she might want to make. But . . . *No,* she told herself firmly. *It would be a mad, bad idea, living in this house, coming back to Oliver's Well. It would.*

"Since when did Danny get to be such a fusspot?" Andie wondered, breaking into Emma's thoughts. "Look, he's catalogued every single book in this room! Even the paperbacks we had as teens. I can't believe Mom held on to them all these years. They're utterly without value."

"Not even sentimental value?" Emma asked.

"*The Mystery of the Flaming Lake? My Dog Ozzy? The Best Boyfriend, Ever?* Do you remember anything about those books other than the titles?"

Emma laughed. "No. That's probably a good thing. Although a flaming lake sounds pretty interesting."

Andie pulled a paperback with a particularly lurid cover off the shelf and tossed it onto the couch. "Danny got so worked up this morning about a little bit of spilled yogurt," she said. "It seems unlike him to be so nit-picky. This whole estate business must really be driving him crazy."

"And what about the remark about the baseboards in the living room?" Emma asked. "What does he think we're going to do, take Magic Markers to them? Or Windex to the Bullock desk?" *If I did buy this house and move back in,* Emma wondered, *would Danny relinquish his control of it or would he be checking up on me daily to make sure I hadn't accidentally burned it down?*

"The family created a bit of a monster in Danny," Andie said with a sigh.

"A loveable one."

"Yes," Andie agreed. "Most times."

The sisters continued to work in companionable silence for a time, and Emma realized once again how she treasured their relationship. To be with Andie was to be with someone Emma trusted and loved entirely. And it had been that way right from the start. Being only two years apart, they had spent a lot of time together as children, playing with their dolls or kicking around a soccer ball or watching Disney movies, or simply being each other's companion on long summer afternoons when it was too hot to do anything but sit close to the air conditioner, hair held up off their sweaty necks. Those experiences, simple as they were, had created a strong bond between the sisters, a bond that continued still, even though their adult lives had taken them in different directions and they rarely got to spend time face to face.

"I was surprised when Danny suggested we come with him and the kids when they go to cut down a Christmas tree," Andie said, breaking the silence. "Like we used to do with Dad, he said. I always felt horribly sad at the destruction of a living thing," she admitted. "Emma? When Danny said we should come along because the kids want us there, did you believe him?"

"Not really," Emma told her. "I mean, I don't think Sophia and Marco would mind us along, but I think Danny is the one with the sudden need for family outings."

"You're right," Andie agreed. "He's nostalgic for our youth. And in some ways our childhood really was idyllic. At least, it seems that way to me now, aside from Mom always telling me to watch my weight. Things only started to go wrong for me when I made the decision to marry Bob. To marry anyone, really. To settle down to a life I wasn't meant to live. But that was no one's fault but my own."

"You felt under pressure from Mom and Dad," Emma pointed out. "They could take some of the blame."

"But why should they?" Andie shrugged. "I own my choices, right or wrong."

Emma thought about that. She thought about the pressure she

had felt to follow in her father's footsteps, even before he'd made her the offer to join him in business, and she realized that she still harbored some residual resentment over her mother's inability to appreciate her decision to make a life elsewhere. It was childish, holding a grudge, blaming her mother for being nothing more or less than who she was. Childish and pointless.

"Look, Andie." Emma pointed to an old-fashioned black metal alarm clock on one of the bookshelves, where it was being used as a prop for a few copies of *National Geographic*. "This was Grandma Reynolds's clock. It's not exactly valuable. In fact, I'm kind of surprised Mom allowed it to be kept around."

"Only because Dad wanted it to be," Andie reminded her. "She'd never deprive Dad of something he really wanted, like his mother's old wind-up alarm clock."

Emma laughed. "Do you remember the awful din this thing made? Really, your eardrum could burst if you were in ten feet of it when it went off."

"I think it can safely go in the trash." Andie raised an eyebrow. "After we ask Danny's permission."

"I doubt he has any memory of Grandpa Andrew or Grandma Alice at all. They died when he was just one. He can't have much of an attachment to what little they left behind."

"Maybe not," Andie agreed. "Still, let's play it safe and check with him before we start loading up the trash bags."

Emma nodded. And she thought of how their Carlyle grandparents had died when Andie was seven, she herself five, and Daniel just three. Daniel had only met William and Martha two or three times and probably had little if any recollection of them, either. "After all the grandparents were gone," she said to her sister, "it really was just the five of us, wasn't it? We were a fairly insular family."

"And now it's just the three. Well, we should include Anna Maria and the three cousins. The next generation. The Reynolds family's future."

"Yes. Oh, look! Remember this?" Emma reached onto another shelf and picked up a small brass elephant from a group of small sculptures in the shapes of animals. "Mom and Dad got this in a flea market in Paris, wasn't it?"

"Yes, I think so." Andie laughed. "Remember how Danny used to mispronounce elephant? 'Ephelant' he used to say."

"That was pretty adorable, actually," Emma said, returning the elephant to the company of his friends.

"You know, I always wished I could go with Mom and Dad on their adventures," Andie said suddenly. "Even when I was very young I knew I wanted to be somewhere *else*. Though it took me long enough to act on that desire."

Emma smiled. "There were obstacles in your way. Like those parental expectations."

"What about you?" Andie asked. "Did you want to jet off with Mom and Dad?"

"No," Emma said. "Not really. But at the same time I felt kind of abandoned when they left. And I absolutely hated having a nanny here with us when Mom and Dad were gone. I felt angry all the time, like what right did this stranger have to tell me what to eat and when to go to bed. They were all nice, I suppose. Still, I couldn't wait for Mom and Dad to come home." *Mostly Dad*, she thought. *It was always Dad for me when I was young.*

"Danny didn't like when Mom and Dad went away, either," Andie said. "I remember one time when he cried for three hours straight. He was little, of course. In fact, it might have been the first time Mom and Dad took a really long trip. I guess the poor kid thought they were never coming back. I remember I felt so bad that I couldn't comfort him. I tried, but nothing seemed to work."

"You didn't mind the nannies, did you?" Emma asked.

"No," Andie said. "I didn't. I did what they told me to do, but I never made any sort of personal connection with them. They didn't even register enough for me to dislike them. I suppose that's odd."

"I think it sounds smart," Emma said. "It was an effective way of coping with a stranger in the house who suddenly had the authority to send you to bed without your supper if you acted up. I wish I had been able to detach like you did, instead of feeling so grumpy about it."

Andie smiled. "You felt what you felt. You were only a child."

"So were you," Emma pointed out. "But you were already on the right path, weren't you?"

Andie shrugged and pulled another paperback from the bookshelves. "*The Count of Monte Crisco: A Chrissy Clarke Culinary Mystery,*" she read aloud with a laugh. "Now, who do you think was reading this?"

CHAPTER 11

"Hi, Jack," Daniel called, though with his window up there was no way Jack Wiseman, driving past going the other way, could hear him. Still, Jack would have seen his wave, as Daniel had seen Jack's tip of his ubiquitous Greek fisherman's cap. It was one of the things Daniel loved about life in Oliver's Well, the strong sense of community.

Daniel was driving back to his home on Little Rock Lane from a private cooking lesson for a young woman recently out of college and sick of eating takeout for dinner. "I can't even make pasta properly," she had moaned. "It always comes out in a lump! My mother tried to teach me the basics, but I never paid attention. Help!" The woman was the daughter of a frequent client, and a good one at that, so Daniel had put on his apron and gone to the woman's rescue.

It wasn't something he did often, give private lessons on the basics of cooking and baking, and he didn't advertise such services, but on occasion someone like this young woman approached him, desperate for knowledge. They were prepared to pay well, and without exception these private students were eager and attentive learners. With a business to grow and two children to raise and someday send to college, Daniel wasn't picky about how he earned his money. Besides, he'd discovered that he enjoyed the teaching experience. It was less physically taxing than catering parties for fifty or more people, and the look of pride on a student's face when he or she managed the first medium boiled egg or apple pie or classic white sauce was ample payment of another kind.

On the subject of teaching, Daniel thought as he came up on the high school he and his sisters had attended. He remembered his high school years as if they had only just taken place. On the very first day of his freshman year, Emma, a junior, had declared that she would look out for him. She briefed him on what teachers gave less homework than others and what food to avoid in the cafeteria and what other kids to stay away from because they were bad news. And she had gone about it all discreetly, so Daniel hadn't felt he was being coddled in public. No teenaged boy wanted his big sister hovering over him, threatening his burgeoning masculinity and very fragile male ego.

Those four years had been happy ones overall. He had done well in his classes, played a fairly important role on the junior and then varsity soccer team, and kissed his first girlfriend by the time he was a sophomore. That she dumped him a month later hardly mattered because two weeks after that another girl caught his eye. Thinking back on his mildly lothario days, Daniel felt a surge of paternal protectiveness. There was no way he was going to let his daughter date until she was at least sixteen. And as for Marco, well, he was going to get a very stern lecture about responsibility and respect for women the moment he hit puberty.

Daniel's attention was briefly caught by what he thought was Emma's car just turning into the parking lot of the one Chinese restaurant in town. But another glance told him that the car was an older model Lexus, not Emma's. *Good,* he thought. *That means she's likely at the house, getting down to business.* Daniel still couldn't shake his irritation, the feeling that his sisters were simply going through the motions, not really *caring* the way he did about the family's belongings, the Audubon prints their father had treasured, the Bullock desk that had been in the Carlyle family for almost two hundred years. Those things were important; in fact, they were more than just *things*. They had meaning. They deserved respect, and only partly because they had been respected by Cliff and Caro. They were . . . they were visible manifestations of continuity.

An ambulance from Oliver's Well Emergency Corp was coming up behind him, sirens screaming, lights flashing, and Daniel quickly pulled the car to the side of the road. At least they had been spared that at the end, he thought, easing back into traffic, the mad dash to the hospital. Caro had died at home, peacefully, in the surroundings she loved, unlike her husband, who had passed away in the ER. Caro had been with her husband at the end; Daniel had been there, too. When the attending doctor pronounced Cliff dead, Caro had asked Daniel to give her a moment alone with her husband. And when a few minutes later his mother had come out of the cubicle where his father was already growing cold, Daniel had seen a profound change. He had known right then and there that Caro Reynolds would not be long for this world.

Daniel's lips tightened. He would never forget the final days of his mother's life. Anna Maria had been a blessing, supportive, kind, willing to do some of the less pleasant work of caring for a dying person when the wonderfully competent private nurse they had hired for Caro took her breaks.

"Do not go gentle into that good night. / Rage, rage against the dying of the light." There had been no rage in his mother's final moments, no protest against the imminent arrival of death. The nurse had left the room to give Daniel and his mother privacy, allowing them to be alone together when Caro breathed her last. She was still beautiful at the end, still the elegant woman Daniel had always loved and even at times had adored.

The nurse, as if sensing her patient's passing, had come back into the room immediately. "I'll close her eyes," she had said softly, but Daniel had refused. "I'd like to do it," he told her, and he had, gently and finally. He remembered thinking, *I'll never see those eyes again. My mother will never look at me again, with all the love she had for me.* It was only then that he had broken down in a wave of hot tears.

Daniel felt his hands tighten on the wheel. He wondered if an adult could be considered an orphan. That's how he felt, orphaned and unmoored now that the anchors of the family, Cliff and Caro, were gone.

His children missed their grandparents, too. Cliff and Caro had been a fixture in their lives since the day they were born. Never a week went by without Sophia and Marco spending an afternoon at the house on Honeysuckle Lane; never a week went by without Grandma and Grandpa having dinner at their son's home. That is until illness and death had gotten in the way.

Not surprisingly, at least to Daniel, Rumi was the grandchild most affected by her grandmother's death; Caro had in some ways been a second mother to her, both before and after Andie's escape from Oliver's Well. If Rumi was a bit spoiled by the attention she got from family members seeking to make up for Andie's absence, well, that was understandable. Daniel had come to feel very protective about his niece. In some way he regarded Rumi as his own child.

Daniel turned onto Little Rock Lane and a moment later pulled into the driveway of his home, noting that Anna Maria's car wasn't there. He looked at his watch. Of course, he thought. She would be taking the kids to pageant practice. He got out of his car and realized he was looking forward to a good cup of espresso before dinner that night with his family. Sometimes, he thought, inserting his key into the lock of the front door, it was the little pleasures that helped soothe the deepest pain.

CHAPTER 12

"**R**umi." Andie smiled and enfolded her daughter in a hug. "It's so good to see you."

Rumi put her arms around her mother for about a second before she pulled away. "It's been a while," she said, not quite meeting her mother's eye.

"Yes," Andie said, closing the front door. "It has. You look well."

Rumi shrugged. "I'm okay." She turned then to greet Emma, with, Andie saw, a lot more enthusiasm than she had shown her mother. Sophia and Marco then gathered around their cousin, each vying for her attention, Sophia with a braided bracelet to present to her, Marco holding up his finger to show Rumi a new blister. Rumi told Sophia the bracelet was awesome and squealed in mock horror over Marco's blister, which was exactly the response he seemed to have wanted. It was good to see her daughter so loved and appreciated by her family. Andie remembered what Daniel had told her about Rumi's determination to keep Caro's George Bullock Regency desk in the family. The Family. It mattered differently to mother and daughter, Andie mused. But that was all right. Rumi was her own person, not meant to be a clone of either parent.

"I'm starved, Uncle Daniel," Rumi said, linking her arm in his. "What's for dinner?"

"Come help me put it out," he said, "and you'll see." Together they headed toward the kitchen.

Emma had set the large dining room table with their mother's everyday dishes, still finer than Andie's own serviceable crockery, and now they took their seats, Daniel at one end, where his father had sat, Anna Maria on his right, Rumi on his left. No one, Andie noted, sat in what had been Caro's place, opposite Daniel.

Daniel had prepared a pork roast with apples and onions, roasted potatoes, and a salad of winter vegetables. Andie brought her own meal to the table, a hearty homemade ratatouille over brown rice.

"My mother always has to be different," Rumi announced. "If suddenly we all went vegetarian she'd be chowing down on a turkey leg before you could say 'pass the gravy.'"

Daniel laughed, but he was the only one. Andie pretended not to have heard her daughter's remark. "That's a beautiful necklace you're wearing," she said to Rumi. "Is the center stone an amazonite?"

"Yeah. It is."

"Did you get the necklace in town?" Andie asked.

"Actually," Rumi said, fingering the stone, "I made it."

"Really?" Emma said. "I didn't know you were interested in crafts and design."

Rumi shrugged. "I'm not. I just like jewelry."

"So do I!" Sophia piped. "Someday I'm gonna have lots."

"I do some beadwork," Andie said, smiling at her niece. "And sometimes I embroider, nothing fancy, things my friends and I use in our daily lives. I find that making something by hand is a good way to open my mind to a larger creative energy. As my favorite poet and prophet says, music, poetry, and dance—all of the arts, really—are a path for reaching God."

"It's not like that for me," Rumi said quickly. "I just do it for fun. It's not like it's important, not like studying to be a dental hygienist." Then she laughed and looked around the table. "I'm not like Mom, always needing to be in the spotlight. I just want to do my job, get paid for it, and come home at the end of the day."

Andie, aware that she had been insulted, but unwilling to argue her daughter's completely untrue remark, simply smiled.

Daniel took a sip of wine and then carefully sat his glass at the top of his plate. Looking at no one in particular, he said, "They say that people who are insecure need a lot of attention from others."

Andie's hand tightened on her fork. But before she could respond to her brother's pointed remark, her sister spoke up.

"They say that, do they?" Emma said, arching her brows. "Well, maybe *they* are right after all. I seem to remember more than one occasion where you, Danny, threw a bit of a tantrum when you thought Mom or Dad or even Andie and I weren't paying enough attention to you." Emma turned to her sister and smiled. "Do you remember the time he dropped to the floor and began kicking his feet because Dad didn't look up from the newspaper fast enough when Danny wanted to show him a drawing he'd made? And the time he threatened to hold his breath 'forever' because Mom didn't notice he'd put his own cereal bowl in the dishwasher?"

Andie, not one to enjoy laughter at the expense of another person, was nevertheless grateful for Emma's deft intervention. She smiled as Sophia and Marco hooted with laughter, oblivious to their father's frown.

"Oh, Danny," Emma said, "don't take yourself so seriously."

Anna Maria, Andie saw, seemed too busy with her meal to get involved with a sibling tussle. Either that or she was simply being smart. Rumi's expression was hard to read; Andie realized she wouldn't be surprised if Rumi suddenly flew to her uncle's defense. To forestall further unpleasantness, Andie cleared her throat and raised her glass. "I'd like to offer a toast," she said.

Daniel was the next to raise his glass. "All right," he said. "To what?"

"To us. To the family. To being here together for Christmas."

The others echoed, Rumi and Daniel loudest in their cries of "Hear, hear!"

To herself, Andie repeated this very important bit of wisdom: "Resolutely train yourself to attain peace."

CHAPTER 13

After dinner had been eaten, the dishes put into the dishwasher, the knives (Daniel's personal set) washed and carefully stowed in their traveling case, and the pots washed, Emma retreated to her parents' bedroom where she now sat propped up in their king-sized bed. The carved frame was made of walnut and must have cost a small fortune, especially for a newly wed couple. Then again, maybe Caro's family had helped with the purchase.

Emma was trying to concentrate on one of the books she had loaded into her Kindle, a biography of the fascinating Frida Kahlo, but her mind wouldn't behave. It kept wandering back to dinner, hearing Rumi's insulting remarks about her mother, watching in retrospect Daniel's whispered asides to his niece. Really, she thought, Daniel was too much of a conspirator with Rumi, encouraging her borderline disrespectful attitude. It annoyed her, but she felt she had no right to intervene—well, except in the rather childish way she had at dinner. Still, she wished *someone* would step in to help mother and daughter get past this difficulty that seemed to have suddenly sprung up. As far as she knew there had never been trouble between them in the past.

Emma wondered what Anna Maria felt about the situation.

She was an emotionally astute woman; at the same time, one who refrained from interfering where her help might not be welcome. Maybe now was a time that Anna Maria *should* interfere, Emma thought. If Daniel would listen to anyone it would be his wife.

"Knock knock."

Andie was standing in the open doorway wearing a voluminous caftan-style garment in a swirling blue and green pattern. "Come in," Emma said, patting the mattress. "Join me."

Andie got into the bed and settled next to her sister. "I could never stay in here," she said, glancing around the room. "Too many memories, like how I would climb up and wiggle down between Mom and Dad when I had a nightmare." Andie laughed. "Mom always told me I was being silly and took me right back to my own bed."

"I don't feel that way," Emma told her. "About the memories. Now that Mom and Dad are gone . . . Well, to me the room feels almost neutral. Free of memories, if that makes sense."

Andie nodded. "Yes," she said. "It makes sense. Just not for me."

"Besides," Emma went on, "I couldn't bear to stay in my old room, not after all the times Ian shared it with me over the years. Don't get me wrong; I'm not at all sorry I broke up with him. It's just that I don't need any reminders of Ian Hayes under the family roof. That part of my life is over. He's been texting and calling me nonstop, by the way."

"What does he have to say?" Andie asked.

"Things like, 'Hope you're having a good time with the family,' and 'How's Danny's business?' and 'Did Andie get there safely?' Nothing weird but . . ."

"Hmm. You told me once he has no family of his own, right?"

"Right."

"Well," Andie said, "*we've* become his family over time. It's normal he'd be reluctant to cut all ties so cleanly. He's in denial. Be patient with him, Emma."

"I'm trying to be," Emma told her sister. "But I don't want to give him false hope by being too friendly."

"I'm sorry to say that's not something you can entirely control.

Right now he'll interpret whatever you say or don't say to mean what he needs it to mean."

Emma sighed. "You're right. Well, I guess I'll just take it day by day. Maybe Ian will meet someone at a holiday party and fall madly in love and forget I ever existed."

Andie laughed. "Dream on."

The sisters were quiet for a time, side by side, peaceful in each other's company, each alone with her thoughts. Emma's mind again wandered back to her brother and his strange behavior toward Andie. She was sure their mother would not have approved, although, Emma thought, Caro probably would have guessed at and understood her son's underlying motives, as odd as they might be. Caro Reynolds had always had a strong connection with her youngest child.

In fact, that was probably the reason Caro had chosen Daniel to take over from her as trustee of the estate about a year before she passed, when she no longer felt capable of handling it properly. As trustee, Daniel, with the counsel of the family's lawyer, Deb Buchanan, and with the advice of the family's accountant, Joe Herbert, had taken on a great deal of responsibility. It had been his job to ensure that there would be enough money for Caro Reynolds to live comfortably for as long as she was going to live. It was also Daniel's responsibility to manage any residual income from Cliff's accounting firm and from retirement accounts; if there had been any debts, it would have been Daniel's job to handle those as well. In short, Emma thought, as trustee, Daniel had been quite literally the Protector of the Family.

At first Emma had been a little hurt by her mother's choosing Daniel over her, a financial professional. Maybe, she had thought, Caro was still holding a grudge against her for not having accepted her father's offer of sharing the business. But Emma had soon let go of the hurt; she was busy enough with her own life, and as long as her brother did a good job caring for the trust, she was content.

"What have you been thinking about?" Andie asked, breaking the long silence. "You've been frowning."

"I have? I was just thinking about Mom having chosen Daniel as trustee of the estate after Dad died," she said. "It seemed an odd choice at first but . . ." She shrugged.

Andie turned to her sister. "Daniel is trustee? Why didn't anyone tell me?" she asked.

"You should have gotten a notice from Deb Buchanan. I did. Mom didn't feel she could handle the finances on her own anymore."

"Well, I do tend to just file papers regarding the estate. And by file I mean stuff them into a drawer unread." Andie paused. "You know, I wonder if Danny's being appointed trustee plays a part in his assumption of the role of patriarch. The lists, the inventories."

"I wouldn't be surprised," Emma said with a laugh. "You wouldn't have wanted that role, would you? Matriarch?"

"No, not at all," Andie said firmly. "I just never thought about Mom's feeling unable to handle her affairs. She always seemed to me to be absurdly competent. Of course, when she died I hadn't seen her for almost a year. I had no idea how quickly she was failing."

"Didn't Danny keep you updated?" Emma asked. "He sent me daily dispatches about Mom's condition, even when there wasn't anything new to tell."

Andie smiled ruefully. "Obviously not as often or as accurately as he did you."

"Well, I have to say that Danny did an excellent job of protecting Mom's assets. She was never in need, and now there's money for those of us still here."

"Whether we want it or not."

Emma smiled. "Be that as it may, Dad would have been proud of his son. Andie? Did you find it odd that Joe Herbert delivered Dad's eulogy?"

"I guess a little," Andie admitted. "I assumed Mom would ask one of us."

"She told me that Dad had requested Joe. Honestly, I would have liked to be the one to speak in Dad's memory. I couldn't help but wonder if he ever forgave me for choosing to move away and start my own business."

Andie put her arm around her sister. "Poor Emma. I know that Dad forgave you, as if there was anything to forgive. I'm sure he was disappointed, but that's all."

"I suppose you're right. But it hurt a bit that it was Joe standing there and not me, or even you or Danny."

"Still," Andie pointed out, "Dad got the tribute he deserved, and that's what really matters."

"You're right about that, too. Joe did a great job, probably better than I could have done. In the last ten or fifteen years of Dad's life it was Joe, not me, who knew him best. Next to Mom, of course."

"You had a life to lead, Emma. Don't waste time on regrets." Andie took her arm from around her sister's shoulders and swung her legs over the side of the bed. "Well, I need to get some sleep," she said.

"How's the couch working out for you?" Emma asked.

Andie smiled. "I've slept on worse."

Emma listened to her sister's footsteps descending the stairs until she heard the sound of the door to the den gently closing. She turned off the bedside lamp, slid down under the covers, and stared into the darkened room. And she thought back to that moment in the den when the idea of buying her parents' house had first occurred to her.

She wasn't a stupid or a reckless woman. She believed that the time for a big change was now, before she started to feel that she was simply too tired to stage a revolution in her life. She had shed Ian and that was a good thing, a step forward into her future. But what exactly came next? The old blueprint she had created for her life needed to be replaced by one to better fit her needs going forward—whatever they might be exactly.

To detach from old habits that had led her to this point in her life, without love. Could that be it; could that be her goal? Except for a few sociable colleagues, her circle of friends in Annapolis was primarily made up of people she had met through

Ian. While they were nice, intelligent, and successful, she had come to realize that she wouldn't miss spending time with any of them, whether she stayed in Annapolis or not. The truth was she had always been a fairly private person, not big on making friends. Except, that is, for Maureen Kline, her old school friend. In fact, they had made plans to meet the next morning.

Emma hadn't seen Maureen since Rumi's party, but they weren't the kind of friends who needed regular face time to feel bonded. Whenever she did see Maureen, even if it was after a full year apart, she felt as if they had been together but a moment before. Still, it would be nice to spend more time with her, sharing one of the massive cinnamon buns at Cookies 'n Crumpets, window shopping at the absurdly high end jewelry store in Lawrenceville, or indulging in a martini at the Angry Squire. Maureen's friendship certainly added a strong attraction to the idea of coming home to Oliver's Well.

But it was just an idea, and often ideas never came to fruition. Emma turned on her side and settled into the ever-comforting fetal position. Before long, she was sound asleep.

CHAPTER 14

The sun was not quite up, but Andie had been awake for some time. As she made her way to the kitchen she noted that but for the ticking of the stately grandfather clock in the living room, the house was absolutely still. Emma was not out of bed; she wasn't meeting Maureen Kline for breakfast until eight-thirty.

Andie made a pot of coffee and when it was brewed she took a cup into the backyard. She pulled her bathrobe more tightly around her and breathed in the cold morning air. How many early mornings had she enjoyed in this yard! She had often snuck out of the house before breakfast to watch the dew dry as the sun came up and to witness her mother's flowers turn from gray to red and pink and white.

For some reason she couldn't identify, Andie suddenly recalled a birthday party at which one of the guests, a boy Andie didn't know very well—but whom for some reason now lost to time she had invited—pushed a girl into a rosebush, where she cut her cheek on a thorn. Andie had never before witnessed an act of violence, and that's what it was, though the boy—what was his name?—had laughingly sworn the shove was "just a joke." She remembered feeling sick to her stomach, unable to enjoy the rest of her party even after her mother had cleaned the girl's cut and covered it with a Band-Aid. Still, Andie had gathered enough courage by then to tell the boy to leave, and surprisingly, he had gone quietly. She had been less afraid to stand up to bullies after that.

Andie took another sip of the cooling coffee, and more memories came rushing to her. As clearly as if he were standing there before her in flesh and blood, Andie saw her father at the charcoal grill, wielding a spatula and laughingly boasting that he was the grillmeister of Oliver's Well. She remembered, too, all the times they had eaten dinner on the patio on a spring or summer's evening, the sun still high in the sky, the sound of laughter from the neighboring houses drifting over them, her father lifting his glass in a toast to his family.

Dad. My wonderful father. It wasn't unusual for her to speak to Cliff now that he had passed on, even though when he was alive she hadn't been in the habit of turning to him for advice or comfort. Sometimes, Andie thought, watching two little birds busily flitting around the birdbath situated near the rosebushes, it was only at a distance that you could see the value of what was once right before your eyes. Sometimes it was only at a distance you could learn to love a person in the way he deserved to be loved.

Now Andie's thoughts traveled into the recent past, touching on Rumi's remarks at dinner about her mother needing to be the center of attention, about her mother having to be different, as if Andie walked at her own pace simply to be perverse. That wasn't at all the way it was, and by now, Andie thought, Rumi should know better. It was upsetting that her daughter didn't seem to understand her—or that she had decided she didn't want to understand her.

Andie sighed, her breath visible in the air. She and Rumi had shared so many good times through the years. There were the early visits to the ashram in a suburb of Baltimore—an adventure Rumi had particularly enjoyed—and later, the books they had read at the same time and talked about via phone, and the times when Andie visited Oliver's Well and they would take turns closing their eyes and pointing to a spot on the map of Virginia and taking a day or overnight trip in Andie's rental car. Such simple fun. Such comfortable companionship. It would be terrible if their relationship were to come to an end over something as trivial as not being around to blow out candles on a cake.

But the fact was that people fell out of love, even parents and children. Maybe, Andie thought, holding her cup of coffee more tightly, this sad fact was something she would have to learn to accept in her own life. Andie remembered how when Rumi started high school she had announced that she would be using her middle name, Caroline, in public from then on. Maybe already she had wanted to disassociate herself from her mother's "otherness." Maybe she had wanted to further the bond with the grandmother who had helped raise her. Or maybe Rumi had simply wanted to "fit in" as teenagers so often do. Andie had never questioned her daughter's decision.

"The wound is the place where the light enters you." Andie believed the message of her beloved poet, but that didn't mean the wound wasn't painful and that it sometimes didn't fester before you could see the brightness or feel the warmth of the healing light.

Her cup of coffee now empty, Andie went back inside the house. She heard the sound of footsteps on the stairs and went about pouring a cup of coffee for her sister. "Good morning," she said, as Emma came into the kitchen.

"Good morning. I saw you out in the backyard a little while ago. What were you doing?"

Andie smiled. "I was calling up ghosts," she said.

"How did that work out for you?" Emma asked, accepting the cup Andie handed her.

"Not well. It never does."

CHAPTER 15

Emma was waiting for Maureen Kline at Cookies 'n Crumpets that morning at a quarter past eight. The bakery was busy with people lingering over artisanal coffee and buttery, jam-filled pastry as well as with people dashing in for breakfast on the go, but she had managed to snag a table for two near the window. She also had managed to scoop up the last of the infamous cinnamon buns.

The door opened and Emma glanced up from her newspaper, the day's issue of the *Oliver's Well Gazette*. A man had just come in and was making his way to the order counter. She thought he was about her age. He was not overly tall; he might even have been a bit shorter than her. His hair was dark blond, and his eyes—Emma only glimpsed them as he walked by—looked to be dark brown. He was wearing dark jeans, brown, unmistakably Italian leather shoes, and a well-cut jacket. But it wasn't his clothing that drew her attention, as nice as it was. It was his . . . It was just *him*.

Emma didn't want to appear rude should he catch her eye, but she couldn't seem to look away. It wasn't that he reminded her of someone she knew back in Annapolis. But it was almost as if she *recognized* him. The feeling was disconcerting but not unpleasant.

The café was small and Emma couldn't help but overhear the man's order—a corn muffin with a side of warm honey and a black coffee. She smiled to herself. *So*, she thought, *he has a sweet tooth*. She was sorry when the man paid for his breakfast and left the café. If he had lingered or taken a seat . . .

Maureen made her appearance a moment later, and with a wave she headed to the counter for her coffee. In the past few years Maureen had made a conscious effort to up her style game. Before that, and especially after her divorce, she had been—and Emma hadn't been thinking anything everyone else hadn't been thinking—downright dowdy. Today, however, she was wearing a white silk blouse with a smart gray pants suit that fit her perfectly. It wasn't couture, but it was a vast improvement on the ancient ill-fitting suits she used to wear. And her hair, once close to a national disaster (that had been Maureen's term for it), was now stylishly cut and the gray professionally disguised.

Emma smiled as Maureen joined her. So many memories! In grammar school they had played with Barbie dolls. In middle school they had spent hours riding their bikes around Oliver's Well, talking about what exciting, adventurous people they were going to be when they grew up. They had double-dated at the high school senior prom. Maureen had visited Emma when she was away at college. Emma had been a bridesmaid in Maureen's wedding. When Maureen's father had suffered a stroke, Emma had gone back to Oliver's Well for a few days to help Maureen care for her parents.

Maureen bent down and gave Emma a hug. "So, back in Oliver's Well for Christmas. Are you staying through New Year's?" she asked, taking a seat.

"Probably," Emma said. "It's great to see everyone. The kids are growing so fast. And Danny's got a full schedule of Christmas activities planned for us!"

"Oliver's Well *is* pretty charming at this time of the year," Maureen said. "Even at my ripe old age, when I see the lights on the trees in the Grove and the pine boughs draped across the windows of the Wilson House, I start to think that maybe there is a Santa Claus after all."

"Your ripe old age is my ripe old age," Emma pointed out.

Maureen laughed. "Oh, right. Our mature youth, I should say."

But time is moving inexorably on. . . . "I was thinking," Emma said abruptly. "I was thinking that maybe I should just chuck it all, my entire life in Annapolis, and move back to Oliver's Well."

"Really?" Maureen raised her eyebrows. "I never thought I'd hear those words coming from your lips."

Emma laughed. "I don't know what came over me. I haven't told anyone else what I've been thinking. And I've only been thinking it for like a nano-second!"

"Hey, we're friends. Besides, I'm the kind of person people tell their secrets to. Must be something about my face."

"You're a natural confessor," Emma said. "It's a talent. Though I suppose it could become a burden."

"Tell me about it. I'll never forget the time I was on line at the dry cleaners, minding my own business, when this woman came in and before I knew it she was telling me all about her skin disorder and how embarrassed she was by it and how people sometimes made fun of her and then—wait for it—she was pushing up her sleeve to show me said condition and pointing out every bump and raw spot and . . ." Maureen shuddered. "I felt sorry for her, of course, but—why me?"

"Talk about too much information! Yikes. I hope she found some relief."

"I hope so, too, but I never saw her again, so I don't know." Maureen frowned. "Hey, wait a minute. What about Ian? If you chucked it all in Annapolis and moved back here, where does he fit in to the scheme?"

"Truth is, I broke up with him a few days ago."

"And you're not telling me until now?" Maureen asked, eyes wide. "Even though I'm a natural confessor?"

"Now we're face to face," Emma said. "It's always best to tell someone big news in person."

"How did he take it?" Maureen asked. "You guys were an item for a long time, except for that one tiny time off."

"I think he doesn't really believe it's over. He was so very pleasant when I told him I wanted to end things. He just kept nodding and saying things like 'okay' and 'well.' And since then he's been sending me countless texts and leaving messages on my voice mail at all hours."

Maureen frowned again. "Sounds creepy. But to give the guy his due, maybe he doesn't believe it's over because of what happened last time. You went back to him almost before he'd had time to process you were gone. Maybe he thinks the same thing is going to happen this time around. Not that it's an excuse for his pestering you."

Emma cringed. "I hadn't considered that."

"It's just an idea. By the way, when are you going to cut that thing in half and give me my share?"

Emma picked up her knife and divided the massive cinnamon bun in two. As she handed half of it to Maureen her phone rattled against the tabletop.

"See what I mean? It's Ian again. This is the second text today and it's only eight-thirty." Emma sighed. "He's not a bad guy, you know that. He's just . . . upset. Andie says Ian's having trouble letting go of his connection, not only to me but also to my family. She says his persistence is denial and that I should be patient with him."

"Well," Maureen said, "that's Andie, always trying to be kind. But I'd be tempted to tell him in no uncertain terms to back off."

"Enough about Ian. Are you still seeing that guy you told me about the last time we spoke?" Emma asked. "The contractor, Jim." That was something else that had changed for Maureen, Emma thought. After her messy divorce she had pretty much shut down her social life and refused even to consider dating. But about the time she had gotten her look in hand—and started taking swimming lessons and adult education courses at the community college—she had re-entered the world of dating. Maureen had told Emma that she felt she had gone from being just "the girl next door" to being someone noticeable in the eyes of Oliver's Well.

"Yup," Maureen said. "Things are going well. Jim's a doll. I can't find anything significantly wrong with him, and believe me,

I've looked. Even his ex-wife doesn't make waves in his life, or in mine. And his son's announced he's staying in California after he graduates college. He's already got a job lined up at the company where he's been interning, so there are no worries about Jim's having to support a disaffected kid. Sorry if I sound so very *practical* about it all, but I'm too old to be saddling myself with someone else's difficult family. Mine can be enough of a challenge. Not Mom and Dad so much as my sisters."

Emma smiled. "I'd say you're being very smart. So what's going on with your sisters?"

"The usual. Fiona's still got middle child syndrome or whatever it is that makes her a drama queen at the age of forty-six. And Kathleen's bossier than ever. I think that when Justin, her oldest, went off to college last year she started to feel, I don't know, redundant. Not a day goes by when she doesn't call one of us to tell us what we should or shouldn't be eating or drinking or doing, all according to her Internet 'research.'" Maureen laughed. "None of us listen, but we pretend to."

"Kathleen was always a bit of a know-it-all," Emma agreed. "So, has Jim met your parents yet?"

"Yeah, and they like him very much. Of course, it's been their fondest wish since I got divorced that I find 'a nice young man' to settle down with. I suspect they'd welcome anyone halfway decent as long as he wasn't an outright criminal."

"Maureen," Emma laughed, "that's awful! Your parents love you."

"I know," Maureen admitted. "I'm exaggerating. Anyway, I'm in no rush to get married again, and though Jim's floated the idea, he seems to accept that I'm just not ready to make that leap." Maureen shrugged. "I might never be."

"Once burned, twice shy?"

"More like why bother? I have a good job, a nice little house, and a few very good friends. Not to mention my adorable goddaughter, Maeve Olivia Fitzgibbon."

"She is pretty cute," Emma agreed. "I saw her in town with her mother when I was here in June. Anyway, love and commitment . . ." Emma shook her head. "I have to believe that a life-long partnership is worth whatever challenges it presents."

Maureen laughed. "Maybe. We'll see how I feel by the time I'm fifty. Maybe by then I'll have decided not to spend my final doddering years alone."

Emma checked her watch; it was a refurbished Rolex she had treated herself to after a very successful year. "Yikes," she said. "I should be getting on. Danny's asked me to check out a few real estate agents and pick one to handle the sale of the house."

"You won't need a real estate agent if you decide to buy out your siblings," Maureen pointed out.

"True. But keep that a secret, okay? It might turn out to be just a passing fancy."

"My lips are sealed. I'll see you again?" Maureen asked, rising from her seat. "I know you're going to be a busy little bee. . . ."

Emma, too, got up from the table. "Absolutely. I'll need you to help keep me sane."

"Families." Maureen sighed. "Can't live with them . . ."

The women parted, Maureen off to her job at Wharton Insurance further down Main Street, and Emma toward the first real estate agent on Daniel's list. But when she got to the door of the Greenfern Agency, she stopped, turned around, and walked back toward the municipal parking lot.

Not yet, she thought, the image of the man she had noticed earlier in the bakery flashing across her mind's eye. There was plenty of time.

CHAPTER 16

It was almost ten o'clock and Andie, Daniel, and Anna Maria were in the kitchen at the house on Honeysuckle Lane. Emma was still out, probably, Andie guessed, paying a visit to one of the real estate agents on Daniel's short list as she had promised to do that morning after breakfast with Maureen.

Her brother and sister-in-law had come by unannounced not long before. After a glance at the contents of the fridge, Daniel had made a call on his iPhone and was still busy with the call several minutes later.

Anna Maria lifted the empty press pot from the table. "Do you want more coffee?" she asked Andie.

"You shouldn't be waiting on me," Andie scolded. "And no, I've had enough coffee, thanks. And two of your croissants, which are even better than those they sell at Cookies 'n Crumpets. Where did you learn to make them so perfectly flaky?"

"Daniel taught me, of course." Anna Maria lowered her voice conspiratorially. "Don't tell him I said this, but the student has surpassed the teacher."

"Who's Danny on the phone with? One of your staff?" Though Andie wasn't consciously listening, she had caught a few words that made her assume the call was related to Savories and Seasonings.

Just then, Daniel ended his call and joined the women at the table. "Bob said he could do the party at the Branley Estate," he told them.

"Bob's working for you?" Andie asked. "But he's on disability. It was that awful injury to his knee that forced him to sell the plumbing business. He shouldn't be carrying heavy trays of food and wine."

Daniel shrugged. "He needs the money. He does what it takes."

"Bob's careful, Andie," Anna Maria assured her. "And he wears a brace on the bad knee."

Andie knew all about the brace; she and Bob corresponded weekly. But she wondered if Daniel or Anna Maria knew that, or if they knew that she regularly sent money to Bob for Rumi's care and education. It wasn't information she would offer, but Bob might have mentioned it in passing to her brother.

"You know," Daniel said, "you really treated Bob pretty badly all those years ago. And he was never anything but good to you."

Andie felt as if she had been hit in the stomach. What was the term? Sucker punched. She saw Anna Maria gave her husband a look of warning. "Daniel . . ." her sister-in-law began.

"What?" he said. "It's true."

"It was better for Bob, too," Andie said quietly, "that our marriage end."

Daniel laughed in undisguised disbelief. "How can you say that? How could you have known that for sure? He was a wreck when you walked out. He loved you."

I shouldn't continue this conversation, Andie thought. *This is wrong.* But she found herself replying. "I'm sorry for hurting him, really. But I—"

"Did you even love him when you married him?" Daniel demanded.

"This is ancient history," Anna Maria said firmly. "Can't we talk about something more happy, something in the spirit of the holiday, like the kids' pageant?"

Daniel shook his head. "I want to hear what Andie has to say."

"I did love him," Andie said carefully. "You don't marry some-one you don't love."

"Well, all I know is that he didn't deserve to be dumped like that."

Anna Maria turned to her, and Andie saw the unhappiness in her eyes. "Andie," she said, "don't let your brother paint you a picture of Bob as someone who needs your pity. He's done just fine for himself. He's not unhappy."

I know that better than anyone, Andie thought. Still, she smiled gratefully at her sister-in-law.

Daniel frowned. "I have to go. There's a crate of vegetables that needs to be picked up from Kramer's Farm and then a case of wine from the liquor store."

He didn't offer a farewell to either woman, and when he was gone they were silent for a long moment. Andie thought about what anyone *deserved* in this life, good or bad. And she wondered if anyone ever had a right to decide what another person did or did not deserve. Daniel was only a teen when her marriage with Bob ended; he had been and still was in no position to judge her.

Suddenly, Andie felt Anna Maria's hand on her shoulder. "Sometimes," Anna Maria said quietly, "he gets overly protective of the people he loves. And I'm sorry about what he said to you at dinner last night, that nonsense about low self-esteem. I should have apologized to you before now."

"What Danny says is not your responsibility," Andie replied. "But I'm sorry it made you feel uncomfortable. Danny shouldn't sit in moral judgment on people. Especially when he doesn't know all the circumstances around the decisions they made. When he doesn't know what was in their heart."

"You're right," Anna Maria said. "He shouldn't, and it's not really like him to . . ." Anna Maria took her hand from Andie's shoulder. "Can I help you sort through this massive box of old school papers Daniel wants taken care of?" she asked.

What Daniel wants . . . "That's all right, Anna Maria," Andie said. "You have enough to do without having to waste your time looking at bad penmanship and old math lessons."

Anna Maria smiled. "I do have to do some prep for a gig before the kids get home from school. Chickens don't debone themselves."

Andie resisted the urge to wince and wished Anna Maria a good day. When her sister-in-law had gone Andie continued to sit at the kitchen table, box of childhood notebooks and spelling tests untouched. *This is not going to be an easy visit to get through,* she thought. *It will be a time to be endured and survived.* But she had been expecting nothing good nor bad, had made no assumptions about what she would find. She had thought she was ready to accept what *was*. But sometimes, Andie realized sadly, she thought wrong.

CHAPTER 17

"Why did Mom keep this old schoolwork?" Emma said, laughing. "I suppose I could understand her wanting to keep the A papers and the 'Great Work!' reports, but look." She held up a yellowed piece of lined paper. "Here's one of my third-grade essays covered in red corrections."

"Not an A effort?" Andie asked. It was later that afternoon and the two sisters were in the den, tending to the contents of the house as they had been instructed to do.

"More like a C." Emma tore the paper in two and dropped it into the small metal trash can that sat by their father's old writing table.

Andie shook her head and peered again into the long white envelope she held.

"What's that?" Emma asked.

"Coupons. I found them in a kitchen drawer and they're all wildly out of date. What's Daniel been saving them for?"

"Maybe he just didn't notice them. Or maybe . . ." Emma shrugged.

"Whatever the reason," Andie said, "they're going right into the recycling bin."

"I don't think Mom recycled," Emma pointed out. "At least, not that I know of."

The doorbell rang then and Emma went to answer it. Rumi stood on the doorstep, dressed in jeans, a nubby blue sweater, and a lightweight puffy jacket. A backpack was slung over her right shoulder.

"Hi," she said. "I just came by to pick up a scarf I left here the other night. At least, I think I might have left it here. I can't find it."

It seemed a flimsy reason for stopping by, but all Emma said was, "Sure, come on in."

Emma led the way to the den, where Rumi dropped her backpack onto the floor. "It's a mess in here," she said. "There are like, papers everywhere."

Andie smiled. "Grandma seems to have been a bit of a pack rat. What brings you by? Come to help us sort through table linens and old spelling tests?"

"No." Rumi shrugged. "I just stopped by to see if I left a scarf here."

"I haven't seen a stray scarf. What color is it?" Andie asked.

"Um, red?" Rumi said, a question in her tone. "But maybe I didn't leave it here after all."

There is no scarf, Emma thought. *Rumi just wanted to see her mother. And hopefully, not to antagonize her.* "Is that another of your necklaces?" Emma asked her niece.

"Yeah," Rumi said, putting her hand to her chest. "I just finished it last night."

"What's the stone?" Emma asked. "It's beautiful. It's almost psychedelic."

"Labradorite," Rumi told her. "I think it's my favorite stone. It helps you to connect to your subconscious and it also protects you from other people's negative energy. And some people say—"

"Some people say what?" Andie asked.

"Nothing." Rumi turned to Emma. "Why isn't Ian here with you?" she asked. "He always comes with you for the holidays."

"We broke up," Emma told her. "Well, I ended things."

"Oh. Sorry. I liked him. Are you okay?"

"I'm fine," Emma said. "Thanks. What about you? Are you seeing anyone?"

Rumi shrugged. "No. There was a guy I sort of liked last summer, but nothing came of it. And right now I'm so busy with school and work I don't even have time to think about having a boyfriend." Rumi looked to her mother. "No need to ask Mom if she's involved with someone."

"I'm still happily and contentedly on my own," Andie said.

Rumi picked up a shallow green marble bowl that Emma remembered had once been used for an ashtray, many, many years ago when people routinely smoked inside their homes or the homes of their hosts.

"I wish Dad would meet someone," Rumi said, turning the bowl over to peer at the underside. "He says he's fine on his own, but I don't believe him. I don't think he's been on three dates since he and Rita got divorced, and that was years ago."

"'Each drop of my blood cries out to the earth. We are partners, blended as one.'"

Rumi looked quizzically at her mother. "What do you mean?" she asked.

"I mean that maybe your father would rather wait until he recognizes his partner than waste time on dating women he knows not to be 'the one.'"

Rumi didn't reply; she returned the marble bowl to the end table and flipped open the cover of the art book sitting there.

"Relationships take work," Emma added. "And they can be fragile. And sometimes, they just shouldn't be in the first place."

Rumi abruptly turned around. "Like the relationship between Grandma and her first fiancé, the one she broke up with to be with Grandpa. Obviously that relationship wasn't meant to be, because she and Grandpa were so happy together. Besides, she told me she never had any regrets, not even for one minute."

"What?" Emma turned to her sister. "Mom actually broke an engagement?"

Andie shrugged. "This is the first I'm hearing of it."

"You mean you guys didn't know?" Rumi said, eyes wide. "Wow."

"So, who was this man?" Emma asked. "I have to tell you I'm absolutely stunned."

Rumi shrugged. "Grandma didn't tell me his name. What she said was that after college she was staying with an aunt and uncle in DC, and it was their job to introduce her to the right sort of man, someone from her social set, someone who would make a suitable husband. So they did, and the guy asked Grandma to marry him and she said yes. And then, she met Grandpa."

"And we know about *that*," Andie said. "Mom and Dad talked about it all the time—that fateful meeting, they called it, two strangers meeting on a city bus, of all places, and falling instantly in love. But they never once mentioned the fact that Mom was already engaged when it happened!"

"Why would she keep it a secret from her own children?" Emma asked. "When did you learn this, Rumi?"

Rumi shrugged again. "About a year before Grandma died, I guess. She told me she'd been dreaming about him—the guy she dumped. She told me that in the dreams she'd be apologizing to him for breaking things up and that he wouldn't look at her. When she tried to touch him he'd turn away. Stuff like that. I told her she shouldn't think about it, that it was all so long ago he'd probably forgotten about her."

"Rumi!" Emma said.

"I didn't say it to be mean!" Rumi protested. "I just didn't like to see Grandma upset about something she couldn't change. For all she knew the guy might have been super happy without her. But as people get older they get haunted by the past, don't they? They can't let go of it. I remember in the last year of his life Grandpa was always talking about how good he was at baseball when he was a kid, but how his parents didn't have the money to pay for a uniform and stuff, so he couldn't play on the school's team. I must have heard that story thousands of times. Well, maybe hundreds."

The past, Emma thought. *How it does prey on us . . .*

"I suppose Mom gave back the ring," Andie said. "It wouldn't be like her not to."

"She tried to give it back," Rumi told them. "But the guy wouldn't take it. He said he still loved her and wanted her to have it."

"Wow." Emma shook her head. "Two men madly in love with Caroline Carlyle. Mom, the most respectable woman who ever lived, the third point of a love triangle."

"Well, she *was* beautiful," Rumi pointed out.

"Yes," Emma agreed. "She was. I wonder what ever happened to the ring."

"Oh, I know that, too. She knew it would be rude to Grandpa to keep another man's ring. So she asked her parents to auction it off for their favorite charity." Rumi frowned. "It was something to do with horses, a sort of retirement or rescue home, somewhere outside Boston."

"I'm still having a hard time processing the fact that my mother told you so much about her personal life, Rumi." Emma smiled a bit. "I think I'm jealous."

"Grandma and I told each other lots of stuff," Rumi said. "We were close. More like . . ." She shook her head. "Never mind."

Emma winced. It was obvious what Rumi had been about to say. "More like mother and daughter." Andie *must* have heard the remark, but she gave no outward indication that she had. Instead, her sister asked brightly, "Do you ever think about pursuing your jewelry making, Rumi? I know the other night you said it's not important and you just make pieces for fun, but I think you might really make a mark with it. It's clear you have an artistic eye."

Rumi laughed. "No thanks. It's just a silly hobby. I'm sticking to a career in dental hygiene. Grandpa always said it's smart to have a steady job. And the last thing I want is to have to depend on other people to take care of me."

Like Mom and Dad took care of Andie and Rumi after the divorce. Emma wondered if this was yet another thinly veiled barb Rumi intended for her mother. But if it was, Andie again seemed unaffected by Rumi's words.

Andie turned back to her daughter. "Well, try not to give up on a creative activity that brings you pleasure. The making of art is so important for a balanced life."

"Maybe," Rumi said, pulling her cell phone from her pocket. "Yikes, I have to go. I'm doing the dinner shift at the Angry Squire and the wait staff gets a meal around four. My friend told me we're getting lamb chops tonight, and I'm totally psyched."

"Enjoy it," Emma said.

"I will. I totally love lamb." And then she colored, ever so slightly. "Sorry, Mom," she said. "I didn't mean . . ."

Andie laughed. "No worries. Be careful driving. And I'll keep an eye out for your scarf."

"What? Oh," Rumi said. "Right. My scarf. Thanks."

Rumi said her farewell, leaving the Reynolds sisters alone again.

Emma sank into the big armchair her father had loved. "Mom was only in her midsixties when she died. These days that's ridiculously young. It makes you think. There's never any time to waste and yet all of us do it."

"Mom seemed older than her years, didn't she?" Andie asked thoughtfully. "After Dad died she seemed to age overnight. She wasted away, lost the will to live."

Emma nodded. "A prolonged death from a broken heart. I know that sounds dramatic, downright Victorian even, but now more than ever I think that's what really did Mom in. Andie? Do you think Danny knows about Mom's first engagement?"

"No idea. But I don't want to be the one to tell him."

"Me, neither. I have a feeling it wouldn't sit well with him. I think Danny always saw Mom as some sort of perfect shining creature, someone a bit above the rest of us ordinary mortals. But maybe I'm wrong."

"No. I suspect you're right about that." Andie sighed. "It's odd. Mom assumed she had a right to know every little thing about me. About us all. And here she was, keeping this huge secret."

Emma shrugged. "All mothers assume they have complete rights to their kids. Even when they know they don't, not really, they still can't help but presume. Perfectly normal, I'd say."

"Maybe it's normal, but I don't like it. I've never felt I had the right to know every detail of Rumi's life. I truly value a person's 'space,' to use a tired old expression. I know it can read at times as lack of concern, but it's not at all. It's respect."

"I know," Emma assured her sister. "I never thought you didn't care, Andie."

"Thanks. You know, I guess it's not really a big surprise, Mom breaking off her first engagement to marry Dad. They were so obviously mad about each other. But why tell Rumi and not one of us?"

Emma thought about the question for a moment. "Because Rumi would have less emotional stake in the knowledge?" she suggested. "Mom guessed that Rumi wasn't going to react like we would have, demanding to know why she hadn't told us about it before."

"Maybe." Andie shook her head. "I wonder who he was. I wonder if he's still alive. Rumi didn't say if he was much older than Mom, but he might have been. I wonder if he's been carrying a torch for Caroline Carlyle all these years or if he's been happily married. Anyway, maybe Mom was ashamed of what she did and wanted to keep it all a secret. And then, when she knew the end was near and that it didn't matter anymore what she'd done forty years in the past, she decided she could safely tell someone and Rumi was an obvious choice. She was *there*."

"I wonder what Mom's parents thought about her breaking her first engagement," Emma said. "I can't believe they were happy about it, not the William and Martha Carlyle we knew, however slightly. And yet they treated Dad well enough. And I never heard Dad say anything against them, not that he would in our hearing."

"I guess the Carlyle clan saw Dad's real worth," Andie said, "just like Mom did. Dad was pretty hard to resist."

"He was." Emma sighed. "It must have taken Mom a lot of courage to defy her parents by choosing her own husband, and someone not at all from her social set."

Andie laughed. "Here I was thinking my mother was a woman who excelled at the expected—which of course she did—when she was really so much more. She was a person who stood up for what she wanted."

"And for what she believed in. Remember the time in high school when my English teacher told us to choose a novel to read over the Christmas vacation and I chose *A Clockwork Orange*? Ms. Tobin told me I had to choose another book because *A Clockwork Orange* was too mature for me."

"I do remember that," Andie said.

"Mom went ballistic. Well, in her usual refined way. She went to the school and told Ms. Tobin and the principal that the administration had no right to censor her daughter's reading. And in the end I got to read what I wanted to read."

"Did you like the book?" Andie asked. "I have to admit I've never read it."

"Hated it. Had nightmares for months. But I appreciated Mom sticking up for me and my intellectual freedom."

"There certainly was a lot about Mom that was admirable," Andie said. "It's just that . . ."

"It's just that what?" Emma asked.

Andie sighed. "I know it's ancient history and that I should let it go. My spiritual training alone should be enough to remind me that clinging to what is gone—and everything goes at some point—is a terrible, self-imposed form of suffering and anxiety. Still, I can't help but wonder. If Mom was courageous enough to defy her parents' wishes, why couldn't she have been more understanding about my leaving Bob?"

"I don't know," Emma admitted. "Do as I say and not as I do? For that matter, I wonder how she would have felt about my breaking off my relationship with Ian, the man she probably expected me to marry."

Andie smiled ruefully. "Another thing we'll never know."

"Like why Mom kept evidence of our failures as well as of our triumphs." Emma picked up another yellowed piece of paper from the box of old schoolwork and tore it in half. "Sorry, Mom," she said. "But some things are best left forgotten."

CHAPTER 18

Daniel put a small bowl of sea salt on the kitchen table, next to a pepper grinder and a dish of butter. He enjoyed setting a table with the staples of a good meal; the simple task gave him great satisfaction.

"Where are Anna Maria and the kids this evening?" Andie asked, as she took a seat.

"They're at her parents' house," Daniel explained, "visiting with some of the Spinelli cousins. Gabriella's youngest daughter has a birthday right about now. I always forget the exact date. I've never been good with dates. Except for my wedding anniversary. Anna Maria doesn't let me forget that, or her birthday."

"Smart woman," Emma said, unfolding her napkin and laying it across her lap.

Daniel brought a platter to the table on which rested a whole fish covered with herbs and garlic. He had already put out a hefty wilted spinach salad with dressing on the side and a crusty baguette he had baked that afternoon.

"This looks amazing, Danny," Emma said, "but you don't have to keep feeding us. I know you're particularly busy this time of the year."

Daniel shrugged. "It's my pleasure. Feeding people is what I

do. I left the bacon out of the salad, Andie. It should be fine for
you to eat."

Andie smiled. "Thanks, Danny."

"You two are never going to stop calling me Danny, are you?"
he asked as he took his seat at the table.

Emma laughed. "Not likely."

Daniel sighed dramatically. "I guess I'll just have to bear with
you. So, Emma, you'll take Mom's silver serving platters to the
Shelby Gallery for evaluation tomorrow?"

"It's on my schedule for first thing."

"Great," Daniel said. "And don't forget the kids' school
pageant the evening of the seventh. Sophia is playing Mary."

"We know," Andie said with a smile. "You told us that at least
three times."

"I just don't want you to forget. This is a big night for her, and
for Marco, of course, even though he's only playing a shepherd.
It's not a speaking part, but maybe next year."

Emma smiled. "So, it's safe to say you're a proud daddy? And
ambitious for your kids."

"Of course." And then Daniel frowned. "But don't think I'm
one of those pushy parents. I mean, first and foremost I want my
children to be happy. And I want them to learn that not everyone
wins all the time. Failing every once in a while is the only way to
really learn. Though my opinion puts me in the minority these
days."

"I agree with you," Emma said. "Trophies for every kid at
every game. It really is an odd notion. Where's the challenge?"

Daniel shook his head. "There is no challenge. I remember
when I was in sixth grade I tried out for the junior basketball
team. I didn't make the final cut and remember feeling seriously
upset about it. I really thought I should have been chosen. I remember going to Dad and asking him to go to the coach and try
to convince him to let me on the team."

"What happened?" Andie asked, spearing a piece of spinach
and chopped egg.

"What happened was that Dad said no, flat out. He said he was sorry I was disappointed, but that if the coach had thought I'd be an asset to the team he would have chosen me. He told me that I'd just have to accept that I wasn't a good enough player and that if I wanted to be chosen next time, I'd have to practice harder and more often."

"Smart advice," Emma said. "But not necessarily what a kid wants to hear."

"Exactly. I was really hurt and angry. I thought Dad was, I don't know, rejecting me. I thought he just didn't care about me." Daniel shrugged. "Eventually I got over it and came to see that he was right in not going to the coach and making a stink."

"Dad loved you, Danny," Andie said. "I remember him always going on about 'my boy' to anyone and everyone who would listen. He was proud to have a son like you."

A son like me, Daniel thought. What did that mean? Maybe his father *had* been proud of his son while he was growing up, but Daniel had never really believed that Cliff had noticed him until he had married, had children of his own, and started his business. Only then, when he had shown that he could equal what his father had achieved, had Daniel finally felt fully visible, fully significant to Cliff Reynolds.

"Earth to Danny."

Daniel looked up from his plate and smiled at Emma. "Sorry. My mind tends to wander a lot these days."

"Where to?" Andie asked.

"The past." Daniel squared his shoulders, as if that gesture could create a barrier beyond which some of the more stressful memories of his younger years could not travel. "The pageant starts at seven-thirty," he said, "but I'd try to get to the school by seven. Parking might be difficult."

"I'm surprised a public school is putting on a pageant with an obviously Christian theme," Andie said.

"Oh, that's not the whole of it. There's a tribute to Passover and Kwanzaa as well." Daniel grinned. "I'm not sure how successful the kids' singing will be, but I think that in this case they'll deserve applause for the effort."

"And hoots and hollers," Emma added. "Danny? Is there any more of the salad dressing? It's delicious."

Daniel rose from his seat. "There is," he said. "I'll get it."

"Thanks, Danny."

"It's my pleasure," he said. And it was.

CHAPTER 19

Emma parked her Lexus in the municipal lot and walked the one block to the Shelby Gallery. The building was one of the many mid-nineteenth-century structures still standing in downtown Oliver's Well. Emma looked up at the sign hanging over the door and for the life of her couldn't recall what had been there before the gallery. A clothing shop? A card store? She shook her head. Another bit of the past lost to, well, to the past.

A bell over the door rang pleasantly when she entered the gallery. The man standing behind the counter had his back to her, but at the sound of the bell he turned. Emma was stunned. It was the man she had seen the other morning in Cookies 'n Crumpets. And in the proverbial split second she realized that he had lost none of his inexplicable fascination for her.

"Good morning," he said. "How can I help you?"

Today he was wearing charcoal-colored trousers with a dove gray tab-collared shirt. And yes, his eyes were definitely dark brown.

"I saw you in Cookies 'n Crumpets the other morning," Emma said, moving across the room of spotlessly clean glass display cases, antique standing lamps, massive armoires, and beautifully upholstered chairs. She put the box that contained the silver serving platters on the counter. "I was at one of the tables by the window."

With mock seriousness he said, "So you know all about my secret vice. The corn muffin with warm honey."

Emma smiled. "Yeah. Sounds like heaven. But I am pretty fond of their cinnamon buns."

"Either one is an indulgence, that's for sure." He put out his hand for Emma to shake. "My name is Morgan. Morgan Shelby."

Emma took his hand. It was a beautiful hand. "Emma Reynolds," she said.

"Of the Reynolds family on Honeysuckle Lane?"

"That's the one."

"I knew your mother," Morgan told her. "Not well, but enough to pass the time of day. She had impeccable taste in clothing, if I'm not being too personal saying that. And she was very knowledgeable about antiques, especially English and American furniture and painting."

"She was brought up to know about such things," Emma explained. "Her family, the Carlyles, have been fixtures in Old Bostonian society since they came over from England in the early seventeen hundreds. My grandparents' house on Beacon Hill was a veritable museum of antique glass and porcelain and furniture. In fact, we still have an original desk by George Bullock, the important Regency cabinetmaker."

Morgan smiled. "Ah, that explains a lot. Your mother was to the manor born."

"In a manner of speaking," Emma said. "I don't remember seeing you at her funeral. There were so many people . . . I was a bit overwhelmed."

"Regrettably, I was out of town at the time of your mother's funeral. A command performance at an aunt and uncle's sixtieth anniversary party."

"I hope it was enjoyable," Emma said. "I mean, an anniversary party trumps a funeral, doesn't it?"

Morgan raised an eyebrow. "Sometimes. So, what's in the box?"

"Take a look. We're in the process of sorting through my mother's effects. I have to say it's not as easy as I thought it was going to be."

Morgan carefully lifted the silver platters one by one from the box. "That sort of thing never is," he said. "These are lovely. Solid sterling, not just plated. By Wilcox and Wagoner Silver Company, out of New York."

"They were a gift at her wedding," Emma told him. "I believe they date from the early twentieth century, but I'm hoping you can tell me more."

"It will be a pleasure," Morgan assured her. "I can tell you right now that Wilcox and Wagoner Silver Company sold to Watson Silver Company in 1905, and Watson continued to use this mark, but I'll try to find out exactly when these pieces were made." Morgan smiled. "But I didn't mean to interrupt you. You were saying it's not easy sorting through the possessions of a loved one."

"Every moment is interrupted by a memory," Emma said. "At least, that's how it seems. And some of the things my mother kept . . . well, I can't understand why. Clearly they must have meant something to her, but for the life of me I can't see *what* they might have meant."

"Like what for example?" Morgan asked, turning the largest platter over to look again at the maker's mark on its base. "If that's not prying."

Emma shook her head. "Not at all. Okay, there are all the silly novels my sister and I used to read when we were in middle school. Every single one is still in the bookcase in the den. And then there's the stack of seed catalogues. There must be at least a hundred of them, all neatly filed by date of publication. It's not as if my mother was a hoarder or a lazy woman, so there has to have been some particular reason for her to hold on to what she did."

Morgan put the large platter carefully on the counter and shrugged. "The books brought back memories of her children when they were growing up. The catalogues help remind her of her annual gardens. Or maybe she simply enjoyed going through them for the pictures."

"Yes," Emma said, "that could be it. Sadly, I'll never know."

"As you might imagine," Morgan said, "I have a lot of experience observing people and their attachment to objects. I can't tell you how often someone comes in and tells me he's been on a search for a table or a chest of drawers or a lamp exactly like the one his aunt or his grandmother had in her living room. Some of these people are so intense about recovering that bit of their past, as if once they get their hands on the object their memories will, I don't know, come to life again. I mean, the good feelings associated with the memories."

"But you can't revive the past, can you?" Emma said wonderingly.

"No. But you can respect and even treasure it . . . if a reverence for what's gone by doesn't get out of hand and prevent you from living in the here and now."

"And," Emma said, "from looking forward to the future."

Morgan smiled and picked up the second largest of the sterling silver platters, and as she watched him mentally assess the condition of the piece, Emma realized that she found it as easy to talk to Morgan Shelby as it was to talk to Maureen.

"So, any further thoughts on Mom's silver?" Emma asked.

"Like I said before, the platters are lovely. And they've been kept in near perfect condition from what I can tell. It won't take me more than a few days to complete an official appraisal."

"That's fine," Emma told him. "We're not in a rush." *Though*, she thought, *my brother might argue that.*

Morgan nodded. "I'll call you when it's done. On another note entirely, would you like to go for coffee sometime, or a drink? Unless your holiday dance card is entirely filled?"

Emma laughed. "That's my brother's plan! He's a veritable Christmas elf. But yes. I'd like that."

"The Angry Squire makes a slew of traditional holiday drinks," Morgan told her. "The consensus is that they're very authentic."

"Sure," Emma said. "I'm always in the mood for grog."

"Grog. Sounds ghastly to me. I'll have the eggnog."

Emma laughed. "Well, to be honest, I wouldn't know grog if it were staring me in the face. That's a frightening thought, grog staring back at you from the cup. I think you serve grog in a cup and not a glass, though I don't know why I think that."

"Maybe we should both stick to wine. How about the evening of the ninth?"

"I'm actually open that night," she told Morgan. Once again she shook his hand, and left the shop. And she realized that she was smiling.

CHAPTER 20

The school's auditorium was already almost full by the time Andie joined her family.

"I had to park three blocks away," she told Anna Maria, who waved her over. "Danny was right. It looks like everyone in Oliver's Well came out for tonight's performance."

Anna Maria smiled. "Something about kids in costumes makes even dyed in the wool Grinches all mushy."

Andie waved to her sister, who was talking to a woman she recognized as the local branch librarian, Lillian Ross. Daniel, a few yards away, was listening to Rumi, who seemed to be telling him something of great importance, if the expression on her face was any indication.

"Andie." Andie turned to find her former husband waiting with open arms. They hugged warmly.

"It's been too long," Bob said, "and that's not a criticism."

"I know." Andie smiled up at him. Bob was a good six inches taller than she was. "You look well."

"As do you." Bob took her elbow and directed her to three empty seats at the end of a row. "I thought we could sit here," he said. "With Rumi."

Andie glanced to where her brother still stood listening to her daughter. And she thought about the unpleasant conversation with Daniel the other morning and wondered why her brother chose to ignore the fact that she and Bob were friends. It saddened her that her brother wasn't able to acknowledge that she was a good person. Still, she had forgiven him for lashing into her about her divorce from Bob. Not that Daniel had asked for forgiveness, but forgiveness was necessary if you were ever to move ahead. And if you ever stopped moving ahead, well, then you'd be dead. In the words of the Buddha: "Holding on to anger is like grasping a hot coal with the intent of throwing it at someone else. You are the one who gets burned."

The lights in the auditorium dimmed, signaling the imminent start of the pageant. Rumi hurried over to sit on the other side of Bob; as she did she nodded at her mother. A moment later the curtain rose on the opening act. Andie assumed that parents had been enlisted to construct the rudimentary scenery—a structure meant to resemble a three-sided barn, a backdrop painted dark blue with a disproportionately giant star to one side—and clearly a child's hand was behind the gaudily decorated pine tree to the right of the barn. *When it comes to Christmas*, Andie thought with a smile, *historical accuracy could always be sacrificed.*

Andie glanced over at Rumi. And she remembered what it had been like to hold her baby daughter in her arms and to feel next to nothing, to feel as if the child was a complete and utter stranger. Postpartum depression. A nice neat phrase to describe an evil thing that deprived a mother of taking joy in her child, an evil thing that deprived the child of her mother's full devotion.

Andie's attention was brought back to the moment by the arrival of Sophia onstage. As the Virgin Mary she was dressed in a long blue robe with what Andie took to be a construction paper halo attached to the back of her head. "There is no room for us in the inn," she told the audience very loudly and very clearly. "What are we going to do, Joseph?" The boy playing Joseph responded in a not so loud or clear voice that they would spend the night in the barn. Andie felt tears come to her eyes. How earnest the children were! And how proud their parents must be.

Andie looked again at Daniel and Anna Maria in the row ahead.

She thought about what Daniel had said to her and Emma the other day, that he and Anna Maria tried to balance protecting their children from unhappiness with introducing them to the fact of life's challenges, and indeed, Andie thought, they had done a fine job so far. From what Andie could tell they were hands-on without being helicopter parents, supportive without being smothering. She saw her brother take his wife's hand and Anna Maria wipe a tear from her eye. And in that one gesture—Daniel taking his wife's hand—Andie saw the true love that existed between the couple.

The first act ended with the baby Jesus safely born and receiving gifts and adoration from the Three Wise Men of the East. The lights came up and voices rose with laughter and praise for the children's performance. Andie looked up to Bob, who put his arm around her and squeezed.

Rumi got up from her seat next to her father. "I played Mary one year," she said to Andie. "When I was in fourth grade."

Andie smiled. "I know," she said. "Your father sent me pictures."

"Oh," Rumi said. "Right. I'm going to go say hello to my old history teacher."

Andie watched as Rumi went off toward the front of the auditorium. How much of her daughter's life she had missed by choosing to leave Oliver's Well—the school pageants, the soccer games, her daughter's first date, that party back in June!

"Want to stretch your legs?" Bob asked, interrupting her melancholic thoughts.

"Yes," Andie told him, rising from her seat and putting out her hand for him to take. "Let's get some air."

CHAPTER 21

During the first part of the pageant Emma had been entirely focused on Marco in his role of shepherd. The entire time he was on stage the poor thing looked as if he was about to bolt. His eyes seemed unnaturally wide beneath the cloth band around his forehead. His costume, a beige bedsheet belted with a wide piece of brown fabric, threatened to trip him up. Luckily his part didn't require him to tramp around too much. His grip on the shepherd's crook—probably made of papier-mâché, Emma thought, something that couldn't do much damage if accidentally wielded—was fierce, as if it alone was keeping stage fright at bay.

With each passing moment Emma's heart had further swelled with love for her brother's children. Having kids of her own had never been a real option for Emma; she had known that about herself from a very young age. But she appreciated children, enjoyed being around them and listening to their often very interesting take on the world, watching how they interacted with people of varying ages. It really would be a wonderful thing to spend more time with Daniel's kids before they were entirely grown. And moving back to Oliver's Well would allow that.

Now, in the second half of the pageant, Emma watched with a smile the students' acknowledgment of Hanukkah. A big poster of a menorah was held high by two boys while a girl gave a brief explanation of the holiday's origins. "It's also called the Festival of Lights," she told the audience, and then a small group of children sang a few songs. Emma recognized "I Have a Little Dreidel," but not a song called "Eight Candles." When the children had taken their bows, another young girl walked onto the stage holding before her a flag in black, red, and green. In a loud and clear voice she explained the origins and meaning of Kwanzaa. "The black in the flag represents the African people," she went on. "The red represents the people's struggle, and the green represents the future and the hope that comes from that struggle." This presentation was followed by the singing of two songs written to celebrate the annual holiday that began on December twenty-sixth and ended on January first. Emma was glad that while Oliver's Well was currently home to only a small group of African Americans, the town made a point of honoring those families' culture.

When this group of children had completed its performance, all of the students who had participated in the pageant crowded onto the stage to take their bows to the thunderous applause of families and friends. Daniel, Emma saw, was literally beaming with pride. When the applause had finally faded away the children came clamoring off the stage in a rush of happy laughter and high spirits.

"How was I, Daddy?" Marco asked, throwing his arms around his father's waist.

Sophia seemed about to jump out of her long blue robe with excitement. "I was so nervous!" she cried. "But I didn't forget my lines!"

"You were both wonderful," Anna Maria assured them. "Just great."

Emma gave her niece a hug. "It was as good as a professional performance, Sophia. Congratulations."

Next Andie encircled Sophia and Marco together in her arms. Emma wondered if it was difficult for her sister, not having seen her own daughter perform in what must have been a very similar production all those years ago. But most likely Andie knew exactly how to handle difficult emotional experiences.

"Come on, everybody. I want a group photo." Daniel called to a man a few feet away, surrounded by his own celebrating family. "Ray, could you take a shot of us?"

Ray smiled and joined the Reynoldses, and Daniel handed him his iPhone.

"Okay, everyone," Ray said. "Squish in."

Andie stood to one side of Bob and Rumi to his other; he had an arm around each woman. Next to Rumi were grouped Daniel and his wife and kids. Emma stood next to them, her arm around Sophia's shoulders.

"Say cheese!" Ray instructed.

Emma shouted along with the rest and shouted again when Daniel's friend asked for a second shot "just in case."

"I'll e-mail the photo to everyone," Daniel promised after Ray had handed him back his iPhone.

Anna Maria put her hand to her neck. "Maybe you should do some Photoshopping first, Daniel. Use the saggy neck filter for me."

"I'll take the crow's feet eliminator," Emma joked.

"Oh, no," he said. "I want this photo to show everyone as he or she really is. This is the *real* Reynolds family."

With the kids dressed as ancient Israelites, Emma thought. But she didn't protest. It was a nice moment. And she realized that she didn't miss Ian being there at all. It had been the right decision, ending things. And it had been the right thing to say yes to her brother's invitation to celebrate Christmas as a family.

"Cake and coffee back at our house," Anna Maria announced. "See you all there in a few."

Emma, grateful the evening wasn't at an end, gathered up her coat and bag and left the school building for the parking lot.

CHAPTER 22

All but Rumi and Bob, who were going to a potluck dinner at a neighbor's house, gathered at Daniel and Anna Maria's house after the pageant. The children were still bouncing with excitement, recounting their big moments and laughing about the near mishap when the Christmas tree on stage had threatened to topple over when one of the Three Wise Men had stumbled into it. Daniel felt as if his heart would burst with pride. He was so very grateful for the gift of his children. For the gift of his entire family, really, even when they didn't conform to the sort of warm or responsible behavior he wished they would.

"Have you met with all the realtors I identified?" he asked Emma, handing her a cup of espresso.

Emma took a sip of the coffee before answering. "No," she said. "Not yet. I decided to do some further research online before I contacted them directly."

Daniel shook his head. "But there's no need; I already did that. I told you, I gave you my short list."

"Okay, Danny. If you feel certain, I'll start interviewing them first thing tomorrow."

Daniel took a seat in the armchair next to the couch. "Good, because the house has got to go. I don't want to spend another year looking after it. It's a drain on my time and energy."

"It will all get done, Daniel," Anna Maria said, passing a plate to Emma and one to Andie. "This is Daniel's famous triple chocolate cake. Or should I say infamous."

"What do you think?" Daniel asked his sisters after they had each taken a bite.

"Decadent," Emma said.

"Divine," Andie said.

Anna Maria smiled. "Delicious."

Daniel felt a surge of pleasure. It meant a lot to him to make people happy, even if sometimes he inexplicably failed. "It's hard to go wrong with triple chocolate anything," he said. "Anyway, I wanted to tell you that Anna Maria and I are catering the holiday party at the Lower Waterville Country Club tomorrow night. It's a last minute thing. The chef was called out of town. A family crisis of some sort. Anyway, we'll get the help of her staff and we get to use the club's professional kitchen, which should be fun. It's at least double the size of ours."

"Congratulations, Danny," Emma said. "Sounds like an important gig."

"If by important you mean it pays well, you're right."

"How long were Mom and Dad members of the country club?" Andie asked.

"Until the day Dad died," Daniel told them. "After that, Mom didn't renew the membership. She had no interest in socializing without him, though it might have done her good to see more people. But then, after the pneumonia and the staph infection that took forever to control, she just didn't have the energy for the drive to and from Waterville, though I would have taken her, of course."

"I never liked going to the country club for Sunday brunch when we were growing up," Andie said. "It felt like an oppressive environment. I was always afraid of doing something wrong, using the wrong fork or spilling my soda."

Emma smiled. "I kind of enjoyed it. I liked being around all the adults. I liked getting dressed up. And I liked looking at the women who wore big jewelry and who carried obviously designer bags. I wanted to be one of them someday. What that says about me, I'm not sure."

"And I liked eating food we usually didn't eat at home," Daniel said. "From what I remember, the menu wasn't exotic, but they did serve some dishes Mom never made, like swordfish. For some reason Mom didn't like to cook swordfish."

"And Mom was good about letting us order whatever we wanted," Emma said. "I first tried veal piccata at the club."

"But I was never allowed a second dessert." Andie grinned. "*That* would have been an outrage!"

"Anyway," Daniel said, "the reason I mentioned the party is that I'd like you both to be there."

"But we're not members," Emma pointed out. "Isn't there a strict policy about nonmembers not being allowed to attend special events?"

"I was able to get two tickets," Daniel said with a shrug. "It wasn't difficult. You are, after all, the Reynolds daughters, and I am saving their necks by stepping in."

"Ah," Emma said. "I see."

Andie scraped the last of the icing off her plate with her fork. "I have to warn you, Danny, I have nothing decent to wear to a fancy event. It was the last thing I thought I'd be doing this holiday season."

"It doesn't matter, Andie," Anna Maria said. "The club has loosened the old dress code. You'll be fine in anything neat and clean as long as it's not jeans and sneakers. Anyway, there's always Caro's favorite store, The Sophisticated Lady. For a few hundred dollars you could scoop up something nice you'll never wear again."

"We'll go to the party," Emma said, "but I think we'll skip The Sophisticated Lady."

"Good. I mean, about coming to the party. Did you get the picture from the pageant?" Daniel asked.

Anna Maria laughed. "Daniel, you just sent it a few minutes ago!"

Emma pulled out her iPhone. "There it is. Thanks, Danny. The kids look so cute in their costumes."

"I remember Mom hiring a seamstress to make a costume for a play I was part of in third or fourth grade," Andie said. "Most mothers made their kids' costumes, but Mom wanted only the best for her offspring."

"What was the play?" Daniel asked.

"*Aladdin and the Magic Lamp.* At least, Oliver's Well Primary School's version of it."

Daniel nodded. "I'm sure Mom and Dad took as many pictures of the production as I did tonight. It's so important to mark special moments, to memorialize them," he said firmly. "Mom and Dad understood that. In fact, we should go through the old films and photo albums while you're both here."

Emma grimaced. "As long as no one laughs at those awful hairstyles I had!"

"I haven't seen any of the family photos or films in years," Andie said. "To be honest, I kind of forgot about them."

"You'll enjoy seeing them, Andie," Daniel said. "I know you will."

Andie turned to Anna Maria. "Would it be outrageous of me to ask for another piece of Danny's cake?"

"No," she said. "And it wouldn't be outrageous for you to eat it, either."

Daniel watched as Andie dug into her second piece of cake and Emma chatted with Sophia and Marco, still excited from their big night. He was sincerely pleased that his sisters would be attending the country club's Christmas party. He had been worried they might refuse. He wasn't exactly sure why it mattered that they be there, but he knew for certain that it did. It mattered a lot.

CHAPTER 23

The following day Emma and Maureen met for lunch at the Pink Rose Café. Maureen was wearing a brooch in the shape of Santa's face. Santa had a very bulbous and lopsided nose. Well, Emma thought, eyeing the piece more closely, it didn't really merit the status of brooch. It was more like a . . . Well, she didn't know what it was like. Emma simply couldn't look away.

Maureen saw her staring. "I know, I know," she said with a bit of a grimace. "But I feel I have no choice but to wear it. Our receptionist makes them and she gave one to each of us in the office. Not everyone wears it, but I feel it would be rude not to. Trouble is I forget to take it off when I'm in public!"

"You're a nice person, Maureen," Emma said. "Better than me! I'd hide that thing in the back of a desk drawer."

They ordered, a chicken salad sandwich for Maureen, a bowl of pea soup for Emma.

"Still hearing from Ian?" Maureen asked after she had taken a bite of her sandwich.

Emma grimaced. "Yeah. But let's not talk about him."

"Deal."

"The man who owns the Shelby Gallery," Emma asked, hoping she sounded nonchalant. "Do you know him?"

"Like I know most people in Oliver's Well," Maureen said. "I know him to see him and we've said hello in passing, but that's about all. I do know from a source I can't disclose that he's an honorable guy."

Emma was intrigued. "You're sure you can't tell me your source?"

"My lips are sealed," Maureen said. "My ability to keep a secret goes hand in hand with my being a natural confessor."

"Of course."

"Why are you asking about Morgan Shelby?" Maureen wondered.

"It's just that he's doing an appraisal for us of Mom's silver serving platters." And maybe, Emma thought, he would be at the country club's holiday party her brother was catering.

"Well, I'm sure he'll give you an honest report." Maureen lifted her water glass and looked meaningfully at Emma over it. "He's single, you know."

"No," Emma said. "I didn't know. How's your mom feeling, by the way? You said she had the flu last month." If Maureen found the abrupt change of topic odd, she didn't say.

"She's fine, thanks, as fine as a woman almost eighty can be after a nasty bout of flu. The older one gets, the longer it takes to recover from sickness or sadness, and that's a fact."

Emma nodded. She knew all about a long recovery—and about those, like her mother, who never managed to achieve it.

"I went to see your mother a few times in the six months or so before she died," Maureen said, as if reading Emma's mind. "I always called ahead." Maureen smiled. "Caro Reynolds was not the sort of person you just dropped in on."

"No, she wasn't," Emma agreed. "That was kind of you, to visit. See? You're a much nicer person than I am."

"I still say that's debatable. Anyway, I'd never really talked to your mother before those visits—I mean talked to her as a person, another woman. She was always 'Emma's mom,' just as my mother is always probably 'Maureen's mom' to you."

"What did you two talk about?" Emma asked.

Maureen smiled. "Well, first thing, she asked me to call her Caro and not Mrs. Reynolds. That took some getting used to.

And mostly we talked about politics. She wanted to know if I voted and I told her that yes, I did. She told me she had been raised to take voting very seriously. Once she asked what I thought about the Syrian refugee crisis, if it was being handled properly and what the U S should be doing to help."

Emma shook her head in amazement. "I never, ever heard my mother talk about world politics, let alone her feelings about civic duty."

"She struck me as pretty well informed," Maureen said. "And sometimes we talked about me. She tried to get me to talk about my love life or lack thereof. She told me she thought I should be married. She said that everyone deserved to be married."

"What did you say to that?" Emma asked. She had never asked her mother how she felt about having a single daughter over the age of forty. She hadn't needed to ask to know that Caro didn't like it.

"I can't remember, exactly," Maureen said. "But I got her to admit that what she really meant was that everyone deserves to be deeply loved and cared for. For Caro Reynolds I suppose that translated to traditional marriage."

"Even though she knew well enough that so many traditional marriages fall short of her ideal." Emma shook her head. "You know, Maureen, in some ways I feel I'm only really getting to know my mother now, after she's gone. It feels . . . odd."

"I wonder if that's the way it always is," Maureen mused, "that once a person is gone people feel it's okay to talk about what they wouldn't have talked about while the person was alive. I don't mean scandal or dark secrets, just daily stuff. Small bits of information that wouldn't have seemed memorable or important enough to share while the person were still here."

"Little gifts of knowledge after the fact," Emma said, partly to herself.

"Only a gift if the knowledge isn't upsetting. Then it would be more of a punishment."

Emma smiled. "Sometimes the truth really isn't meant to be known, at least not by everybody."

"Exactly," Maureen said.

When they had finished their lunch, Maureen went back to her office and Emma once again headed to the Greenfern Real Estate Agency. Even if she was vaguely floating the idea of buying her parents' house herself, it wasn't right to ignore her brother's request to choose an agent to handle a sale to a buyer out of the family. She had made a promise to her brother and she would keep it.

Promises. Duty. She had told Maureen she didn't want to talk about Ian, and she didn't. She didn't even want to think about him, but now, as she walked down Main Street, she wondered if she had a duty to help Ian recover from the loss of a person he genuinely loved—and Emma believed that Ian did love her. She wondered if she had a duty to help him separate from the family he had come to consider his own.

Could she really have a moral responsibility to the man? But how could that be? How could she have a responsibility toward someone she had chosen to eliminate from her life, someone she had, in brutal fact, rejected? It was confusing, and Emma didn't like confusion. Maybe, she thought, she should talk to Andie about what she did and did not owe to Ian. She felt bad that Ian was upset, but not bad enough to reverse the new course she was setting for her life just to soothe his hurt feelings. Her life was her own to live, and if she didn't live it honestly, then she would be the only one to blame for her unhappiness.

Emma reached the Greenfern Real Estate Agency. This time, she pushed open the door without hesitation and went inside.

CHAPTER 24

Andie poured herself a glass of orange juice while she waited for Emma to finish a phone call with her second-in-command at Reynolds Money Management. Emma's work was as mysterious to Andie as her own work had been to her parents. Interestingly, Andie thought, all three siblings had chosen service careers. While Emma and Daniel helped people with the basic comforts of life—food and financial security—Andie provided, or tried to provide, the less tangible but no less important spiritual comforts. In that way, the Reynolds children were firmly united.

The real family. It wasn't the first time Andie had found herself thinking about Daniel's comment after the children's pageant. He had wanted to take a picture of the "real family," sagging necks, crow's feet and all. But what was the "real" family? There was no fixed, unchangeable entity; everything was always in flux and every person saw and experienced a different reality. But maybe Daniel couldn't understand that.

Andie finished her juice, put the glass in the sink, and wandered out to the living room where that ghastly portrait of her parents confronted her. She didn't know why it bothered her so, but it did. Still, she forced herself to look at the painting now, and as she did she felt a rush of emotion. *The real family.* Cliff and Caro's presence would have made the Christmas pageant, that enjoyable family event, entire. But she of all people knew there was never any good in thinking of what might have been.

She turned away from the image of her parents, those estimable people. She was glad—if that wasn't too insensitive a word—they weren't going to be guests at the country club's holiday party. Andie was a pro when it came to public appearances, but this would be different and she would not have wanted her parents to suffer any potential awkwardness. The fact was there would be plenty of people at the party who had known Andie Reynolds since birth and who had witnessed her "scandalous" departure from Oliver's Well. Of course, they would likely be too well behaved to snub her or to speak ill of her in her presence. And some might be happy to forget about her dubious past—leaving her child behind, a mother's greatest sin—in order to be able to tell their friends they had chatted with a celebrity. Andie had experienced fawning before. She understood it was something certain people needed to do; she just didn't feel compelled to like it.

Emma came jogging down the stairs and rejoined her sister in the living room. "Sorry," she said. "Bit of a crisis. It took me longer to troubleshoot than I thought it would. Maybe I'm losing my touch."

"More like you're exhausted from a busy year with no break," Andie noted.

Emma shrugged. "Maybe. Anyway, what are we supposed to be doing now?"

"Come with me," Andie said, leading Emma to the den. "This entire row of oversized art books. I was thinking that whatever volumes we don't want would make a nice addition to the public library."

"In Mom and Dad's memory?"

"Or they could be given anonymously. I like the idea of anonymous donations."

Emma smiled. "What does it say in the New Testament, something about doing charitable works without advertising the fact?"

"Whitewashed sepulchers, corrupt on the inside but present-

ing a pristine facade. That's sort of the same thing, isn't it?" Andie
paused before going on. "How did Rumi seem at her birthday
party?" she asked her sister. It wasn't as random a question as it
might seem.

"To be honest," Emma said, "she was very emotional. I think
it was Mom not being there. She told me it was the first birthday
she could remember without her grandmother."

The real family. "Not the first birthday without me," Andie
pointed out. "Her mother."

"I'm sorry, Andie," Emma said. "I didn't mean anything accusatory, really."

Andie smiled. "I know. It's just that it would have been better
if I were there for her. I apologized, of course, several times, but
I don't think she's forgiven me for being a no-show."

"It was only a party, Andie," Emma pointed out. "I know she
misses Mom, but I think she's making too big a deal of things.
Besides, her friends were there. It's not like she was miserable.
She was, after all, the center of attention."

"And Rumi does like being the center of attention." *Even if,*
Andie thought, *she teases me about my public presence.* "Remember
what Rumi was about to say the other day?" Andie asked. "That
she and her grandmother were so close they were more like mother
and daughter. I suspect she said that to hurt me. I don't like to
think that about my child, that she intended to wound me, but . . ."

Emma shook her head. "She didn't actually *say* it, Andie. She
stopped herself."

But the intention, Andie thought, had been there. "Danny
laid into me the other day, you know," she said. "Anna Maria
tried to stop him, but he went on and accused me of treating Bob
shabbily when I asked for a divorce." Andie sighed. "I was the
one who filed because Bob suggested I be the one. He was being
absurdly, sweetly old-fashioned about it. We both knew the marriage was over, and there was no animosity at all, but he didn't
want me to appear as the wife who'd been cast off."

"You never told me that. Why?" Emma asked.

"I don't know," Andie said. "I suppose it's because I try not to dwell on that difficult time. And because what Bob and I have is so . . . Well, so special and private. It felt like such a violation when Danny got all judgmental about our relationship."

Emma frowned. "Danny should let the past alone. He's allowing it to obsess him. And he shouldn't criticize something—or someone—he doesn't understand."

"I agree," Andie said. "But he seems to be under a lot of strain."

"He does at that. He's like the proverbial tightly wound spring. And the trouble with a tightly wound spring is that you never know when it's going to spin off and hit you in the face." Emma slit open a cardboard box she had unearthed from the floor of the closet. "Oh, look!" she cried. "I haven't seen this in years! Mom used to keep it in the china cabinet, didn't she? I wonder why she put it away."

Andie peered down into the carefully packed box and pulled aside more of the wrapping. "Mom's Lenox. The pattern is called Buchanan. Huh. Just like our lawyer."

Emma smiled and lifted a bundle that proved to contain a teapot and its lid. "I wonder if the entire set is here," she mused. "It's very sophisticated with its cream and tan and touch of cobalt blue."

"Mom didn't buy the entire set. She only bought pieces for tea and dessert." Andie dug into the box and pulled out the largest bundle. "Look, here's the two-tiered serving platter. Gosh, I loved this piece when I was little and Mom and I used to have a fancy tea together. It seemed so exotic, pretty little cakes and cookies arranged on the two levels. I remember thinking we were probably the only ones in Oliver's Well to have something so special. I . . ."

"What?" Emma asked, rewrapping the teapot in its bundle.

But Andie couldn't speak, not yet. With something akin to shock she realized that she wanted the tea service. She needed it. Again came that wave of nostalgia, something Andie didn't often experience. Yes, she would like to have this tea set in her own home. She would like to serve tea to her friends. She would like to revive the soothing, civilized ritual her mother had introduced her to all those years ago. *The real family . . .*

But maybe Emma or Daniel wanted the tea set. If that were the case, then she would keep her desire for it to herself. "The Buddha said that to live a pure and unselfish life," Andie recited silently, "one must count nothing as one's own in the midst of abundance."

"Earth to Andie? You okay?"

Andie startled, then laughed. "Oh, sorry," she said. "Just wool gathering. Here, let me help you stow this box back safely in the closet. And then let's get started on those tomes."

CHAPTER 25

The Lower Waterville Country Club's annual Evergreen Ball. Andie looked around the dining room that had been decorated for the event and suppressed a smile. She never thought she would find herself back here, the scene of all those uncomfortable family meals, when all she'd wanted to do was to go running out of the room, tearing off her restricting, irritating panty hose as she fled.

Still, it wasn't terrible being there now. The dining room was festive enough, even if the tree that had been given pride of place by the DJ was made of some sparkling white, no doubt toxic material and topped with a glittery red star. *Mom would shudder*, Andie thought, remembering Caro Reynolds's refined taste in decor.

"It's a real family affair," Emma noted as they watched Rumi pass among the guests. Both Rumi and her father were acting as circulating waiters, and Anna Maria was acting as her husband's sous chef and supervising the club's kitchen staff.

"Waiting is hard work," Andie noted. "I hope Danny can afford to pay his workers a decent wage."

"I'm sure he pays them well," Emma said. "Danny is nothing if not scrupulously fair."

Except when he's being testy and unfair, Andie thought, but she kept that thought to herself and instead admired her sister's appearance. Emma had had little problem putting together an outfit suitable for the Lower Waterville Country Club's big event. She was wearing a cream-colored cashmere sweater over a slim gray pencil skirt and houndstooth fabric pumps. Emma always looked effortlessly and perfectly put together. Obviously, she had gotten that talent from their mother.

"I stick out like a sore thumb," Andie said. "Not that I thought there'd be anyone else here wearing a bright red dress with an image of Ganesh around the hem and Sanskrit printing across the bodice."

"You're definitely more comfortable than that woman by the bar in that sequined number," Emma whispered back. "How does she breathe? And she must be sweating like mad. I guess she's never heard the term 'overdressed.'"

A waiter approached the sisters with a tray of blinis topped with sour cream and caviar. Andie politely refused while Emma took one of the appetizers. Daniel hadn't provided many vegetarian options, Andie thought. Then again, there was a good chance she was the only vegetarian in this crowd. She knew she shouldn't make assumptions, but this one seemed likely to be correct. The men and women gathered at the party seemed to Andie all versions of her parents, respectable, conservative in their tastes and probably their politics, not the sort to want to be seen as different in any way at all. Well, Andie thought, each to his or her own.

"Here comes Rumi," she said, as her daughter made her way toward them carrying a tray of appetizers. "No unpleasant guests I hope?" Andie asked when Rumi had joined them.

"Not so far," Rumi said. "Sometimes a man can get gropey at these events, in a discreet sort of way, of course."

Emma frowned. "That's disgusting. How do you handle it?"

"I tell him, quietly, that if he attempts to touch me again I'll go straight to his wife. That type always seems to come with a wife. Poor woman. Imagine being married to a creep?"

"No," Emma said. "I can't."

"I'm sorry you have to deal with bad behavior," Andie said. "It's so unfair."

Rumi shrugged. "It could be worse. And I can take care of myself. Hey, Mom, anyone ask for an autograph yet?"

"No," Andie said, managing a smile. "And I'd be happy if no one did, not at Danny's event. The spotlight should be on him."

"Come on, Mom," Rumi said with a laugh. "You love being sought after."

Andie ignored her daughter's comment. "How's your father doing?" she asked. "I worry about him reinjuring his knee, carrying those heavy trays."

Rumi rolled her eyes. "He's not a weakling, Mom. He's fine."

"Still, you'll keep an eye on him?" Andie asked.

"He can take care of himself, too, Mom. He's never had a choice about it. Look, I have to keep moving."

When Rumi had gone off Andie turned to her sister. "I think that comment about Bob's having to take care of himself was meant for me."

Emma frowned. "You think? And that comment about your wanting to be sought after? She's definitely got a bee in her bonnet. I wish for your sake she'd just come out and say what's bothering her. She's toying with you, Andie, and I don't like it."

Andie chose not to reply to her sister's comment. "The Evergreen Ball," she said instead. "A euphemistic name for what amounts to a cocktail party."

"It was a real ball at one point in time," Emma pointed out, "with a live band, not a DJ spinning rap versions of classic carols. How do the older people here tolerate it? Anyway, there's no harm in keeping the name. The Evergreen Ball. It has a nice ring to it."

"A nod to the past?" Andie said. "I'm not so sure that's always wise. But in this case I think you're right. There's no harm in a bit of nostalgia." She remembered how she had felt when she had unearthed her mother's Lenox tea set earlier that day; the flood of emotion was too strong to be denied or tossed off as mere sentimentality.

"And we're here, so we might as well enjoy ourselves, and more of Danny's cooking. The meatballs are fantastic. Sorry. I know you can't eat them."

"Not can't," Andie said. "Choose not to. Look, here comes Bob."

"Evening, ladies," he said with a grin. "Can I interest you in a shrimp puff, Emma?"

Emma took one from Bob's tray. "Going well, Bob?" she asked.

"It's a job and not an unpleasant one."

"Well, you look quite dapper in that white shirt." Emma sighed dramatically. "There's something about a man in a buttoned down white shirt that always gets me. I know, how boring!"

Andie raised an eyebrow. "Not boring at all. You're drawn to the notion of restraint, to the idea of a man's reigning in his dangerous masculine energy with starch and cuffs and collar."

Bob cleared his throat. "I'm glad I could generate such an interesting topic," he said, "but I'd better get back to work. Mrs. Duran, the woman standing over by the coffee urns, the one in the bright green dress, has a thing for Daniel's shrimp puffs. She's already had four and she's been following my every step since I last passed her way."

"I wonder if Rumi tells her father about the gropers," Andie mused when Bob had gone off.

"My guess is no. What could he do about them anyway? Though he might be tempted to have a stern word with the offender."

"I'd be tempted to do more than that," Andie said, "and I'm staunchly antiviolence. When it's your own child at risk, pacifism tends to wear thin."

Emma put a hand on her sister's arm. "Let's talk about something more pleasant. Like how silly that man over by the ice sculpture looks. Does he really think we can't tell he's wearing a toupee, and a bad one at that?"

"Now, Emma," Andie said, with mock sternness. "We shouldn't make fun. But it is really awful, isn't it?"

"Do you remember that client of Dad's," Emma said suddenly, "the man with the blindingly white teeth?"

"How could I forget? They looked as if they would glow in the dark. What on earth do you think he was putting on them to get that effect?"

"Bleach?" Emma shuddered. "I wonder what ever happened to him. He left Oliver's Well ages ago."

"Whatever happened to him," Andie said darkly, "I bet he's wearing dentures now."

CHAPTER 26

Emma breathed in the chill December air. She had gone outside to get away from the DJ's questionable taste in holiday music only to find at least five of the party guests standing around smoking a cigarette or a cigar. She wasn't one of those people who demonized smokers. It was just that the smell had always made her feel slightly nauseous. So she had made her way around the building and down to the dock, where the boats gleamed whitely against the night sky.

Morgan Shelby hadn't made an appearance and, given the fact that the party had been in full swing for over an hour, Emma doubted that he would now. She was disappointed but not unduly so. She was having fun being at the country club, in spite of the bad music. Memories had begun to surface . . . people coming up to Cliff and Caro to say hello, to admire Caro's outfit, to shake Cliff's hand and thank him for his sound financial advice. For years Emma had enjoyed basking in her parents' reflected light. Once she became fifteen or sixteen, her interest in being her parents' satellite had waned and she found all the attention paid to them simply annoying. Who cared if Caro had gotten her dress at the Saks Fifth Avenue in Boston? Who cared if Cliff had saved someone a few thousand dollars on their taxes? Typical teenage crankiness, Emma had come to realize. Nothing more than that.

After a few minutes in the night air Emma went back inside the club. She didn't want to leave her sister on her own for too long. There had been a lot of talk in Oliver's Well back when Andie took off to study in the East, leaving Rumi with her father. Emma was already living in Annapolis by then, but Maureen had kept her posted and Caro herself had been openly critical of Andie's decision. Cliff, as always, had said little, but often enough his silence spoke volumes.

Not that her sister couldn't handle criticism or worse, condemnation, but she certainly didn't deserve either. Thankfully, the people they had spoken to that evening had been nothing less than gracious.

"I'm back," Emma announced, joining Andie, who was seated at one of the small white-clothed tables set around the periphery of the room.

"Got your fill of fresh air?" Andie asked with a smile.

"Yes. And I love looking at boats bobbing at their moorings. There's something so peaceful about the sight."

"If you're not the type to be seasick," Andie pointed out.

Emma laughed. "Look," she said. "There's Danny. He's finally emerged from the kitchen to make a round of the guests."

Emma watched her brother with admiration. He had successfully forged a unique and important place in Oliver's Well and the neighboring towns. And she thought again about what her life would be like if she did decide to move back home. She probably wouldn't be joining the country club—she and Andie were the youngest guests that evening by a good ten years—but she would have to become a genuine part of the community, and that would take some effort. The burning question remained: did she want to make that effort?

"Working the room, shaking hands, no doubt graciously accepting compliments. Danny's a bit of a celebrity himself." Andie nodded. "You know, I think that's why he wanted us here, to prove that to us. To prove he's done well for himself. To make us sit up and take notice."

"I think you're right. It's kind of sweet, really," Emma said.

"Little Danny still wanting to make his big sisters pay attention to him. Like the time when he found a fifty-cent piece when he was about five and wouldn't stop showing it to us. You'd have thought he'd found a cache of diamonds he was so excited."

"Or the time he won that poster contest at school. I think the theme was conservation of forests or water."

"Gosh, I'd forgotten about that. He talked about winning that contest for weeks! But it wasn't bragging as much as it was making sure we'd noticed he'd done something good."

Andie smiled. "It was pretty cute. But it shouldn't matter to Danny at this point in his life what we think of him. His opinion of himself should be important. Providing it's not too distorted, of course. You know, one branch of Buddhism teaches that only if we can see through the delusion of an individual self will we be able to experience nirvana. But I don't think nirvana interests our brother all that much."

"Doubtful," Emma agreed. "And the bottom line is that our good opinion does matter to Danny whether it should or not. Of course, he'd be the last person to admit it. I wonder if it's always that way with the youngest child, wanting to be recognized by his older siblings."

"It seems likely." Andie sighed. "Honestly, I don't know why Danny would want my good opinion when he seems not to have much respect for me these days. But desires and needs among family members are complicated things, ever variable."

They certainly are, Emma thought. Daniel had been perfectly nice to their sister at Caro's funeral. Whatever had changed for him seemed to have happened only recently, within the past fourteen months. But nothing ever stayed the same. Daniel would get past this current state of dissatisfaction; he *had* to get past it. Emma only hoped it happened soon. Andie would be the first to say that their brother's belief that people never lived up to his expectations would make him increasingly miserable.

"We've got company," Andie said under her breath. It was a moment before Emma could put a name to the vaguely familiar faces of the couple coming toward them.

"I don't know if you remember us," the woman said, extending her hand first to Emma and then to Andie, who had both stood. "Marcia and Terry Parker."

Mrs. Parker was wearing a dark green A-line dress with a red and brighter green silk scarf artfully draped around her neck. Diamonds sparkled in her ears. Mr. Parker looked dapper in what Emma would have put money on was a Brooks Brothers blazer—navy, of course—white dress shirt, red tie, and gray wool slacks.

"Of course," Emma replied. "I went to school with your youngest son, Robin. It's so nice to see you both again."

"And I went to school with your middle son," Andie told the couple. "Ned."

"Oh, it's so nice that you remember!" Mrs. Parker glanced around the room and then looked back to Emma and Andie. "It's a nice party, isn't it?" she went on. "Not what it was in the old days, but then again, everything changes and so often not for the better."

Mr. Parker made a noise of agreement and smiled at the Reynolds sisters.

"And the club is certainly not the same without Cliff and Caro Reynolds." Mrs. Parker put her hand to her heart. "They really lit up a room. It was such a tragedy they died as young as they did."

Mr. Parker spoke for the first time. "Now, Marcia," he said, "there's no need to—"

"Yes," Andie said. "It is a tragedy."

"Will you be selling the house?" Mrs. Parker went on. "It's such a lovely place. I used to drive by just to see Caro's garden. I suppose someone's been tending it since—"

"Yes," Andie said again. "My brother has been wonderful about taking care of everything."

Mrs. Parker clasped her hands before her. "It's so lucky," she said, "that Daniel stayed on in Oliver's Well, especially with you girls moving so far away and you, Andrea, living such a carefree sort of life. *Someone* had to be there for Cliff and Caro, even if it was the son and not one of the daughters."

Mr. Parker cleared his throat in a meaningful way. "Marcia, we really should say hello to the Bakers."

"Are they here? Well, good-bye, girls. It was so nice to see you both again."

Mr. Parker led his wife away by the elbow.

"Not the most tactful woman," Emma commented. "Or the nicest."

Andie sighed. "Oh, she's all right. So many people start babbling or say the wrong thing when someone dies. I'm sure she didn't mean to be insensitive."

"Maybe not. Look, here comes Danny."

"Enjoying the party?" he asked. He was wearing a chef's coat, pants, and clogs. His face was flushed and Emma thought he looked almost exuberant.

"The music could be better," she said with a smile, "but the food is wonderful."

Andie nodded. "You've outdone yourself, Danny. And not for the first time, I'm sure."

"I saw the Parkers descend on you a moment ago. He's a sweetheart, but she can be a bit . . ."

"Yes," Emma said. "She can. She thinks Andie lives a carefree sort of life. I wasn't aware such a thing existed."

Daniel grimaced. "But she did tell me she'd never tasted a more delicious preparation of ahi tuna in her life, so I personally can't complain."

"One of your legion of fans," Andie said.

Daniel laughed. "I don't know if I have an entire legion, but I do have some."

"So, no complaints?" Emma asked her brother. "No one claiming the chicken satay is undercooked or the savory tartlets are too salty?"

"Not that I've heard, but I'll quiz the staff when we're through here. Someone might have picked up a critical comment or two. I do try to pay attention to the comments, good and bad. It's the only way to learn."

"Unless the commenter is completely uninformed or simply a troublemaker," Andie pointed out.

"You've probably had your fair share of people going after your work," Daniel said. "And worse than Mrs. Parker." Emma thought he sounded genuinely sympathetic. She was pleased. Andie had been enough of a punching bag lately.

"More than my fair share," Andie told them. "I've been called everything from a quack to a criminal. But you try to keep your focus away from the haters and firmly on the people you've touched in a positive way."

"Easier said than done," Emma remarked.

"Thanks for being here tonight, guys." Daniel briefly put a hand on each woman's shoulder. "It meant a lot. Well, I'd better get back to the kitchen. I'll see you both tomorrow."

Daniel walked purposely off to rejoin Anna Maria and the other kitchen staff.

"We were right," Andie said with a smile. "He did want to show off for us."

Emma slipped her arm through her sister's. "I think we can go home now," she said. "And you must be hungry. Let's raid the fridge. I think there's a pint or two of ice cream in the freezer with our names on them."

CHAPTER 27

Bob yawned widely and clamped a hand over his mouth. "Sorry," he said. "Didn't get enough sleep."

"What time did you get home last night?" Andie asked. She had arranged to meet Bob this morning at Cookies 'n Crumpets; they had only been there about ten minutes and already Bob had consumed a large coffee. Clearly it hadn't done the trick.

"Just before midnight. Could have been worse. We didn't get off site at a party last month until almost two o'clock."

Andie frowned. "That's too late for people our age."

"Andie," Bob said with a laugh, "I'm not decrepit. And neither are you. Don't worry so much. Hey, I saw your latest book at B and N the other day when I went in for a new collection of crosswords. I always make sure there's at least one copy on the shelf with the cover facing out, to catch a person's eye. *The Root of the Root of Love*. It's a good title."

Andie smiled. "Rumi, of course. Hey, remember how I never could finish a crossword puzzle? I don't have the right sort of brain, I guess."

"My dad used to do them all the time. But you know that."

"I do. Are your parents still enjoying retirement life in Florida?" Andie asked.

"They are. I get down there as often as I can, which hasn't been very often lately."

"What about Rumi?" Andie asked. "When was the last time she saw her grandparents?"

"She and a friend took a road trip to see Mom and Dad right before the fall semester started." Bob smiled. "But you know she was always partial to her Reynolds grandparents."

"They were pretty charismatic people," Andie admitted. What she didn't say was that she wished they hadn't spoiled Rumi quite so much. But wishing was a ridiculous waste of time. "How is your knee this morning?" she asked. "Is it really worth working for Danny if there's a risk of reinjuring it?"

"Actually, the knee feels pretty good these days," Bob told her. "Daniel's a good boss. He'd never ask an employee to do something that might put him in danger."

"I know, but I worry." Andie toyed with her coffee spoon for a moment before blurting, "The other day Danny asked me if I loved you when we got married."

Bob's eyes widened. "What made him ask that? And all these years later, too."

"I don't know," Andie admitted. "Anyway, I told him that of course I loved you."

"As I loved you and still do."

Andie reached across the table and squeezed Bob's hand. "At least that part of my life is blessedly simple. Our love for each other." *True love*, she thought, *is born of understanding.* The Buddha had preached that.

Bob smiled. "Ain't that the truth!"

"Still . . . I wish I had known myself better back then. I wish . . ." Andie laughed. "There I go again, wishing."

Bob leaned in. "What were you going to say, Andie? Go ahead."

There was never any point in keeping things back from Bob, Andie realized yet again. "Getting married and having a family," she said, almost as if she was talking to herself. "It was what I was brought up to do. And face it, Bob, I never showed any particular promise academically or musically and certainly not athletically! I guess I thought, what else was I supposed to do?"

"Why are you dredging all this up now, Andie?" Bob asked, his tone urgent. "What's going on?"

"I guess it's being back here in Oliver's Well. I guess it's both Mom and Dad being gone. I guess . . ."

"I don't have to tell you, Andie, that it's not healthy to dwell on the past. Especially not now, when your life is so good."

Is it? Andie thought. "What about Rumi?" she asked. "Clearly she's upset with me."

"You're a fine mother, Andie. You're too hard on yourself."

"Why shouldn't I be hard on myself?" she argued. "We should all hold ourselves to standards of good conduct."

"But the standards you've set for yourself are so awfully high."

"And I seem to have fallen seriously short of them lately."

"If you set your standards too high, aren't you just setting yourself up for failure?" Bob challenged.

"Not necessarily," Andie argued. "I think we need to aspire to be perfect. Even if we never achieve perfection."

Bob looked intently at Andie. "I'm going to tell you one very important truth right now, Andie, and I want you to really hear me. Your daughter needs you."

"Does she?" Andie asked ruefully.

"Of course she does. Why else would she be punishing you for missing a silly party? She wanted you to be there. And she'll get over being miserable." Bob smiled. "She's my own child, but I'll be the first to say she can be a bit of a drama queen. Now, enough of Rumi. Tell me more about you. Are you still walking through the world alone?"

"Not alone but on my own, yes. There's something about me that allows me to do well without a partner. A self-sufficiency. I haven't suffered, Bob, you know that. At least, not because of being unattached."

"I'm glad. Suffering is never good." Bob raised his hand. "Now, don't go all spiritual on me and say that sometimes suffering is good, because I just won't change my mind on that one."

"All right," Andie conceded. "I won't argue, but I can't agree with you. You know, Danny mocked me the other evening about being a vegetarian. I wasn't going to bother you with that tidbit, but I can't seem to stop myself from confessing all when we're together!"

"People always mock what they don't understand," Bob said. "It's not right but it happens. I wouldn't take it personally."

"But he's a chef, Bob. He of all people should be open-minded about food cultures. How can I not take it personally? Besides, it's not like my being a vegetarian is news. I've been one for the past nine years and he's never said a word before."

"'Ignore those that make you fearful and sad,'" Bob said, "'that degrade you back toward disease and death.'"

"I wonder how successful Rumi was in living his own words of wisdom."

"Who knows? Anyway, I'll agree that Daniel hasn't seemed his usual self lately. I put it down to the business expanding almost too quickly for its own good and his needing to get your mother's house off his back."

"So, you really like Danny?" Andie asked.

Bob raised an eyebrow. "What's not to like?"

"Well, he can be self-righteous about his place in the family. A bit holier-than-thou."

"He doesn't see it that way," Bob argued. "He takes his role in the family very seriously. He's gone out of his way. I think he feels entitled to recognition for all he does. That's different from being self-righteous."

"Maybe," Andie conceded. After all, Bob spent far more time with Daniel than she did, as brother-in-law, friend, and employee. His assessment was valid and quite possibly more accurate than hers.

"Do you ever hear from Rita?" she asked.

"No. Rumi has been in touch with her lately, though."

Andie felt a twinge of jealousy. But wasn't love, after all, the whole point of this world? And Rita had been good to Rumi and for that Andie was thankful.

"So," Andie asked, "Rita is happy?"

"I hope so. I should never have married her just to provide

Rumi with a mother figure. Someone who could be there for her when I had to be at work, someone who could talk to her about girl things as she got older. Pretty stupid, huh?"

"Not the impulse," Andie said firmly. "Not the love behind it."

"Maybe, but I rushed into it. Rita might have been good for Rumi, but she wasn't good for me and I wasn't good for her. Luckily we didn't have kids together. Our divorce was tough enough on Rumi. Well, my two divorces."

Andie shook her head. "We both seem to be in a reminiscing mood today. What about the present, Bob? Is there anyone on the horizon? Rumi said you weren't seeing anyone but . . ."

Bob laughed. "She worries about me. But no, there's no one special. I'm not concerned about it."

"Good. We're all sufficient on our own. We have everything we really need for a happy, fulfilled life already inside us."

"But it's nice to have a friend, Andie."

"Yes," she said. "We all need friends. Bob, do you really think Rumi will forgive me for not being at her party?"

"I'm one hundred percent sure. It's just that she took her grandmother's death pretty hard and I think she doesn't know what to do with her grief. She seemed to bounce back pretty much until her birthday came around, the big two-oh, no longer a teenager. Since then I think a lot has been preying on her mind. On Caro's birthday in July I found her holed up in her room, going through every card she'd ever gotten from her grandmother. I tried to get her to talk about what she was feeling, but she said she didn't want to talk."

"Poor thing." Andie sighed. "Emma also suspects that Rumi's being so emotional about her birthday this year had to do with losing her grandmother."

"Mourning takes as many forms as there are people to mourn, Andie, you know that. Anger, lashing out, depression, lethargy, overeating, self-starvation. It's all hard to witness, harder still to experience."

Andie smiled. "And I'm the so-called life coach!"

"I learned from a pro. You might have heard of her, Andie Reynolds?"

"Vaguely." Andie looked at her watch, a Timex she had been wearing for the past twelve years. The leather strap had been replaced twice, but the watch itself still kept perfect time. "I'd better be going," she told Bob. "Danny wants me to sort through something or other today, I can't remember what."

"And I've got to let in the electrician. I might know a lot about pipes but not about wires."

Andie paid for their coffee, and with a warm hug they parted. She watched as Bob walked down Main Street toward where he'd parked his car, and she knew without the shadow of a doubt that she was so very, very blessed to know and to love Bob Dolman.

CHAPTER 28

Emma parked her car in the municipal lot and headed toward the Angry Squire. The evening was a cold one; she had read earlier that the overnight temperature was expected to drop to thirty. But being a person for whom preparedness was an ingrained habit, she had brought a suitably warm three-quarter-length coat with her from Annapolis, along with a beige cashmere scarf, both of which she was wearing.

Andie hadn't asked where she was going, and Emma hadn't offered her sister an explanation of why she was heading downtown at seven in the evening. And Daniel and Anna Maria were catering a private party that night for close to ninety people. The only thing her brother had time to be concerned with at the moment was cold shrimp, mini quiches, and making sure there were enough wineglasses to go around.

Morgan was already at the restaurant when she arrived, at a table for two in the bar. She smiled as she joined him. "No grog?" she asked, taking her seat.

"I figured I'd wait for you before ordering anything, grog or not grog related."

A waitress appeared and took their drink order, a glass of Prosecco for Emma and a shot of Jameson's for Morgan.

"I love this place," Emma said when she had gone off. "It's so unbelievably cozy."

Morgan agreed. "I've been to England several times on buying trips," he said, "and let me tell you, Richard Armstrong has done a bang-up job reproducing the atmosphere of the classic English pub."

"And he hasn't skimped with the Christmas decorations, either," Emma noted. "I love the fact that it's not at all gaudy but still festive. Simple evergreen wreaths, bowls of pinecones, that lovely tree in the lobby, decorated only in blue and red ornaments."

"Richard Armstrong," Morgan said, "is what my mother would call a class act."

Emma smiled. "My mother used that expression, too."

Their waitress arrived with their drinks. "May I propose a toast?" Morgan asked.

Emma raised her glass. "Sure," she said. "To whom? Or to what?"

"To Cliff and Caro Reynolds."

Emma was moved. For a very brief moment she thought she might cry. "To Mom and Dad," she said, touching her glass to Morgan's.

"So, Emma Reynolds," Morgan went on, "who are you? I mean, aside from being Cliff and Caro's daughter."

That was a very good question, Emma thought. Who was she, really? It was what she needed to find out. It might even be why she was here in Oliver's Well, to discover the answer to that question.

Emma told Morgan as succinctly as she could about her career in Annapolis, that she owned a condo there, and that she had recently broken up with someone after ten years together. "Most people start to glaze over when I go any further, so I'll spare you."

"I'm sorry," he said. "Even if it's for the best, I'm sure it wasn't easy."

"Easier than you think, for me at least," she admitted. "See, it was something I should have done long ago. It was overdue. I feel bad about not having let Ian go long before, so that he could get on with his life."

"I don't think anyone ever gets relationships—the beginning, the middle, or the end—completely right, do you?"

Emma shrugged. "I guess I wouldn't know. Before I met Ian I'd never had a serious long term relationship. I guess I was too busy establishing myself, finishing grad school, working hard, saving up to buy a home, all of that." Emma laughed. "There were years when I might have gone on one date, tops." Then, though she already knew the answer, she asked, "But what about you? Are you involved with anyone?"

"I'm single at the moment," Morgan told her. "It's been a long moment. About two years back I started to fall in love with someone I shouldn't have. Thankfully I came to my senses. Since then, there's been no one special."

Emma remembered what Maureen had told her, that Morgan was an honorable man, and guessed that Morgan had begun to fall in love with a married woman. But she didn't feel she had the right to ask. The past, after all, was the past, and it was private. It could only harm you if you insisted on digging it up. "Children?" she asked.

"No. You?"

"No."

"It was a deal breaker in an early relationship, actually," Morgan went on. "The woman I was involved with in my early twenties really wanted a family and I really didn't. I still don't. I'm sure I don't need to tell you that sometimes love alone isn't enough when it comes to making a marriage work over time. So many other elements have to be in place, shared moral outlook, shared values, compatible goals." Morgan smiled. "And a hefty dose of luck."

Emma nodded. Ian had never mentioned having children, she thought. For that matter, neither had she. "Did she leave you?" she asked. "I'm sorry. I don't mean to pry. . . ."

"Oddly, no," Morgan said. "I was the one to end the relationship. She said she would give up her desire for a family for my sake, but I knew that if we stayed together it would have been a disaster. I'd be constantly feeling guilty for not giving her children, and she'd come to resent or even to hate me for forcing her to make such a sacrifice. She'd come to see her decision to stay together and give up on her dream of a family as my fault."

"It must have been a difficult breakup," Emma said sympathetically.

"It was. It was a mess for both of us because we really were fond of each other." Morgan smiled. "But I'm glad to report that she's now married and mother to two boys, so there's a very good chance that she's happy. I hope so. On another topic entirely," Morgan went on, "I meant to tell you, I was a guest at a small garden party your brother catered this past summer. He's very talented. He could easily head up a good restaurant—if he were crazy. From what I hear, catering is tough, but it's far more sane than the restaurant world."

"I'm not sure Danny's ever seriously considered opening a restaurant of his own," Emma admitted. "I've never asked him about it. He catered the Evergreen Ball at the Lower Waterville Country Club last night. He got tickets for my sister and me to attend. Supposedly there was a serious run on the shrimp puffs."

Morgan smiled. "I've had his shrimp puffs and I'm not surprised. You know, I can't say I've ever taken to the idea of belonging to a country club. It might be because most of my family—the generations before me at least—are die-hard country club members and in my opinion, pretty obnoxious about it. Plus, I have an aversion to anything even remotely political, and I can't tell you how many times I've witnessed conversations over cocktails and canapés get heated over some ridiculous issue like a new traffic light or an empty promise of a tax cut. That was all back in the days when I was dragged along to country clubs by my Important Old Maryland Family."

"My parents belonged to Lower Waterville," Emma told him. "After my father died my mother let her membership lapse. Actually, I used to enjoy going with them for Sunday brunch. I liked the pomp and ceremony, the sense of it being a special occasion. But the idea of actually becoming a member of a country club at this point in my life doesn't appeal." Emma smiled. "Maybe it's the fear of fisticuffs and flying cocktails over a new traffic light or the empty promise of a tax cut."

"Do you know, I've just remembered something? I'm sorry it didn't come to me before. It was about a year, maybe eighteen months after I moved to Oliver's Well. My car died out by the Joseph J. Stoker House. I was about to call AAA when your father happened to drive by. There was no need for him to stop—I waved that I was fine—but he did stop, and he insisted on giving me a jump." Morgan smiled. "Problem solved and a heck of a lot less expensive than AAA."

Emma laughed. "Dad fancied himself a mechanic. I think it was his secret wish to have his own garage!"

"But was he happy being an accountant?"

Emma considered this. "Yes," she said, "he was. He liked to be needed. And he really helped people by sorting through their money problems and keeping them out of financial trouble. He provided a service and he was proud of that." Emma leaned forward and folded her arms on the table. "You know," she went on, "it's kind of fascinating to hear someone's impressions of your parents. Both my niece and my friend Maureen told me things about my mother recently that took me totally by surprise. As children, even adult children, we see our parents with such a narrow perspective; we view them through such a blurry lens. I don't think it's possible for us—for children—to ever know a parent as a whole human being."

Morgan nodded. "I agree. Knowledge of a parent as a fully rounded individual is impossible, no matter how long you have them in your life."

"And I didn't have mine for all that long, did I?"

Morgan smiled sympathetically. "It must be tough losing your parents so young. I might complain about my parents on occasion, but at least they're still alive."

"Thank you," Emma said. "It is difficult, and not only because it makes you so brutally aware of your own possibly limited mortality. And it seems so unfair that someone who had achieved as much as my parents had in life shouldn't enjoy a more extended period of, well, of relaxation. I don't mean to glamorize old age. It's not, I hear, for wimps."

Morgan laughed. "My grandmother reminds me of that every time I see her. Sometimes I think she blames me for having the nerve to be young in her presence. And from the way she tells me how challenging it is to get old, I think she's implying that I don't have the nerve to hack it."

"Yikes. Your grandmother sounds . . . formidable."

"That's one way of putting it. And formidable women run in my family. Some day I'll tell you about my Aunt Agatha."

"Still," Emma went on, "I know my parents would have loved to spend another ten or twenty years together. They would have been a comfort to each other during the difficult times."

"Mortality. It's a very good reason to make every single moment of your life count. I know that's an almost impossible thing to achieve, but it's certainly worth a try."

"My sister and I were saying the same thing the other day. Frankly, she beats me hands down when it comes to living consciously and, well, fully."

Morgan smiled. "Tomorrow is a new day?"

"Yes. So, tell me more about yourself," Emma requested. "Where did you go to school? What do you do when you're not hunting down antique armoires and armchairs?"

"Well, I went to a small liberal arts college called Ryder in Massachusetts. It's a Shelby family tradition. See, my great-great-grandfather endowed the science wing a million years ago so . . ."

Emma smiled. "You really had no choice?"

"None. I'm an only child, so it was up to me to keep the old ways. Anyway, I got an undergraduate degree in painting and then went on to the Rhode Island School of Design, where I got a master's in American furniture. After that I came back to Baltimore and worked in a few antique shops learning the ropes; you could even say I was a good old-fashioned apprentice in some ways. And then, when I was thirty, I came to Oliver's Well and opened my own place."

"And you like living here?" Emma asked.

"I do," Morgan said. "Very much. I've been a local for almost eight years now. I've got an apartment over my gallery. It's got great views and enough space for me to keep dabbling in my painting."

"Do you show your work locally?"

"Honestly," Morgan said, "I haven't tried to place anything in years. For now, I just enjoy the process."

"I took a painting course in college," Emma told him. "I had such high hopes for myself, but I was just awful. Sadly, I've got no creative talent whatsoever. I like to think I have taste and that I appreciate fine work, but as for making it . . ."

Morgan laughed. "Those of us who are makers seriously appreciate those who can appreciate us!"

A sudden chorus of "Happy Birthday" rose from the dining room next to the bar. Emma smiled. "I haven't heard that done in ages."

"It happens here pretty much every night, I'm told. Celebrations. Anniversaries, engagements, you name it. The Angry Squire is the place to be when you have good news to share with the community."

Emma smiled. "So, Oliver's Well. Any dirty local politics?" she asked. "I remember vaguely there was some scandal when I was a kid, but I couldn't tell you what actually went on."

Morgan shook his head. "If there's anything dirty going on I don't know about it and, like I said, I don't want to know about it. Politics and I don't mix."

"What about crime?" Emma asked.

"Petty theft on occasion, a few DUIs each summer, and that's about it. Most people who live outside the immediate downtown area don't even bother to lock their doors at night. The police chief and his deputy have probably the cushiest jobs in the state of Virginia."

"And the school system? I have a niece and nephew in grammar school and I haven't heard my brother or sister-in-law complain."

"It's solid," Morgan said. "Respected. A town with a good

public school system is a town in which any person might want to live, parent or not." Morgan smiled. "Why all the questions?" he asked. "Are you thinking of moving back to your hometown?"

Emma shrugged. "Just curious. It's been ages since I've lived here and things can change so quickly."

"Not in Oliver's Well! In fact, a few years back the OWHA began a Day in the Life project. Are you familiar with that sort of thing?"

"I think so," Emma said. "It's where a photograph is taken every day at the same time and place and then catalogued."

Morgan nodded. "Right. Anyway, it's the brainchild of Mary Bernadette Fitzgibbon, the grand old lady of the OWHA. You must know her."

Emma laughed. "Who doesn't? She's been angling for that George Bullock desk I told you about for ages. Besides, our family lives on the same street."

"Oh, right! Anyway, I have to say I'm not the only one to think it's a bit of a silly project for a town where nothing much ever changes."

"Don't you think there might be some value in things staying the same?" Emma asked.

"Sure," Morgan said. "Depending on what things you're talking about. Scientific exploration? Medicine? Human rights? Animal rights for that matter. All things that should change, and for the better." Morgan smiled and looked around the bar. "But places like the Angry Squire? I'd like this place to stay the same for a long while."

"Me, too," Emma said.

The rest of the evening passed as pleasantly as it had begun, and at almost ten P.M. Emma and Morgan parted ways outside the restaurant with a warm handshake. Emma realized that she had just spent by far the most enjoyable few hours of the entire year.

She was home within minutes and tucked into her parents' bed only minutes after that. Before she plugged her iPhone into its charger she checked for any new media messages or voice mails. And there it was. Ian had sent her a text. He was watching a movie on Amazon and had thought of her. He knew she would love the movie. He wished her pleasant dreams.

With a sigh, Emma turned off the light and slid down under the covers. *Why can't he leave me alone?* she thought. She didn't want Ian to care about her, not now. Not ever again.

Especially, Emma realized, not after tonight.

CHAPTER 29

A few minutes after Daniel arrived at number 32 that morning, Andie left the house for a walk.

"For exercise?" Daniel had asked her, plopping his tool bag on the counter next to the sink.

"For peace of mind," his sister had replied. "Walking is a form of meditation for me. If it helps to keep my arteries clear, all the better."

Daniel had been about to say something to the effect of, "Well, some of us aren't lucky enough to have free time to exercise, let alone meditate," but his phone had rung just then. It was one of his long time clients and he promptly answered the call, all thoughts of his sister and her privilege forgotten.

"I thought I heard you come in."

Daniel turned away from the sink to see Emma in the doorway of the kitchen. "I noticed the sink wasn't draining properly, so I thought I'd give it a look."

"Any luck?" his sister asked, leaning against the counter.

"I think so." Daniel turned on the cold water faucet and watched for a moment as the water drained smoothly and quickly.

"You really are a jack of all trades!"

Daniel put the drain-clearing snake back in his tool bag before replying. "Sometimes," he said, "you have no choice but to just tackle the job at hand."

Emma briefly put her hand on Daniel's arm. "Like you did with Mom," she said.

Daniel didn't know what to say, so he busied himself filling the kettle with water for a pot of coffee.

"Those last days with Mom must have been so hard on you, Danny," Emma went on. "I really did feel for you. I still feel for you. You gave the family an enormously important gift by being with Mom in her last moments."

Daniel felt tears pricking at his eyelids and willed them away. "I didn't want her to die alone," he said simply, turning on the gas under the kettle. "Though at the very end I don't think she really knew I was there. If she did, she was beyond letting me know."

"That's so sad," Emma murmured.

"Last Christmas . . ." Daniel shook his head. "It was like it went by in a blur. I felt as if I was living through a haze, not really *there*, not fully taking in the fact that Mom was gone. But this year . . ."

"I think I know what you mean, Danny," Emma said. "It was the same for me last year. The holidays came and went and though I went through the motions—parties and presents—they barely registered with me. Just like Mom's being gone hadn't quite registered."

"Yeah. For months after Mom died I'd drive by the house half expecting to see her in the front yard, pulling up a weed or watering the roses. I hardly even missed her because I couldn't really believe what had happened."

"But her death didn't come as a huge surprise, did it? I mean, we knew she was failing. It wasn't a sudden or accidental thing."

"Death is always a surprise," Daniel said forcefully. "At least, it's always a shock, even if you've been expecting it. It's just so . . . It's just so final. And yet," he went on, "sometimes still in my dreams, I turn a corner or open a door and there's Mom, healthy and smiling, and I say, 'There you are! I knew you were here somewhere,' and for that moment, I truly believe that she didn't die, that I'd made a mistake. And then, my head tells me that I'm dreaming and that my mother is indeed dead. And that's that. Final."

Daniel felt surprised by his own forthcoming mood. He hadn't planned on sharing his feelings in this way with Emma, with anyone, really. But it didn't feel so bad, opening up, and opening up was something Anna Maria was always encouraging him to do.

"I remember so clearly the time I last saw Mom alive," Emma said then. "It was about two weeks before she passed."

"I remember, too," Daniel said. "I was glad that you came."

"She seemed to have rallied since my previous visit. I really thought she would be with us for at least a few more months. I had absolutely no sense that the end was so near." Emma sighed. "After she'd died I thought that maybe she'd put on a bit of a show for me, that she hadn't wanted me to see how bad she really was. That she hadn't wanted me to see her die. I thought that maybe my being around at the end would have been embarrassing for her. I don't know."

Daniel smiled. "Funny," he said, pouring boiling water into the press pot into which he had already dumped the coffee beans he had ground earlier. "Anna Maria said much the same thing to me recently. She said that Mom might not have wanted her daughters to witness her in such a vulnerable state. That maybe it was better that you and Andie weren't around more."

"Oh." Emma's face seemed to fall. "I'm not sure how I should take that. . . ."

"All Anna Maria meant," Daniel added hurriedly, "was that Mom was always so conscious of making a good impression on people, especially her daughters. . . . I don't know for sure why Mom died exactly when she did, Emma. All I know is that she's gone, and hopefully, she's with Dad."

"Danny? What were Mom's very last words? I mean, coherent words? I never asked you before now because"—Emma shook her head—"maybe I was afraid to hear them."

"You really want to know?"

"Yes. I do."

Daniel cleared his throat. He had only told Anna Maria this bit of the story, and then it was with copious tears. "Well," he said, "I got up from the chair at one point and leaned over her in the bed. I remember I took her hand with my left hand and braced myself against the bed with my right. Suddenly, I thought, she looked . . . upset. 'Mom,' I said, 'are you okay? Are you in pain?' "

Emma put her hand to her heart. "What did she say?"

"She looked right at me and said, clear as a bell"—Daniel paused and arranged his face in a suitably grim expression— " 'You're leaning on my leg.' "

A laugh of shock burst from his sister. "Danny, no!"

Daniel laughed, too. "I felt awful, of course. Seriously, I wanted to kick myself. But Mom sort of smiled and . . . and about forty minutes later she was gone."

"Have you told Andie any of this?" Emma asked.

"No. She's never asked about the details of Mom's passing." *And,* he thought, *it's because she doesn't really care what I went through in those hours.*

"Look, I don't mean to pry, but are things okay between you and Andie?"

"Why shouldn't they be?" Daniel countered; he knew he sounded defensive.

"I don't know. It's just that you seem a bit annoyed or impatient with her."

Daniel shrugged. "She gets on my nerves sometimes, that's all. She always has. Look, don't forget about the concert tonight."

"I won't," Emma promised. "I haven't been inside the Church of the Immaculate Conception since someone's funeral back when I was in high school. I remember it being beautiful. All that scrolling plaster and gorgeous artwork."

"And the choir has won several awards in statewide competitions," Daniel said enthusiastically. "We're in for a real treat."

Emma smiled at her brother. "I'm glad I'm here, Danny. I just want you to know that. Thank you for suggesting we all come together this Christmas."

Daniel, suddenly uncomfortable, turned away from his sister to take cups from their cabinet over the microwave. "You're welcome," he said. "Just don't forget to get a real estate agent signed up."

CHAPTER 30

Andie couldn't remember the last time she had been inside the Church of the Immaculate Conception. It might have been as long ago as her primary school days, when one of the class trips was to the local places of worship. She remembered being so excited about visiting the various churches and the synagogue in neighboring Westminster. She had loved learning a bit about the different religions and their traditions, and though the variety of religions practiced in and around Oliver's Well wasn't particularly large, still, she had gotten a tantalizing taste of something far bigger than her own little life.

The entire family but Bob were in attendance at the concert that evening; he was having dinner with old friends in Smithstown. Andie smiled to herself. Bob had always been the social butterfly of the two. He had been the one to introduce them to the neighbors when they moved into their little house just after the wedding; he had been the one to suggest they host an open house that first Christmas as husband and wife.

Andie slipped into the pew next to her family and glanced around the crowded church. Maureen Kline and her parents, Jeannette and Danny, were seated a few rows ahead, next to several members of the Fitzgibbon clan. And there was Joe and Jenna Herbert and their two kids. Andie didn't immediately rec-

ognize anyone else, though she suspected that she would remember more than a few people if they spoke to her at intermission.

The program ranged from jovial secular songs like "Santa Claus
Is Coming to Town" and "Frosty the Snowman" to the more lovely
sacred hymns like "Hark! The Herald Angels Sing" and "O Come,
All Ye Faithful." All were recognizable, and though the members
of the chorus might not welcome the "help," Andie noted that
many of the audience were singing along under their breath. She
felt a happiness flow through her, a happiness laced with that
new friend, nostalgia.

At the intermission, Andie followed Rumi and Daniel out into
the vestibule, filled to bursting with people of all ages.

"Are you enjoying the concert?" Andie asked her daughter.

"Yeah," Rumi said. "But isn't it a bit weird for you, Mom? I
mean, you're pretty much a Buddhist these days, aren't you?"

Daniel laughed. "Can a Buddhist commit blasphemy or say
something heretical? They don't believe in God, right?"

Knowing that her brother was not truly informed about her
practice, Andie ignored his questions. This was not a teaching
moment for Daniel. "I'm not immune to celebration," she told
her daughter, "or to beautiful music. Besides, for me religion is
largely a personal experience, not limited to creeds."

Rumi shrugged. "Whatever. I'm going to sit with some friends
for the second half," she said. "See you guys."

"You know," Andie said, looking to her brother, "I really wanted
to say a few words at Mom's funeral. I know we weren't always
close, especially after I left Oliver's Well, but I would have welcomed the opportunity to honor her by speaking publicly about
her life. She really was extraordinary in some ways."

"She was extraordinary in all ways," Daniel said with some
heat, "and you could have honored her more if you'd shown up
when she was dying, or even as soon as you were given the news
that she had passed. Why didn't you come back to help me with
the details, the church and the undertakers?"

"Danny," Andie said patiently and quietly, "you know I was in

Vietnam. I couldn't get back immediately. It cost me a small fortune to get back as quickly as I did."

"The point is that *I* was the one on the scene," he went on. "It was my right to give Mom's eulogy and I did. What's done is done. Emma was fine with my decision. Why can't you be?"

Andie wondered if her sister was indeed fine with Daniel's usurpation of rights. Well, usurpation was too strong a word. Still, when Andie had suggested that all three siblings might say a few words at Caro's funeral her brother had rejected the idea out of hand.

Leave the past where it belongs, Andie told herself. *In the past.* She shouldn't have brought up an old grievance. Daniel could be self-righteous at times (if not in Bob's opinion, then in hers), but he was also always the one willing to do the dirty work, and that counted for something. It counted for a lot.

Andie looked at her brother's face, now set in a grim, joyless expression, and felt sorrowful. *Oh, Danny*, she thought, drawing again on the wisdom of the Buddha, *you will not be punished for your anger, you will be punished by it.*

"You did a good job, Danny," she said. "Keeping Mom happy and safe."

Daniel stuck his hands into the pockets of his pants. "Thanks," he said shortly.

"Come on. The choir is filing back into the church. We need to take our seats."

CHAPTER 31

Emma spotted a familiar figure at the opposite end of the vestibule. Yes, it was Morgan Shelby, wearing a beautifully tailored topcoat. Just as she was considering making her way through the crowd to say hello to Morgan, Maureen waylaid her.

"Hey," she said. "I'm here with my parents and the Fitzgibbon clan. Well, those who live in Oliver's Well. I'm guessing you're here with your family?"

"Yeah, the whole gang's here except for Bob. I'll try to catch your mom and dad after the concert," Emma promised. "I haven't seen them since my mother's funeral."

"Here we go," Maureen whispered. "Mrs. Fitzgibbon is coming our way."

Mary Bernadette joined them, her famous dazzling smile firmly in place. Emma hadn't seen Mrs. Fitzgibbon since Caro's funeral, and then she had been struck by how straight and elegant she still looked, in spite of having suffered both a stroke and a heart attack the year before. Now, if you looked closely, Emma thought, you could see small signs of age finally beginning to catch up with her, a slightly thinner frame, her eyes a little less intensely blue, her once gloriously thick hair not quite so thick.

Still, Mary Bernadette was dressed as elegantly as she always had been, in a navy dress with a narrow black patent leather belt at the waist, a strand of pearls around her neck, and small but what looked like very good pearls in her ears. Emma almost smiled remembering how she had always suspected a fashion rivalry between Mrs. Fitzgibbon and Caro Reynolds, each out to outshine the other in simple sophistication.

"Hello, Mrs. Fitzgibbon," Emma said. "It's good to see you."

"As it is you." And then, to Emma's surprise, the older woman abandoned small talk. "I'm sure your brother has told you how very interested we at the Oliver's Well Historical Association are in your mother's fine desk. We would be greatly honored if your family decided to donate it for display at the Wilson House."

"I'm sure you would be honored, Mrs. Fitzgibbon," Emma replied smoothly, "but the family hasn't yet decided what to do with the desk."

"You will be sure to let me know if you do decide it should pass out of the family?"

"Of course."

Mary Bernadette went off to rejoin her husband and family, but not before reminding Maureen that intermission would soon be over and that she shouldn't dally.

Maureen rolled her eyes. "That woman is like a dog with a bone. Don't get me wrong," she added hurriedly. "I like her and I respect her. She's my mother's best friend you know—and my goddaughter's grandmother—so I think I understand her a bit more fully than the people in town who just see the sort of intimidating grande dame."

"I like her, too," Emma admitted.

Maureen went back to her seat. Emma glanced around the vestibule, but Morgan Shelby was lost to sight. She did see Andie and Daniel talking; her brother looked agitated and Andie looked distressed. She thought about how during that wonderfully open conversation she'd had with Daniel about Caro's final days she had tried to get him to talk about his feelings toward

Andie. Her brother's answer had been dismissive—it had told her nothing—and there was no way she believed Daniel was suffering just a case of mild annoyance with his oldest sister.

Well, hopefully her brother would allow the good will of the season to overtake any ill feelings. Emma went back to her seat inside the church, next to Anna Maria and the other family members; her siblings joined them a moment later. She glanced around and was finally rewarded with the site of Morgan Shelby several pews ahead. He seemed to be alone, but she couldn't be sure. What mattered was that she had missed the chance to say hello. She was disappointed, but then she realized not inordinately so. After all, she would be going back to Annapolis shortly after Christmas, most likely not to return to Oliver's Well for anything other than a weekend here and there. Her future, whatever form it might take, most probably did not include Morgan Shelby.

Emma folded her hands on her lap. But what, she thought, as the organ came to life, what if it did?

"It was nice tonight, wasn't it?" Emma asked her sister. They were curled up in the living room, lights low and a Diana Krall CD on the player. "I kept remembering all the times we went to Christmas concerts when we were growing up."

Andie smiled. "It was always a big occasion, another chance for the Reynolds family to be seen in all their glory! Do you remember Mom dressing Danny in a suit and bow tie when he was small?"

Emma laughed. "A suit with short pants, yes! It was more than a bit old-fashioned, but he did look awfully cute."

"He probably hated it. Most little boys hate being stuffed into suits of any kind. I have a friend with a four-year-old son and she can barely keep him in his play clothes. He prefers to be naked."

"That could be awkward!" Emma laughed.

"Oh, I'm sure he'll grow out of the naked stage. At the very least he'll be taught to conform enough to be allowed to attend school without causing a riot. Any word from Ian?" Andie asked.

"I can't help but remember how he enjoyed—how he probably still enjoys—dressing for an occasion."

Emma sighed. "His latest text said, 'thinking of you.' The one before that said, 'miss you.'"

"Did you reply?"

"No. I am feeling a bit guilty about that," Emma admitted, "but like I told you, I'm afraid he'll read too much into common courtesy. So I suppose I'm being cruel to be kind." Emma hesitated before going on. "I don't mean to be nosy," she said, "but I couldn't help but notice that you and Danny seemed to be having a, well, a bit of a heated discussion at intermission."

Andie smiled ruefully. "I made the mistake of mentioning to Danny that I would have liked the opportunity to say a few words at Mom's funeral. I guess I was feeling—emotional."

"What did he say?" Emma asked.

"In effect, he said, 'tough luck.' He was the one on hand for Mom, so he had the right to deliver the eulogy. Honestly," Andie said, "I can see his point."

"Though he could have been more open minded about your suggestion that we all say a little something," Emma argued. "Lately I think he's stopped . . . Well, I was going to say 'stopped caring about anyone but himself,' but that's wrong. I guess what I mean to say is that he seems to have lost track of the fact that other people have feelings, too, and that it might be a good thing to show some respect for those feelings."

Andie sighed. "He's suffering anxiety, the stress of trying to hold on to things as if they were tangible and not constantly changing. It's a terrible state to be in, and none of us are entirely immune to it. Well, unless we're great spiritual masters, and that leaves me out, no matter what my book jackets say."

"You're more of a spiritual master than Danny or I will ever be, that's for sure!"

"Well, you're entitled to your opinion. By the way, what time are the others coming over tomorrow to go through Mom's clothes?" Andie asked.

"Around ten." Emma got up from her chair and stretched. "Well, I'm off to bed. Good night, Andie. Sleep tight and don't let the bedbugs bite."

Her sister laughed. "Bedbugs? In Caro Reynolds's house? Never!"

CHAPTER 32

A ndie ran her finger over the intricate brocade on the collar of a jacket Caro Reynolds had worn for occasions like a dinner party at the house of one of Cliff's more important clients, or one of the OWHA's fund-raising evenings. And what Andie was thinking about was not the fine workmanship that had gone into creating the jacket, but rather the strange power people accorded the things that outwardly defined a person, rather, the things that a person chose to outwardly define her self, to render herself recognizable and distinct from everyone else. The clothing and jewelry; the hairstyle and trademark lipstick shade; the big dark sunglasses and head scarf.

And what was it all worth in the end? What did it all come to? Nothing, Andie thought. At least, nothing of real importance.

Together Andie and Emma had laid out most of their mother's clothes on the bed; the closet stood open and largely empty, though Caro's camel-colored wool topcoat still hung on its padded hanger, next to her classic belted trench coat, one very similar to the one worn by Caro's friend or nemesis (depending, Andie thought, on whom you talked to), Mary Bernadette Fitzgibbon. On the shelf above the coats sat three hatboxes. Though she hadn't opened the boxes yet, Andie knew their contents by heart. First, there was the elegant straw picture hat, trimmed with a pale blue ribbon, which Caro had worn for Easter. Next, there was a larger, floppier version reserved for bright summer days; it was, Caro had said, excellent protection against the harming rays of the sun.

Finally, there was her mother's mink beret. Andie had always had an aversion to the hat; she remembered how she had actually scolded her mother for wearing "a dead animal," long before her own vegetarian beliefs had taken shape. Come to think of it, it was shortly after her impassioned speech that Caro had stopped wearing the mink, at least, in her daughter's presence. *Could Mom actually have put it away out of respect for my feelings?* Andie wondered. It was a striking thought.

Andie laughed and picked up a pair of lightweight wool pants. "There's nothing here I would wear. Mom and I had completely different taste in clothes."

"I might be able to fit into some pieces," Emma said, "with a little alteration here and there, but most of it isn't really my style, either. Everything is a bit too elegant for me, a bit too overtly feminine. The silk dresses, what she used to call her dress slacks. Though some of the blouses are beautifully tailored. . . ."

"What about the scarves and bags?" Andie said. "There's an entire dresser drawer full of silk scarves."

"Mom always said the details made an outfit. A good silk scarf artfully draped or knotted could elevate a look. She was right. If it's all right with you and Danny, I'll probably choose a few accessories to bring home with me."

"It's fine by me," Andie said. She looked down at the batik print scarf draped haphazardly around her neck and hanging almost to her knees. "This thing I'm wearing," she said, "certainly wouldn't meet with Caro's approval."

Emma smiled. "No, it wouldn't. And Mom's shoes. Her feet were so narrow! I hope there's someone around who can squeeze into them. Look at this pair of navy pumps. They're really gorgeous. And every single shoe here is in perfect shape. Mom must have been the cobbler's best customer."

"There's a cobbler in Oliver's Well?" Andie asked.

"Not that I know of, but there might be one in Lawrenceville. These days most people just throw something out when it starts to show some wear. Mom had the right idea. Repair what could be repaired and buy good quality in the first place. She liked to spend money, but she wasn't wasteful."

Andie opened another drawer of her mother's dresser. "Her jewelry boxes," she said, opening each one in turn. "Two for the good pieces, and this one for the costume."

"I think we should deal with all the jewelry some other time," Emma suggested. "It might be fun to go through it all and try it on."

"Sure," Andie agreed, as her sister went over to their mother's vanity table. The surface was bare of all but a silver-backed comb and brush set. Andie watched as Emma opened the table's shallow drawer and shook her head.

"Her makeup is still here," Emma said. "Danny never threw it out."

"We'll do it," Andie said briskly. "Did I ever tell you about the time Mom introduced me to makeup?"

"I don't think so, no."

"It was bad enough I had to endure her poking and prodding me about my unruly hair and my weight, but then she had to start on my face." Andie could hear the note of distress in her voice and it bothered her.

"Andie," Emma asked, frowning. "What happened?"

Andie took a calming breath before she began. "I must have been about thirteen," she said, "when Mom decided it was high time for a lesson in what she called 'the art of concealment.' She sat me down right here at this vanity table, and I'll never forget what she said. 'The point of using this powder, Andrea, is to conceal the flaws.'"

"And?"

"And I was genuinely puzzled. I told her I didn't have any flaws. To which she replied, 'Everyone has flaws.' And then she pointed out this tiny red spot on my chin and dabbed some cream on it and then some of that powder she always used. 'Now,' she said, 'no one can see it.' "

"What did you say?" Emma asked.

"I said that the spot was still there. And Mom said, 'Not if it can't be seen.' " Andie laughed and shook her head.

Emma grimaced. "Mom's logic wasn't always, well, logical. But that's all in the past now, Andie. You—well, all of us—really should let go of the unhappy memories."

"I know," Andie admitted. "But the sorry truth is that I still get upset about Mom's always trying to change my appearance. And I'm disappointed that I haven't been able to outgrow all childhood resentments. I have to keep reminding myself why Buddhism is called a practice. You have to work at achieving and then maintaining necessary detachment."

"Well, if it's any consolation, you're not alone in hanging on to old hurts, even those not intended to be punishing. The things parents say to you when you're growing up matter so very much. I doubt any parent realizes that every time he or she opens a mouth to comment or criticize, the effect of their words is likely to be very deep and very long lasting." Emma laughed. "Parenthood is fraught with traps! It must be exhausting."

"What do you hang on to from the past?" Andie asked.

Emma sighed. "For one, Mom and I were often mistaken for sisters, at least until she was in her midforties. Mom didn't mind in the least, of course; I could see that clearly enough. But it always made me feel annoyed, like why wasn't she content to be my mother? Why wasn't that good enough? It still makes me upset when I think about it."

"It appealed to her vanity to be thought your sister."

"I know, and I didn't like that about her. Not that I don't have my own share of vanity. It's not entirely a bad thing, but sometimes I thought Mom took it one step too far."

"And Dad didn't help," Andie said, "always telling her how beautiful she was and saying he felt like he'd married a model and that he was the luckiest man in the world."

"Well, he really felt that way, I think, like the luckiest man in the world. We can't blame him for loving Mom."

"No," Andie agreed, "of course not."

Just then Andie heard the front door open, and Anna Maria called out, "Hello, we're here."

Andie went to the door of her parents' room. "We're upstairs," she called back.

A moment later Anna Maria, Rumi, and Sophia joined the sisters.

"We started without you guys," Andie explained. "There's so much to go through. Hi, Rumi."

Rumi murmured a greeting and went immediately over to the bed on which Caro's clothes were laid out. Andie couldn't help but recall Rumi's remarks about her being a Buddhist at the concert the night before, not so much what she had said but the dismissive and disrespectful way she had said it. She wondered if her daughter was feeling a pang of conscience for the way she had been behaving toward her mother. But unless Rumi spoke, there was no way for Andie to know for sure. Guessing was as useless as wishing.

"Remember the dress Mom was buried in?" Emma asked suddenly. "The pale lilac one? She'd chosen it, of course, months before she died. Mom always liked to be in charge of her image."

"It was a very pretty dress," Rumi said to her aunt, a bit defensively, Andie thought.

"It was," Emma agreed. "I didn't mean anything negative by my comment, Rumi."

Rumi turned away and seemed to be finding a pile of cashmere sweaters of great interest.

Andie went to the foot of her parents' bed where a large cedar chest had stood for as long as she could remember. "What's inside, I wonder," she said. She removed the carefully folded gray light wool blanket from the top and set it on the bed.

"I don't remember Mom ever showing us what she kept inside it," Emma told the others.

"I don't remember ever asking to see." Andie undid the brass latch and slowly opened the chest. The pleasant scent of cedar met her as she did. "It's her wedding dress," she said with some surprise. "Mom's gown." Carefully she lifted it from the chest and spread it out on the bed atop the elegant suits and dresses and cashmere sweaters.

"It's so narrow," Anna Maria said. "I've seen the pictures of it, of course, but to see it in person is such a different experience. Caro must have been terribly slim when she married."

Emma nodded. "Even when she was well into her fifties Mom used to boast that she could still fit into her wedding dress."

"She was obsessed with her weight," Andie said. "I suppose women of her class often were, and probably still are. Like being thin is a badge of honor, proof of a strict control over the passions. Ladies who lunch but who, in fact, don't."

Sophia frowned. "Why wouldn't a lady have lunch?"

"Because she's silly," Emma said.

"Grandma wasn't *obsessed* with her weight," Rumi said suddenly. "She just cared about how she looked." She turned then to her mother. "Why didn't you wear Grandma's dress when you got married?" she asked, the challenge in her tone unmistakable.

Though the answer was obvious to anyone with eyes, Andie chose not to take offense. "I was *always* bigger than Mom," she said lightly, "ever since I hit puberty. Look at the waist of this thing! I could barely get my arm into it. Plus, I'm about four inches shorter than she was."

Andie waited for her daughter's reply, but Rumi wandered over to the open closet and took down the hatbox that contained Caro's Easter bonnet.

"The question now," Emma said, "is, what do we do with the dress? It could be altered if Rumi or Sophia wants to wear it someday. Or we could give it to the charity shop or put it on consignment. Otherwise, it's just going to sit here. I can't believe it's held up as well as it has. Leave it to Mom to know how to protect a treasured item."

Anna Maria shuddered. "I've seen wedding dresses after the preservation process dry cleaners offer. They give me the creeps. There's something—funereal—about them lying stiff in a box under a hard plastic shell. Anyway, I know Daniel would love it if Sophia wore Caro's dress someday."

"That would be fun!" Sophia said. "It's so pretty. I love the picture of Grandma on her wedding day. She looks like a princess."

Andie laughed and glanced at the wedding portrait on her mother's dresser. "An empress, you mean. Mom was the only person I've ever known who could wear a tiara and not look slightly ridiculous in it."

"Grandma wore a tiara?" Sophia asked, eyes wide.

"She did indeed," Andie said. "When I was about seven she and Grandpa went to a costume ball at the country club. They dressed as British royalty, no one specific as I remember, but their costumes were definitely early nineteenth century in style, and your grandmother wore a tiara."

"There must be a picture around here somewhere," Emma said. "Mom and Dad documented everything. We'll probably find it when we go through all the old albums."

Rumi abruptly turned to face the group again. "What did you do with your wedding dress, Mom?" she asked.

Andie thought a moment. "I don't know," she admitted. "Mom might have kept it. I suppose it might be in the attic."

"That figures," Rumi said with an unpleasant laugh. "Don't you have any sentimentality?"

Andie flinched. "Of course I do," she said. "Of course I have sentimentality."

"I doubt it! Is that why you didn't come home for my twentieth birthday?" Rumi challenged. "Because you just don't care?"

Here it is, Andie thought. She had half expected a showdown was coming. She just wished it wasn't happening in front of other family members. She kept her eyes on her daughter as she spoke, but she was all too aware of their audience.

"I told you I'm sorry for missing your birthday," she said. "I really am. You know I was on a book-signing tour. I'd made a commitment."

Rumi folded her arms across her chest. "I guess for some people career is more important than family."

"Work," Andie said calmly. "Good work. That's important to me. Not more important than family, but important."

"If family is more important than work why did you move so far away from Dad and me all those years ago?" Rumi demanded.

Andie chose not to respond to that question, not now. She reached out to take her daughter's hand, but Rumi, arms still folded, took a step aside. "I sent a card for your birthday," Andie went on. "I sent you a gift. I called, and when you didn't answer your phone I left a message. Again, I'm sorry." She knew that she must sound pathetic, but she couldn't seem to stop herself from apologizing. And with every passing moment she was more aware of the silent witnesses to this upsetting exchange—Emma watching, her lips tight, Anna Maria staring fixedly at the wedding dress laid out on the bed, Sophia looking confusedly from her aunt to her cousin and back again.

"You knew it was my first birthday without Grandma," Rumi said. "You should have put my needs before your own, for once in your life. Even Rita called me and sent me a present. My ex-stepmother made more of an effort than you did!"

Andie felt her heart sink. Did Rumi really think she had shuffled her aside as unimportant or irrelevant? All those years of phone calls and visits and long handwritten letters, had they all been forgotten? "I'm sorry my absence caused you pain, Rumi," she said carefully. "I truly am."

Rumi's eyes blazed. "But you'd do it again, wouldn't you?" she challenged. "If something important was happening for me and some stranger begged you for help, you'd see it as your duty to help him rather than me."

"Rumi, that's not—"

"I don't want to hear any more excuses for your . . . for your neglect. I'm out of here."

Rumi grabbed her cloth bag from where she had tossed it onto a chair and stormed out of the room. The sound of her feet thudding down the stairs, the sound of the front door slamming behind her, tore at Andie's heart. It was the sound of loss, the sound of the impossible actually happening, her daughter rejecting her once and for all.

Anna Maria sighed. "She's just upset, Andie," she said. "She'll calm down."

Andie smiled weakly. "Will she?"

Sophia looked on the verge of tears. "Why is Rumi so mad at Aunt Andie, Mom?"

Anna Maria put her arm around her daughter's shoulders. "She's got a lot on her mind, Sophia. That's all."

"I'm okay, Sophia," Andie said. "Really." But her niece hung her head and wouldn't meet her eye.

Emma's expression was grim. "You didn't deserve that," she said. "Do you want me to talk to her? She can't be allowed to be abusive to her mother."

But at that moment Andie didn't know what she did or did not deserve from Rumi. "No," she told her sister. "But thanks. I'll talk to Bob about . . . about the situation."

"So," Anna Maria said briskly. "The wedding dress. Obviously it can't stay here if we're selling the house. Why don't I bring it to my place? I suppose I should bring the chest, too. It's kept the dress safe for all these years. . . . I'll ask Daniel to hire one of our young waiters to help move it."

Andie smiled gratefully. "Thank you, Anna Maria. I'd appreciate that."

Emma nodded. "Me, too. And I'll finish going through the rest of the clothes and take them to that good thrift shop in Lawrenceville. I think it's called Style Revisited. Now," she said, "why don't we have some lunch? And maybe a glass of wine with it, for medicinal purposes."

Andie slipped her arm through her sister's. "A glass of wine would be very welcome," she said.

Emma nodded. "Good. And a cupcake for Sophia. I think I can manage to whip up a batch pretty quickly."

"All right, Sophia?" Andie asked gently. The girl finally raised her head and gave her aunt a shy smile.

CHAPTER 33

"Darn." Daniel shook his head and jiggled the on/off switch of the standing mixer. With a grating sound the mixer came back to life. It had been acting up since the end of summer and really should have been replaced before now, but not until his parents' house was finally sold and he received his part of the estate could Daniel finally afford an upgraded model.

"Can I help?" Bob asked. "I've been known to coax a dead blender back from the grave."

"Sadly, no," Daniel told him. "But thanks."

Daniel was trying out a new recipe for dinner rolls, that ubiquitous but so often bland and tasteless accompaniment to a meal, and Bob, who had an excellent palate for everything from exotic spices to good basic breads, was acting as his taster. Already they had rejected two recipes—one as too crispy; the other not crispy enough—but Daniel had tweaked this and adjusted that and was now feeling more confident of success in spite of the wonky mixer.

"Did you hear what happened at the house this morning?" he asked, scraping the current dough mixture onto the floured work surface. Anna Maria had reported the incident after lunch, and though she had sworn Rumi's attack had been unprovoked, Daniel didn't really believe it.

"If you mean the argument between Andie and Rumi," Bob said, "yes, I heard."

"My sister has become so selfish," Daniel said forcefully as he began to knead his dough. "So single minded, as if only she matters."

Bob shook his head. "Well, I heard Rumi's version of the tussle, and let me tell you, I took it with a grain of salt. If Rumi's got a problem with her mother she needs to talk it through one on one, not drag other people into her drama. She knows better, Daniel. Andie and I have taught her better."

"*You* taught her, Bob. You were here, Andie wasn't."

"Daniel," Bob said, "you might find this hard to understand, but Andie and I both actively parented our daughter. Maybe we're not the most conventional family, but we're a family."

"You're right," Daniel said. "I don't understand. Not really."

"It's to everyone's benefit if Rumi and her mother reconcile," Bob went on. "It's only a bump in the road, but if we all don't support the idea of peace it might become something bigger and more destructive."

Daniel shrugged. "Well, of course it would be nice if Andie and Rumi got along again, but do you really think my sister has anything to offer Rumi at this point in their lives?"

"Yes," Bob said firmly. "I do. And forgive me if I'm frank, but family harmony seems to matter an awful lot to you, Daniel, and I think that's really great, but when it comes to Andie you seem unwilling to keep that in mind. You weren't always so harsh with her. What's going on?"

Daniel opened his mouth to deny the accusation, but closed it again. How could he deny the truth? He *had* been unwilling to entertain his sister's point of view on much of anything for some time now. And he thought about his close attachment to his children and how horrible it would be if one or both turned against him. He experienced a moment of pity for his sister. . . . But just a moment.

"Okay, Bob," he said finally. "I'll give it a rest." He knew he would try—he was a man of his word—but he wasn't at all sure that he would succeed.

"Good. Well, I'd better be off. That is, unless you still need my taste buds."

"No, I think I'm closing in on perfection."

Bob smiled. "I'd be careful reaching after perfection," he said. "I hear it's pretty elusive."

When Bob was gone, Daniel found himself wondering what Emma had made of that morning's tussle between Rumi and her mother. He felt almost certain that Emma would side with him. After all, she had cared enough to ask about the final moments of their mother's life and to express her sympathy and her thanks for all her brother had done. And yet, Daniel thought, a frown coming to his face, Emma still hadn't chosen a real estate agent to handle the sale of the house. Words were all well and good, but deeds were what mattered in the end. And neither sister had finished going through the books in the den and neither had given an opinion on whether the family should hire an auction house to handle an estate sale or tackle it on their own.

It will all come down to me, Daniel thought, setting the dough aside to rise. *I'll be stuck with all the work, just like I always am.* He was aware he was being a bit self-pitying, but he felt so very strongly that achieving this closure for the family was vital, and that it would lead the Reynoldses into the next phase of their life as a happy family.

Family cohesiveness. That was the priority his parents had established and the goal they had largely achieved; it was why, Daniel thought, they had been so rattled by his sisters' choices, each girl seeming to want to break apart the family unit, to separate out from the rest, to forge an entirely independent life.

Daniel looked around at the kitchen he and Anna Maria had worked so hard to afford. He thought about the business they had struggled to build, a business that served the community his parents had served. He thought about how he and his wife had chosen to raise their children right here in Oliver's Well. And thinking about all these things, Daniel felt proud. *At least*, he thought, *one of us didn't let Mom and Dad down.*

CHAPTER 34

Emma steered her car onto Market Street. Morgan Shelby had called a little while earlier to say that he had completed the appraisal of the silver serving platters and that she could retrieve them at any time.

But her mind wasn't entirely on the task at hand. She couldn't get Rumi's words to her mother out of her mind. She had accused Andie of neglect; she seemed to have become so unfair and un-generous. And if Emma was worried about her niece she was even more worried about her sister. After lunch, when Anna Maria and Sophia had gone home, Andie had grown even more dejected, and as far as Emma knew, that was not a mood common to Andie Reynolds.

Emma slowed at a crosswalk to let a young woman pushing a stroller and gripping the hand of a child about the age of four cross the street. And she wondered if Rumi knew anything about her mother's postpartum depression; if she did know, Emma wondered if she felt an ounce of compassion for what her mother had suffered and sacrificed. Rumi needed to get past the fact of Andie's missing the birthday and deal with whatever issue was really feeding her anger.

And suddenly, with a blinding flash of memory Emma recalled a time when she had been completely unwilling to forgive her mother for a perceived failure. She had been in sixth grade, old enough to be conscious of her family's standing in the town, old enough to feel she had something to prove or to uphold. She remembered, too, that it was a sensitive stage in her life, a time she had spent seeking her mother's attention with more than usual persistence.

The Oliver's Well Historical Society had announced its first ever Mother-Daughter Luncheon, an event that hadn't proved to have much staying power over time. The meal was to be served at the Wilson House, with fine china and good flatware and food delivered from what was then Oliver's Well's premier restaurant. Emma had asked her mother if they could attend. Maureen and her mother were going, she had told Caro. "Everyone will be there. And we can get dressed up and maybe there'll even be champagne!" Emma remembered her mother laughing. "Of course we'll go," she said. "But no champagne for you!"

But then, two days before the luncheon, Caroline had gotten a bad stomach virus and no amount of moping and tears and questions—"Are you sure you're not better, Mom?"—could make her well enough to attend. "I'm sorry, Emma," her mother had told her, sweat standing out on her pale brow as she lay in bed. "Maybe we can go next year."

"Next year's not good enough!"

Emma cringed at the memory of her stomping out of her parents' bedroom. It had been incredibly stupid to get angry about something her mother couldn't have prevented if she had tried. *Oh*, she thought, *the impossible standards a child sets for a parent!*

She parked once again in the municipal lot and made her way toward the Shelby Gallery, passing another of the real estate agencies she should already have visited. *Tomorrow*, she thought. *Tomorrow*.

Morgan greeted her as she came through the door. "Well, hello," he said. "Beautiful day, isn't it?"

"It is. I saw you at the concert the other night," Emma told him, walking over to the counter. "At the Church of the Immaculate Conception."

"You were there?" Morgan smiled. "I'm sorry we missed each other. It was quite the turnout." He reached below the counter, retrieved a stapled sheaf of papers, and handed it to Emma. "The appraisal," he said. "So, what's next on your agenda? I mean, in terms of settling your mother's estate."

"Oh, there's a lot still to do. And we'll be selling the house, of course. As it is the three of us who own it equally, Danny, Andie, and I."

"I've always liked the house," Morgan told her. "Most of the houses on Honeysuckle Lane, in fact. There's something solid yet graceful about those old homes. It all comes down to proportion."

Emma nodded. "I've always felt that, too." She looked down at the papers Morgan had given her. "Thanks again for doing the appraisal. I have to say your fee seems very reasonable."

Morgan smiled. "Friends and family discount."

Before Emma could respond to this interesting remark—did Morgan genuinely consider her a friend?—the bell over the door to the gallery rang. Emma turned to see a middle-aged couple coming through. "Hello," Morgan said to them. "Welcome back."

"We've decided on the dining set," the woman said excitedly.

Emma smiled at Morgan. "You're busy," she said quietly. "I'll be on my way."

She left Morgan attending to his customers and walked back to her car. As she was stowing the box of the silver serving platters in the trunk her cell phone rang. Distracted by thoughts of her latest conversation with Morgan, as well as by a passing UPS truck that was rattling alarmingly, Emma answered before realizing that what she had heard was Ian's particular ring tone.

"Emma, at last." Ian laughed. "I thought you'd fallen off the face of the earth. Have you gotten my messages?"

Emma cringed. *Damn*, she thought. She didn't want to be having a conversation with him on a sidewalk. She didn't want to be having a conversation with him at all. "Hello, Ian," she said. "I've been busy."

"How are things going?" Ian asked. "Any progress on the sale of your mom's house? You guys are going to sell, aren't you?"

"Things are fine," Emma said. And she thought: why should he care about the sale of her mother's home? He was no longer a part of this family. He was no longer a part of *her*.

"And how's your brother doing?" Ian went on. "You said before you—"

Emma cut him off. "Ian," she said, "I've got to go. I have an appointment with a real estate agent in a few minutes." She hated to lie, but there were times when it seemed harmless enough, and more importantly, expedient.

"Call me later?" he asked.

Emma hesitated and then ended the call without a reply. Maybe now, she thought, he would understand. Hanging up on Ian was rude, but frankly, his persistence, his stubbornness, his cheery denial of what had happened between them a few nights back was starting to feel like too heavy a burden for her to bear. There were other people that mattered more to her at the moment, like Andie and Daniel.

Like Morgan Shelby?

No. Not yet, anyway.

CHAPTER 35

"I wish the bartender wouldn't keep refilling this dish of nuts," Emma said to Daniel, frowning at the salted cashew between her fingers. "When it comes to mixed nuts I have no self control."

Getting together with her brother at the Angry Squire that evening had been Emma's idea; she wanted to talk to him again, but this time away from "the family house." The place seemed to have a hold on Daniel in some unhappy way. When Daniel had asked why they couldn't talk at number 32 Honeysuckle Lane, Emma had shrugged and said, "I'm in the mood for a festive environment."

The bar was busy and Emma had immediately recognized the old geezer sitting at the very end; she remembered seeing him around town when she was a kid.

"Mr. Hazan," Daniel whispered. "He's rumored to be closing in on one hundred."

Emma raised an eyebrow. "Good for him," she said. "He's a regular?"

Daniel grinned. "He comes in every day around this time for a shot of whiskey and then takes himself off. Hey, did I ever tell you that Richard Armstrong approached me a few years back about coming on board as his head chef?"

"No, really? Wow."

"I told him no, of course. I wouldn't have been free to expand the menu the way I'd have wanted to. Richard understood. You can't suddenly go serving your loyal steak and baked potato customers a hot Indian curry."

"I guess not. Still, it's nice to be appreciated, isn't it?"

"Anyone ever try to lure you into joining forces?" Daniel asked.

Emma shrugged. "Once. It probably would have been a very lucrative move, but I wasn't interested in a partnership. I wanted to stay on my own." Emma took a deep breath. "Look, Danny," she said, "I want to talk to you about Andie."

"Is that why you lured me here?" Daniel asked, and Emma couldn't quite gauge the extent of his annoyance.

"Yes," she said. "And I had a hankering for this excellent Beaujolais."

"What if I say I don't want to talk about Andie?"

"Tough." Emma playfully slapped her brother's arm. "I'm your big sister and I'm pulling rank. Come on, Danny, I promise it won't hurt."

Daniel sighed. "All right," he said. "You win."

"First, I don't know what you heard about what happened this morning at the house, but I was there and I have to tell you that Rumi behaved badly. Andie was very upset after, though of course she didn't make a fuss."

"Anna Maria told me," Daniel admitted. "And Bob and I talked about it later. Maybe Rumi shouldn't have blown up at Andie in front of you guys, but she had a point."

Emma decided not to pursue that particular line of argument. "Danny," she said, "what do you really know about Andie's marriage to Bob?"

"What do you mean?" he asked with a frown.

"Look, I don't think I'm spilling a secret I shouldn't when I tell you that it was Bob who suggested Andie be the one to file for divorce. The decision to split was entirely mutual, but he didn't want her to be seen as the betrayed woman."

Daniel nodded. "That's like Bob. He's a gentleman. But the fact is that Andie left her child. The divorce is nothing compared to that. I just can't wrap my head around it. I'd do anything rather than walk away from my kids. Anything. And her being a *mother* . . ."

"Men walk away from their children all the time, Danny," Emma pointed out. "Don't be hard on Andie just because she's a woman. And why is this bothering you so badly now, after all these years?"

Daniel didn't respond. Maybe, Emma thought, he didn't know how to respond.

"Anyway," she went on, "it's not as if she abandoned Rumi. She's always been in close touch with her daughter, as well as with Bob. You know that."

"Bob said as much to me this afternoon," Daniel admitted. "He swears he and Andie coparented even after she left Oliver's Well."

"Believe him, Danny. They're a family. They're going through a rough patch, but they're close at heart. And they certainly don't need anyone from the outside stirring the pot."

Daniel smiled a bit. "Are you saying I'm interfering?"

"Yes," Emma told him. "That's exactly what I'm saying. You shouldn't encourage Rumi when she's rude or disrespectful to her mother. Think about it, Danny. How would you feel if I started to encourage Sophie or Marco to turn against you or Anna Maria?"

"I'd be furious."

"And I'd be in the wrong."

Daniel sighed. "It's just that when I think of how Andie lives her life I can't find any connection between my sister and my mother. Mom would never, ever have turned her back on her husband and children to pursue her own interests. It never even would have occurred to her."

"Of course it wouldn't have occurred to her, Danny," Emma said, trying to keep the frustration out of her voice. "Mom was happy with her life the way it was. Look, just because Andie did something that Mom would never have done doesn't make it wrong. And face it, we really don't know what Mom might or might not have done in different circumstances, if she had been unhappy with Dad and her life in Oliver's Well. No one ever knows another person well enough to accurately predict their behavior one hundred percent of the time."

Daniel frowned down at his beer, as if assessing the truth of what she had just said. *Poor Danny*, Emma thought. In her brother's eyes, their mother could do no wrong, and that sort of adulation could bring with it difficulties. She wondered again what her brother would think if he knew that Caro had broken her first engagement. She suspected he might put his own spin on the story, paint the fiancé as a monster his mother was well rid of, rather than accept that she had followed her passion—just as his oldest sister had followed hers. For a split second Emma was tempted to tell her mother's secret, but she got the better of herself. To tell Daniel might be to further upset him, and what good would that do for any of the family?

"Have you chosen a real estate agent to list the house?" Daniel asked suddenly, looking back at her.

"Not yet," she said, "but I'm close. Hey, Danny, do you remember the time we went with the Klines to Worthington Lake for the day? I was just thinking about it last night. Remember how we kids, Maureen's sisters, too, went into the woods at one point and tried to build a fort with fallen tree limbs?"

Daniel laughed. "And Kathleen tried to control the construction, which is probably why it failed. And later, Fiona pretended to fall into the lake and drown."

"She always was an attention seeker, even as a little kid. I'm surprised Jeannette and Danny put up with it."

"We parents do tend to overlook our children's foibles at times. Sometimes to our—and their—detriment."

"I don't see anything too terrible in your kids, Danny."

"If you lived with them you might see differently!" Daniel smiled and then glanced around the bar. When he spoke again his voice was low. "Look, I know I'm a professional chef and I'm supposed to only eat the best quality food, but I suddenly have a craving for very greasy onion rings. There's a dive about a mile out of town. Are you in?"

Emma grinned. "Oh, yeah. A gal can only eat so many salted nuts."

"Great. But let's keep this to ourselves. I've got a reputation to maintain."

Emma laughed. "You sound like Dad. Every time he would do or say something goofy or slightly off color he'd say exactly the same thing. 'Don't tell anyone. I've got a reputation to maintain.' "

"I remember. I remember an awful lot of the things he used to say and do. Like how he used a good old-fashioned brush and shaving foam instead of an electric shaver or a razor. Sometimes it's as if he never died, I see him so clearly."

Emma took her brother's arm as they left the Angry Squire. Her brother, she thought, was truly suffering, maybe more even than Andie at the moment. "Onion rings are on me," she said. "And remember, you're not allowed to say no to your big sister."

CHAPTER 36

Bob had lived in the little house on Bertram Road since just before Rumi's tenth birthday. He had bought it as a fixer-upper and had truly transformed the one-story structure into a charming home for himself and his daughter.

"Thanks for having me over," Andie said, turning from the small watercolor she had been admiring. "Sorry to invite myself."

"My pleasure." Bob smiled. "You know you're always welcome, Andie. I'll go make us some tea."

Andie waited for her former husband in the living room, a small but welcoming room with walls painted a soothing blue and homey touches like a brightly colored crocheted afghan tossed across the back of the couch and a vase of fresh white carnations on the coffee table.

With some difficulty she resisted going down the hall to take a peek into Rumi's bedroom. She hadn't seen it for years and she wondered what she might find. She wondered if there would be evidence of Rumi's jewelry making, stones she had selected for their healing properties as well as for their beauty. She wondered, too, if Rumi had kept the things she had sent her through the years, like the books and the prayer beads. Andie had always believed that a gift should be given freely, without expectation even of thanks; still, she hoped her daughter had kept and cherished at least some of the items her mother had sent her.

More importantly, Andie wanted to touch the pillow on which her daughter laid her head each night, and to see whatever it might be that Rumi saw first thing each morning. She wanted to see evidence of her child's daily life, a life she had not witnessed firsthand for most of the past twelve years.

But she remembered what she had said to Emma about a parent respecting a child's privacy and she refrained from satisfying her curiosity. If she wanted to know more about her daughter's life, she should simply ask her. Assuming Rumi was still talking to her. Andie hadn't heard from her since she stormed out of the house on Honeysuckle Lane the morning before.

Bob came back from the kitchen carrying a tray with teapot, cups, and a plate of ginger snaps. Andie smiled. Bob loved ginger snaps. They sat side by side on the couch and Bob poured their tea.

"I hope you like this," he said. "It's a new blend I discovered at the Eclectic Gourmet. They've got a specialist in tea; he's always coming up with new combinations."

Andie took a sip. "Mmm. That's lovely. What's it called?"

"Seahawk's Dream."

Andie laughed. "That's creative."

"So, what did you want to talk about?" Bob asked. "Though I think I can guess."

Andie took another soothing sip before answering. "Rumi is so angry with me, Bob, more so now than ever. I can't help but wonder if it's more than just missing her grandmother. It's almost as if she's been listening to nasty stories about my being . . ."

"Being what?"

Neglectful. But Andie couldn't say the word aloud—the word Rumi had used to describe her mother. "Never mind. But it's like she's determined to misinterpret everything I say."

"I've never spoken ill of you to our daughter, Andie. You can believe that."

"I do, Bob," she said. But she wondered if her brother had been subtly poisoning Rumi's thoughts. . . . No, she decided. Daniel would never do such a thing. It would be far too cruel. "Has Rumi ever asked you why you married me?"

"Where did that come from?" Bob smiled. "But as a matter of fact, yeah. When she was about fifteen she had a crush on a boy at school, and I guess she had fantasies about marrying him at some point. It was painful to witness. Hormones masquerading as young love."

And I wasn't here to help.... "What did you tell her?" Andie asked.

"I said that I asked you to marry me because I loved you."

"The simple answer."

"And a true one."

Andie sighed. "Sometimes," she said, "I wonder if the postpartum depression was partly the result of my knowing that I wasn't the right kind of wife to you. If I couldn't properly love the father of my child as a wife should love him, how could I properly love the child?"

Bob shook his head. "Gosh, Andie, I don't know the answer to that. But I do think you might be allowing Rumi's mood to make you feel gloomy. And I don't want you to feel gloomy or to dwell on what's gone. The past can take care of itself."

"I wish I could always believe that." Andie smiled ruefully. "I truly never meant any harm, Bob. But I caused it. Sometimes I think I'll never be able to fully forgive myself. Ironic, isn't it? The teacher can't practice what she preaches! As Rumi says, 'Everyone is overridden by thoughts; that's why they have so much heartache and sorrow.' The question is, how do you let go of thoughts?"

Bob smiled gently. "I'll get back to you on that one."

Andie took a bite of a ginger snap, and as she chewed her eye returned to the small watercolor painting she had been admiring earlier. "That painting by the door," she said. "It's charming, but I'm not sure I noticed it before today. Where did you get it?"

"Your mother gave it to me about a year before she died," Bob told her. "It was a birthday present. I think she said she'd gotten it at a craft fair a short time before your father passed away." Bob shrugged. "For some reason she wanted me to have it."

"Because she loved you, Bob," Andie said. "She wasn't entirely sure about me, but she knew that you were a quality person."

"Now, Andie, your mother loved you."

"Maybe. But she considered me a flake at best."

Bob sighed and put his cup on the coffee table. "Caro didn't understand you," Bob said gently, "but then again, none of us ever really did. None of us *do*, not entirely, not even me. Now, that's not a criticism of you. It's our failing. Maybe we lack imagination. But, Andie, your mother *did* love you. You have to believe that. She even admired you, one she got past the shock of your leaving Oliver's Well after Rumi came to live with me. I remember her saying to me once, just after you published your first article in a national magazine, that she never thought you were the child who would prove to have such nerve."

Andie laughed a bit sadly. "Kind of a backhanded compliment, don't you think?"

"Only if you choose to take it that way," Bob argued. "The point is that she was proud of you. If she was surprised by your success, it was only because you were, and these were her words, a late bloomer. What she didn't have to say—what she probably couldn't say—was that you only really blossomed after our divorce."

"And after you took over Rumi's care," Andie pointed out. "In an important way, Bob, I have you to thank for what I've managed to accomplish in my life. You gave me the freedom to leave Oliver's Well."

Bob smiled. "You would have found another way out on your own, I'm sure of it. It might have taken some time, but you would have succeeded in the end."

"I suppose it was nice of my mother to tell you she had some respect for my work," Andie admitted. "But I would have liked to hear it from her own lips."

Bob shrugged. "She was who she was, old fashioned, in spite of having witnessed the sixties and seventies. She probably didn't know how to talk to you. Or she thought she didn't know how. So she kept quiet rather than flounder and embarrass the both of you in the process."

"You're probably right, Bob. Still . . . I wish I had known how she felt when she was still alive."

"Well, now you do know," Bob pointed out. "Better late than never."

"Yes. You're right. And I hope that knowledge will help me going forward."

And Andie thought: *Why are the important things left unsaid? Why do we waste so much breath—so many words—on the trivial, the mean spirited, the critical? How often in my own life I've been guilty of this! Because to be human is to fail others, as well as to serve them.*

"Any thoughts on what can be done to bridge the gap that's opened up between Rumi and me?" she asked her dearest friend.

Bob sighed. "I don't have any bright ideas, if that's what you're looking for. This is a difficult time for her. We were lucky her adolescent years were relatively smooth. The biggest bump in the road was when she had to get braces for a year. She threw a bit of a tantrum about that until her best friend of the moment also got them, and suddenly braces were cool."

"I just wish she weren't so *angry*," she said. "Anger frightens me, Bob. It always has. It makes me feel physically ill."

"Be patient, Andie. Why don't you ask her to visit you in Woodville Junction sometime?" he suggested. "Let her see where you live, meet the people who share your day-to-day life. They're important to you, and maybe she needs to witness that."

"I don't know, Bob. She used to enjoy our visits to the ashram and to the retreat center outside Charleston, but she was so much younger then. Do you really think asking her to visit me is a good idea? Especially now, when we're in such a bad place?"

"Maybe not right yet." Bob sighed. "But some day."

Andie laughed a bit desperately. "I certainly hope so."

Later that afternoon, back at the house on Honeysuckle Lane, Andie thought about what Bob had told her—Caro Reynolds had been proud of her oldest child's achievements. Bob was right;

knowing this now was better than never having known it at all. And suddenly Andie recalled the time many years earlier when she had been presented a humanitarian award from a foundation to support and promote the work of spiritual guidance and study. The reason? She had donated one hundred hours of her time to work with victims of PTSD and help them master the skills needed for a more peaceful life going forward. Her father, she remembered, had called her from Oliver's Well to congratulate her. "It's more of a recognition than an award," she had told him, feeling a bit awkward accepting his praise. "Still," he had replied, "I'm so proud of you."

It wasn't something Cliff often did, Andie recalled, tell his oldest child that he was proud of her. He was more likely to praise Emma or Daniel. . . . But maybe, like Bob had said, that was because he had more easily understood and recognized their achievements than he had Andie's.

Andie felt a lightening of spirit—her parents had respected her!—and decided just then that she would host a feast for the family that night. She couldn't remember the last time she had made a meal for any of her family; certainly it had been years and years. And it was such a caring and generous thing to do, to cook for people you loved. She would send a text to Rumi and also ask Bob to encourage her to join them; the invitation might be better coming from both of her parents. Andie might not succeed in getting the Reynolds family to join hands in a prayer of thanks, but at least she would have the satisfaction of giving a gift.

Andie pulled out her iPhone and sent a text to Anna Maria, Bob, and to Rumi, inviting them for dinner at six-thirty that evening. Emma had left a note that she would be back soon; Andie would tell her directly. And then she would make a shopping list and head into town. Any ingredient she couldn't find at the grocery store she might be able to secure at the Eclectic Gourmet.

Andie heard the front door open and shut. A moment later Emma came into the kitchen, carrying a bag from the local independent pharmacy. "I took the last of the aspirin that was in the bathroom cupboard," she said. "So I thought I'd better replace the bottle before Danny decided he'd pay for that, too."

Andie smiled. "Speaking of Danny doing things for us, I thought I'd give him a break and cook dinner here for everyone tonight."

Emma smiled. "Just don't expect to make a convert out of Danny. I don't think he'll be giving up his red meat any time soon."

Andie laughed. "I'm not that naive." But, she thought, reaching for her bag, if she could at least accomplish a pleasant meal around the family table, she would be happy.

CHAPTER 37

"What time is it?" Andie asked, wiping her hands on the apron tied around her middle. Emma remembered her mother wearing the apron; until Andie had put it on earlier that evening it had remained spotlessly clean. Now it was splattered with stains. But what, Emma thought, was an apron for if not to get dirty?

"It's six-forty," Emma told her. She hadn't needed to check her watch. Andie had asked the same question less than two minutes ago.

Andie frowned. "I don't want to hold dinner for long. The children are probably starving."

"There's no reason we can't start without Rumi," Emma said, in what she hoped was a comforting tone. "I'm sure she'll be along soon."

"I hope nothing's happened," Andie said worriedly.

Bob, who was putting the final touches on a salad of mixed greens, walnuts, and goat cheese, said, "I'm sure she's fine, Andie. Probably just running late. I'll send her a text."

Andie went off to the dining room, and a moment later Emma saw her brother-in-law frown at his phone. "What is it?" she asked.

"She said that something came up. She knows better than to behave this way," he said quietly to Emma. "Come on, let's get the food on the table."

Emma picked up a platter and followed Bob out of the kitchen. Andie hurried back into the kitchen and joined them a moment later at the table, carrying a large covered tureen Caro had often used on the holidays. "Did she reply?" Andie asked Bob.

"Looks like she can't make it after all." He hesitated and then, shooting a look at Emma, he said, "She apologized."

The stricken look on Andie's face told Emma that her sister didn't believe that Rumi had done any such thing. If Daniel or Anna Maria had caught Andie's expression, neither commented.

"We'll get started then," Andie said stoutly. "I've made an Indian vegetarian meal. We'll start with the carrot ginger soup."

"I like soup," Sophia announced. "It's one of my favorite things to eat."

"I like sandwiches best," Marco added. "Especially peanut butter and jelly. But the jelly can't have seeds in it. They stick in my teeth."

Emma smiled at her niece and nephew. "Maybe you guys will follow in your father and mother's footsteps and go into the food business."

Sophia took a spoonful of soup before saying, "Nope. I want to be a doctor. I think." Marco was too busy destroying a piece of naan to reply.

The soup, which Emma thought was excellent, was followed by curried potatoes with cabbage, a lentil stew, a cold cucumber salad with a creamy dressing, and something Andie explained was called *mysore bonda*. "They're fried dumplings made with flour, yogurt, and spices and traditionally served with coconut chutney. Unfortunately," she said, "I couldn't find any coconut chutney in town, so this mango chutney will have to do."

"Where did you find the naan?" Emma asked.

"I made it. I used a recipe that doesn't require a tandoor or oven."

Emma nodded. "Impressive." So far no one had mentioned Rumi's absence; she wondered how long they could go on avoiding the very large elephant in the room.

"This stew is delicious, Andie," Daniel said, scooping up another forkful. "Really flavorful. I'm sorry I've been a bit of a jerk about your being a vegetarian. I do know better; it's a perfectly valid and healthy option. Though I doubt a vegetarian restaurant would be a success in Oliver's Well."

"You never know," Anna Maria said. "Not that we have the capital to give it a go!"

"Or the interest in taking on more work," Daniel added. "We're spread thin enough."

Emma felt a flash of guilt; the sooner the house was sold the sooner her brother and sister-in-law would get the money they needed to put into their business. And because of her the house wasn't even on the market yet.

"Were you ever a vegan, Andie?" Anna Maria asked.

Andie shook her head. "No, but I have friends who are. Having such a restricted diet can be a bit isolating, but they feel it's worth the trouble."

"I admire people with a passion," Bob said, spooning chutney onto a *mysore bonda*. "I'm not sure I've ever really had a firm commitment to anything other than reruns of *Seinfeld*."

Andie laughed. "Oh, Bob, don't be silly!"

"What was the weirdest thing you ever ate, Aunt Andie?" Sophia asked.

Andie considered for a moment. "Well," she said, "I guess it would have to be something called *gutka*; I was offered it when I was in India for the first time. Mind you, it wasn't weird to my hosts."

"What is it?" Marco asked.

"It's a preparation of crushed betel nut, tobacco, and sweet or sometimes savory flavorings. These were in the shape of little hearts and came wrapped in bright paper. It looked like candy— but it didn't taste like candy, at least not to me."

"That sounds awful," Emma said. "Eating tobacco?"

Andie smiled. "If I had known what was in it I would have passed as politely as I could have. Later I learned that the stuff can cause oral cancer, like chewing tobacco does."

"But what did it taste like?" Sophia asked.

"Like nothing I'd ever eaten before or since," Andie told her.

"The weirdest thing Dad said he ever ate," Daniel said, "was blood sausage when he and Mom were in Portugal. Blood sausage isn't all that weird or even unusual, but I guess to Dad it was. And the weirdest food Mom said they ever saw was being sold at street markets in China."

"Like what?" Emma asked. "Or do I not want to know?"

"Like lollipops filled with worms and grasshoppers. And there was a mention of duck heads."

Marco scrunched up his face. "Ew! That's disgusting!"

"I have to say I agree." Daniel shuddered. "When I was at the CIA there was a guy who was always challenging the rest of us to eat something outrageous he'd cooked up, like fried wasps and spiders. It drove me nuts. Not to say it sometimes made me ill."

"Is he a working chef?" Emma asked.

Daniel laughed. "Let's hope not!"

"I was thinking just the other day about our Italian holiday," Andie said. "I remember it as such a magical time."

"Me, too," Emma said. "Every day we spent in Italy is burned into my memory."

Daniel nodded. "I'll never forget the fried squash blossoms. I think I decided to become a chef at the very moment they were brought to the table one night. They were so gorgeous and, of course, delicious."

"It was all about the gelato for me," Andie said. "It still pretty much is."

"The art," Emma added. "The architecture. There was beauty everywhere you looked, even in the narrowest lanes and in the smallest little farmhouses. A true celebration of life."

"Can we go to Italy, Dad?" Sophia asked.

"Some day, absolutely. Your mom still has family there."

Anna Maria nodded. "I've never met them, but I think it would be fun to pay a visit."

"Birthday cakes," Emma said suddenly. "Each of us had a particular cake we asked Mom for year after year."

"Chocolate cake with vanilla icing," Daniel said. "That's what you always wanted, Emma."

Andie shook her head. "No, that was what I asked for. Emma always asked for the reverse. White cake with chocolate icing."

"Really? Why do I have that backward?"

"You're getting old, Danny," Emma teased. "We all are."

Daniel laughed. "Well, I'll still always be younger than you two."

"What kind of cake did you like best, Dad?" Marco asked.

"Hazelnut torte. Hands down."

"Mom didn't even attempt to make *that* from scratch," Emma remembered. "She would special order one from the French bakery in Lawrenceville."

Anna Maria grinned. "Anything for her son. The *figlio d'oro*."

"What does that mean, Mom?" Sophia asked. "It's Italian, right?"

"Right. The golden son. It means that Daddy was special to his mother."

"I liked the cake Dad made for Rumi's big birthday party," Sophia said. "You should have seen it, Aunt Andie. It was huge. It took two people to carry it into the restaurant. And it had all these sugar flowers on top, all of Rumi's favorites, those purple ones . . . yeah, irises."

"Speaking of favorites," Emma said brightly, eager to steer the conversation away from Rumi and her now infamous birthday party, "Andie, what's in these dumplings? I can't quite put my finger on the spice combination, but it's the most delicious thing I've tasted in a long time."

"There's cumin, ginger, green chili, and cilantro. All pretty basic." Andie looked to the others. "Would anyone like more curried potatoes and cabbage?" she asked.

"Yes, please!" Marco said.

While Andie served her nephew, Bob leaned close to Emma and whispered, "That birthday has assumed far more significance than it deserves. Thanks for changing the subject."

Dinner finished with a bang. Andie had bought several pints of ice cream in a variety of flavors, from chocolate chip to peanut butter cup, from good old vanilla to strawberry swirl. She put the containers on a large tray in the middle of the table and suggested that everybody help him or her self.

"Are there any sprinkles left from when Sophia and me made cookies the other day?" Marco asked eagerly.

"Sophia and I," his father corrected. "And you don't need sprinkles."

Marco frowned, but Emma noticed that his appetite for the dessert was not diminished by the absence of sprinkles.

Daniel and his family left soon after the meal, followed by Bob. "It will be all right," he said to Andie when she walked him to the door. Emma saw him kiss her on the cheek.

Finally, the sisters were alone. The evening had been pleasant overall, Emma thought, as she helped Andie bring the dishes and glasses and silverware back into the kitchen. If only Rumi had shown up as she had promised, real progress toward togetherness might have been made. At least no one had commented on Rumi's absence.

Andie closed the door of the dishwasher after pressing the start button. "That went well, I think," she said.

The determinedly cheerful note in her sister's voice saddened Emma. "It went very well," she told her. "And I'm sorry Rumi couldn't make it. I know you really hoped she would be here."

Andie shook her head. "Well, I'm pooped. I think I'll read for a while and then turn in."

Emma watched her sister leave the kitchen. She thought her shoulders looked a bit stooped, as if the weight of her disappointment was a physical burden. Emma wasn't prone to violence, but at that moment she wanted to shake some sense into her older niece.

But what good would that do? she thought as she turned out the lights on the first floor and followed her sister up to bed. People only made a change when they were ready, not when other people wanted them to. That was an undeniable truth.

CHAPTER 38

By nine fifteen the following morning Emma was driving through downtown Lawrenceville, her destination Style Revisited. She had been to the shop before and knew that it offered both a consignment option and accepted donations; a good portion of the money earned by the donated clothing went to a food bank run by one of the local churches. The proprietors of the shop were particularly strict about the sort of clothing they would accept. Not only did the clothing need to be in pristine condition, it had to meet certain standards of style and quality. You would find no slogan T-shirts from Old Navy or pink sweatpants from Victoria's Secret at Style Revisited. Some of the best clothing for sale—like fur or leather coats—was wired to a rack against theft. *An appropriate place for Mom's treasured wardrobe to find itself*, Emma thought.

She parked as close as she could to the store and wondered for a moment why she hadn't thought to bring a hand truck or a dolly with her. The boxes filled with her mother's clothing were heavy; Daniel had come by the house early that morning to help her load them into her car. *Oh, well*, Emma thought, wrangling the first box from the backseat and then the other from the trunk. *This is my exercise for the day.*

The woman at the receiving desk was impeccably if simply

dressed in a classic blue pinstriped Oxford shirt, tucked into a pair of navy pants. Her accessories were few and all gold. Emma knew a bit about jewelry—she had built a decent jewelry wardrobe over the years—and guessed the earrings and chain and rings on her fingers were eighteen karat. They had that rich, warm color not usually found in a lower karat gold.

"How may I help you?" the woman asked.

"I've brought in some clothes for donation," Emma told her, indicating the two large boxes she had lugged into the store and left near the entrance. "They were my mother's. She died last year." Then, she laughed. "I don't know why I told you that last bit. It's not as if you need to know."

The woman smiled kindly and asked if Emma would like a receipt.

"Yes," she said, "for the estate taxes." Emma handed her the descriptive list she had made of each item.

The woman glanced at the list. "A very nice collection," she said approvingly. "We should be able to sell these easily. Sarah?" she called to a much younger and fairly strapping-looking woman straightening a rack of blouses. "Will you bring those boxes up to the desk?"

Sarah did so, and the woman behind the desk unfolded the flaps of the first box. Carefully she lifted out the top few items. "Oh, yes," she said. "These will spend hardly any time in the store. And just look at this jacket. This is really lovely."

Emma swallowed hard. The woman was holding a boxy tweed jacket with gold buttons, reminiscent of the classic Chanel style. Her mother had bought it on a trip to DC when Emma was in high school; she remembered eagerly awaiting Caro's return from her journey so that she could see what treasures her mother had scooped up in the big city.

"I'm sorry," Emma blurted. "I just can't let this jacket go. I so vividly remember my mother wearing it. It's not really my style and it'll probably sit in my closet for the next ten years, but . . ."

"But you need to keep it," the woman said with sympathy. "I know."

"I suppose you've seen this sort of behavior before. Someone changing her mind."

"People react in all sorts of ways when they hand over the relics of a loved one," the woman said. "Sometimes they walk through the door all calm and collected, and the next minute they're sobbing like the world had come to an end. And I suppose it really feels that way for them—the end of something so very important. Sometimes, people leave with every single one of the items they intended to give up. Sometimes they fairly toss a coat or pair of trousers on the counter and they're gone, quick as a shot."

Suddenly, Emma found that there were tears in her eyes. "I'm sorry to be so emotional," she said, reaching for the pack of tissues she kept in her bag. "Thank you. You've been very kind."

Emma took her receipt and her mother's jacket and left the shop. When she got to her car she realized that she was in no fit condition to drive. So she walked a bit further to a wrought iron bench set under a magnolia tree before an ice-cream shop and sat.

And she thought of the things she might have said to her parents but hadn't, things like "thank you for giving me life." She thought of all the lost opportunities for understanding and connection. She thought of the covered tureen Andie had used at dinner the night before and remembered all of the occasions on which her mother had brought it to the table, a proud smile on her face. She thought of her mother in her spiffy gardening outfit, high-waisted tailored chinos, a pale blue blouse tucked in neatly, the floppy wide-brimmed hat on her head, the fitted gloves on her hands. She thought of her mother in the casket, in that lovely lilac dress, her hands artfully folded, her wedding rings not yet removed.

And then Emma thought of Morgan Shelby. She had no good reason to stop at the gallery on her way home. And she didn't feel that she had a right to turn to him in a moment of emotional need. Not yet. Still, she remembered what he had told her about people coming to the gallery seeking to replace or to revive a memory, and about how he understood the complicated process of letting go of—and holding on to—the past.

Emma sniffed and glanced at her watch. She really should get back to Oliver's Well. Norma Campbell's annual open house Christmas party was that afternoon and she would need time to change her clothes to something more appropriate for a festivity. And she would definitely need to clean off and then reapply the mascara that was most likely smudged all over her face.

With a fortifying deep breath and one last swipe at her eyes with a now soggy tissue, Emma got up from the bench and, carrying Caro's tweed jacket, she walked back to her car.

CHAPTER 39

Daniel adjusted his tie. He only wore a tie for special occasions, and Norma Campbell's annual open house certainly counted as a special occasion. Still, the tie would come off the moment he got back into the car. His father hadn't liked to wear a tie, either, though he had dutifully worn one to the office every day of his working life. *Like father like son,* Daniel thought. *I wonder how much like me Marco will turn out to be.*

Bob and Rumi had gone to a movie theater in Somerstown to see a screening of *Holiday Inn,* and Sophia and Marco were spending the afternoon with their Spinelli cousins. So it was just the four of them at Norma's, Daniel and Anna Maria, Andie and Emma. The room in which the party was being held—the "ballroom"—was vast. Three enormous chandeliers, dripping faceted crystals, hung in a row from the center of the ceiling. Between the tall rectangular windows along the right wall stood massive urns filled with artful arrangements of red and white roses, feathery pine boughs, and red and white poinsettias. Over the doorway to the ballroom—and at the entrance to the house—were hung large sprigs of mistletoe.

Per usual, Norma Campbell had hired a band to play standards from the American songbook, including what Daniel remembered to be some of his parents' favorite songs—"Smoke Gets in

Your Eyes" and "Moon River" and "The Twelfth of Never." And, of course, there were the holiday standards—"I'll Be Home for Christmas" and "Blue Christmas" and "White Christmas"—sung by a man whose voice, Daniel thought, was perfectly suited to handle the songs the famous crooners of the forties and fifties had performed so beautifully.

And the food! The term "groaning board" came to Daniel's mind. There were tables and tables laden with food. Roast beef. Roast turkey. Baked ham. There were baskets overflowing with breads and rolls of all descriptions, from brioche to baguettes. There were chafing dishes of savory baked vegetables and a large selection of cheeses, from the soft to the hard, from mild to pungent. And the desserts . . . Daniel had never been a fan of chocolate fountains, but Norma's guests seemed to be enjoying this one, and the mounds of insanely large strawberries to go with it. There were traditional Christmas puddings complete with brandy sauce, and good old American fruitcake. Four elaborate gingerbread houses stood side by side, surrounded by plates of cookies of every description. Waiters in white shirts, black pants and vests, circulated with finger foods and glasses of champagne. Daniel didn't know where Norma Campbell got her money, but she certainly was generous with it.

"I don't mean to be critical . . ." Daniel peered suspiciously at the mini quiche he held in his hand.

"Yes, you do," Emma said with a smile.

"All right then, I do. But this food doesn't stand up to what Anna Maria and I do. It's not awful by any means, but . . ."

Emma nodded. "I agree. The turkey is a bit dry and the broccoli casserole is a bit soggy."

"To be fair, it's not easy catering a party this big," Anna Maria pointed out.

"But we could do better," Daniel said. "I know we could."

"You'll just have to work on getting Norma's business, Danny," Andie said. "Spread the word of your excellence."

Daniel raised an eyebrow at his sister. "I didn't think that you of all people would advocate bragging. Aren't you a fan of humility?"

"Yes, but I'm not talking about bragging," Andie corrected. "I'm talking about simply stating the truth. Telling someone that you do good work. There's nothing wrong with being justly proud of your achievements."

Daniel didn't argue with his sister. He couldn't. Andie had actually used the word "excellence" and Andie wasn't one to choose her words casually. He was moved. "Thanks, Andie," he said. "You're right."

"Don't look now," Emma whispered, "but it's the Fitzgibbons senior descending upon us."

Mary Bernadette Fitzgibbon was wearing a skirt suit in a soft gray, with an even paler gray silk blouse. There was a small diamond stick pin in her right lapel. The woman, Daniel thought, fairly emanated elegance and resolve. Mary Bernadette's husband, Paddy, wore a suit in a conservative cut, with a white shirt and red tie. Daniel was sorry to see that Mr. Fitzgibbon had visibly aged in the past few months. *Well*, Daniel thought, *age comes to us all. If we're lucky.*

"It's nice to see the Reynolds siblings all together again," Mrs. Fitzgibbon said, flashing her trademark dazzling smile. Daniel, though used to the smile, could still sometimes find himself weakening in its presence, ready to give Mrs. Fitzgibbon whatever it was she wanted of him, even a discount on his catering services. But not his mother's treasured Regency desk.

"It's nice to be back in Oliver's Well," Emma said. "Danny's been treating us like royalty."

Daniel felt himself color slightly. "I wouldn't go that far," he said.

"Norma puts on a pretty good shindig, doesn't she?" Paddy laughed and patted his stomach. "And she certainly doesn't skimp on the food! There's even Yorkshire pudding!"

Daniel smiled at the older man. He might be aging, but he certainly hadn't lost his good humor and pleasant personality. It wasn't surprising that Cliff Reynolds had deeply liked and ad-mired Paddy Fitzgibbon.

"Have you tried the strawberry tarts, Mr. Fitzgibbon?" Andie asked. "I've already had two!"

Before Paddy Fitzgibbon could reply, his wife was talking. "Have you given any further thought to the future of the George Bullock desk?" Mary Bernadette asked the siblings. "Did you know that in 1805 Mr. Bullock supplied furniture for Chol-mondeley Castle?"

Paddy beamed proudly. "My Mary is the most persistent per-son I know! And she certainly knows her history!"

Daniel restrained an impulse to answer brusquely. "I'm afraid the desk is still not available, Mrs. Fitzgibbon," he said politely. "It will remain in the family as my mother wanted it to."

Amazingly, Daniel thought, Mary Bernadette didn't persist, merely bowed her head in acknowledgment.

Paddy put his hands in the front pocket of his pants. "You know," he said, "just the other day I was thinking about how I met your father. It was so many years ago now, back when he was starting his business and wanted to get involved in the Chamber of Commerce."

"You were a great help to Dad," Andie said. "You taught him a lot."

Daniel smiled. "Dad often used to say your advice was worth more than what some people paid for in business school."

"I don't know about that!" Paddy demurred. "But I do know we had some fun." Mr. Fitzgibbon lowered his voice and leaned in closer to Daniel and his family. "We used to sneak away from some of those chamber meetings and go to this little pub in Smithstown and talk about how we'd gotten to where we were in our lives." Paddy laughed. "Your father used to tell me how he worked two or three jobs at a time while he put himself through college. In the afternoon he washed dishes in the school's cafete-ria, and at nights he worked at a packing plant, driving a forklift. Oh, and for a short time he mowed the lawns of the professors who lived near campus, until the work got too much for him. But you kids must know all that."

Daniel felt tears threaten. He hadn't known any of it.

"This is the first I'm hearing of Dad's part-time jobs," Emma replied.

"Me, too," Andie said.

Mary Bernadette shook her head. "Clifford Reynolds had such a zest for life. He never let that silly heart problem slow him down." Her attention seemed to be caught by someone or something behind Daniel's right shoulder. "Excuse me," she said then. "I must go and greet Father Robert."

Mrs. Fitzgibbon sailed off, her husband at her side, like a stately ocean liner with her trusty tugboat companion, Daniel thought. He stood there for a long moment feeling oddly dislocated and left out. He thought he knew everything there was to know about his parents. He—

"Danny, are you there?"

It was Emma. "Sorry," he said, forcing a smile and a jovial tone. "I was just thinking. Can you see Dad washing dishes? He never did a bit of housework when we were growing up! The house was totally Mom's domain."

"She wouldn't let him near her domestic arrangements," Andie pointed out. "I'm sure he would have pitched in if she'd let him."

"And driving a forklift in a packing plant." Emma shook her head.

"Well, Cliff never was afraid of hard work," Anna Maria said. "I'm not surprised he took what jobs he could to get by, even the job mowing lawns. That must have stressed his heart, but he gave it a go."

"Yes," Daniel said. "Dad was a hard worker."

Emma lowered her voice. "I'll never forget the times when Mom and Mary Bernadette found themselves in the same room, like when one of them gave a party. It was Queen Elizabeth and Mary Queen of Scots all over again, not that those two ever met in person. The two rival rulers of Oliver's Well society."

"Mom always came out on top, of course," Daniel said firmly. "Though I'm not sure Mary Bernadette—or her husband—would agree."

Andie shook her head. "How silly, competing over social standing."

"It's not silly," Daniel argued. "You have to understand Mom's context. In many ways the rarified world into which she was born had already passed. It must have been difficult for her to adjust to such radically changing social mores."

"Of course." Andie said. "You're right, Danny. I didn't mean to be critical."

"Well, you sounded critical. You—"

Anna Maria laid a hand on Daniel's arm, and he refrained from finishing his comment.

"You know," Emma said, "since being back in Oliver's Well this Christmas season, I've learned so much about Mom and Dad that I never knew. I was talking to Maureen the other day and—"

"And what?" Daniel interrupted. "What did Maureen have to say?"

"It seems she unearthed Mom's keen interest in politics and civic duty. I'm not even sure I knew that Mom voted!"

"When did this happen?" Daniel demanded. "When did Maureen talk to Mom alone?"

"She told me she visited Mom a few times in her last months," Emma explained. "And they talked about all sorts of things. Didn't you know they used to meet?"

"No," Daniel said shortly, realizing that he was frowning. He felt . . . He felt upset that Maureen Kline, a relative stranger, should know about his mother's interest in politics while he had been left in the dark. It was one thing for his father not to have shared every detail of his early life with his children; men like Cliff Reynolds were often silent on the subject of the struggles they had endured for the sake of building a career. But for his own mother not to have shared with her son something she considered important . . .

"Danny?" Emma asked. "You okay?"

"Yeah," he said. "Just thinking."

"Well, it's a party," Anna Maria said robustly. "Try not to think so much and just enjoy."

Daniel forced a smile and lifted his glass. "A toast to Mom and Dad's memory," he said. Anna Maria, Andie, and Emma lifted their glasses to his. And as they each sipped their drinks, Daniel added silently, *To the people I thought that I knew.*

CHAPTER 40

Shortly after the Fitzgibbons had gone off to greet Father Robert, Andie wandered away from the others to look more closely at one of the large landscape paintings that hung in the ballroom. The painting depicted a rugged mountain scene with a spectacular waterfall cascading violently to the plunge pool below. It was a powerful and atmospheric image, like those wonderfully romantic paintings done by artists of the Hudson River School. Andie wondered vaguely where Norma Campbell had found it.

It was terribly nice of Norma to open her house to the entire community. Andie had always believed that generosity was an innate quality. It was hard to learn how to be truly generous unless it really came from the heart. Giving with no strings. She and Bob had always believed that and had taught it to their daughter. . . .

Not that Rumi always followed her parents' good advice, like honoring the importance of forgiveness. In the past few hours Andie had left Rumi a voice mail and sent a text and an e-mail, all of which had gone unanswered. And she knew that Bob had tried several times to get Rumi to apologize to Andie for having stormed off the other day and for having been a no-show at dinner, but Rumi was refusing to budge. Andie sighed. You couldn't force someone to forgive, or to let go of her grief. Still, if there was some way she could help her daughter to move forward into a happier place, she would.

Andie turned from the painting and spotted Emma chatting with Lucy Burrows, one of their neighbors on Honeysuckle Lane. She couldn't imagine what the two women might have to talk about. Lucy Burrows, in her cobalt blue velveteen tracksuit, was as unlike Emma, in her winter white sweater and slacks, as another woman could be. But both were nice people and niceness could bridge almost any divide, if only temporarily.

Poor Emma, Andie thought. Her sister had taken their mother's clothing to the resale shop that morning and it had proved far more difficult than she'd imagined. "I found myself unabashedly crying in the store," she told Andie before they left for Norma's party. "And then again once I was outside."

"Do you think it was a cathartic experience?" Andie had asked, to which her sister had shrugged.

"I honestly can't say. I felt so horribly aware of what I've lost. Is it ever cathartic to realize how much and how often you've failed the people you love?"

Andie hadn't been able to find the words to answer her sister's question. Her own sadness over her daughter's unprecedented rejection was weighing on her too heavily to allow clear thought.

"'The sky where we live,'" she whispered to herself, "'is no place to lose your wings, so love, love, love.'" But Hafiz's words of encouragement were of no help in blocking out the sudden wave of unhappiness that swept through her, alone among the crowd in Norma Campbell's ballroom.

"Mommy? What is that?"

Andie turned back to see a woman and her daughter, about five or six years old, Andie guessed, standing before the image of the waterfall. The mother quietly began to talk to the child about the picture before them. The girl, wearing a pink velvet dress with a matching ribbon in her hair, was clutching a giant cookie. Her eyes were wide with wonder as she listened to her mother. And Andie suddenly recalled a time when Rumi was about that age and they had gone to see a show of traveling acrobats in Lawrenceville.

Rumi had been transfixed by the performers, to the point of bursting out in tears when the show was over. But that was so long ago. . . .

Andie turned away from the mother and her little girl, her heart sore, to be confronted by two women passing not yards away, champagne glasses in hand. "Mom," the younger woman said, linking her arm through her mother's, "why don't we say hello to Doctor Herbert. She was so good to you last month when you fell, wasn't she?" The older woman smiled and nodded, and together they went off, still arm in arm, to where Jenna Herbert, Joe's wife, was talking with three women wearing garish holiday-themed sweaters.

Andie felt her throat tighten. Would she and Rumi ever be there for each other as time brought inevitable challenges along with joys, sorrows along with celebrations? Suddenly Andie felt besieged by the memory of the happiness that had been and tortured by the fear of what unhappiness might come.

The clinking of glasses, the din of the crowd, the determinedly nostalgic selection of music was too much for Andie. Sweat began to break out on her chest. She realized that she badly needed to be alone. She had driven to the party on her own, so she was free to go whenever she wanted. She would go straight back to the house and try to work on the article she was preparing for the inaugural issue of a small magazine. Work, thought, prayer, and imagination were all saving graces.

Andie scanned the crowded ballroom. She couldn't locate Emma among the guests, but she did spot her brother and sister-in-law; they were facing away from her but it was unmistakably them. At least she could tell Daniel that she was leaving the party. She made her way toward them, and when she was close Daniel suddenly turned so that she could see his profile. Once again, he was frowning. And then she heard her brother say in a loud, angry whisper, "I don't know why I bothered to ask Andie to come home for Christmas. She's been of no help whatsoever in finalizing Mom's estate. She doesn't have a practical bone in her body."

"Daniel," Anna Maria hissed. "That's entirely untrue. Really, sometimes you go too far."

Fighting nausea, Andie turned and walked almost blindly toward the door of the ballroom. She felt humiliated. She felt like a fool. And after the nice evening they had shared over the meal she had prepared . . . Had her brother's good mood toward her last evening all been just a lie? Andie tried to take a deep, slow breath. Daniel's unkind words said more about him than they did about her. She knew that, but still, the words hurt. "The wound is the place where the light enters you. . . ."

Norma Campbell, resplendent in a red silk dress, was chatting with a man Andie didn't recognize. It was rude to leave without thanking the host, but at that moment Andie simply didn't have it in her to play the part of gracious guest. She would send Norma a handwritten note of thanks and hope that it sufficed.

As she approached the front hall and the massive doors to the house, Andie began to run.

CHAPTER 41

Emma discreetly wiped a bit of cream from the corner of her mouth with a paper cocktail napkin. Whatever valid criticisms Daniel might have of the catering service, she doubted he could fault the pastry chef. The mini profiteroles were the most delicious Emma had ever tasted.

After her totally unforeseen breakdown that morning at the resale shop in Lawrenceville, Emma had wondered if she would be able to enjoy Norma Campbell's open house, but she had succumbed to its festive spirit with ease. Earlier in the day Andie had asked her if what she had experienced giving away their mother's belongings had been a cathartic experience, and at the time Emma hadn't been able to say. But now, a few hours later, filled with good food and surrounded by happy people, Emma thought that maybe it *had* been a cathartic experience. Difficult but cathartic.

Emma stifled a yawn. She probably should have left the party when her brother and sister-in-law had gone home, but the hope of Morgan Shelby showing up had kept her at the festivities. Whether she would tell him about her emotional experience that morning remained to be seen; at the very least she would simply like to see his face.

A woman about Emma's age smiled at her in passing, and

Emma smiled back, though the woman wasn't familiar to her. She glanced again around the crowded ballroom and realized that she knew so few people in Oliver's Well anymore, certainly not to talk to about more than "how time had flown this year" and "who could believe that it was almost Christmas." Too bad Maureen wasn't at the party, Emma thought, but Maureen was babysitting her goddaughter, PJ and Alexis Fitzgibbon's first born, so that they could enjoy Norma's party without having to worry about a toddler escaping their clutches and reaching out with a sticky hand to touch a precious object.

Emma looked at her watch and reconsidered leaving the party—she *had* been there almost two hours—but at that moment her patience was rewarded by Morgan's arrival. She resisted the urge to wave; it might seem too eager. He saw her immediately, in any case, and came directly across the room to join her.

"I'm glad I found you here," he said. Today he was wearing a camel wool blazer, a cream-colored mock turtleneck, and well cut navy pants.

Emma smiled. "Me, too."

"The size and splendor of Norma's parties always amaze me. They make me feel—insignificant."

Emma laughed. "And yet I don't get the impression she's out to lord it over us mere mortals."

"No," Morgan agreed. "She's a nice woman, truly humble."

A circulating waiter offered them a glass of champagne, and Emma took one. It was her second, but she had eaten so much food she seriously doubted it would impair her ability to drive. Especially, she thought, eyeing the dessert table, if she had another profiterole.

"Have you chosen a real estate agent yet?" Morgan asked when the waiter had moved off.

"No, I'm afraid I haven't," Emma admitted. "I've . . . I've been busy with other things. I brought my mother's clothes to a resale shop this morning. It was more difficult than I imagined."

"I'm sorry it was a trying experience," Morgan said feelingly.

"Thank you," she said. "I suppose I should have expected it."

She would not tell him that after leaving the resale shop, clutching her mother's tweed jacket, she had wanted so badly to see him. At least, she wouldn't tell him yet.

"You know," Morgan said. "I've never been inside number 32. Well, I suppose there was no reason I would have been. I wasn't a close friend of your parents."

"The house has some charming touches," Emma told him. "Otherwise, structurally it's much the same as the Fitzgibbons' house. And the decor doesn't come anywhere near Norma's taste in furniture and trappings!"

Morgan smiled. "Some of the pieces are not to my taste—I could never get into rococo!—but Norma's got a good eye and the money to put that eye to good use. She invited me to tour the entire house shortly after she settled in, which I thought was very nice of her. And she's bought a few small pieces from the gallery in the last year or so."

"And still no one knows where she got her money?" Emma asked.

Morgan lowered his voice dramatically. "It's a deep dark secret, though I've often wondered how Mary Bernadette hasn't managed to ferret out the truth! By the way, I saw your brother leaving earlier, as I was handing my car keys to a valet. Was that his wife with him, the woman in the red blouse?" Morgan asked.

"Yes, that was Anna Maria. And you missed my sister, too," Emma said. "She left shortly before my brother did. She seemed to be in a bit of a hurry. So much of a hurry she didn't even say good-bye."

Morgan laughed. "Is my reputation that bad? No, really, I'm sorry that I missed her. She's forged quite a life for herself from what I've heard around town."

"Have you also heard the nastier gossips slam Andie for having left her child with her ex-husband so she could go off gallivanting or smoking strange substances or performing bizarre rituals 'God knows where'?"

Morgan frowned. "One old biddy tried to buttonhole me in the gallery not long after I opened. I don't know why she felt it necessary to fill me in on a so-called scandal that took place years in the past. I was polite, but I managed to shut her down."

"And if you knew Rumi," Emma said, "Andie's daughter, you'd know that she turned out just fine." In spite, Emma thought, of her current unhappy behavior toward her mother. That was private. And hopefully, it would pass.

"Small town life," Morgan said. "It's got its good and its bad points. Still, I'd say the vast majority of people in Oliver's Well feel proud of Andie Reynolds being one of theirs."

Emma smiled. "I'm glad. I'm certainly proud of my sister."

"I know. I can tell. It's in your voice."

"Good. We were always close as children," Emma told him. "We grew apart a bit when she got married and had Rumi, but I think that was because our lives were suddenly so different. She was here in Oliver's Well, eventually living back with our parents for a time, changing diapers and working at whatever job she could get, and I was off in Annapolis, trying to establish a career."

"But you grew close again?" Morgan asked.

"Yes." Emma smiled. "Interestingly it was when Andie finally left Oliver's Well and went off to establish her own life on her own terms. Then we seemed, I don't know, on more equal footing."

"Apropos of nothing, that's a beautiful ring you're wearing."

Emma looked down at the gold and black diamond ring on her right hand, holding the glass of champagne. "I'm afraid it was a bit of an indulgence," she said. "It's funny, but I'm more comfortable buying presents for myself than receiving them from others."

"And what was the occasion for this present?" Morgan asked.

Emma didn't answer right away. She remembered how she had asked Ian not to get her anything special for her fortieth birthday; she hadn't wanted to feel indebted to him even then. "My fortieth birthday," she told Morgan finally.

"I think it's a good thing we treat ourselves to what makes us happy, as long as it's not at the expense of others. And happy belated birthday."

Emma smiled. "That was two years ago. But thanks."

"Look," Morgan said, with a quick glimpse around the ballroom, "I don't know about you, but I feel I've spent long enough here not to seem like I'm being a rude guest, just in and out for the drinks. And I spoke to Norma and at least three other people on my way to the ballroom. Would you like to stop back at the Angry Squire for a bit? Unless you've got to be home."

"No command performance this evening," she told him. "Sure. I've got my car, so I'll meet you there. Though I'm not sure I'll be able to eat another bite!"

"Good. If I get there first I'll try to get our table." Morgan briefly touched her arm and made his way back through the crowd of Norma Campbell's guests.

Our table, Emma thought. That had a nice ring to it.

CHAPTER 42

Daniel was in the den alone the next morning. Emma was taking a shower and Andie was on a call with her editor. Both promised to join him as soon as possible to help with what was beginning to feel like a never-ending task. Every time Daniel opened a drawer or uncovered a box in his parents' house, he seemed to find something else he hadn't noticed before. *So much for my complete inventory,* he thought, flipping through a spiral notebook that contained jottings on grilling techniques and temperatures in his father's handwriting. Yet another thing about his father he hadn't known until now.

He put the book back into the right-hand drawer of his father's writing table and sighed. He had thought a lot about what Anna Maria had said to him just before they left Norma Campbell's party the day before; she had taken him to task—again—for being unfair where his oldest sister was concerned. Anna Maria was right. He hadn't been nice to Andie lately, or nice about her when talking to the other members of the family. Emma had asked why Andie's choices were bothering him now, so many years after the fact. He hadn't answered her and still wasn't entirely sure he knew *how* to answer. And he had told Bob that he intended to change his behavior toward Andie. If he were to be honest with himself, he hadn't made one effort to treat her with more respect and understanding.

Daniel rubbed his eyes. He felt so very tired. He could, of course, put his general impatience with his sisters down to the stress of the holiday season. But he knew that his impatience had a deeper root. . . .

Daniel went over to the intricately carved red lacquer box his mother had bought while in China. He ran a finger along the deeply cut curves and swirls. How many times had he dusted this precious object, both before and after Caro's death, unwilling to let anything scar the beauty of one of his mother's treasures? Countless times, and yet he had never looked inside. Somehow to open the box—as to go through his mother's vanity table—had seemed a violation of the privacy of a woman who'd already had so much taken from her. But now . . . Carefully Daniel unlatched and lifted the lid of the box. Inside was a stack of postcards, all from a woman named Susan, all sent to Caro between fifteen to twenty years earlier. One card had been posted in Venice, another card from Cairo, yet another from Buenos Aires. Daniel shook his head. He had no memory of his mother having a friend named Susan. Who was she? And why had his mother kept the cards all these years? "Wish you were here, Caro. What fun it would be if we were in this fabulous city together. Thinking of you as I watch the glorious sunset over the basilica." Whoever this Susan was, she had meant something to his mother. And his mother had meant something to her.

Daniel returned the postcards to the box and closed the lid. And as he had at Norma's party he felt a sense of dislocation, a sense of alienation. Susan. His mother's interest in politics. What else about Caro Reynolds did he not know? Daniel had thought he was the closest to her after Cliff's death. He had just assumed. . . . He had assumed what? That he had been in the privileged position of partner; that he had been his mother's dearest friend and confidante. Had he really been so wrong?

"What did I miss?"

Daniel turned to see Emma, her hair still damp, coming into the den. "Did you know that Dad kept notes about what techniques and temperatures to use when grilling different meats?"

"Really?" Emma laughed. "Yet another bit of the puzzle falls into place."

Andie joined them a moment later. Daniel thought she looked drawn or tired. "Things okay with the publisher?" he asked.

"Fine," she said.

"That really was a great dinner you made for us the other night, Andie," Daniel said with a heartiness he didn't feel. "I still can't get over how you managed to pull together the entire meal at the last moment."

Andie smiled a bit. "Thank you, Danny."

Daniel wasn't at all sure that Andie had believed his compliment. *Well,* he thought, *could you blame her?* "I'll continue going through Dad's writing table," he said briskly. "You guys can get to work on something else."

Daniel opened the top drawer of the desk. Three perfectly sharpened number two yellow pencils. A clean pink eraser. A small box of staples. He wondered if his mother had ever sat at this table after her husband passed. Or had that seemed too painful for her? It was yet another thing he would never know.

"What's this?" Daniel lifted a folded piece of newsprint from the very back of the drawer. Carefully he unfolded it and scanned the article and then handed it to Emma. "I don't remember this at all. I wonder why Dad kept it."

"The trial of Brian Dunn," Emma said. "Well, the headline says it all. GUILTY! Seems this Mr. Dunn was convicted of stealing a huge amount of money from the charity for which he was the CFO." Emma handed the clipping to Andie. "Do you remember this story?" she asked. "You were about eleven when it happened."

"Yes," Andie said. "I do. It seemed like everyone was talking about it, even the kids in school. I remember someone saying that it was 'the trial of the century' and that nothing that exciting had happened in Oliver's Well for generations. I also remember Mom and Dad arguing about it. Dad knew this Mr. Dunn and said there was no way he could be guilty of such a crime. He wanted to put himself forward as a character witness at the trial, and Mom thought it was a bad idea. She said something about Dad putting the business at risk if he came out for someone accused of embezzling funds from a charity dedicated to the welfare of children. I think it was the only time I heard them argue. It really upset me."

"That's not true," Daniel said stoutly. "Dad would never have stood up for a criminal, and Mom and Dad never argued, ever."

"But I remember it," Andie said, her voice calm. "I remember it clearly. In the end Dad didn't come to his friend's defense. And the man was found guilty. I'm not saying the conviction was Dad's fault. I'm just telling you what I know."

Daniel felt his heart begin to race. Why did Andie always need to stir things up? Was it any wonder he wasn't able to treat her like a normal person? "You're wrong," he said.

"It's not uncommon for siblings to remember a particular event in completely unique ways," Emma said in what Daniel found to be an annoyingly soothing tone of voice. "Everyone experiences reality differently. No one here is lying. No one here is wrong or right."

"Maybe I am wrong," Andie said quietly. "Maybe I misremembered after all." She turned away and picked up a small crystal owl. It seemed to fascinate her. Daniel hoped she wouldn't drop it.

"Mary Bernadette called me this morning about the George Bullock desk she wants for the OWHA," he announced, turning to Emma. "Just yesterday I told her to her face that it wasn't up for grabs. You heard me at Norma's party. Talk about tenacity."

"She's just doing her job," Emma said. "You can't blame her for trying, though it must be annoying, having to fend her off all the time."

"She's polite enough," Daniel admitted, "but yeah, it's annoying."

"Maybe if I talked to her I might—"

"No," Daniel said, shaking his head. "I'll deal with her."

"Excuse me."

Daniel was startled; he had almost forgotten Andie was in the room. "What is it?" he asked.

"I need to go out for a while," she said. Andie put the crystal owl back on its shelf and left the den.

"I hope she's all right," Emma said with a frown. "She's not herself today."

Maybe, Daniel thought, *we should be thankful for that.*

CHAPTER 43

"Shouldn't you be home sifting through silverware and table linens?" Maureen asked. Emma and Maureen were window shopping in Somerstown later that afternoon and enjoying the unexpectedly balmy day. Emma's coat was open and she had slipped off her scarf and folded it in her bag.

"Danny will probably kill me when he sees I haven't finished packing up the silk flowers Mom collected," Emma admitted. "I swear she must have bought a bunch once a month for years; there are so many, and all in perfect shape, not even a speck of dust."

"She wasn't a fan of fresh flowers in the house?" Maureen asked.

"Dad was allergic to lots of stuff," Emma explained. "Anyway, I did manage to pack up a big box of almost brand new towels to donate to the local animal shelter. Those kitties and doggies are lucky—if any animal in a shelter can be considered lucky. My mother was adamant about only using super-high-quality towels."

Emma's phone, set on vibrate, alerted her to a text message from her second-in-command at Reynolds Money Management. "Sorry," she told Maureen. "I have to answer this."

"Do you ever regret doing what you do?" Maureen asked when Emma had sent her reply and stuck her phone back in the pocket of her coat. "It can't be easy, handling other people's money. There's got to be so much risk."

"No, it's not always easy," Emma admitted, "but then again, not much worth doing well *is* easy. Still, I used to love my work, really love it. It's challenging and interesting. Some clients are unpleasant to deal with, mostly because they're used to bossing people around from morning till night, but somehow I've always been able to handle those types."

"But?" Maureen asked, as the two women stopped at a storefront with a display of handcrafted wooden nutcrackers in the shape of Old World soldiers in red coats with gleaming brass buttons, Santa Clauses of various types, elves with distinctly mischievous looks on their faces, and jolly, rotund bakers, complete in tall white hats and aprons, a baguette tucked under an arm.

"But lately," Emma went on, only vaguely noticing the fanciful collection before her, "lately, I don't know, I find myself thinking of Joe Herbert sitting at the desk that was supposed to be mine. . . ." Emma smiled ruefully. "Well, the desk my father wanted for me, I should say."

"And you feel?" Maureen prompted.

But Emma didn't answer her friend's question right away. Instead she said, "I used to love going to my father's office when I was a kid, sitting in that big leather chair at the big oak desk and admiring Dad's shiny pen and pencil set and the brass paperweights. Everything was solid and sure, and I used to fantasize about working there with him, side by side."

"So what happened?" Maureen linked her arm through Emma's and they strolled on. "Why didn't you go into practice with him? I guess I never really understood."

Emma sighed. "I left because it was expected of me to stay. I left because Dad's offer felt like someone else's demand, rather than my own choice. I wanted to be independent."

"As simple as that?" Maureen asked.

Emma simply shrugged. Nothing was ever *that* simple.

"And now you want to claim your heritage, or maybe I should say your legacy."

"The legacy I didn't want and really have no right to now. I'm not entirely sure."

Maureen came to a halt at another storefront, this one featuring a Christmas village with houses, a post office, a church with a tall white spire, and a tavern. "Charming," she commented. "I've always wanted to collect a Christmas village, but the pieces are so expensive." She shrugged and the women moved on. "So, tell me more about what's going on inside that big brain of yours."

Emma laughed. "Maybe a big brain but a tired one."

"You work too hard. It's a silly thing to say to someone, especially to someone who owns her own business. But it's true."

"I can't argue," Emma admitted. "You know, I used to go to Dad for advice when I first started out on my own. To be honest, I wasn't at all sure he would want to help me, after I rejected the idea of becoming his successor. But I asked, and he was generous with his advice. He was a kind guy, not one to punish people unnecessarily."

"Your father was a favorite for sure." Maureen smiled. "A bunch of us had a crush on him in about seventh grade."

"Really? Wow. I had no idea."

"We kept our squealing in public to a minimum," Maureen said dryly. "So, what else is going on at 32 Honeysuckle Lane?"

"Well," she said, "Rumi's not talking to her mother for some reason or another. Andie made a special dinner for us the other night, and Rumi was a no-show."

Maureen frowned. "That's not like her, to be rude to one of her parents."

"I know. It's getting to Andie. She seemed particularly subdued this morning and she left Norma's party pretty suddenly yesterday. I saw her almost running toward the door, and when I called out to her she didn't look back."

"Maybe she's feeling under the weather," Maureen suggested. "Where is she this afternoon? She could have come with us."

Emma shrugged. "I don't know. She'd left the house before I could suggest she join us."

"And Danny? What's going on with him?"

Emma sighed. "Still being Keeper of the Flame. This morning he accused Andie of lying about an argument between my parents she swore she remembered."

"Does he seem happy?" Maureen asked. "Danny is a sensitive soul, far more than he lets on, I've always thought. And sensitive souls can make themselves—and everyone around them—miserable at times."

"He is sensitive," Emma agreed, "and no, I don't think he is happy, not really. His marriage is solid, from what I can tell, and he adores the children. But..." Emma shook her head. "Enough about the Reynoldses. What I really want to know is when I'm going to meet Jim."

"Soon, I promise. But at the moment there's something far more important on my mind."

"What's that?" Emma asked.

"Lunch."

CHAPTER 44

A ndie had left the house with no destination in mind; for the
past hour she had been wandering the back roads of Oliver's
Well in her rental car, barely aware of the passing scenery. She
knew she was remembering the events around the trial of Brian
Dunn clearly. Daniel would have been too young even to notice
that the town was abuzz. She just couldn't understand why he
had to accuse her of lying, or why he couldn't accept the fact that
his parents had argued. It was normal for people to disagree; it
was to some degree even healthy.

A large hand-painted sign announcing the sale of homemade
candles—a big red arrow pointed toward a small house set far
back from the road—barely registered with Andie, so preoccupied was she with her unhappy thoughts. Yes, she was worried
about her brother, but she was more worried about her own state
of mind. Being home this Christmas was proving toxic. Maybe
because Oliver's Well wasn't really *home* and it hadn't been for a
very long time.

Tired of wandering aimlessly, Andie decided she would head
into the heart of town and stop at the Eclectic Gourmet for a
packet of herbal tea, something to calm her nerves. Bob had said
the store had an expert on staff; surely he would be able to rec-

ommend just the thing. Andie found a driveway into which she could pull and turn around. Just as she was about to get back onto the road, her iPhone, on the seat next to her, alerted her to an e-mail. She didn't recognize the sender, but almost automatically she picked up the phone to view the message. Too late and with dawning horror Andie realized that the e-mail had been sent to her by a troll. Her heart began to beat heavily. She felt as if she would be sick to her stomach. Hastily she opened the driver's side window and tried to breathe normally.

This person, this awful person, had found it necessary to tell her that her latest book was garbage. This self-appointed critic chose to remain anonymous. And he couldn't spell. And his grammar was awful. But still, this person had succeeded in wounding the flesh and blood woman who had taken so much time and expended so much heartfelt effort into writing the best book that she could write at that moment in time.

Andie tossed the phone onto the seat; it bounced onto the floor of the car. *Take this for what it is*, she told herself. Mentally she reached for the words of the Buddha. "Hatred," he had taught, "does not cease through hatred at any time. Hatred ceases through love. This is an unalterable law."

A life based in nonattachment was what Andie tried her best to achieve, but oh, sometimes it was so hard to do. And one took a risk forging a career in the public eye, attracting random hate, becoming an easy target for cowardly commentators who thought it was acceptable to insult and drag you down because they could get away with it without having to own their hateful, shameful behavior.

Andie shivered and quickly closed the window. And going a bit too far over the speed limit, she drove into town. She felt . . . strange. She wondered why she wasn't just going home. Well, not home. Number 32 Honeysuckle Lane was not home. Nowhere was home. Was that the message she had been missing? Maybe, Andie thought, that anonymous critic was right and she didn't really know what she was talking about. Maybe she really was just a self-deluding fraud.

Andie parked her car in the municipal lot and, grabbing her bag—leaving her phone on the floor—she climbed out. She began to walk purposefully until she arrived outside the Wilson House, home of the Oliver's Well Historical Association. And then she climbed the stairs to the front door. A volunteer at the reception desk told her that Mary Bernadette was in her office and pointed the way. Andie knocked and was summoned inside.

Mary Bernadette was wearing a simple fitted maroon dress. It reminded Andie of a dress her mother had owned. "You're too stockily built for this sort of thing," Caro had told her daughter. "Better stick to more forgiving, less formfitting shapes."

"Good morning, Ms. Reynolds," Mary Bernadette said, rising from her desk and coming around to greet Andie with a hand-shake. "This is an unexpected pleasure."

"I'm sorry to just drop in like this, Mrs. Fitzgibbon," Andie said, her hand sitting limply in the older woman's. Her voice sounded odd to her ears, both too close and too far, both too loud and too soft.

"It's perfectly all right," Mrs. Fitzgibbon said, returning to her seat behind the desk. "The OWHA always welcomes visitors. What can I do for you?"

"It's about the George Bullock desk," Andie went on. "My mother's family's heirloom. We've . . ." Andie wondered. Would it really matter what happened to the desk? It was only a bit of wood, after all. It meant nothing in and of itself. It could burn up in a fire and nothing essential about the world would change. Right?

Mary Bernadette folded her hands before her. "Yes?" she said.

"We've decided that the OWHA can have it."

The moment the words left Andie's mouth she came crashing back to earth with the realization of what she had done. She could feel the color drain from her face and her body began to shake. She put her hand on the back of the guest chair and hoped that Mrs. Fitzgibbon was too excited to notice that her benefactor was ready to faint.

Mary Bernadette smiled beatifically. "This is a most generous gift, Ms. Reynolds, and one deeply appreciated. Would you like to have a seat and we can talk details of the transfer?"

Andie sank into the offered chair. She barely heard Mrs. Fitzgibbon's questions about the desk, its provenance and its condition. Paperwork. There was something said about paperwork.

"I'm sorry," Andie blurted. "I'm not really the expert on the piece. I'm sure another one of my family can answer all of your questions."

"Of course," Mrs. Fitzgibbon said.

Andie rose unsteadily. Sweat was pouring down her back and chest. "There's one other thing," she said. Once again her voice sounded as if it was coming from far off. "Could I ask that you not make the announcement of the gift until after Christmas? This is an emotional time for my family, and as some of them aren't entirely happy about the Bullock desk going to the OWHA . . ."

"Of course, Ms. Reynolds," Mrs. Fitzgibbon said. "Of course."

The women shook hands again, and Andie found herself back on the sidewalk before she realized she had actually left the Wilson House.

Make the announcement after Christmas, she thought. *After I'm gone from Oliver's Well, never to return.* Regret and embarrassment flooded her, but she could not bring herself to go back inside and recall the offer she had had no right to make. She began to walk, on the verge of tears. *What just happened to me?* Andie cried silently. She had never acted without careful thought; she had never done anything so utterly bizarre and against her own interests. A terrible thought occurred to her. Could it be that for the first time in years she had acted out of hate or spite? Was her promising something she had no right to promise an act of revenge on the brother who seemed to find enjoyment in belittling her? On the daughter who . . .

No. No, Andie thought desperately, *that couldn't be right! It could not be right.* She was not like that troll who had attacked her with hate. She was not.

But what if she *was* just like that hate monger? Tears began to slip down Andie's cheeks and she prayed she wouldn't have a breakdown in view of downtown Oliver's Well. She vaguely remembered there was a small park on a side street somewhere nearby; maybe it was a place she could take refuge until she felt calm enough to drive. She wasn't at all sure she could find the park and thought it was a miracle when she did. She dropped gratefully onto a wooden bench and clasped her hands tightly in her lap. And then it was impossible to block the memories of a time she usually tried very hard not to remember.

She had gotten pregnant a few months after her wedding. She was pleased. She felt she had done something right. Her parents were all warm approval and well wishes. Bob was over the moon. His mother started a quilt. Emma bought a big plush frog for the baby. Daniel seemed almost embarrassed in Andie's presence; then again, he was only a teen and the thought of his sister having sex was probably anathema to him.

The pregnancy was almost ridiculously easy; she didn't even suffer once from morning sickness. Bob painted the tiny room that was to be the baby's in shades of lilac and purple. He built the crib himself. Andie taught herself to knit and made a trousseau fit for a royal infant. They decided to name the baby Rumi if a girl or a boy. This was a nod to Andie's nascent interest in things spiritual and other. By other, she meant things that didn't interest her parents, like, she assumed, the quality of the inner self.

When the pregnancy was well under way, she thought, *This is my life. I have a husband and he's a good man. We have a cute little home. We're having a child and maybe, in a year or two, we'll have another.* Why not? Bob intended to expand his father's business. Maybe someday, when the children were grown, she would go back to school, take some courses in Buddhism and meditation. Maybe someday she would . . .

But there was enough to occupy her in the present.

Labor was brief and the birth easy. Bob was with her when their daughter first saw the light of day, and they both cried tears of joy when Rumi was laid on her mother's breast.

Life was good.

And then it was not.

The changes were almost imperceptible at first—a lessening of interest in her favorite TV shows and authors, an erratic appetite, odd changes in her usual sleep pattern. Andie initially chalked it up to the exhaustion of being a new parent. It was Bob who first saw the changes for what they were, signs of depression in a woman who had never before been depressed and didn't know how to identify the symptoms. Increasingly Andie felt as if she were living under a heavy, low hanging cloud that no one else could see. Colors weren't as bright as they had been. She lost track of her body in the space it occupied and frequently tripped or bumped into objects.

Days passed excruciatingly slowly. From the moment Bob left the house each morning to go to work—after feeding and changing the baby, making coffee for his wife, kissing her forehead and smoothing her hair, telling her that "things will be all right"—until the moment he walked in the door at four each afternoon, Andie desperately awaited his return. Worse than anything was that the little helpless baby, her own flesh and blood, seemed an utterly foreign being. Andie felt almost entirely detached from the child she had helped to create. It was a cruel thing to know that she should care but that she was unable to care.

She struggled to understand why she was the way she was. She never thought: *I want to hurt someone.* She did think: *I want to die.*

Finally, Bob insisted they talk to a doctor, a sympathetic woman who spoke gently to the couple, explaining the causes and symptoms and likely duration of postpartum depression. The doctor gave Andie a mild antidepressant—"not a magic pill, but something that will help over time," she explained—which Andie took obligingly. They said nothing to Cliff or Caro of what their daughter was experiencing. Andie felt ashamed of her failure.

She began to have panic attacks where the sweat would pour from her, soaking her clothing, much as it had in Mrs. Fitzgibbon's office just moments before. Once, she fainted dead away in the middle of the kitchen. She lost interest in food and dropped a good deal of weight. Her mother, not seeing—refusing to see?—the pain in her daughter's eyes, told her she looked better than she ever had. "I didn't think it would happen for you," she said, casting an approving eye over Andie's slimmed frame. "I didn't think you would get your old body back, let alone a better one."

When the depression had finally lifted, when the marriage was amicably over, still the guilt lingered. The guilt of failure. The shame of having succumbed to weakness. The embarrassment of having to move back in with her parents. Caroline Carlyle Reynolds had never failed. She had never succumbed. *But I am nothing like my mother,* Andie had thought. *Nothing at all.*

Andie came back to the present moment with a start. Her hands felt numb with cold. How long had she been sitting on that bench, lost in times past?

"The mind is everything. What you think, you become."

Andie shivered. The words of the Buddha had never sounded so frightening. She wondered if she was becoming clinically depressed again. She had suffered a second episode of depression in her midthirties, triggered by nothing other than the chemicals in her brain. By then she had her beliefs and her peers to help her survive the time of distress and unease.

But now, at this particular moment in her life, at the age of forty-four, Andie felt cast away, cut adrift, unsupported. Vulnerable. She knew that wasn't really the case, but at the moment it *felt* that way, and sometimes no amount of mental or spiritual discipline could budge a *feeling*.

Abruptly, Andie got up from the bench. She couldn't sit alone in this park all day. With what little determination she could muster, she continued on to the Eclectic Gourmet on Market Street. Maybe doing something as ordinary and mundane as buying a packet of loose tea would help reorient her in the moment. Andie opened the door of the shop and stepped inside. Immediately, as if he had been waiting for her, a man approached. He looked to be in his early thirties and was wearing a distinctive tweed cap.

"You're Andie Reynolds, aren't you?" he asked, his expression eager.

For a moment Andie was too stunned to reply. Finally, she said, "Yes."

"I recognize you from your book jacket," the man went on. "I knew you grew up in Oliver's Well, but I'm pretty new to town, so I've never seen you in person before."

"I'm here for Christmas," Andie said automatically. "My family . . ."

"May I have your autograph?" The man pulled his wallet from his pocket and began to poke through it. "I know I have a piece of paper in here somewhere. Here, this should do."

He handed her a receipt and then took a pen from his jacket pocket. As Andie signed her name, the man went on. "I can't tell you how much this means to me," he said earnestly. "You really helped me through a difficult time of my life. I really didn't know where to turn or what to do, and then I heard you speak on the radio and I thought, I want to hear more, so I went right out and bought your first book. I swear you practically saved my life. My name is Ralph, by the way."

"I'm very glad I could be of help, Ralph," Andie said. She managed a smile and handed the signed paper and the pen back to the man.

"Thank you," he said. "And have a very merry Christmas!"

And she stood there as he went off, feeling again like a complete fraud. For a moment she couldn't remember what she had come into the store to purchase. Yes. Tea. A packet of herbal tea.

She smiled bravely at the friendly girl behind the counter, bought the tea, and left the shop. For a moment she wished she could magically transport herself to the house on Honeysuckle Lane. But she wasn't a magician and her car was parked blocks away, so there was nothing for it but to walk back to the municipal lot and run the risk of encountering another fan or worse, a foe.

I don't have to be possessed of magical powers to get on a plane, she thought, hands stuffed into the pockets of her coat. *There's no rea-*

son I can't go back to my home and my friends right now and let Danny and Emma handle the dispersing of the estate. Like her brother had said at Norma Campbell's party, she was of no use. And while it had been their mother's wish that all three of her children make decisions about the estate together, there was no way Daniel could enforce that wish. She, Andie Reynolds, was a free agent. "Ignore those that make you fearful and sad . . ."

No, Andie thought. No. She would *not* indulge in self-pity or give in to fear. "We are shaped by our thoughts; we become what we think." And she would not think like a coward or like a person in despair. She would stay in Oliver's Well and do what she could to restore peace in her family and to right the wrongs she had committed, however innocently. She thought of what the man in the Eclectic Gourmet had said, that she had helped him in a time of serious trouble. Well, why couldn't she help herself in a time of serious trouble? "You yourself, as much as anybody in the universe, deserve your love and affection." The Buddha had said as much, and she would be wise to heed his words.

As Andie was passing End Quote, Oliver's Well's only independent bookstore, a young man wearing a gray cardigan over baggy corduroys came dashing out.

"Ms. Reynolds," he said. "I don't know if you remember meeting me. . . ."

Again, Andie managed a smile. "Of course I do," she said. "It was at the booksellers convention in Nashville two years ago. You'd just bought End Quote from the previous owner."

The man nodded and extended his hand. "That's right. Chris Owens. Look, I know this is last minute, but when I saw you passing by I thought, I just have to ask. I hope I'm not imposing on your family time, but do you think you might possibly do a reading or give a little talk sometime before Christmas Eve? I can't pay you what you're probably used to," he added worriedly, "but—"

"There's no charge, Chris," Andie said quickly. "And I'd be delighted."

Chris Owens looked thrilled. "Thank you so much," he said.

"Your books are very popular in Oliver's Well; I can hardly keep them in stock. You're our very own celebrity!"

Andie forced another smile. "Let me check my schedule," she said, "and I'll call you this afternoon to set up a time and date."

Chris Owens thanked her again and hurried back into the shop. Andie walked on toward the municipal parking lot. She thought of what the Buddha had so wisely taught his followers. "No one saves us but ourselves. No one can and no one may. We ourselves must walk the path."

Andie unlocked the door to her rental car and slid into the driver's seat. She knew she was being tested. She just hoped she could pass the test. And she hoped that in her present suffering she would find the hidden gift.

CHAPTER 45

"Let's get the atmosphere going," Emma suggested. "I'll put on some music."

The family was gathered to decorate the Christmas tree, a Virginia pine that Daniel and the children had cut down earlier that day. After securing the tree in its stand, he had gone to the kitchen to make hot chocolate with marshmallows, all made from scratch.

"The tree is enormous!" Emma commented when he returned to the living room, carrying a tray of the hot sweet drinks. "How did you manage to get it on and off the roof of your car?"

Daniel shrugged. "I managed," he said. "I like to do the holidays right."

"Daniel has always been of the more is more and less is a bore school of thought," Anna Maria said, helping herself to a mug of hot chocolate.

"You should have come with us this afternoon when we went to the tree farm," Daniel said to his sisters. "It was fun. What were you doing?"

"I spent the afternoon with Maureen," Emma told him. "We did some Christmas shopping."

"Andie?" Daniel asked.

Andie looked at her watch and said, "I was in town, running

some errands. My cookies must be ready." She went off to the kitchen at a trot.

Emma thought her sister looked stressed, and not just because of the threat of burnt cookies. Rumi hadn't yet put in an appearance, although according to Daniel she was planning to join them.

"This is my favorite song," Marco shouted as the opening strains of "The Little Drummer Boy" reached their ears. "I want a drum set."

His father frowned. "And you're not getting one."

Before Marco could protest the unfairness of this decision, Andie returned to the living room bearing a plate piled high with treats. "I don't know if these cookies are as good as the ones Sophia and Marco made the other day. . . ."

Sophia and her brother dashed over to their aunt and each took a cookie. "This is yummy," Sophia said. "I love raisins and chocolate chips together. And that dinner you made us the other night was really good, too, Aunt Andie."

Andie smiled at her niece. "Thank you," she said. "I'm glad you liked it. Where I live we take turns cooking dinner and we all eat together. You get to learn a lot about different kinds of food that way."

"That sounds like fun," Sophia said.

"What if you're not in the mood to eat with the group?" Emma asked her sister. "I know sometimes after a long day at work I just want to hole up by myself and eat whatever's hanging around in the fridge."

"As long as you're not sneaking out on your night to prepare the meal," Andie explained, "you're perfectly free to have your dinner in your own place."

"Dad never makes vegetarian stuff," Marco announced, reaching for his second cookie.

"But we eat a lot of vegetables and fruit. Mom says we have to. Aunt Andie, when you're a vegetarian do you—"

Before Sophia could finish her question, Daniel said, "Andie, don't fill her mind with that—"

Emma shot a look at her brother and he closed his mouth. And she recalled his vehemently denying that Andie's memory of an argument between their parents was indeed a real memory. She went over to her sister, put an arm around her shoulder, and squeezed. "You were always a good baker, even when you were a kid," she said. "I remember those bundt cakes you used to make in high school, the kind with a coconut filling. Yum."

The doorbell rang then and Anna Maria went to answer it. It was Rumi, a long striped scarf wound around her neck. She gave the family a general greeting and went into the hall closet to hang up her coat. When she returned Andie offered her a cookie. "They're just out of the oven," she said. "It's one of my favorite recipes."

"No thanks," Rumi said, without, Emma noticed, even the courtesy of meeting her mother's eye. "Is this Uncle Daniel's homemade hot chocolate?" she asked, already reaching for a mug. "I'll definitely have this!"

This is ridiculous, Emma thought. She wondered why Rumi had even bothered to come to the tree trimming if she had so little use for her mother—unless, of course, she had come specifically to antagonize Andie. *Rumi is basically immature,* Emma thought. *She can't fully cut the cord that ties her to the role of child to be taken care of, noticed, and pampered.* It was too bad, after all the good guidance her parents had offered her.

"Me and Sophia are the luckiest people," Marco suddenly announced. "We get to decorate two trees, this one and the one at home!"

"Sophia and I," Daniel corrected.

Emma gave her sister's shoulder one more squeeze, for which she received a grateful smile, and said, "Let's get started."

With Daniel's help Emma had hauled the cardboard boxes that contained the family's Christmas decorations from the attic. The boxes had been carefully sealed with tape and each item within had been individually wrapped in tissue paper.

"Mom had such respect for everything in this house," Emma said, as she knelt by one of the opened boxes, "from the most insignificant piece of flatware to the most precious of items, like that Lenox dessert service Andie and I uncovered."

Daniel nodded. "She knew about value. She understood what it means to be house proud. Wow," he said, holding up a long marquise-shaped ornament. "I haven't seen this stuff since Dad was alive. After his death Mom pretty much ignored the holidays." He looked to Emma. "Remember how she used to love to decorate every room in the house? But without Dad around, she just lost interest."

"I'm sure that's not unusual," Emma said. "Sad, but not unusual." She lifted the next package from the box she was emptying and unwrapped the tissue paper from it. "I remember these," she said. "Mom had these monogrammed stockings made for us at the yarn shop that used to be downtown. The Cable Company, I think it was called. It was only there about a year."

Anna Maria laughed. "No wonder it closed, with a name like that!"

Emma continued to explore the box and after a moment unearthed the delicate German glass ornaments that had belonged to the Carlyles. There was one in the shape of a rotund American style Santa Claus and another in the image of the older European Father Christmas. There were several in the shapes of animals— a graceful swan, a proud rooster, a roly-poly pig, and a mischievous kitten.

"Handle these carefully," Emma told Sophia and Marco, who had abandoned the glittery chain they had been untangling and had come to join her. "They're very fragile. And if they break you could get a nasty cut."

"Look," Andie said, breaking her long silence. "Here's the glass peacock. Its tail is still perfect. Mom said I could have this one day if I wanted."

"Really?" Emma asked, looking at the little ornament her sister was holding.

"Yes," Andie said. "Why?"

Emma shrugged. "It's just that Mom knew the peacock was my

favorite ornament. Every year I wanted so badly to be the one to hang it on the tree."

"I didn't know that," Andie said. Then she got up, crossed the room, and handed the peacock to her sister. "Here, Emma, you should have this for your own. Take it home with you after Christmas. It really means nothing to me."

Rumi, sprawled on the couch, laughed. "My mother doesn't care about possessions. She's above all that. Although I'm surprised the peacock isn't her favorite, too, with the crazy, colorful way she dresses."

Emma restrained a sharp reply. She was aware of Anna Maria's unhappy expression; she didn't want to see Daniel's. Andie, ever Andie, calmly responded. "Possessions aren't wrong," she said mildly, "but they can get in the way of more important things. If you have possessions just to have them they begin to own you."

Rumi rolled her eyes. She got up from the couch and left the room. Emma, still holding the peacock ornament, crawled to her feet and followed her to the kitchen. Rumi took a glass from its cabinet and turned on the cold water faucet.

"You missed a delicious dinner the other night," Emma said. It wasn't what she wanted to say—which was something on the order of "grow up!"—but this supposedly enjoyable family event wasn't the place for a confrontation.

Rumi shrugged. "I've had vegetarian food before. It's no big deal."

"Maybe, but your mom is a good cook."

"Is she?" Rumi laughed. "I wouldn't really know. She hasn't cooked for me since I was eight."

Emma could barely restrain her annoyance. "Come on, Rumi, surely that's an exaggeration and you know it."

Rumi shrugged, drank the water and put the glass in the sink. Without another word the two went back to the living room, Emma all too aware she had accomplished absolutely nothing. She watched as Rumi went over to Anna Maria and gave her a big hug. Andie had to have seen it, even from the corner of her eye.

"Dad liked this sled ornament," Daniel was saying. "I think it belonged to his father when he was a boy. You know, after listening to Paddy Fitzgibbon at Norma's party I've been wondering what else he might be able to tell us about Dad."

"Or what Joe Herbert might be able to tell us, for that matter," Emma said. "Or anyone else in this town who knew him well."

"We're all strangers to one another," Andie said quietly, almost to herself. "Even to those who know us best."

Rumi laughed. "Some people just don't try to understand the people in their lives."

"You're right, Rumi," Emma said with what she hoped was a meaningful look. "Some people don't."

CHAPTER 46

The following morning Emma paid a visit to another of the real estate agents Daniel had chosen as finalists. *As if it were a contest,* she thought. Well, she supposed in a way it was—free market competition, with number 32 as the prize. She was less than impressed by the personal manner of this agency's representative, who was brusque to the point of being unpleasant, but as Emma was still considering buying the house herself, asking smart questions of the agents under the pretense of hiring one could only help her think through the logistics of a purchase. After all, if she decided to buy out her siblings she would have to make them a fair and market competitive offer.

When she had gone a few yards in the direction of her car, Emma spotted Joe Herbert coming out of the post office just ahead. She waved and he waved back. Joe was a year or two older than Emma, and a great deal taller. She thought he might be close to six and a half feet tall. His eyes were keen and observant; his smile was ready and transformed what might have been a stern face into one that you couldn't help but deem trustworthy. Even in the warmest of weather Joe wore a long-sleeved dress shirt and his signature bow tie. He had one in just about every color and pattern a person could imagine. Today's bow tie was celery green embroidered with tiny sprigs of parsley.

"We were just talking about you last night," she said when she joined him.

Joe laughed. "Ah, that's why my ears were burning! Do you have a question about the estate's financial health?"

"No, actually, we were wondering what you could tell us about our father that we don't know. I mean, you worked side by side with the man for years. You knew him uniquely."

"As did you," Joe pointed out. "And Daniel. And Andie."

"Yes," Emma admitted, "that's true. It's just that parents conceal so much of themselves from their children, purposely or not. It can be interesting to learn about your mother or father from someone who interacted with them outside the bounds of family."

"The trouble with asking questions about someone you love is that you never know what the answers are going to be—disturbing or pleasant."

"And in Dad's case?" Emma asked.

Joe smiled. "Entirely pleasant."

"So, how's business?"

"To be honest," Joe said, "it's almost too good. There are nights when I can't get out of the office before eight. I wouldn't mind so much but for my kids. I mean, I didn't become a father not to see my own children. And my long hours put a strain on Jenna, who has enough on her plate caring for her patients."

"That *is* a danger of success," Emma said. "Losing the rest of your life in the process." *And I*, she thought, *should know.*

Joe frowned. "That's exactly what I'm afraid of. But I just have to hope that a solution will present itself before too long." And then he smiled. "After all, nothing stays the same for long, does it?"

"Even when we wish it would! You know, Joe," Emma went on, "I have to admit that at first I was puzzled when Mom chose Danny to be trustee of the estate. Frankly, I seemed like the better choice, at least the more obvious one. But he's done a fine job of it all, with your guidance. I really appreciate all you've done for the family. We all do."

Joe shrugged. "It's just my job."

"No," Emma said. "It's more than that."

"Okay," Joe admitted. "It's my vocation."

Emma nodded. "I understand. Helping people manage their money is, well, it's almost an intimate experience. It's such a matter of trust. You're privy to someone's hopes and dreams, to their successes and failures. It's a bit like being a doctor or a lawyer in that way, I imagine."

Joe smiled. "I'll ask Jenna and get back to you on that one." He checked his watch and whistled. "Look at the time. I've got a client coming to the office in ten minutes. Good to see you, Emma."

"You, too, Joe. Have a merry Christmas." Emma watched for a moment as Joe hurried off toward his office, then continued on to her car. And as she drove back to Honeysuckle Lane she thought about what Joe had said about being overworked, and the glimmer of an idea began to take hold.

It's not an outrageous notion, she told herself, steering the car along. After all, if she were to move back to Oliver's Well, wouldn't it make sense that she and Joe join forces? It would probably be to the benefit of each of them; she couldn't see any obvious downside, at least not at the moment.

But nothing was set in stone, Emma reminded herself, as she passed the local bank branch, still housed in a fairly elaborate nineteenth-century building. She had not yet made the commitment to return to the scene of her childhood, and indeed, might never make that commitment. Still, joining forces with her father's former apprentice and partner was an idea she would keep hold of, if lightly.

Because as Joe had said, nothing stayed the same for long.

CHAPTER 47

Daniel pulled up in front of the Unitarian Universalist Church. He recognized Reverend Fox's ancient Volvo in the lot and smiled. How that thing was still running was anyone's guess. *Maybe*, Daniel thought in a moment of whimsy, *God is his mechanic.*

While the family had been decorating the Christmas tree the day before, Daniel had got to thinking of how his father had loved to add the strands of silvery tinsel in great big handfuls, and if his mother later edited her husband's handiwork, he never seemed to mind. It was always Caro who climbed the ladder to place the star atop the tree, after which Cliff would applaud and declare the Christmas season officially begun.

And it had occurred to Daniel that a nice way to commemorate the senior Reynoldses and their love of Christmas would be a good old-fashioned candle-lighting ceremony. So he had set up today's meeting with Reverend Fox to discuss the logistics. Though his mother had grown up in the Episcopal Church, she had embraced membership in the Unitarian Universalist Church her husband preferred. Daniel had often wondered how his mother's parents had felt about her choice. Why, he wondered, had he never asked her?

He was alerted to a text from the reverend; he was running a bit late and would Daniel mind waiting about five minutes? Daniel texted his reply—**no worries**—and, as the day was mild, he decided to wait for Reverend Fox on the front steps of the building. And for what seemed like the hundredth time in the past few days, he thought about the article he had found in his father's writing table, the one about the trial and conviction of a man named Brian Dunn. He had tried to put what Andie had told him about his parents' argument out of his mind, but it was no use. The fact that they had differed so strongly about what came down to an issue of ethics—of right behavior and loyalty—bothered him. And why in the end had his father not come forward as a character witness for Brian Dunn? Had Cliff Reynolds simply bowed to his wife's opinion? Had it been to keep the peace in the home or had he really come to change his mind and agree with Caro, that his coming forward on Dunn's behalf might seriously hurt his business? Had his father chosen his family's financial security over an act of altruism for a friend? Daniel had to admit it was probably what he would do in a similar circumstance.

And all this speculation was based on the assumption that what Andie said had happened had indeed happened. The truth in all its large and small detail about what transpired all those years ago was another thing lost to Daniel and he would simply have to accept that. *Easier said than done*, he thought.

The front door of the building opened then, and Reverend Fox beckoned Daniel inside. "Daniel," he said, extending his hand. "Hello. Sorry to keep you waiting."

Reverend Fox was about Daniel's age; he and his life partner, Matt Lehrmitt, lived in a restored farmhouse not far from the Joseph J. Stoker House, only one of the many historical sites the OWHA had helped to preserve.

"Reverend Fox," Daniel said, shaking the man's hand. "Thank you for seeing me on such short notice."

"It's my pleasure. How are you, Daniel? I haven't seen you at a service since your mother's funeral."

"I'm afraid I've been busy," Daniel said. And then, he laughed a bit awkwardly. "I know. A person should never be too busy for God."

Reverend Fox smiled. "Joining the congregation on Sundays isn't compulsory. I didn't mean to make you feel guilty of negligence. So, why don't you tell me what you have in mind for this memorial ceremony?"

What Daniel had in mind was something very simple; he didn't, he told Reverend Fox, even want the distraction of music. "It will be just my wife and sisters," he explained. "I thought we might light candles in my parents' memory and each say a few words. And, of course, if you could offer a prayer. . . ."

Reverend Fox agreed to a date and time for the ceremony. Daniel thanked him and took his leave. Just before he left the building he stopped and turned to look at the giant quilt that had been made by members of the Women's Institute back in 1908. He flashed back to Andie's wedding, which had taken place in this very room, under that very quilt. He remembered how happy she had looked, and how pretty. She had been so young and hopeful then. . . .

And then Daniel remembered how promptly Andie had offered the peacock ornament to Emma, and how she had hosted that lovely meal for the family. And he remembered Rumi's rude remark about Andie's colorful clothing, and the criticisms of her mother's behavior and beliefs. He felt truly ashamed of how he had been treating his sister—and of how he'd been encouraging his niece to treat her. What he had said about Andie to Anna Maria at Norma Campbell's party was inexcusable. He felt a genuine tenderness for his oldest sister in that moment, a feeling that was very new to him. And he remembered again his promise to Bob, Emma, and to Anna Maria that he would treat his sister with more respect and kindness. . . .

So much for promises, he thought guiltily. But tomorrow was another day, wasn't it? Andie would say that it was never too late to change. . . .

Daniel turned away from the massive quilt under which his oldest sister had taken her marriage vows and left the building. *Mom,* he thought. *Dad. I'm trying my best. I truly am. But I don't think that my best is good enough.*

CHAPTER 48

"This place certainly seems to be a success. I think it must have something to do with the rosy colored walls. Pink makes everyone feel good, doesn't it?"

Andie smiled. She and Emma were at the Pink Rose Café, sharing its version of the classic afternoon high tea. On a three-tiered plate were laid out small thin sandwiches and an assortment of petite cakes and pastries. Andie thought of her mother's Lenox tea set. Would it ever belong to her? she wondered. And if it didn't, would it really matter so much?

Yes, she thought. It probably would. Just as it would matter to Daniel and to Rumi if the Bullock desk were to leave the family.

"I ran into Joe Herbert this morning," Emma said. "He's such a nice guy."

"What was his tie like?" Andie asked.

"Celery green with sprigs of parsley. And speaking of color, thanks again for letting me have the peacock ornament."

"My pleasure." Anyway, Andie thought, from now on she would associate the peacock with her daughter's unpleasant remarks. She would work hard not to hang on to that memory, but given her current weakened state of mind and emotion . . .

"What was your favorite ornament from when we were kids?" Emma asked.

"That's easy," Andie said. "It would have to be the Victorian balloon. It seemed so exotic to me, so appealing to be able to take off into the sky and have all sorts of adventures." Andie smiled ruefully. "I suppose Danny would say that even as a child I had my head in the clouds."

Emma frowned. "It would do our brother good to lighten up and float a bit."

Andie didn't reply to her sister's comment. Instead she voiced a question that had long been on her mind. "You know, I've never really understood why Mom left her wedding rings to me. I mean, I'm the divorced child, the wild child, at least in her eyes. Maybe she still held out hope that I would suddenly see the error of my ways and settle down and marry again."

"Well, you are the oldest daughter," Emma pointed out, licking a bit of powdered sugar from her fingers, "and Mom was a traditionalist. I suppose she thought leaving the rings to you was 'the thing to do.'"

"Sure, but it would have made more sense to leave the rings to you. Or why not leave them directly to Rumi?"

"I guess we'll never know. By the way, what ever happened to your wedding ring?" Emma asked. "The one Bob gave you?"

Andie smiled. "I sold it not long after the divorce. I needed the money. Bob couldn't afford much in the way of child support."

"But you were living with Mom and Dad."

"I hated being so dependent on them," Andie said. "So I decided to sell the ring to supplement my measly income. I didn't get much for it—it was a pretty narrow band—but it helped pay for diapers and mashed carrots for a while."

"I'm sorry, Andie."

"Don't be. I was okay with it. So was Bob; I told him what I'd done and he admitted he'd done the same thing with his. We laughed about it. But when Mom found out . . ."

"How did she find out?" Emma asked.

"I kept the ring in a box in the top drawer of my dresser. I don't know what Mom was doing snooping around my room, but one day she noticed that it was missing. She asked me about it and I told her. She was shocked."

"It was your ring to do with as you wanted," Emma said. "Why do you think she was so upset?"

"I know why she was so upset, because she told me. The ring was sacred; it represented the union that had created my daughter. There was more in that vein. Mom put more importance on my wedding ring than I did."

Emma nodded. "The traditionalist. Still, you and Bob were divorced. Her attitude doesn't make a whole lot of sense."

Andie shrugged. "To Mom it did. Remember, not only was a she a traditionalist, she was a real romantic at heart, defying her family's choice of husband for the sake of love. It really was a courageous thing to do."

"I wish I was as courageous as Mom," Emma said ruefully. "I should have ended things with Ian a long time ago, instead of just letting the relationship slide along. I took the lazy way out."

Andie shook her head. "I don't think you're lazy or a coward, Emma. I suspect that for whatever reasons you simply weren't ready to leave the relationship. And then, you were ready and you acted. As Rumi says, 'There is a candle in your heart, ready to be kindled.'"

Emma smiled. "Is there?"

"Yes," Andie said. "I think that there is."

While Emma poured them each more tea, Andie let her mind wander. She had no idea if Mary Bernadette would keep her promise not to advertise the gift of the Bullock desk until after Christmas. Maybe it would serve Andie right to be shamed with the truth before she could make things right by telling Mrs. Fitzgibbon that she had been misguided in giving the desk to the OWHA. Coming clean before more time passed was the mature option. In fact, she could tell her sister right now what she had done and then, make amends. Promises could be broken, even if they shouldn't be.

But looking across at Emma with her perfect posture, always calm and in control of her emotions, Andie felt simply too embarrassed to confess. She had long ago realized that one could never underestimate the power of embarrassment. It could render a person speechless, immobile, and unable to do the right thing.

"I wonder if I've accomplished anything by coming back to Oliver's Well this Christmas," Andie said suddenly, with a bitter laugh. "I certainly haven't succeeded in mending my damaged relationship with my daughter."

Emma smiled kindly. "You've helped me with going through Mom's belongings. I couldn't handle all that on my own. Not that Danny would have let me. And you've helped me understand why Ian might be clinging to what no longer exists. And you've helped me by simply being who you are. My sister. My friend."

Andie reached for Emma's hand and gave it a squeeze.

"Hey," Emma said, "let's do something fun when we've finished here. Let's do something that has nothing at all to do with estate sales and damaged relationships. I read about a vintage store in Somerstown that exclusively sells clothes and memorabilia from the eighties. It's called Time after Time. Remember the Cyndi Lauper song by that title?"

Andie laughed. "I do. I love that song. But the eighties are already vintage?"

"Guess so. How about it? It should be pretty cringe-worthy. Massive shoulder pads. Big plastic earrings. Ripped fishnet stockings."

"Sure," Andie said. "I've always had a soft spot for Boy George."

CHAPTER 49

Daniel smiled as he surveyed the crowd that had gathered in the heart of town this evening. The weather had consented to be as near Christmas-like as possible; temperatures had fallen rapidly since the late afternoon and had now settled at about thirty-five, encouraging the appearance of goofy holiday-themed hats, brightly colored mittens, and furry ear muffs.

The Christmas Parade and Festival was arguably the biggest annual communal event in Oliver's Well. Shop owners were happy to participate in open house hours, with merchandise on deep discount and window displays to rival those found in big city department stores. Restaurants and cafés provided happy-hour-priced wine, hot chocolate, and free snacks. The Wilson House welcomed those who wanted to visit the displays of Oliver's Well artifacts and to view the videos the OWHA had produced through the years, chronicling the founding and the development of the association. About a dozen performers set up on various street corners and played guitar or violin, juggled balls and pins, or performed simple magic tricks. And each year a different member of the Chamber of Commerce volunteered to play Santa Claus; like Santa at the end of the famous Macy's Thanksgiving Day Parade, he was pulled along Main Street in a sled set upon a float decorated with papier mâché reindeer, noisily jangling jingle bells, and a blanket of artificial snow. The most popular part of the float, Daniel thought, was not Santa but the handful of local children dressed adorably as elves, complete with pointy hats and shoes. When the float passed the yarn shop at the end of Main Street, it was then time to look forward to the ultimate event of the evening—the lighting of the massive fir tree that had been erected at the small square at the intersection of Main and Market streets.

People came from all the neighboring towns to stroll, eat, chat, and to buy. It wasn't unusual for a shop to make more money on this one night than it did in the three weeks leading up to Christmas. Richard Armstrong of the Angry Squire had told Daniel that the restaurant was routinely completely booked for dinner as early as the first of December.

Daniel found himself alone with Rumi, Marco, and Sophia; Anna Maria, Andie, and Emma had gone off to check out the sales, and shopping held no interest for Daniel and the youngest Reynoldses. He estimated there were close to four hundred people gathered in the center of town, and though he wasn't particularly worried about criminals—there hadn't been a violent crime in Oliver's Well in almost twenty years—he didn't want either of his children to come to any harm in the throng.

"Sophia, keep an eye on your brother," he told his daughter. "I don't want him getting lost in the crowd. You know how he tends to dash off."

"I'm on it, Dad," Sophia assured her father, every inch the responsible older sister. She took her brother's hand—under great protest—and steered him toward a juggler dressed in a bright and motley assortment of garments.

Daniel smiled at his niece. "I can't tell you how I used to look forward to this night when I was a kid," he told her. "I swear I started obsessing about it in August."

"Uncle Daniel," Rumi said, taking his arm, "you're such a sentimentalist."

"Guilty as charged. I'm a sucker for anything that tugs on the heartstrings."

"It's what makes you such a good dad." Rumi sighed. "Too bad my dad couldn't be here tonight. But he really wanted to see his old friend Tom. He's got some sort of cancer, and Dad said he's really been down."

"Your father is a good man." And Daniel remembered the feelings of tenderness toward his oldest sister he had experienced after his meeting with Reverend Fox that morning. "And your mother's not so bad, either," he added with a smile. "Try to go easy on her."

"It's just that she can be so frustrating," Rumi said with a sigh, removing her arm from his. "She's always quoting some guy who's been dead for like a thousand years. Sometimes I wish she were just an ordinary mother, boring and predictable."

"But only sometimes?" Rumi shrugged and Daniel decided not to pursue the subject. "So, what's your favorite part of the festival?" he asked.

Rumi's face took on a distinctly sheepish look.

"What?" Daniel prodded. "What's going on?"

"Well, I didn't tell anyone, but the Artful Soul agreed to show a few of the bracelets and necklaces I made recently. You know they have that section of the shop for new local artists and craftspeople to showcase their work. And tonight is my debut, so I guess *that's* my favorite part of the festival."

Daniel smiled. "Good for you! But why keep it a secret?"

"I don't know," Rumi admitted. "I guess I'm kind of scared. What if nothing sells? What if I told Aunt Emma or Mom and they each bought something just to make me feel good? I don't want that happening."

"I understand. But you know your mother and aunts might see your work if they happen to stop in at the Artful Soul."

"I know. I guess I can't do anything about that."

"Well," Daniel said, "I wish you success. Maybe you'll make some money."

"I don't really care about the money," Rumi said. "Honestly. If I do make some money I'll use it to buy more materials so I can make more pieces. And maybe before long I'll be able to afford a course in metalworking."

She's more like her mother than she knows, Daniel thought. "So it's not about profit," he said, "at least, not at the moment."

Again Rumi shrugged, and again Daniel decided not to pursue his questioning. Suddenly, the kids came dashing toward them, no mean feat in such a crowd.

"Dad," Sophia cried, "can we go into Billet-Doux? My friend Rebecca just told me they have awesome hot chocolate."

"Yeah, Dad, can we?" Marco echoed. "They put peppermint sticks in it!"

Daniel shrugged. "Sure. We'll all go."

Together the four members of the Reynolds family made their way to the specialty card and gift store, where Rumi wandered off to look at the handmade notebooks and Sophia and Marco got on line for their hot chocolate. Daniel was idly looking at a rack of greeting cards when he became aware of a man standing next to him.

"Daniel," the man said, extending a hand. "It's so good to see you."

For a second Daniel didn't recognize the man. And then it came to him; it was Reggie Beaton, Cliff's childhood friend. Mr. Beaton had left Oliver's Well over twenty years before for a job in New York City.

"Mr. Beaton, hello," Daniel said, shaking the man's hand. "I'm sorry, but it's been a while."

Reggie Beaton laughed. "And I've gained at least thirty pounds since I last saw you. And you've grown a few more inches!"

"What are you doing back in Oliver's Well?" Daniel asked.

"I decided to retire here in my old hometown." And then Mr. Beaton moderated his jovial tone. "I was very sorry to hear of the death of your parents. My wife and I sent condolences, but I'm afraid both times I was working at our office in Basel and couldn't get back in time for the memorial services."

Daniel felt tears threaten. "Thank you," he finally managed to say. "It was a shock with Dad, even though we knew about his heart condition. And with Mom . . ."

"I know," Mr. Beaton said with sympathy. "I heard. It's a great loss to our community. I'm sorry I won't be able to spend my retirement years in your parents' company. You know, it's funny how the people who are your friends in the early years of your life are so often the ones you want most to spend the last years of your life with. I grew up with Cliff. I guess I expected to grow old with him, too."

"Thanks," Daniel managed again. But he couldn't bring himself to say more.

"Well, the wife is waiting for me at the candle shop. It was good to see you, Daniel. I'm sure our paths will cross again."

Mr. Beaton went off, leaving Daniel experiencing a disturbing mix of emotions—sadness warred with fond nostalgia and pleasant memories.

"You okay, Uncle Daniel?"

Daniel startled; he hadn't been aware that Rumi had joined him. "Yeah," he said. "I'm fine."

Rumi looked at him worriedly. "Sure? You look sad all of a sudden."

"It's nothing," he assured her, with an attempt at a smile. "I just saw a ghost is all."

Rumi laughed. "Well, if *that's* all it was! Come on. I think you need a hot chocolate."

CHAPTER 50

In spite of the distraction of the streetlamps and the bright lights of the shops, Emma could make out a few stars in the sky. She felt it was a good sign, though why she couldn't exactly say. *Maybe*, she thought, *I'm just wallowing in nostalgia, seeing good omens and dreaming of a future that was as perfect as the past seems now.*

Emma turned to her sister "Remember that one year—gosh, it must have been when we were still in grammar school—when all the lights on the tree sputtered out just after they were turned on? The collective groan," she told Anna Maria, "was probably heard in Washington!"

Andie smiled. "And then the lights came back on, just like magic."

Emma grinned. "More likely someone corrected a technical malfunction."

"Look." Anna Maria nodded. "The Shelby Gallery is just ahead. Why don't we stop in?"

Emma opened her mouth and then closed it. What had she been going to say? Of course she would like to see Morgan Shelby, but the thought of chatting with him in the company of members of her family struck her as potentially . . . awkward. Would Andie and Anna Maria, both astute women, be able to tell that Emma had feelings for him? *Yes*, Emma thought. *They will be able to tell. I'm a terrible dissembler.*

"You two go on," she said. "I want to stop in the Eclectic Gourmet. I'll meet you in about ten minutes?"

"Okay," Andie said with a shrug, and she and Anna Maria went into the gallery. Emma made her way into the specialty food store—a store she did in truth like—feeling more than a bit foolish. *Really,* she thought, *what am I hiding? Who am I hiding from?* Whatever the answers to those puzzling questions, the fact remained that at the moment Emma felt the need to keep her nascent relationship with Morgan (if that's even what it was) to herself.

After a few minutes mindlessly browsing the store's vast selection of spices and dried herbs and handmade pastas, she rejoined the others on the sidewalk. Andie was wiping her lip with a paper cocktail napkin decorated with an image of a poinsettia. "That was the best brownie I've had in an age," she said. "Emma, you should have come in with us."

"The brownies were good, but I was more taken with the nineteenth-century sideboard Morgan just got in," Anna Maria said with a sigh. "If Savories and Seasonings ever makes it really big I think I'd like to have a sideboard like that at home. Of course, it might not actually fit in the living room, let alone through the front door!"

"Morgan asked for you," Andie went on, stuffing the napkin in the pocket of her jacket.

"Did he?" Emma said. "Oh."

"I told him you were around. Maybe we'll bump into him later. He seems very nice."

"Yes," Emma said, affecting what she hoped was a tone of nonchalance. "Maybe we'll see him later."

"Look, here comes Maureen. Who's that with her?" Andie asked.

"It must be her beau," Emma said. Maureen was wearing a lightweight down vest over a bright red sweater. Emma was glad to see that the awful clay brooch of Santa Claus was nowhere in sight.

"Emma!" Maureen called, waving to them. "Andie. Anna Maria. Let me introduce you to Jim."

The women took turns shaking Jim's hand. *He has a nice face,* Emma thought. *An honest face.*

"It's great to meet you all," Jim told them. "Maureen's met my friends, and I was beginning to think there was some terrible reason she was keeping me from her oldest buddies."

Maureen playfully slapped his arm. "Remember," she said, "the Reynolds gals don't live around here. We only get to see each other once or twice a year at best." Maureen smiled then at Anna Maria. "And Anna Maria is a busy mom and businesswoman. Her schedule isn't exactly wide open."

The others chatted for a few minutes, but Emma found herself not quite able to join in. In the midst of the proverbial crowd she felt a sharp twinge of loneliness. It was difficult not to compare Maureen's happy situation with her own uncertain relationship status. Not that she begrudged her friend the joy she had so obviously found with Jim. No, Maureen deserved whatever bit of happiness she was able to find for herself.

"Looks like the whole town is out tonight!" Maureen said with a cheerful laugh that broke through Emma's melancholy reverie.

Jim nodded. "All we need is some snow and this would be a perfect night! And speaking of perfect," he added to Maureen, "didn't you say you wanted to check out the sales in some dress shop?"

"I almost forgot! Maybe we'll see you guys around the tree later."

When Maureen and Jim had moved off, arms linked, Andie said, "Well, he's a huge improvement over that loser she married. I hate to use that term, 'loser,' but in Barry's case I think I'm justified."

"And I was her maid of honor," Emma told Anna Maria. "I

cringe when I think of how I didn't see the truth about him before it was too late."

"You might have been able to warn Maureen that she was marrying a bad seed," Anna Maria pointed out, "but that doesn't mean she would have heeded you."

Emma managed a smile. "You're right. The mistakes we make for love."

"If you have to make a mistake," Andie said, "and being human, we all do, making the mistake in the name of love isn't the worst thing."

Before Emma could reply—and she had no idea what she would say to Andie's observation—she spotted Joe Herbert and his family gathered by a young man and woman playing fiddles. She had last seen Jenna at Caro's funeral, but she hadn't seen the children in at least three years. The boy, Edward, would be around seven or eight now, she thought. The girl, Alice, must be ten or eleven. They were an attractive family and, if the fact that they were all laughing proved anything, a close family. She remembered Joe telling her that he was working too many hours, and she thought, *With a family like that to come home to, who in his right mind would want to spend crazy hours at the office?*

Emma ambled on alongside her sister and sister-in-law, feeling a tiny bit like a fraud. She hadn't even told Andie that she was considering moving back to Oliver's Well. Why? Was she afraid that Andie would tell her she was being crazy, abandoning the safe life she had built in Annapolis? No, she thought. Andie was firmly for change and growth. So was the reason she had kept her thoughts from her sister because voicing the idea of coming home to Oliver's Well to anyone in the family would make it *too* real?

A loud burst of laughter and applause caused Emma to look toward a small crowd gathered around a magician—he had to be a magician, what with the black cape and the wand from the end of which was sprouting a bouquet of silk flowers. And in that crowd stood Morgan Shelby, a classic Burberry wool scarf wrapped around his neck. He must have closed the gallery early, Emma thought, or have hired someone to man the counter while he took some time to enjoy the festivities.

"I'm just going to pop into the Hyatt Gallery," she told her sister and sister-in-law hurriedly. "If I lose you we'll meet later at the tree."

Anna Maria looked slightly suspicious—at least, Emma thought she did—but said only, "Okay." Andie simply nodded, and Emma went off, wondering if she was becoming paranoid as well as childishly secretive.

When she was within a few yards of the magician's audience a very attractive young woman joined Morgan with a cry of greeting. Morgan bent down to let the woman kiss his cheek, and then he kissed hers in return. Emma stopped in her tracks and felt a surge of jealousy that stunned her. It was something she had never once felt in relation to a man. *What is happening to me?* she thought. *It's as if . . . It's as if I'm really waking up for the first time in my life. . . .*

She wanted to turn away but couldn't. Instead she allowed herself to be tortured by the sight of them chatting animatedly, the woman putting her hand on Morgan's arm in what Emma saw as a gesture of possession. Finally, she could stand no more. Emma abruptly turned away and went in search of her family. She had no claim on Morgan. She knew that. But now she thought that she might want a claim. She thought that she would like to matter to him. She remembered what Andie had said to her at the Pink Rose Café. She had said there was a candle in her heart, waiting to be kindled. Making her way through the throng of revelers in search of her sister, Emma thought that Andie might just be right.

CHAPTER 51

A ndie looked up at the huge, old-fashioned, round-faced clock mounted on a black post just outside the bank. She and Emma and Anna Maria had been strolling the streets of downtown Oliver's Well for almost an hour, and if anything, the crowds were even more animated than they had been at the start of the festivities. *Wine and sugar and adrenaline,* Andie thought. She realized that the sweet treats she had consumed were making her feel a bit twitchy and swore she would indulge no more for the rest of the evening. She needed to keep her wits about her; it was entirely possible that she would run into Mary Bernadette Fitzgibbon this evening, and if she did she hoped to find the courage to explain that the Bullock desk would not be going to the OWHA. But courage was a slippery thing to hold on to these days, Andie thought sadly, let alone to find in the first place.

"Look, there's Danny," Emma said suddenly, pointing across the street. "Oops, I lost him. I've never seen so many people out and about."

"Did you get to say hello to Rumi earlier?" Anna Maria asked as they walked on in step with the other revelers. "She and Daniel and the kids took off pretty quickly."

"Not really," Andie admitted. "I think she gave me a half smile, but I'm not sure it wasn't a grimace."

Emma sighed. "I'm so sorry that things are at an impasse. It's such a waste of precious time."

"I suppose I could talk to Rumi if you think it might help," Anna Maria offered. "Maybe I'm at enough of a distance from the family—not a blood relation at least—for her to listen to me."

"Thanks, Anna Maria," Andie said, "but no. Honestly, I don't know what to do, but the situation is between my daughter and me. We'll have to figure out a way to peace by ourselves." *And that*, Andie thought, *might take a miracle.*

"Mom and Dad loved this festival," Emma was saying. "For Mom I think it was primarily another opportunity to go on parade. She liked the attention she got when displaying a new coat or hat for the first time."

"She did at that," Andie agreed. "And I think Dad just ate up the joyous spirit of the evening. That and the candy apples they used to sell at the bakery before Cookies 'n Crumpets! What was the name of that bakery?"

"I think it was Pat's Pastries, wasn't it?" Emma shrugged. "Something like that."

"After Cliff died," Anna Maria told them, "Daniel and I tried every tactic we could think of to persuade Caro to come with us, but she just wouldn't budge. Maybe she couldn't handle being around so much cheer and good spirit, the others not feeling her loss as keenly she did."

Andie couldn't help but wonder what her father would have done if Caro had gone before him—if he would have fared better, continued to find some joy in life, if he would have accompanied his son and family to the Christmas festival and not wasted away so quickly. But that, too, was something no one would ever know.

"Let's go in here," Andie suggested as they reached the Artful Soul. "I've never been inside."

The three women entered and were greeted by the enticing aroma of cinnamon, nutmeg, clove, and orange. "Pomander balls," Andie said, pointing to the bowls of spice-studded oranges on several counters.

"How pretty," Anna Maria cried.

Indeed, Andie thought, the store did look beautiful, with its array of pine swaths and spindly sprays of branches painted white and sprinkled generously with silver sparkle. She noted but refrained from partaking in the refreshments on offer—classic colorful ribbon candy; candy canes in red, white, and green; and little squares of fudge and caramel.

"Oh, my gosh, look!" Emma grabbed Andie's arm and pointed to a section of the display case to their right. "Look at the sign," she said. "Handcrafted by Rumi C. Dolman!"

Andie felt her heart speed up, and it wasn't due to the sugar she had consumed earlier. Carefully she lifted a bracelet from the display. It was made with irregularly shaped labradorite beads—Rumi's favorite stone, Andie recalled—and the clasp bore the mark of sterling silver. The bracelet was simple and lovely. "I had no idea Rumi was showing her work to the public," she said. She was surprised—and pleased—that her daughter had chosen to use her first name rather than her second, Caroline, by which she was familiarly known to her peers and much of the community.

"Neither did I," Anna Maria admitted. "She's been so dismissive about it all."

Looking at the selection of bracelets and necklaces, fifteen pieces in all, Andie felt a surge of pride. Clearly Rumi's creative outlet meant more to her than just a hobby, even if she denied its importance to her mother. She was sorely tempted to buy a bracelet or necklace, but then better sense took hold. The shop owner would be sure to tell Rumi who had purchased her work, and the fact that it had been her mother might not sit well with Rumi at the moment.

"Guys," Emma said, looking at her watch. "It's almost seven-thirty. The tree is about to be lit. We'd better get out there."

Andie followed Emma and Anna Maria out of the store and together they made their way toward the massive fir tree that stood magnificently at the intersection of Main and Market streets. It was decorated with red, white, green, and blue lights that would soon be switched on to the enthusiastic singing of the crowd.

Volunteers were already distributing sheets of lyrics to popular Christmas songs to those people still gathering, and Andie took the one offered to her. She wondered how many present really needed the lyric sheets; a quick glance at the papers in her hand told her that the words she had learned as a child were still firmly with her.

A little boy standing close by with his parents tugged on his father's coat. "This is the best night of my life," he said quite solemnly. Andie smiled. Though she mourned the unhappiness that seemed to have engulfed her daughter in the past few months, she was struggling mightily with her own dark thoughts and the great misdeed of having given away something she'd had no right to give, she couldn't help but be moved by the general good feeling of the crowd.

At seven-twenty the master of ceremonies—another member of the Chamber of Commerce, Andie guessed—began to lead the crowd in singing the first carol. At seven-thirty precisely, the tree became a blaze of color and a great cheer interrupted the singing of the much loved standard "O Christmas Tree!"

Andie felt a flood of emotion, too intense to sort through. Emma leaned into her and smiled. Anna Maria put her arm through Andie's and continued to sing in her strong soprano. Andie, tears in her eyes, wished that Bob was there with her. But he wasn't, and that, she thought, was all right, because the moment—both painful and joyous—was good enough just as it was.

CHAPTER 52

"I had so much fun last night," Emma said when she and her brother and sister were seated at Cookies 'n Crumpets. The only thing that would have made the Christmas festival any better, she thought, was if she had actually worked up the nerve to talk to Morgan Shelby. But she wouldn't share that regret with Andie or Daniel.

"Anna Maria and I have a big holiday lunch party at a small office park in Middleton," Daniel told them, ignoring his sister's comment. "It's at least an hour ride, so I have to be out of town by ten. Anna Maria will go on ahead with Bob."

"Well, this shouldn't take long. We don't have too much to discuss this morning, do we?" Emma asked.

Daniel shook his head. "There's always a lot to discuss, but at the moment I want us to come to a decision about hiring an auction house to evaluate the estate and proceed with plans for the sale. I know it's going to cost us money," he said. "But honestly, the thought of handling a sale on my own once you two go back to your lives elsewhere gives me a migraine."

"Hiring an auction house is fine by me," Andie said. "We're not professionals. We don't know what we're doing."

Emma nodded. "I agree. Maybe we should ask Morgan Shelby to recommend one."

"Good idea. Well, that's a relief. One less thing to worry about."

"What about the Bullock desk?" Emma asked her brother. "Are you still determined not to sell it?"

"I'm still determined to keep it in the family," Daniel said stoutly.

"I guess I'm fine with that. Andie?"

Andie cleared her throat. "Are you sure you wouldn't consider loaning it to the OWHA, even just for a year or two?"

Daniel sighed. "I know Mom used to say she couldn't stop us from giving it to Mary Bernadette after her death, but that doesn't mean it's the right thing to do."

"But a loan is not a permanent gift," Andie pointed out.

"I don't believe it's what Mom would have wanted," Daniel said, and his tone was stubborn.

Emma's phone buzzed. "It's my assistant," she said.

"Do you really have to answer that now?" Daniel asked with a frown.

"Sorry, I'll make it quick."

Emma got up and walked a few feet from the table. As she listened to her assistant relate the latest message from a particularly irritating but important client, she watched her siblings sitting at the table in silence. Daniel was checking his phone, a frown of concentration on his face. Andie was toying with a bit of the muffin she had ordered but had barely touched. At that moment Emma wished nothing more than to see her brother and sister sharing a laugh. Even a smile would do.

After calming her worried assistant and promising to call the client in question herself later that day, Emma ended the call and returned to the table.

"Everything okay?" Andie asked.

"Yeah. Nothing a bit of groveling won't fix."

"I've arranged a memorial candle-lighting ceremony at the Unitarian Universalist Church for tomorrow at ten A.M.," Daniel announced suddenly. "Reverend Fox will say a prayer or two first. Then I thought we could each say a few words about Mom and Dad."

Emma looked to Andie; her sister seemed as surprised as she was.
"What made you think to hold a memorial ceremony, Danny?"
Andie asked.

Daniel frowned. "Are you opposed to it?"

Andie shook her head. "Why would I be opposed?" she asked,
and Emma thought her sister sounded weary. Well, why wouldn't
Andie be weary of Daniel's changing moods?

"I wish you'd given us a bit more notice," Emma said. "I'm
terrible at speaking about important things off the cuff."

"You don't have to say anything if you don't want to."

"No, I do want to. It's a nice idea, Danny."

"Good. Any other business on the agenda?" Daniel asked.

Emma thought that Daniel should be the one telling his sisters what they next needed to discuss, not the other way around.
"I've got nothing," she said.

"I have something to say," Andie told them. "The owner of
End Quote, Chris Owens, asked me if I would give a reading,
and I said that I would. I know it's last minute, but I'd appreciate
it if you all could be there. It's late afternoon, the twenty-third."

"Moral support?" Emma asked her sister.

"Something like that. Danny?"

Daniel tapped his index finger against the table, as if, Emma
thought, to indicate the seriousness of his words. "I can't really
make a commitment, Andie. This time of year can be crazy. People suddenly realize they can't handle the party they've announced they're giving and they call us, frantic for help. If
possible, we say yes."

Emma smiled. "What are you afraid of, Danny? That you'll be
forcefully converted to Buddhism or suddenly convinced that
meat is murder?" She turned to her sister. "I'll be there, Andie."

Emma's phone indicated that she had just received a text. It was
from Morgan Shelby. He had scored two tickets to the Oliver's Well
Players' production of *A Christmas Carol* that evening. Would she
like to join him?

"More work-related stuff?" Daniel asked.

Emma shrugged. "Nothing that need concern you," she said, typing her answer. **Would love to.**

"Well, I'm out of here." Daniel gathered his belongings and with a wave, he was off for Middleton.

"So," Emma said to her sister, taking a final sip of her coffee. "What do you think of this memorial service?"

Andie didn't answer for a moment. "I think," she said finally, "that the last thing Danny needs at the moment is another walk down memory lane." And then she waved her hand dismissively. "But what do I know?"

CHAPTER 53

The Oliver's Well Players were known to be the best of the area's amateur theatrical companies. The current director had worked in New York for many years with innumerable respected off-Broadway companies before retiring to Oliver's Well to devote her energies to her hometown's theater fans.

Daniel and Anna Maria and the kids were at their own home that evening; they were hosting a potluck dinner for their neighbors on Little Rock Lane. "We all take turns," Anna Maria explained. "This year everyone is gathering at our house." Emma hadn't mentioned her own plans for the evening.

"I'm going to see *A Christmas Carol* at the playhouse," Emma had told her sister before leaving the house. She didn't mention that she would be attending the play with Morgan Shelby, though of course being at the theater with him would likely get back to the family. So what if it did, she thought. And then she felt a twinge of embarrassment. She should have told Andie the entire truth; she should in fact have tried to get a ticket for her sister as well. When it came to Morgan Shelby, Emma thought, remembering the wild surge of jealousy she had felt at the festival the night before, she was acting like a moody, love-struck teenager.

Emma met Morgan in the lobby, as arranged. He was wonderfully turned out, as always. The word "dapper" came to Emma's mind; Morgan was never flashy but always noticeable.

"I'm sorry I missed you last night at the festival," he said right away. "Andie told me you were around, and I was hoping we'd bump into each other."

Emma almost blushed at the memory of her strong emotions on seeing that woman kiss Morgan on the cheek. "I'm sorry, too," she said. "But it was such a madhouse. . . ."

"I hear it was the best turnout in the history of the festival," Morgan told her. "And that's saying something." Morgan looked at his watch, a vintage Breitling. "We'd better take our seats," he said. "The curtain rises in a few minutes."

Together they went into the noisy theater and took the seats Morgan had scored. And as soon as the lights were dimmed and the curtain began to rise on the first scene of the play, Emma felt an overwhelming desire for Morgan to take her hand. She knew she didn't have the nerve to take his. This sense of expectation, the sense of sheer *romance* was something she had never felt with Ian, not even in the beginning of their relationship. It was something she had never felt with *any* man in her past. *Gosh*, she thought. *I don't even recognize myself!*

Emma was soon absorbed in the unfolding of the famous Christmas story. The woman playing Belle, Ebenezer Scrooge's poor fiancée, brought a truly plangent note to the role, and the man playing Scrooge himself was perfection, evoking in Emma a troubled mix of anger and pity. The Players' costume people had done an excellent job and the set the designers had created was appropriately atmospheric. When the lights went on at intermission, Emma turned to Morgan with a smile. "It's as good as any performance I've seen in Annapolis," she said.

Together they walked back to the lobby and joined the throng of audience members chatting and laughing. Morgan went to the refreshment table for two glasses of wine, and Emma let her mind wander back to the Christmas concert she and her family had attended at the Church of the Immaculate Conception. Like this evening it had been an event that had drawn together young and old to celebrate not only the holiday season but also the community of Oliver's Well. Emma thought about how different things were back in Annapolis. There, none of her close acquaintances had children; those of her colleagues that did weren't in the habit of socializing with childless couples like Emma Reynolds and Ian Hayes. And no one she knew regularly spent time with significantly older friends. Maybe, she thought, the people she knew didn't have friends of a different generation, and if they didn't, why didn't they? For that matter, she thought, why didn't she?

If she moved to Oliver's Well she might very well be able to establish more of a warm and inclusive social life. And, as she had realized the night of the Christmas pageant, she could be closer to her nieces and nephew, share more of their childhood and young adulthood before they were off to live adult lives of their own.

Morgan returned with their wine and said in a whisper, "Don't look now, but it's Mary Bernadette Fitzgibbon and she's heading our way." He took Emma's arm and hurried her back into the theater. "Just in the nick of time," he said as they took their seats. "I'm sure no one will throw us out for bringing our drinks into the theater."

"How did you know she wanted to talk to me?" Emma whispered.

"The Regency desk. Everyone in Oliver's Well knows that Mary Bernadette has been after the George Bullock piece for the past thirty years or so. I just assumed you didn't want to be bothered on a night out."

Emma smiled. "She really is persistent. Thanks for being my knight in shining armor."

The second act proved as wonderfully absorbing as the first, and when the little boy playing Tiny Tim finally proclaimed, "God bless us, everyone!" Emma felt tears flood her eyes. She felt embarrassed until the lights in the theater came on and she saw that Morgan was unabashedly wiping his eyes.

"Gets me every time," he admitted with a laugh. "No one can pull a heartstring like Charles Dickens. Talk about sentimental."

"Good thing I always carry tissues!" Emma handed one to Morgan and wiped at her own eyes with another.

"How about a nightcap at the Angry Squire?" Morgan suggested when they reached the lobby.

"I'd love to," Emma said. And then, she took a risk no moody teenager would take. "It's becoming our place, isn't it?"

Morgan smiled. "Richard will be screwing metal nameplates to the backs of our chairs before long."

When Morgan held out his hand, Emma took it.

The restaurant was crowded and cheery, the perfect setting, Emma thought, for the end of an evening of sentiment and joy. Richard Armstrong himself was circulating among the people in the bar, shaking hands and patting backs. When he had moved on from Emma and Morgan's table—their usual—Morgan said, "He's the perfect publican, to use a British term. He makes everyone feel like a regular even if they're just passing through, while at the same time he keeps an eye on potential troublemakers."

"Has there ever been a troublemaker at the Angry Squire?" Emma asked.

"Nope. Thanks to Richard!"

When they had ordered a drink and a bowl of warm assorted olives to share, Emma told Morgan about the candle-lighting ceremony her brother had arranged for the next morning. "I don't know why it's so important to him to do this now," she said, "but it is."

"Didn't you say this is the first time the three siblings have been together since your mother's funeral?" Morgan asked.

"Yes, that's probably it. Danny's a big one for memorials and ceremony."

"Nothing wrong with that, I suppose."

"No," Emma said. "But sometimes people can lose track of what they're supposed to be memorializing or honoring and get caught up in the pomp and circumstance of ceremony."

Morgan took a sip of his red wine before saying, "I'm not sure that's always a bad thing. Maybe allowing the pageantry of an event to take over allows people to survive a moment or even a memory of grief."

"I suppose you're right. Pageantry might have a cathartic effect." Emma smiled. "Maybe that's why human beings love to give parties! Frankly," she went on, "I'm nervous about what I'll say. I want to say something meaningful, something that's *true*, but the idea of trying to put my feelings about Mom and Dad being gone into words frightens me."

"I don't blame you," Morgan said. "I've already told my parents they can look elsewhere for a eulogist. I'm hopelessly bad at creative writing, and the last thing I want to do is speak off the cuff at something as important as a funeral."

"Were they upset?" Emma asked.

"No. They understand I mean no disrespect. Besides, my mother told me they'd already had their eye on my cousin. He's a formally trained actor and regularly performs the big guns, everyone from Shakespeare to Mamet." Morgan shrugged. "I guess they feel they can't go wrong with a guy who can handle playing Hamlet."

Emma smiled. "Well, Andie isn't an actor, but she'll have something wonderful to say. She's always been good with voicing the important stuff, emotions and feelings. Even if she's quoting someone else, she knows how to choose just the right message. And knowing Danny, he's been drafting his speech for weeks!"

"A chance to shine?"

"Yes, though I know his heart is really in this. Oh," Emma said, "I've been meaning to ask you. Do you think you could recommend a reputable auction house to handle an estate sale for us? With the exception of a few items, particularly the Regency desk, we'd like to sell most of the contents."

"Of course," Morgan told her. "A few come to mind immediately, but I'll do a little asking around, see if I can determine the one best suited for the Reynoldses."

"Thank you." Emma hesitated but only for half a moment. "My sister is doing a reading at End Quote the afternoon of the twenty-third. Would you like to come? That is, if you're not busy."

"Sure," Morgan said eagerly. "You know, I have two of her books and I've been meaning to buy the most recent one. She really is a gifted teacher. And a pretty good writer, too."

"That she is. A far better writer than I am!" Emma finished her wine and suddenly realized that the bar had emptied significantly. She looked at her watch. "Look at the time! The pumpkin coach will have come and gone without me. And I've still got to come up with something to say at the memorial service tomorrow morning."

Morgan paid their bill. Emma thanked him. She had long ago made peace with the idea of allowing someone else to pay her way on occasion.

Together they left the restaurant. "The beauty of living in the heart of town," Morgan said, "is that I can be home in minutes. Would you like me to walk you to your car?"

"That's all right," Emma said. "I'm just in the municipal lot."

And then, Morgan leaned in and kissed her gently on the lips. Emma responded readily.

"Good night, Emma," Morgan said softly, pulling slowly away.

"Good night," she breathed. And then he turned toward his apartment above the gallery, and she turned the other way and began to walk toward the parking lot. *He kissed me*, she thought, and a very big smile broke across her face.

Chapter 54

"I think the lunch went well today, don't you?" Anna Maria asked. She was wearing the nightgown Daniel liked best. It was a shade of pale green that made him think of lilies of the valley; he thought the gown made her look like a sprite in a spring fantasy.

"The blinis could have been a little thinner," he told his wife as she climbed into the bed next to him, "but no one seemed to notice but me. At least, no one complained."

"That's because they were delicious. There was nothing wrong with them, Daniel. You're just a perfectionist."

Daniel shrugged. "It was a long way to travel for a gig, but the Sumner Group could become an important client for us. I'm glad Bob was able to help us all he did."

"He's a dream. Oh, we were so busy—what with the gig and then the potluck—I never got to ask how your meeting with Emma and Andie went this morning."

"It went well," Daniel said honestly. "We decided to hire an auction house. Emma will talk to Morgan Shelby about it. But Andie still thinks we should loan Mom's Regency desk to the OWHA for a period of time."

Anna Maria nodded. "Personally, I think it's a nice idea, but I'm not a Reynolds, so my opinion doesn't count."

"You are a Reynolds!" Daniel protested. "And your opinion always matters to me. I love you, Anna Maria, more than anyone. How can I thank you for all you've done for me and my parents?"

"You can make that monkfish dish I love," she said promptly. "The one with marsala wine."

"Deal. Anna Maria? A few days ago Emma told me I was wrong to encourage Rumi's bad behavior toward her mother. She said I was interfering. I feel pretty foolish about it all," Daniel admitted. "I really never wanted to cause trouble." *Or did I?* he wondered. "Anyway, I suggested to Rumi at the festival that she try to treat her mother with more patience and kindness, but I'm not sure my suggestion was accepted."

"Maybe you should say something to Andie, apologize or try to explain yourself."

Daniel shook his head. "No. I don't want to make an even bigger deal of it. I think I should just watch my behavior going forward." *Besides,* he thought, *how can I explain myself when I'm not even sure why I've been acting the way I have?*

"Good. You know, I've been thinking about Emma, too. She seems . . . different. More herself than she's seemed in a long time, if that makes sense."

"Maybe it's being done with Ian," Daniel suggested. "Maybe it was the right decision, after all."

"That's probably part of it," Anna Maria agreed. "And maybe— now, don't jump down my throat about this—but maybe now that both Cliff and Caro are gone she's able to, I don't know, relax a bit. I always got the feeling that Emma was trying to impress them, always trying to prove herself to them. Cliff and Caro could be formidable. Nice, but . . . strong."

"I know." Daniel found himself sighing. "Kids needing to prove themselves to parents. I know it's something I suffer from, even now that Mom and Dad are gone."

Anna Maria smiled. "None of this is news to me, but I'm glad you're talking about it."

"But what about Andie?" he wondered. "It's like she set out to do exactly what might make Mom and Dad disappointed in her.

Well, at least until she made it big and they finally had to take notice."

"Andie did what she had to do. I don't see her as a person who set out to rebel for the sake of rebellion. In fact, if I understand your sister, and I think that I do—thanks to Bob, mostly—her marrying when she did was a rebellion against her true nature. And that's always the wrong thing to do."

Daniel looked at his wife with a combination of wonder and love. "You're so much smarter than I am," he said, leaning over to kiss her gently.

"About some things, yes," Anna Maria replied readily. "But this isn't a competition, it's a marriage."

"It's a good marriage, isn't it?" Daniel asked, and he could hear the slight note of worry in his voice.

"Yes," Anna Maria said. "It is. I'm happy."

"That makes two of us." Daniel kissed his wife again and turned off his bedside lamp. He was a bit anxious about the memorial service the next morning. Would he break down? Would one of his sisters fail to show up? For a moment he wondered if he would actually be able to fall asleep. But then he felt Anna Maria take his hand in the dark and before he knew it his eyes were closing.

CHAPTER 55

The next morning found the Reynolds siblings along with Anna Maria gathered at the Unitarian Universalist Church, from where Cliff and Caro had been buried, and where Andie herself had been married. As they pulled into the parking lot, Andie had a sudden, distinct memory of her wedding day, how nervous Bob had looked, wearing a suit bought specially for the occasion, a white carnation in his buttonhole. Her mother had looked so proud and content, satisfied that she had successfully steered her older daughter in the right direction. And her father, well, Andie believed he had simply been happy.

"You're a million miles away again," Emma said, opening her door.

"I was visiting the past," Andie told her. "It's been happening a lot since I've been back. I don't want to go there, but I do."

The sisters approached the imposing brick building that had gone up over a century and a half earlier as a private girls' academy. After having been abandoned and left derelict for almost twenty years, it had finally been sold and converted to a mixed-use building; currently the church shared the space with a co-op of local artists. The sisters went inside and joined Daniel and Anna Maria. Daniel was wearing the suit he had worn at Caro's funeral. Andie usually didn't take notice of such things, but for some reason she remembered her brother's suit.

Reverend Fox greeted them, and when they had gathered around a small table on which had been placed three white candles, he said a prayer for Cliff and Caro Reynolds, as well as for the living members of the Reynolds family.

"I'll leave you alone now," he said after the prayers, "as Daniel requested." When his footsteps had died away, Daniel took the lighted taper from its holder and held it to the wick of one of the three white candles arranged in a row. Then he passed the taper to Emma, who lit the second candle and then handed the taper to Andie. When all three candles had been lit, their bright flames dancing in the relative darkness, Andie felt tears threaten.

"Emma," Daniel said quietly. "Why don't you speak first?"

Emma took a piece of paper from her bag and unfolded it. "I know Mom and Dad liked this poem by Christina Rossetti," she said, "so I thought I'd read it aloud, rather than come up with something of my own I know would be inadequate." She began in a soft but clear voice to read. Then she stopped for a moment and said, "I know these lines were Dad's particular favorites."

Andie recited the lines silently as her sister continued to read aloud. " 'Nay, weights and measurements do us both a wrong. / For verily love knows not 'mine' or 'thine,' / With separate 'I' and 'thou' free love has done, / For one is both and both are one in love. . . .' "

As Emma read through the final lines of the poem, Andie took her sister's hand.

"That was beautiful," Daniel said, an unmistakable catch in his voice.

"Danny?" Emma said. "Why don't you speak next?"

Daniel nodded and folded his hands before him. "I loved and respected my parents," he began, "and they truly deserved love and respect. They were the most wonderful people I've ever known. I just hope that when my time comes I'll be able to look back on my life and know that I lived up to their example."

"I know that you will, Danny," Emma said. "Andie?"

Andie cleared her throat. "I'd like to read a few words by the poet Rumi," she said. " 'Good-byes are only for those who love with their eyes. Because for those who love with heart and soul there is no such thing as separation.' And to those words," she went on, her voice trembling slightly, "I'd like to add that I'm forever grateful to my parents for the gift of life."

"Thanks, Andie. It's not as good as getting to say the eulogy," Daniel said. "But I hope this ceremony made up for it somewhat."

"Thank you, Danny," Andie said gratefully. "It did."

And Andie hoped that this ceremony would help her brother shrug off the tension and unhappiness he so obviously had been carrying. But she remembered his words—that he hoped to live up to the example set by their parents—and wondered if her brother would ever be entirely free of a crippling sense of duty.

"Let's go to their graves," Daniel suggested then. He led the others out of the church and to the small private cemetery on the lot next to the church building, where Cliff and Caro Reynolds were buried side by side. Neither, Andie remembered, had ever entertained the notion of cremation. Her mother had thought it vaguely pagan. "The Vikings burned their dead," she had said often enough. "I'm a Christian, not a Viking." Come to think of it, Andie couldn't recall her father actually voicing an opinion on the subject. It was likely, she thought, that he had simply acceded to his wife's wishes for an in-ground burial.

The family stood in a half circle around the two marble headstones. Neither Cliff nor Caro had opted for a quote, just the dates they had been born and had died and the simple inscription Loving Husband and Father, Loving Wife and Mother. There was a certain dignity to the stones, Andie thought. She planned to be cremated when she passed and had left instructions for her ashes to be scattered to the winds, but she had no trouble understanding the very real need many people had for a physical memorial to their lives. *My name was Cliff and I was here. My name was Caro and I, too, lived in this world.*

Daniel brushed a leaf off the top of his father's stone. "I come here once a month," he said. "It's always well tended, but I like to be sure."

"Do you talk to them, Danny?" Emma asked.

"Not when I'm here, no. I suppose that's odd, because I do sometimes find myself talking to them, like when I'm watching one of Dad's favorite movies or when I'm making a dish Mom used to ask for. I find myself saying things like, 'This is the part you liked, Dad,' and 'Do you think the sauce came out a bit too thick, Mom?'" Daniel smiled. "Half the time I think I hear them answer."

"What about you, Andie?" Emma asked.

"I talk to Dad sometimes," Andie said. "I ask him questions about important things going on in my life. That's definitely odd, because when he was alive I rarely, if ever, went to him for advice or input."

Anna Maria, silent until now, said, "Do you hear him reply? Do you feel he hears you?"

Andie smiled. "Most times, yes."

"So, what about you, Emma?" Daniel asked. "Do you ever talk to Mom or Dad?"

"No. I think about them, sure. But I don't talk to them. I guess I don't feel the need to."

But I do, Andie thought. *Dad,* she said, *I've done something wrong. Not evil, not even irreparable, but misguided. The burden is weighing terribly on me and yet I can't seem to take the steps to throw it off.*

But this time, Andie couldn't hear her father's voice in reply. Perhaps it wasn't there to be heard.

"We have to get going," Daniel said abruptly. "We've got a lunch gig at one. We'll see you at the house this evening." And with a wave, he and Anna Maria went off.

Silently the two sisters walked back to Emma's car. "You okay?" Emma asked as the sisters buckled themselves in.

Andie made it a point to speak truthfully, but she couldn't quite bring herself to tell Emma just how miserable and fraudulent she felt. "I'm fine," she said. "Just fine."

CHAPTER 56

Emma picked up her phone from where it sat on the kitchen counter. "It's Morgan Shelby," she told her sister. "I won't be a moment."

Morgan was calling to tell her that he had found what he thought was a suitable auction house in Westminster. "It's called R. W. Simons," he said. "I could make an appointment for you to meet with them, if you like. And I could come with. Just remember to bring along a copy of the inventory your brother put together and any additional information on items you might have unearthed."

"Thanks, Morgan," Emma said. "That would be great. I have no experience at all with auction houses. Having an expert along will lessen the anxiety."

Morgan promised to let her know the date and time of their appointment, and Emma ended the call.

"Morgan found an auction house for us," Emma told her sister, who was sitting at the kitchen table, her shoulders drooping. When Andie didn't respond, Emma asked, "Andie? Did you hear what I said?"

"Yes," she replied. "An auction house. Good."

"Is there something else worrying you besides the situation with Rumi?" Emma asked gently. "You seem a bit preoccupied these past few days. A bit weary."

Andie smiled and sat up straighter in her chair. "No, I'm fine. I was just thinking about this morning's service."

"It was nice, wasn't it? I'm glad Danny organized it. It actually felt kind of healing. Funny, I hadn't even realized I needed healing."

"We all need healing," Andie said. And then, more quietly, she added, "Some of us more than others."

Emma let her sister's comment pass. She didn't believe for a moment that Andie's mind was troubled by her daughter's mood alone, but she had never been one to push for a confession. "I suppose we should get started organizing things for tonight," she said. "Gathering all the photo albums and videos Danny's so eager for us to see. We'll have to divvy it all up when the house is sold unless one of us wants to be the archivist and hold on to the entire lot." *And if I decide to buy the house,* she thought, *it could all stay just where it is.*

"And we should start getting dinner ready." Andie got up from the kitchen table and went to the fridge. "Daniel seemed a little dubious when you suggested we just eat leftovers."

Emma laughed. "What's he worried about? He made most of the food! All we're doing is heating what needs to be heated."

"You know Danny," Andie said. "He needs to be in charge."

"Poor guy. It must really wear him down sometimes."

"Yes, but it might be a good thing in terms of his business," Andie commented with a wry smile. "Unless he drives Anna Maria and the staff up the wall with his perfectionism."

"I hope not. How about we eat dinner in the kitchen and then afterward we can go into the living room to watch the videos on the big screen TV."

"Sounds good." Andie opened a plastic container that held a good portion of ratatouille. "For some reason, I have absolutely no appetite. Oh, well." Andie put the lid back on the container and set it on the counter. "Maybe I'll drop a pound or two. Mom would be pleased."

Emma turned away to take plates off a shelf over the microwave. *No doubt about it,* she thought worriedly. *Something big is bothering my sister.*

CHAPTER 57

"The casserole didn't hold up as well as it might have," Daniel said with a frown. "Did you remember to heat it at three hundred and fifty for twenty minutes?"

"Yes, Danny," Emma said. "And I thought it was as delicious tonight as it was the other evening."

Daniel shrugged. "At least there was enough to go around."

As it had been at the morning's ceremony, only the Reynolds siblings and Anna Maria were gathered. Bob was spending the evening with his brother while Rumi had taken Sophia and Marco to see one of those lavish animated Christmas movies that popped up every year.

Daniel poured himself another glass of wine and went over to the old VCR. "This is labeled First Day of School," he said, choosing one of the videotapes onto which his parents had long ago had the old family films transferred. "Let's give it a go."

After inserting the tape into the machine and pressing the play button on the ancient remote, Daniel took a seat in his father's favorite chair.

"This is original," Anna Maria noted immediately. "Not an old transferred film. Look! It's Daniel! Oh, you were so cute!"

Daniel felt himself blush. "I was pretty adorable, wasn't I?"

There were about four minutes of Daniel, dressed in shorts

with a striped T-shirt neatly tucked into the waistband, standing outside the grammar school, waving to the camera with one hand and clutching a small backpack with the other. The rest of the tape, they discovered, was blank.

Emma laughed. "Well, my first day of school doesn't seem to be here, or Andie's. You always were Mom's favorite, Danny."

Daniel didn't refute his sister's observation; it was, after all, the truth. Instead, he got up and chose another and then another of the videotapes, and for the next forty minutes the past was once again alive before their eyes. And as he watched the birthday parties and Christmases long gone, as he was presented with the faces of those now dead—not only his parents but their parents as well—Daniel felt the small degree of calm and release he had achieved that morning at the memorial ceremony fade away, and in its place came into his heart a sharp pain of loss. Daniel poured himself another glass of wine and drank it greedily.

"It's like after I turned ten I disappeared," Andie was saying. "Except for that split second of my high school graduation."

"I remember someone taking video at your wedding, Andie," Emma told her. "It must be on one of these tapes somewhere."

"Caro stopped taking pictures of any kind when Cliff died," Anna Maria put in, "and I suspect nothing has been organized properly since then. After Andie mentioned Caro's wearing a tiara at a costume party, I went looking for a picture to show Sophia, but I couldn't find anything."

"Look," Daniel directed loudly. He drained his glass of what little wine was left and raised the volume. "Here's Anna Maria's and my wedding reception. There's Mom dancing with my best man, Sam. She looked absolutely gorgeous."

"Not as gorgeous as your bride," Emma pointed out. "That was such a lovely gown, Anna Maria."

"I was the third person in my family to wear it! The first was my cousin Lisa, and the second was my sister Gabriella."

"Your first dance as husband and wife. 'Sea of Love.'" Andie shook her head. "You know, sometimes I can't even remember what song Bob and I danced to."

"Don't let Rumi hear that," Daniel said shortly.

"No," Andie said. "I won't."

"Gabriella made such a funny maid of honor toast." Emma looked over at Daniel. "Do you remember it, Danny?"

But Daniel ignored his sister's question. The video was now showing Andie talking with one of Anna Maria's aunts. As the cameraperson approached, both women smiled and waved.

"What was that you were wearing, anyway?" Daniel asked his sister. "It looks like a silly costume out of a silent film about some ancient desert sheik!"

"Daniel," Anna Maria said sharply. "It does not. I thought it was lovely, Andie."

"Thanks. It was a gift from a fellow student in my meditation class at the time," Andie explained. "She was also studying dressmaking methods from around the world."

Daniel laughed. "Well, you certainly stood out. But look," he said, pointing to the TV screen. "How cute is Rumi, dancing with her father. You were just about to leave Oliver's Well for good, right, Andie? And I don't think you saw any of us again for almost two years." Daniel raised his wineglass to his mouth before realizing it was empty. *And I doubt*, he thought, *she ever thought much about us, either.*

Emma laughed. "Ooops," she said. "Whoever Mom and Dad hired to put these videos together had a continuity problem. Here's your wedding shower, Anna Maria!"

Daniel frowned. A wedding shower that neither Emma nor Andie bothered to attend. Andie had gone off to take a ten-day course in some arcane and useless topic in the wilds of Pennsylvania. And Emma had cancelled at the last minute, claiming a case of the flu. *More like a case of something more interesting on her social calendar*, Daniel thought. *A party for some visiting corporate bigwig or free tickets to an opening night at the ballet.*

"You guys really should have been at the shower," he said, vaguely aware that he was speaking loudly. "It should have been a priority. I know Mom was embarrassed that neither of her daughters was there."

"That's all in the past," Anna Maria said quickly, smiling at Andie and Emma and putting the video on hold. "Though you guys did miss some awesome food. My uncle Dominic is famous in my family for his *cassata* cake. We usually only have it at Easter, but as it's my favorite and it was a special occasion . . ."

"Here," Daniel said, picking up and passing an open album to his sisters. "Look at these." The photos pasted to the pages showed Cliff and Caro dressed to the nines, clearly heading out for a formal event. "Doesn't Mom look elegant?"

"Who took these?" Andie asked, looking up at Daniel. "I must have left Oliver's Well by the time these photos were taken."

"I don't remember ever seeing them," Emma said. "I must already have been living in Annapolis."

"Joe Herbert took the pictures," Daniel told them. "There was a business awards dinner that night, something to do with a society of accountants. Joe had also been invited and he'd offered to drive Mom and Dad. When he got to the house, Dad asked him to take the photos."

"You know, I've never regretted my decision to leave Oliver's Well all those years ago, but seeing these photos, well . . ." Emma shook her head.

"Well what?" Daniel asked.

Emma shrugged. "I don't know. I guess I would have liked to be with Mom and Dad that night. Maybe if they had told me about the dinner I could have come back for it."

"Assuming you were able to wrangle an invitation," Daniel pointed out. "You weren't part of their crowd. There might not have been a place for you at their table."

Emma frowned. "Thanks for pointing that out, Danny."

Well, Daniel thought, *all I said was the truth.* "I'll be right back," he told the others, heading for the kitchen to retrieve another bottle of wine. It was the third they had opened that evening. Usually he didn't drink much at all, but it had been an emotional day, and tonight, what with the revival of his feelings of loss, he felt the need for something to help him relax and . . . And there was something else he needed help with, but he couldn't quite put his finger on what it was.

"Danny," Emma said when he returned to the living room. "Look at what I just found sticking out from behind this picture." Emma held up a piece of slightly yellowed paper.

"What is it?" he asked.

"It's a love note from Dad to Mom. It was written before they were married. Listen."

"'My beloved Caroline,'" Emma read. "'I'm counting the days—no, the minutes—until we are joined forever as husband and wife. You've already made me the happiest man alive. I can't imagine what additional happiness there is to come, and yet, I look forward to it with all my heart. Your Cliff.'"

"That's lovely," Anna Maria said. "Isn't it, Daniel?"

Daniel didn't respond. He felt . . . Well, he realized, he didn't know exactly how he felt or why. A little bit angry suddenly, but with whom? Sad. Proud. And something else . . . Emma passed the note to Andie, who then passed it to Anna Maria.

"Mom and Dad knew what love and commitment meant," he said finally, and firmly. "They knew what was important. They knew the meaning of family."

Anna Maria passed the note back to Andie, who handed it once again to Emma. "We know that, Danny," Emma said quietly. "You don't need to remind us."

Daniel put his hand out. "I want to keep that note." His sister handed the paper to him without a word. "I'll keep it safe." To himself he added, *I'm the only one who can keep it all safe.*

CHAPTER 58

A ndie watched her brother carefully fold his father's love note to his bride to be and place it in his wallet. Something was wrong with Daniel this evening. For the first time in her life she felt vaguely frightened of her brother. For one, he was drinking way too much and way too quickly. But she felt helpless to do or to say anything. *I'll only make things worse*, she thought. *Again.*

"What's in here?" Emma said, opening an album with blue leather covers. "Pictures of Rumi," she said. Andie looked down at the photos on the open pages. "Rumi's ninth birthday party," Emma read. "That's Mom's writing, isn't it?"

Andie nodded. Slowly Emma turned the pages of the album, and together the sisters watched Rumi's childhood unfold. Rumi in Halloween costumes; Andie recognized her daughter's witch costume but not the big green frog. Rumi in a bathing suit on Virginia Beach. That was the time Bob and his parents had taken her there for vacation, Andie remembered. And then there were the many photos of Rumi with her grandmother. Rumi seated on Caro's lap. Rumi holding Caro's hand. Rumi and Caro with their arms linked.

Of course Rumi is still mourning the loss of her grandmother, Andie thought. *Of course she doesn't like me very much.*

"This is a cute picture," Emma said, pointing at the left-hand page. Rumi looked to be about ten or eleven; she was sitting cross-legged around a campfire with several other girls. Each of the girls was smiling and holding a stick on which a marshmallow had been speared for toasting. Suddenly, Andie became aware of Daniel looming over her.

"It's really too bad you weren't here that summer she went to Girl Scout day camp," he said. "She had so much fun learning how to cook over an open fire and how to tie knots. The girls even went canoeing. But you know all that, Andie, don't you?" Daniel laughed. "Then again, maybe you don't."

Anna Maria cleared her throat. "Daniel. Don't you think—"

But Daniel cut off his wife in midsentence. "I'm sure Bob sent you photos, but there's nothing like being there to watch your child experience the world for the first time. It's all so fleeting. It's a crime to miss it."

"Yes, Danny," Emma said, her voice tight. "That's enough of that."

For a moment no one spoke. Andie stared down at the picture of Rumi seated at the campfire. She thought that now the image would be forever burned on her brain. And suddenly she felt so very tired of feeling guilty and hurt, tired of being battered around by her brother's switching from critical mode to loving sibling and back again. She felt . . . she felt wounded. She felt as if she were bleeding out. If someone asked what her motives were for speaking then, she would honestly have to say sheer exhaustion.

"You're right, Danny," she said, and she could hear the note of defeat in her voice. "You're right about all of it. And you might as well know it from me, before the news gets around town. I spoke to Mary Bernadette Fitzgibbon the other day and promised her the George Bullock desk for the OWHA."

Andie braced herself against the storm she knew was about to strike. Her brother stepped back from the couch. Andie looked up at him and saw the look of horror on his face.

"But we'd decided what to do with the desk!" he cried. "We'd decided *not* to sell it and *not* to give it away! How could you have done something so . . . something so stupid!"

"Daniel," Anna Maria said loudly. "Please."

"There's an easy solution to this, Danny," Emma said quickly but calmly. "If Andie didn't sign anything promising the desk to OWHA we can simply not deliver it. We can tell Mary Bernadette that we've changed our minds."

"I didn't sign anything," Andie assured her family. "It was a verbal agreement. I know a verbal agreement has value but . . ."

Emma took her hand. "Don't worry, Andie. I'll stop by the Wilson House tomorrow and take care of it."

Daniel, it seemed, was not to be appeased. "I want to know why you ignored the family's decision," he demanded, his face growing red. "I want to know what in God's name made you so carelessly give away our mother's most cherished possession!"

Andie said nothing.

"It's all right, Andie," Anna Maria said. Andie saw with sorrow that her sister-in-law looked as if she had aged ten years in the past few minutes. "No real harm was done. Daniel—"

But once again he cut off whatever it was his wife was about to say. "If anyone has the right to go against Mom's wishes, which all three of us agreed on—how to dispose of the important items—then it's me." He jabbed his chest with his forefinger. "I'm the one who's been doing all the hard work since Dad died!"

"Oh, Danny, not again," Andie murmured.

"You're not in the least bit sorry for what you did, are you?" Daniel demanded.

Andie took a deep breath. "I *am* sorry. It was wrong of me. I was upset. I wasn't thinking clearly. That's not an excuse, just the truth."

Daniel waved his hand in a gesture of disbelief.

Anna Maria got up from her chair and sat on Andie's left. Andie felt grateful for her show of support; still, she felt guilty that she was the one responsible for this terrible scene.

"You've never cared about the family," Daniel went on, pacing in front of the couch. Behind him on the television screen was the stilled image of Anna Maria and Caro at the wedding shower Andie had not attended.

"That's not true," Andie answered quietly, trying to ignore the taunting image.

"Yes, it is. At the ceremony this morning you couldn't even find something original to say about our parents. No, you had to quote that stupid dead poet again!"

"I thought the words were lovely," Emma said firmly, "and entirely appropriate. And my words weren't original, either. Be fair, Danny."

Daniel shot her a frown and turned back to Andie. "And the way you just gave away Mom's desk—our very *heritage*—as if it means nothing!"

Andie folded her hands tightly in her lap and said as calmly as she could, "You're obsessed with things, Danny. You're held prisoner by the material. The concern you show for the most minute and inconsequential contents of this house, envelopes stuffed with out of date coupons, soup spoons and fish forks, that ridiculous desk. Danny, let it go. It's making you so unhappy."

"Things have meaning," Daniel argued. "They hold our memories."

Andie sighed. "Things are nothing, Danny. The memories are inside you."

Anna Maria stood abruptly. "This—this conversation," she said, her voice trembling, "is leading nowhere. I suggest we call it a night and—"

"Mind your own business, Anna Maria," Emma cut in. "This is between siblings. And Andie is right. Danny's behavior is troubling. I for one am tired of it."

Andie was shocked. She had never heard her sister use such a tone or such words to their sister-in-law, to anyone. She tried to catch Emma's eye, but Emma wouldn't look up from her lap.

There was a moment of heavy silence. Andie half expected

Daniel to defend his wife against Emma's harsh words, but he didn't. Instead, he turned and stalked off toward the kitchen. "I need another drink," he said, letting the kitchen door slam behind him. And instead of going after her husband, Anna Maria quietly returned to her chair.

CHAPTER 59

Emma felt that every breath was a challenge. She was shocked and embarrassed by how she had spoken to her sister-in-law; she had never been so rude to anyone in her life. She lifted her head and turned to Anna Maria, who was sitting in the armchair she had occupied earlier. Anna Maria looked stricken, almost ill. Emma was about to apologize sincerely and profusely when Daniel came storming back from the kitchen, clutching a half-empty bottle of wine by the neck.

"And you're not much better than Andie," he said, pointing a finger at Emma.

This is getting worse by the minute, Emma thought. *I've got to stop this.* But she realized she had no idea of how.

"Joe told me about the conversation he had with you the other day," Daniel went on. "He told me that you were upset Mom chose me to be the trustee of her estate and not you, the big expert. How could you have doubted my abilities, my honesty?"

Emma shook her head. "I never doubted your honesty, Danny, not for a moment, and I certainly never told Joe that I had. And my wondering about your qualifications was my problem," she argued, "not yours. You did a great job. I just felt—"

"You felt that I was incompetent. You felt that I'd make a mess of the estate."

Emma could deny it no longer; her brother was now clearly drunk. It would be best, she thought, to keep her mouth shut and let Daniel run out of steam. There was never any use in arguing with someone under the influence.

"And you still haven't chosen a real estate agent like I asked you to!" Daniel said, gesturing with the open wine bottle and sloshing some of the wine onto the carpet. "The one thing I asked you to handle and you let me down."

"I'm working on it, Danny," Emma said quietly.

"How hard can it possibly be, especially after I did all the real leg work? Are you just lazy, is that it?"

Emma said nothing. She could feel Andie's distress; it was emanating from her like a wave of heat. Her own distress had made her grow cold. She could only guess at how bad Anna Maria was feeling.

Daniel had more to say. He put the bottle of wine onto the coffee table with a thud. "I don't know how I put up with the two of you. You didn't even want to take part in this morning's memorial service."

"That's simply not true!" Andie protested, her voice strained.

"Danny," Emma said, now seriously angry and insulted, "cut it out. You're acting like an insane person."

Daniel chuckled and shot a pointed look at Andie. "Me, the insane one? I think you're talking about our sister. I was the one Mom and Dad turned to and trusted, right from the start. I was the one who mattered to them."

Emma could hold her tongue no longer. She didn't care that Daniel was drunk. She didn't care what he thought or said about her at this point, but she would not allow her sister to be defamed and mocked yet again. Still, she was hardly aware of the words that spilled from her mouth. "You think you know everything about our parents, but they were *ours*, Danny, not yours exclusively."

"I was *here*."

Emma laughed and shook her head. "I bet you don't even know that Mom broke her first engagement to some high society type to marry Dad." She felt her sister's hand on her arm, but restraint was no good now. The words were out.

Daniel's face became even more alarmingly red. "You're lying!" he cried.

"Why would I lie, Danny? What possible good could it do for me to lie about something like that?"

And then the unthinkable happened. Daniel stalked over to the fireplace and with one violent movement he tore the portrait of Cliff and Caro off the wall and threw it across the room. The painting landed against an end table, a corner of which tore through the canvas, leaving a brutal looking slash from Cliff's forehead down through Caro's shoulder.

Emma's hand flew to her mouth. She was horrified. She thought she might be sick. An unpleasant tingle ran through her from head to toe, as if she had experienced a bad electric shock. She glanced at her sister and thought she had never seen such a genuine look of fear on anyone's face. Anna Maria had gone deadly white.

After what seemed like an eternal moment, Daniel, breathing heavily, but in a very controlled voice, spoke. "Why don't the two of you just pack up and go back to where you came from," he said. "I was stupid to think that I needed you here. Leave and I'll take care of everything like I always have and let you know what I decide. If you even care to know."

With that he turned and began to stalk toward the front door. Anna Maria leapt from her seat and reached for his arm. "Daniel, no," she cried, but he yanked his arm from her grasp and snatched his coat from the hall closet, sending the hanger clanging to the floor.

Anna Maria was crying now, and without looking at Emma or Andie, she grabbed her own coat and followed her husband out of the house.

The house seemed steeped in silence, a heavy, thick thing that threatened to choke Emma. She thought she would almost rather the sound of voices raised in anger to this shocking quiet.

Finally, she found her voice. "I guess we should clear all this away," she said, helpless to say anything important, anything meaningful.

Andie got up from her chair. "It will wait until morning," she said, and she left the living room without another word.

A moment later Emma heard the door to the den close firmly and quietly. She surveyed the wreckage of the evening, the wine stain on the carpet, the destroyed portrait, the photo albums strewn on couch and chairs and coffee table, the videos separated from their cases. Andie was right, she thought. There was nothing here that couldn't wait. With some effort she got up from the couch, turned out the lights, and slowly climbed the stairs to her bed.

CHAPTER 60

Emma looked down at her empty plate. "I'm surprised I have an appetite after last night's scene," she said to her sister. "I literally devoured those eggs."

"I think my finally confessing to promising the desk to the OWHA revived my appetite," Andie said ruefully, eyeing her own empty plate. "More's the pity."

"And I slept like the proverbial log. I was sure I was going to be wide awake, replaying every awful moment of the argument."

"The calm after the storm?" Andie wondered. "Or simply our bodies being smart enough to take over in order to give our minds a much needed rest."

"I wonder if Danny was able to get any sleep." Emma shook her head. "Until last night I didn't fully recognize the depth of his pain. He must have seen our behavior toward the whole question about the sale of the estate and the future of Mom's desk as an insult."

Andie nodded. "I agree. I mean, I knew he was under a lot of pressure, self-imposed or not, but I had no idea he was *so* near the breaking point. I feel bad. I should have seen what was really going on."

"Still, throwing the painting . . ." Emma shook her head.

"It was pretty extreme. Danny's never shown a temper like that. He must have been building up to that for weeks, months."

"It's funny," Emma said, "but I thought he seemed calm and at peace at the memorial service. I thought that maybe he'd let go of some of the tension he seemed to be holding. I guess I was wrong."

"The calm *before* the storm?" Andie grimaced. "I have to say I always hated that painting of Mom and Dad. I don't know why."

"You, too?" Emma asked. "It really was pretty awful. I suppose it was technically good, but there was something off about it. Anyway, I shouldn't have used the fact of Mom's first engagement as a weapon. It was childish of me, even mean. I wanted to hurt Danny. I wanted to shock him out of his complacency, his assumption of status as Keeper of the Flame."

"None of us acted beautifully last night," Andie said. "Except for Anna Maria. You have to admire her loyalty to Danny. She could have justifiably walked out on him when he threw the painting."

Emma shook her head. "If Ian had ever behaved like Danny did last night I probably would have walked out on him for *good* at that very moment."

"The difference is that Anna Maria loves Danny. You never loved Ian. Sorry," Andie said. "That's educated guesswork."

"No, you're right," Emma admitted, toying with her fork. "I thought I loved him for a while, but it wasn't really love, not the right kind anyway. Still, there are limits to what someone should put up with, love or not."

"I don't think Anna Maria is suffering at the hands of a violent lunatic, Emma. Danny's going through a crisis, a dark night of the soul maybe, that's all. I believe that."

"Like what Rumi is going through?" Emma asked carefully. "And you?"

Andie sighed. "Maybe."

Emma reached across the table and put her hand on her sister's arm. "Andie, I wish you had told me about promising the desk to the OWHA. I could have gone to Mary Bernadette before Danny had to know and told her there had been a mistake. I can handle her. I'm my mother's daughter. No one could intimidate Caro Carlyle Reynolds and no one can intimidate me. Well, almost no one."

Andie smiled. "I *should* have gone to you. I was tempted to more than once, but honestly, I was just so embarrassed by what I had done. I was paralyzed."

"You don't have to be embarrassed with me. Remember when I was in college and I thought I was pregnant and came crawling to you, begging for you to help me out? And you did. You were great. You didn't try to make me feel ashamed that I'd been stupid enough to have unprotected sex."

"I just did what any big sister would do. And thanks for the offer of talking to Mary Bernadette, but that's something I need to do on my own."

"If you're sure."

"I am. Anyway, I think Bob should know what happened here last night," Andie said. "I'll call him a bit later. But no one else."

"You mean not Rumi. Of course."

"Yes. Well, what do we do now?"

"I'm completely out of ideas," Emma admitted. "I think we should call Anna Maria and let her advise us about how to go forward."

Andie nodded and reached for her phone. "I'll call her right now."

CHAPTER 61

Andie and her sister met with Anna Maria at Cookies 'n Crumpets at two that afternoon. After ordering—an herbal tea for herself, a latte for Emma, and a decaf coffee for Anna Maria—the women sat at the table furthest from the others.

"Privacy," Anna Maria said, "is hard to come by in this town. I suppose we should have met at the house but..." She half laughed. "I've had enough of Thirty-Two Honeysuckle Lane for the moment."

"Thanks for agreeing to see us at all after last night's . . . I don't even know what to call it," Andie admitted.

"Debacle? Meltdown?" Emma shrugged. "Whatever it was, I'm glad it's over."

Anna Maria sighed. "Me, too. But things can't magically go back to the way they were before Daniel became so . . . It's just that he's so emotionally invested in the family. In the *idea* of family. He wasn't always this way. It's only since Cliff died and Caro became ill that he became, well, became obsessed. The family means so much to him, too much at times."

"It must be hard on you," Andie said. "You must feel ignored. You must feel that sometimes Danny doesn't really see you."

"Honestly," Anna Maria admitted, "yes, it can be hard, and yes,

I do sometimes feel ignored, though I know that Daniel loves me. Since Caro's passing he's been ratcheting up. Frankly, when he told me he was going to insist you both be here for Christmas I was worried. I half suspected something like what happened last night was going to happen."

Andie put her hand on her sister-in-law's arm. "You couldn't have done anything to stop it, you know that. Danny was angry. He wasn't focused on the truth. He was focused on himself."

Anna Maria shrugged. "Maybe I couldn't have stopped it. Still . . ."

"I'm sorry I told you to butt out when you tried to calm things down," Emma said. "Only days before I was hoping that you would take a more vocal part in our crazy family matters. I shouldn't have spoken to you so harshly."

"It was the heat of the moment," Anna Maria said. "You're forgiven. And maybe I shouldn't have tried to butt in. It's the peacekeeper in me."

Andie shook her head. "You should have thrown a bucket of cold water over us all. How is Danny today?"

"Besides a bit hung over? Miserable. He's not a drinker. I don't know what possessed him last night, but I think he learned his lesson."

Andie smiled. "Danny did us a favor actually, destroying that painting. Emma and I were saying this morning that neither of us liked it. Dad's eyes seemed to follow you around the room. And the expression on Mom's face made her look like she was about to be sick to her stomach."

"Daniel wants to get it repaired," Anna Maria told them.

"That would cost a fortune," Emma said. "He shouldn't bother, really."

"I agree," Anna Maria said. "I think that if he can manage to let the painting go, it might be a symbolic gesture, something that helps him to let go of his grip on his parents as people he still needs to please and impress. Maybe he can finally live out from under their shadow."

Andie nodded. "I think you're right. It would be good for

Danny to let the painting go. But for now it can stay in the hall closet where I put it this morning."

"So, how do you think we should approach Danny?" Emma asked.

Anna Maria frowned. "He should be the one to approach you. He owes you both a big apology and he knows it."

"It doesn't matter who approaches whom," Andie said, "as long as we all make peace."

"Will you tell him that we three talked?" Emma asked. "I don't want him to think Andie and I are actually going to leave Oliver's Well before Christmas because of a stupid fight."

Anna Maria smiled. "I doubt he really meant that you should go. He so wanted to spend Christmas with you both. Not all of his reasons had to do with the estate. He genuinely misses you two. "

"We *will* spend Christmas together," Andie said. "Emma and I aren't going anywhere." *At least*, she added silently, *not yet*.

CHAPTER 62

Emma was tired but she hadn't wanted to go back to the house quite yet, so after dropping Andie off she drove out to Shepherd Pond at the very edge of Oliver's Well. There was a good walking and running path around the pond, and at a time like this, when quiet thought seemed necessary, it was the perfect destination.

The air was chill and the sky was a dead sort of gray; Emma smiled at how well the weather seemed to mirror her own mood. As she walked along the groomed path she thought about the conversation she and Andie had had with Anna Maria, and what they had learned about their brother's increasingly troubled state of mind this last year. And she wondered again if moving back to Oliver's Well was a good idea after all. Would she, too, find herself sucked into the trap of the past her brother seemed to have been sucked into? No, she thought. It was highly unlikely. She and Daniel were very different people. She had wanted and needed in equal measure to leave the proverbial nest far behind, and a return at this point would be a very conscious choice. Besides, that nest was no longer what it had been. It had changed; she had changed; everything had changed. As Andie would say, the only sure thing in life was impermanence.

Emma stopped at one of the stone benches along the path and

looked out over the still water, steely gray in the December light. She felt her breathing slow and a sort of calm come over her. At the very least, she thought, she would stay in Oliver's Well for a few more days. If things got really unbearable—if in spite of Anna Maria's assurances, Daniel refused to apologize or to accept an apology—she would go back to Annapolis and spend Christmas alone. It wouldn't be the first time. And it wouldn't preclude the eventual possibility of a permanent move back to Oliver's Well. . . .

A group of ducks waddled their way out of the water's edge and onto the path only yards from where Emma stood. Though they looked well fed, she wished she had brought some bread for them. Next time, she promised as, hands thrust in her pockets, she turned back toward her car. But when would that next time be?

As for Morgan, well, she would be reluctant to leave before getting some sure sense of what or what might not be happening between them. She knew it would be difficult to get to know Morgan from Annapolis; long distance romances were never easy. Assuming, of course, Morgan wanted a romance with her. Yes, he had kissed her, but a kiss wasn't necessarily a promise.

Emma gazed once more at the pond before getting behind the wheel of her Lexus. No, she thought, a kiss wasn't necessarily a promise. But it had been a very nice kiss.

CHAPTER 63

Daniel was making dinner for his family. *My family*, he thought, slicing cucumbers for a salad. *My wife and my children. Maybe the only family I have left.*

Anna Maria was sitting at the kitchen bar, her laptop open in front of her. She was balancing the family's personal checking account, one of the many chores she routinely undertook, as was managing the finances of their business.

"I can't believe I actually threw that painting," Daniel said to his wife, his voice low. The last thing he wanted was for the children to get wind of what had happened the night before. To lose their respect would be devastating. "I've never done anything like that in my life. It frightened me."

"It frightened me, too," Anna Maria replied, closing her laptop with a small sigh. "Daniel, this . . . this fixation with the family has got to stop. You've got to get some perspective."

"I know. I think it was hearing about my mother's first engagement that just—that just made me lose it. Why it should matter is beyond me, but at that moment . . . I've got some serious thinking to do, don't I? I've got to settle some big emotional issues concerning the family. I guess I've known that for a while, but just couldn't. . . ."

"You'll do it, Daniel," Anna Maria said encouragingly. "And I'm here to help if you need me."

Daniel felt tears come to his eyes; he put down his knife and reached for his wife's hand. "I always need you," he said. "And I always will."

"I spoke to your sisters earlier. We met for coffee."

Daniel cringed. "Do they hate me?"

Anna Maria laughed. "Daniel, don't be ridiculous. They love you. They want to make peace."

"Can you imagine what Mom would have thought if she knew I'd destroyed the portrait? She would have been so disappointed in me. Dad, too, but especially Mom. She . . . She expected so much of me."

"Daniel," Anna Maria said, "it shouldn't matter what your mother would have thought. She's gone. You're here. You have to let her go, your father, too. I need you to come back to me, Daniel. To me and to the children."

As if summoned by his wife's words, Sophia and Marco came thundering into the kitchen. "I'm starving, Dad," his daughter announced. "When's dinner?"

"I'm *famished*!" Marco added.

Daniel laughed. "Where did you hear that word?"

"On TV. I was watching one of those cooking shows you say are so silly."

"Well, I guess not all of them are silly if they help increase your vocabulary. What other new words have you learned?"

Marco scrunched up his face in thought. "Succulent," he said. "And daube. That's French."

"Are you sure you don't want to be a chef when you grow up?" Daniel asked.

"I'm one hundred percent certain, Dad. That's another way of saying I'm sure."

Anna Maria laughed. "Maybe you'll be a writer, Marco."

"Do they make a lot of money?" he asked.

Daniel shrugged. "Some of them do, I guess."

"Then I'll consider it. That's another way of saying I'll think about it."

"So, like half an hour?" Sophia demanded. "My stomach is literally growling."

"Half an hour," Daniel promised. Satisfied with his answer, both children ran from the kitchen.

Daniel picked up his knife again and got back to preparing the meal. And for some reason he suddenly remembered that popular expression from long before his time, "let go and let live." The message there was pretty wise. He smiled. What would Andie say if she knew he was turning to the world of forty-year-old self-help for guidance?

"What's got you smiling?" Anna Maria asked, opening her laptop again.

Daniel shrugged. "Life," he said. "Broccoli or peas tonight?"

CHAPTER 64

The meeting with the people at R. W. Simons in Westminster had gone well; Emma had been grateful for Morgan's professional presence. They had taken only one car, Morgan's, for convenience, and on the ride back to Oliver's Well Emma realized that neither of them had said a word for a full ten minutes. Just as she was about to rectify that, Morgan spoke.

"You seem a bit preoccupied today," Morgan said. "Anything the matter? You said you thought the meeting went well."

"I did say that and I meant it." Emma hesitated, but only for a moment. "It's just that there was a big to-do at the house the other night. Let's just say a lot of old grievances were aired, some of them kind of surprising, others, not so much."

"Sounds upsetting. I've never been one for controversy or confrontation."

"It *was* upsetting," Emma said. "It wasn't a pleasant scene for any of us, but mostly for Danny. He's been under such strain these past few years, taking care of my mother and the estate on his own. He pretty much accused Andie and me of neglecting our duty to Mom."

Morgan sighed. "Ah. Habits and family dynamics die hard. And slowly."

"Yes, they do," Emma said ruefully. "Anyway, enough of my drama. I've been meaning to ask what you're doing for Christmas."

"I'll be spending Christmas with my parents and the dreaded Aunt Agatha in Baltimore." Morgan glanced over with a grin. "Seriously, she's the definition of the Formidable Aunt."

"What do you mean?" Emma asked.

"Have you ever read the Jeeves and Wooster stories, or seen the TV adaptation with Hugh Laurie and Stephen Fry?"

Emma felt her eyes go wide. "You're not saying she's like Bertie's Aunt Agatha?"

"Yes, I am, minus the little white dog. Aunt Agatha's got the meanest, most ornery cat I've ever had the displeasure of meeting. Anyway, I suppose she means well, but she dominates the entire family, even the others of her generation." Morgan laughed. "She holds us in fear and trembling by the terror of her ways."

"A slight exaggeration?"

"Yes," Morgan admitted, "but only slight. Well, here we are."

Morgan pulled up to number 32 Honeysuckle Lane and took Emma's hand in his. "Call me if you want to," he said. "Any time, even after I've gone to Baltimore."

"Thanks," Emma said. "It's very kind of you."

Morgan laughed. "There's something in it for me, too. I always appreciate a break from Aunt Agatha and her cat from hell!"

He released her hand after a final gentle squeeze, and Emma got out of the car. She watched for a moment as Morgan drove away. Yes, she thought with a smile, in spite of the challenges, she was glad she had stayed on in Oliver's Well.

And now, there was an apology she had to make.

Emma found her brother in his professional kitchen, what was formerly the garage, chopping a mound of leeks. There was a tantalizing smell of sautéing onions in the air, and though she had eaten lunch after Morgan had dropped her home, Emma felt her stomach growl.

"Hey," she said.

Daniel looked up from the chopping board, clearly startled. "Oh. Hi," he said. "I didn't hear you come in."

"You were absorbed with your work. I'm sorry to disturb you."

"You're not disturbing me. Here, have a seat." Daniel put down his knife and gestured toward a stool that stood next to the main work counter.

"I just came from the auction house in Westminster," Emma told him. "Morgan was nice enough to come with me. He thinks they're perfect for our needs, and from what I learned today, I agree. And their price is competitive."

"Good," Daniel said. "Thanks."

Emma thought she had never seen her brother look so awkward or pained. "Danny," she said, without wasting more time, "what I really came here to tell you is that I'm sorry for my behavior the other night. And for my words. I'm sorry for using that information about Mom and her broken engagement like a weapon."

Daniel ran a hand through his hair and sighed. "I'm sorry, too, Emma," he said. Emma thought he sounded both weary and relieved. "I don't know what came over me. Well, yes, I guess I do. At least, I'm working on figuring it all out."

"Family can be . . . It can be difficult, both the reality of it and the idea of it. All the expectations and assumptions and misperceptions that go along with trying to find our place in it, in trying to break away from it. All the hurt feelings. All the loss. All the anger." Emma shook her head. "And yet, where would any of us be without family?"

"I have absolutely no idea," Daniel admitted with a smile. "I should have come to you, Emma. I'm sorry."

Emma smiled. "Does it matter? We're here now, together."

"And I am sorry for being a bit of a jerk all around since you and Andie have been back home."

"You're forgiven. Though you did have me worried. It was so unlike you to be, well, jerky."

Daniel managed another small smile. "I think I worried myself, too! So, Mom really left her high society fiancé for Dad?"

"That's what Rumi tells us."

"It's actually pretty impressive of Mom, to realize true love when she saw it and not to be afraid of changing the direction of her life so radically."

Emma nodded. *As I'm doing?* she wondered. "I agree."

"I miss Dad and Mom," Daniel said bluntly. "I can't help it. I do."

"I think that's perfectly normal, Danny."

"And I'm angry they died. I'm angry they were ultimately unknowable."

Anger, Emma thought. *It was anger at our parents, not Andie and me, that made Danny throw that portrait.*

"I'm sorry, Danny," Emma said gently.

"Do you miss them?" he asked.

"It's odd," Emma said, "but I don't. It's almost as if they were enough of a force in my life. If I'm honest, almost too much of a force at times. Now that they're gone, I breathe more easily. The memories are enough for me."

"I think I envy you. You know, I shouldn't have accused you and Andie of not caring about Mom or Dad. It's just that I've been under so much pressure for so long. . . ."

"Even when we choose a role in life," Emma said, "it can become suffocating. We can feel trapped by our choices because, let's face it, even at its best, life is never easy."

Daniel smiled. "That's putting it mildly. By the way, do you find that you're missing Ian the closer it gets to Christmas? This is your first holiday season apart in a long time, and I can't imagine *that* is easy."

"No," Emma said. "I'm not missing him at all, and that confirms I made the right choice. A liberating choice, finally."

Daniel put both hands on the counter on either side of the cutting board and hung his head, as if the board itself held something far more interesting than cut vegetables.

"What is it, Danny?" Emma asked gently.

Daniel continued to stare at the board as he spoke. "The first time I saw Mom in one of those humiliating johnnies, the first time she got sick after Dad died, her arms so thin, the skin almost papery, it was like something in me just shattered. It was like my childhood, something I thought had ended long before, only ended at that moment, abruptly, almost violently. Even though I had married and was raising a family and had started a successful business, I was still a child, my mother's child, until I was confronted by the sight of her in that hospital bed. And then I finally realized that she was no longer the woman I had known all my life, not really. And after that, every time I sat with her in a doctor's waiting room or paced the hallway waiting for her to come out of the exam room, I felt . . . I *felt* every emotion so strongly." Finally, Daniel looked up at Emma. "I'd never realized just how much I loved her," he said, his voice trembling, "how much I wanted to be the one to take care of her, even when it was difficult or inconvenient, which it was at times."

Emma felt her heart break a little for her brother. "Oh, Danny," she said. "I'm so sorry."

"It's hard being sick, you know. A patient is so vulnerable, so utterly dependent. It's a half-life really, being ill. Mom didn't talk much about it, but I could tell she felt . . . demeaned. Useless."

"Surely not unwanted though, not with you there?" Emma asked.

"No," Daniel admitted. "I think she knew she was still wanted. Just not . . . necessary."

Emma shook her head. "I wish you had told me these things, Danny. I wish you had let me know how stressed you were feeling. I would have listened. And I would have tried to help." Emma considered for a moment. "Though I probably should have been the one to ask if you needed help. I'm sorry, Danny. I let you carry the full burden of Mom's care."

"I *wanted* to carry it," he told her. "I *wanted* to feel indispensable. I just didn't think about how trying to do it all on my own was going to affect me in the end. It took its toll, didn't it?"

"Yes. But you don't have to bear that weight any longer, Danny. Mom and Dad are gone, but the family still exists, and it will go on existing in some form or another without your having to exhaust yourself to keep it alive."

"I guess I'll have to learn to believe that. Emma?" Daniel said. "Do you think Andie will forgive me? I've been pretty rotten to her, as you, Bob, and my wife have pointed out to me."

"I'm sure she already has forgiven you," Emma said with a smile. "You know our Andie. She's as close as a Reynolds is ever going to come to being a saint."

"But she's still a human being," Daniel said. "Vulnerable. Easily hurt. Sometimes I forget that when I think of her. I see her as, I don't know, as a troublemaker, I guess. Anna Maria has told me it's unfair of me to think that way. I know she's right, but I still have a hard time letting go of all these assumptions I made about Andie years ago. That she was cold. That she was selfish. That she shakes things up just to get a reaction out of us."

Emma wasn't entirely surprised to hear these words from her brother. But it did sadden her that Andie had been so deeply misunderstood—and that poor Daniel had been drained by such uncharitable opinions. "I think," she said, "that Andie feels more than any of us. I think she feels things more *immediately*, if that makes sense. By the way, did you tell Rumi that Andie promised Mom's desk to the OWHA?"

"God no," Daniel said, eyes wide.

"Good. I don't want Andie to suffer anymore than she already has this holiday, and I suspect that if Rumi found out about what her mother did she would react badly."

"I'm afraid you're right. And that's partly my fault, too, trying to drive a wedge between mother and daughter, and for what?" Daniel shook his head. "For my own childish needs."

"Now, stop being so hard on yourself, Danny," Emma said, getting off the stool. "What's done is done and we're all moving on. I'll let you get back to whatever delicious dish you're preparing."

"Cream of leek and potato soup."

"And who are the lucky people getting to eat this luscious-sounding soup?" she asked.

"The guests of Mr. Neal Hyatt and Mr. Gregory Smith. By the

way, Neal is a member of the OWHA. I doubt he'd approach me about the Bullock desk when I'm at his home on a professional basis. But if he does . . ."

"If he does," Emma said, "just demur. Andie wants to be the one to tell Mrs. Fitzgibbon the offer no longer stands."

"Agreed."

Emma gave her brother a hug—which he returned warmly— and went out to her car. The conversation had gone so much better than she had expected, and she felt grateful that Daniel had trusted her enough to share his thoughts and feelings again. Now, she thought, starting the engine of the Lexus, if only her brother would make a pot of cream of leek and potato soup for her.

CHAPTER 65

Andie was sitting on the couch in the living room, flipping through one of the art books she had found in the den—this one featured the paintings of the Italian Renaissance—and sipping a cup of the tea blend she had bought (somewhat blindly) at the Eclectic Gourmet.

Emma had gone to meet Maureen for dinner at the Angry Squire. She had told Andie that she and Daniel had reconciled that afternoon and that he had apologized for his behavior toward both sisters, but Andie found that she couldn't quite work up the energy to face him just yet. The intensity of her brother's anger the other evening still weighed on her; she needed a bit more time to let the memory of that anger dissipate so that she would be able to speak clearly and, more importantly, to listen carefully.

Andie turned the next page in the book to find an image of Raphael's *Madonna of the Chair.* The warm and intimate family portrait of Mary, her baby son, Jesus, and a young Saint John the Baptist, was one of Bob's favorite paintings. Andie sighed. Bob, too, had been deeply troubled by Daniel's outburst, surprised by Andie's promising the Bullock desk to the OWHA, and distressed about Emma's so callously revealing the fact of Caro's first engagement. But he had also voiced his sincere compassion for all three of the siblings. "Don't forget," he told Andie, "the holidays often bring out the pain we thought we had safely buried." And in that, Bob Dolman was absolutely right.

Suddenly, there was a loud and insistent knocking on the front door. Andie put her cup of tea on the end table, the book on the cushion next to her, and got up from the couch. She opened the door to find her daughter standing there, her expression grim.

"I need to talk to you." Rumi strode past her mother and into the living room.

Andie's heart sank. She knew why her daughter had come. The truth about her foolish action had come out. Very little in a small town could stay hidden, and certainly not something as ill considered as she had done. "All right," she said. "Why don't we sit down?"

"I'll stand," Rumi said. Her voice was hard. "I ran into Joyce Miller just now, when I was coming out of the Angry Squire. Imagine my surprise when she told me how happy she was that my mother had given Grandma's heirloom desk to the OWHA. And imagine how totally stupid I felt when she realized from the look on my face that I knew nothing about it."

For a moment Andie was speechless. She had no clear idea how to explain why she had done what she had done. She couldn't admit that she might have promised Mary Bernadette Fitzgibbon the desk in retaliation for her brother's hurtful remarks about her, or that . . .

"Well?" Rumi demanded. "What do you have to say for yourself? Does Uncle Daniel know about this?"

"He knows," she said. "So do Emma and Anna Maria. Look, Rumi, I'm so sorry. Sometimes I . . . Sometimes I don't get things right. Sometimes I act foolishly. But don't worry. I'm going to tell the OWHA there's been a mistake. Grandma's desk isn't going anywhere."

Rumi laughed a bit wildly. "But you can't change the fact that you did what you did. You gave it away!"

"No," Andie said, "I can't change that fact. But I can make reparation."

"Not everything can be fixed, Mom. Some things just stay broken."

"Rumi, I—"

Rumi shook her head in obvious disgust. "I'm out of here," she said.

"Rumi, wait!" Andie cried. "Don't run off like this!"

But Rumi ignored her mother's pleas. She stalked out of the living room, slamming the front door behind her.

Andie sank into the nearest armchair and put her head in her hands. The words of her favorite poet came to her then to ease the passing of grief. "Suffering is a gift. In it is hidden mercy." But this time, the words failed to support her.

The sound of the front door opening startled her; she wiped futilely at the tears now coursing down her cheeks. It was Emma. "Andie, my God," she said, hurrying to her sister's side. "What's wrong?"

A sob escaped Andie in place of words. Emma knelt and put her arms around her sister and began to smooth her hair away from her forehead. "It's all right," she whispered soothingly. "It's all right."

But at that dreadful moment, Andie felt that nothing would be all right ever again.

CHAPTER 66

"Bob? It's me."

"Good morning, Andie. Sleep well?" he asked.

"No," she said, her grip on her phone tightening. Her eyes were still swollen from crying so much the night before, and there was a dull ache in her forehead. "I'm sure you know by now that Rumi found out about my offering my mother's desk to the OWHA."

Bob sighed. "Yes, I know. I got an earful last night."

"Bob," Andie asked, "will you come with me this morning to see Mrs. Fitzgibbon? I have to make this right before more time passes."

Bob agreed and an hour later the two of them were standing on Haven Street, looking up at the Wilson House.

"It looks particularly imposing this morning," Andie said, with an attempt at a laugh.

Bob squeezed her shoulder. "There's no reason it should. There's nothing inside this building that can hurt you, Andie, not unless you let it."

Andie sighed. "I know. Well, let's get this over with."

Together they climbed the steps and went inside. The volunteer receptionist—the same woman whom Andie had seen days earlier—welcomed them and sent them off to Mary Bernadette's office. Mrs. Fitzgibbon was dressed much as she had been at

Nora Campbell's party, in a conservative but pretty skirt suit in a pale neutral color.

"What can I do for you, Ms. Reynolds?" Mary Bernadette asked, nodding as well to Bob, who stood a little behind and to the right of Andie, a silent but sure support.

With a deep breath Andie began. "I regret," she said, "that I have to withdraw the offer of the George Bullock desk to the OWHA. I misunderstood my family's intentions. I'm so sorry for any inconvenience I've caused."

The expression of pleasant expectation on Mrs. Fitzgibbon's face didn't budge. "Yes, well," she said after a moment, "I'd be lying if I said this isn't a disappointment. But the OWHA will go on without the addition of the Bullock piece."

"Thank you," Andie said. "Again, I apologize."

"Of course, if you ever change your mind . . ."

Andie nodded, and she and Bob left the Wilson House behind. "I think," Andie said, as they walked toward the parking lot, "that was one of the most difficult things I've had to do in a long time."

"But you did it and survived. Look," Bob said, when they had reached Andie's car. "I'll tell Daniel that you spoke to Mrs. Fitzgibbon. And I'm going to suggest that he seriously consider your idea of loaning the heirloom to the OWHA for a few years. Maybe he'll listen to me since he's not been in the habit of listening to his sisters."

"That might be about to change," Andie told him. "Emma says she had a very good conversation with him yesterday afternoon. He apologized for having treated the both of us unfairly."

Bob smiled. "Still, it can't hurt for me to chime in."

Andie smiled back gratefully. "Thank you, Bob, for everything."

"You going to be okay?" he asked.

"Yes," she said. "I will be." And she *did* believe now that she would be okay.

Andie got into her car and watched in the rearview mirror as her former husband, the father of her only child, her dearest friend, got into his own car and drove out of the lot.

CHAPTER 67

Daniel had inspired Emma to try her own hand at making cream of leek and potato soup, and Andie had readily volunteered to help with the prep. While Emma peeled and sliced potatoes, Andie washed and chopped the leeks.

And while Emma performed the simple and oddly soothing task of peeling and slicing, she found herself trying to imagine Morgan, gentle, nonconfrontational Morgan, standing up against the formidable Aunt Agatha, whom she now pictured as looking exactly like the character in the Stephen Fry and Hugh Laurie version of P. G. Wodehouse's stories, complete with antiquated dress and stern frown.

"What's got you so happy?" Andie asked, pausing in her chopping. "You're smiling."

"Oh, nothing," Emma demurred. "I just remembered something funny I heard on TV the other night." *Really*, she thought, *why don't I just tell Andie what I was imagining? Why the need for adolescent secrecy?*

"Thanks for taking care of that wine stain on the living room carpet," Andie said. "I wonder if Danny even remembers spilling the bottle."

Emma smiled. "I doubt he does or he would have had a professional cleaning service here by now." She hesitated a moment before asking, "No word from Rumi?"

Andie shook her head. "No. And I don't expect there to be, not for some time anyway."

Emma sighed. "I'm so sorry the rift between you and Rumi has widened. But I'm glad you talked to Mrs. Fitzgibbon this morning. I'm sure it wasn't easy."

"It wasn't," Andie said, "but with Bob at my side, I managed. And though Mary Bernadette might be intimidating, she's extremely polite. I didn't fear that she was going to subject me to a tongue-lashing. And I don't think she's the type to go around bad-mouthing me to others after the fact."

"I agree. I expect she'll put a very genteel spin on the story. After all, she won't want to look like someone who was duped."

Andie visibly cringed. "Gosh, I hope she doesn't suspect me of purposely fooling her about the desk!"

"I'm sure she doesn't," Emma said hurriedly. "By the way, I told Maureen last night about what happened here with Danny. Not all of it, just enough for her to get the gist. I felt I could really use the perspective of someone who isn't family but who knows us well."

"Was she helpful?" Andie asked.

"She listened, and that's the most important thing. "

"That well might be. Does Maureen know about my promising Mom's desk to the OWHA?"

"Yeah. Remember, her mother is a board member and Mary Bernadette's dearest friend. There are no secrets in that bunch."

"Yet another scandal for me to live down in Oliver's Well."

"Hardly a scandal."

"Just an embarrassment. You know," Andie said, "I've been wondering why Mom put that love note from Dad behind a photo in an album and not somewhere more private. I'm sure it was something she cherished."

Emma shrugged. "Maybe she was rereading it one day while looking through some pictures and the phone rang or someone came to the door. She might have just slipped it behind a photograph for temporary safekeeping and then forgot where she'd put it."

"That sounds plausible. I wonder what Danny will do with it."

Andie's cell phone rang. "It's Bob," she said, looking at the screen. "I should take this." She put down her knife and walked off a step or two; after a moment Emma saw her sister nod and heard her say with some doubt in her voice, "All right, Bob. If you think it's a good idea. I'll see you later."

"What did he have to say?" Emma asked when Andie had closed her phone.

"He's invited me to dinner tonight. Rumi doesn't know I'm coming. He thinks it's best. He said that normally he hates the idea of an ambush—as do I—but drastic times call for drastic measures."

Emma nodded. "He might be right. This situation has gone on long enough."

"And he thinks it's high time we tell our daughter everything. I mean, about my postpartum depression. We never said anything about it before. I guess we thought we were protecting Rumi from a difficult truth."

"I've been wondering how much she knows of those early years," Emma admitted.

"Maybe we did the wrong thing by keeping her in the dark to the extent we did." Andie nodded firmly. "But I think Bob's right. Now's the time, if ever."

"Bob is forcing the moment to its crisis. Brave man, and smart."

And maybe, Emma thought, she should take a lesson from her brother-in-law, a lesson about forcing the moment, taking charge of one's life, taking the leap of faith.

"I'm ready to sauté these leeks," Andie announced. "That's the best thing about this recipe. We get to use butter."

Emma sighed. "Sometimes," she said, "life can be pretty darn good."

Chapter 68

Andie's first thought on seeing Rumi that evening at Bob's house was: *she's suffering.* Her daughter looked so deeply unhappy. There were dark circles under her eyes and her mouth was fixed in a frown. It broke Andie's heart to think that she was the cause of this distress, however unwittingly. In her mind's eye she saw the image of a little girl seated cross-legged by a campfire. . . .

"Hello, Rumi," Andie said.

Rumi stood stock-still in the doorway to the kitchen. She looked for a moment like a cornered animal, about to make a desperate dash for freedom. Then she turned to her father and said in an accusatory tone, "You didn't tell me she would be here."

"I know," Bob said simply. "I didn't tell you because I wasn't sure you'd show up. Now, come to the table. We're going to share a meal and I want the three of us to talk. Not yell. Not storm off. Talk. And listen. As the Buddha said, and he was right: 'In a controversy the instant we feel anger we have already ceased striving for the truth and have begun striving for ourselves.'"

Rumi, her face a storm cloud, took a seat at the table, and Andie took the seat between Bob and her daughter.

"Let's get some food in our stomachs first," Bob said, and he began to pass around the serving bowls. "No one should have to talk about anything important on an empty stomach."

The family ate in silence for a few minutes, Rumi picking at her dinner, Bob eating with his usual gusto, as if, Andie thought, determined to instill a state of normalcy to the gathering. And though she was nervous at the thought of what might come, Andie did her best to focus on the moment, on the gift of the meal, and to enjoy it.

After a time Bob put his napkin next to his plate and said, "Now, we'll let our dinner digest before we have dessert. And we'll talk."

"Dad, I don't—"

But Bob cut off his daughter's attempted protest. "It hurts me, Rumi, to see you punishing your mother for your own grief. You have to own your emotions, Rumi. You have to accept responsibility for them, not try to make them go away by blaming someone else for their origin. You're mourning the loss of your grandmother, and that's what you're angry about. The fact of death. Not the fact that your mother couldn't make it to a party."

Rumi was silent for what seemed like a terribly long time. Andie could see that her expression had changed subtly during that time, but she couldn't quite interpret its meaning. And then, Rumi put down her chopsticks, with which she had been moving around her beans and rice, and sighed. "All right," she said, looking to her mother and then her father. "I shouldn't have bagged out of dinner the other night without even a phone call. That was rude. I'm sorry. And I guess I've said some pretty nasty things to you lately, Mom. I'm sorry about that, too. Dad's right. I shouldn't blame anyone else for my own feelings."

"Thank you for the apology," Andie told her. "And you're forgiven."

Bob took Andie's hand in his. "Rumi," he said, "there's something we never talked to you about. Keeping silent seemed like the right thing to do but . . . But now we think it's important you know that your mother suffered several months of severe postpartum depression. I'll admit there were times when I despaired of her ever being free of the sadness."

Rumi looked stunned. "Why didn't you tell me that you were sick?" she asked her mother. "I've read about postpartum depression. It's awful. And being sick is nothing to be ashamed of."

"I thought it for the best," Andie explained. "I didn't want to burden you with that knowledge. And I was deeply ashamed of what I saw as my weakness and failure. By the time you were old enough to understand, well, it was so far in the past and . . . There just didn't seem to be much of a point."

"I agreed with your mother," Bob told Rumi. "It was a terrible time for her, though she always did her absolute best to care for you. And, of course, I was there, even after we separated, as were your grandparents."

"But there are drugs for depression," Rumi said, "and all sorts of therapy. Didn't you get any help, Mom?"

"Yes, of course. I was under a doctor's care, thanks to your father figuring out what might be wrong. But depression is not something you can will away," Andie explained, "no matter what some people might believe." Andie turned to Bob and smiled. "But eventually, I was out from under the cloud."

"Did it come back?" Rumi asked. "The depression? I've heard that most people who experience an episode of serious depression are likely to have another one."

"Yes," Andie said. "When I was in my midthirties I went through another bad experience. But by then I knew more about what to expect and I knew that the depression would lift, so I didn't feel as hopeless and as guilty as I did the first time, when I had a baby to care for, a baby I felt I was failing. And I had the help of my spiritual beliefs."

"Do you think . . . ?" Rumi hesitated a moment before going on. "Do you think that's why you went to Mrs. Fitzgibbon about the desk? Do you think you might be getting depressed again?"

"I think," Andie said carefully, "that I've been feeling very distressed and sad. If that's not exactly depresson, it's close enough to it, and yes, it can cause a person to make mistakes."

"And when I went to live with Dad?" Rumi asked. "When you left Oliver's Well. What really happened then? Was it like what you told me? You didn't just leave without telling anyone, did you? Because some people have said . . . " Rumi pressed her lips together.

"Gosh, no," Andie said, looking to Bob and then back to her daughter. "Your father and I made the decision together, just like we told you. I knew that my calling lay elsewhere. I'd been preparing for it for a long time. You know about that. The courses of study, the retreats. Finally, it was time for me to move on. It was time for me to give back to the world." She looked again to Bob. "Your father understood that. He believed in me. He's always believed in me."

Bob nodded. "And my belief proved to be rightly placed. Your mother brings so much peace and joy and wisdom to so many people. It would have been supremely selfish of me to try to hold her back and keep her just for the two of us." Bob reached for his daughter's hand as well. "You've been happy until now, haven't you, Rumi? You've felt loved?"

Andie tightened her grip on Bob's other hand. So much depended on Rumi's honest answer to this question.

"Yes," Rumi said, looking from her mother to her father. "I have been happy. I have felt loved. I still do." And then she slipped her hand from her father's and rose slowly from the table. "I need to think things through," she said, "Leave the dishes, Dad. I'll do them later."

They watched as she went off to her room and heard her softly close the door.

"It'll be all right," Bob said, releasing Andie's hand with a final squeeze. "I think things went well."

"Hafiz, another great Sufi poet, says, 'Love sometimes wants to do us a great favor: hold us upside down and shake all the nonsense out.' "

Bob laughed. "I always get a headache when that happens."

"It's what you did for us tonight, Bob," Andie went on, "for the family. You acted with love and for the sake of love. Thank you."

"It was my pleasure," he said, "and my duty."

"Now, wish me luck with Danny. I know I need to face him soon. It's ridiculous to be hiding from each other."

"Danny might be hiding, but you're not. You're just waiting for the right moment."

Andie wasn't entirely sure she agreed with Bob, but she didn't protest. She declined dessert—she thought it best she not be around when Rumi emerged from her room later that evening—and helped Bob to bring the plates to the sink before heading back to Honeysuckle Lane. *Tomorrow morning,* she thought as she drove through the quiet, darkened streets of Oliver's Well, brightened here and there by sparkling Christmas lights strung on houses and shops and trees. *First thing, I'm going to visit my brother. From this moment on, fear has no place in my life.*

CHAPTER 69

Daniel took a deep breath and knocked on the front door of number 32. He did not use his key this morning. He no longer believed he had a right to use it, not with his sisters in residence.

After a moment Andie opened the door. He thought she looked thoroughly surprised to see him. *Well*, he thought, *of course she would be surprised*. And, he thought, maybe even a little bit scared.

"Hi," he said. "Can I come in?"

Andie stepped back to allow him past. "I was just coming to see you," she said, indicating the jacket she held in her hand.

"I'm saving you the trip." Daniel attempted a smile. "Where's Emma?"

Andie shrugged. "I'm not sure. She said she was going for a drive. Do you want some coffee? I could make another pot."

Daniel shook his head. "No, thanks," he said. "Look, could we sit down?"

"Sure." Andie led him to the kitchen and they took seats at the table. Daniel saw that while his sisters' breakfast had been cleared away, the dishes still sat in the sink. He restrained the urge to comment on the housekeeping. After all, he was here on a mission of peace and tolerance.

"I came here to apologize to you," he said abruptly. "I've been completely out of line since you came back to Oliver's Well. I've behaved miserably toward you and I really am sorry for it. Will you accept my apology?"

Daniel watched his sister closely in an effort to gauge her reaction to his words before she spoke, but he could tell nothing from Andie's expression of what he could only describe as calm detachment.

"Yes," she said finally. "I accept your apology. And I apologize for any of my words or behaviors that might have hurt you. I promise it was never—I promise it *is* never—my intention."

"I know," Daniel admitted, with a sigh of relief. "I know you always mean the best. And thank you."

Then Andie took a deep breath and Daniel tensed. Clearly, there was more to come. . . . But he would just have to be brave.

"I overheard what you said about me to Anna Maria at Norma Campbell's party," his sister told him. "About my being useless. It hurt."

Daniel rubbed his forehead. "I'm so sorry, Andie. I should never have said you were useless. I should never even have *thought* something so cruel and untrue. I hope we can go on from here. I hope this isn't the end of our relationship."

Andie finally smiled. "Danny," she said, "don't be silly. We're stuck with each other whether we like it or not."

"Blood is thicker than water?"

"That's what the experts say. But tell me, Danny. Why were you so angry with me? You didn't always feel so—so combative—toward me, did you?"

Daniel frowned. He wasn't sure he could properly put his feelings into words that would make sense to Andie, but he would have to try. "No," he said, "I didn't. It sounds so ridiculous, but I started feeling put upon. I had convinced myself that you and Emma had been taking me for granted, relying on me unfairly to take care of Mom and Dad and then their estate, when the truth was I *wanted* to be the caretaker. But then . . . I think my grieving took a wrong turn after Mom died. It became . . . it became all about me, if that makes sense. I kind of stopped realizing that every one of us was struggling with losing our parents, not just me."

Andie leaned across the table and put her hand on Daniel's arm. "I do respect you, Danny," she told him, her tone earnest. "For being a good human being. For being a fantastic father and husband. For being the best darn cook in the kitchen! I'm sorry if I haven't succeeded in showing you that respect."

"My feelings aren't your responsibility, or Emma's or anyone else's," Daniel said firmly, putting his hand over his sister's. "When I think about it all rationally I can see that you've never treated me with disrespect. I can see that you've always thanked me for being here for Mom and Dad. Still . . . I guess I just . . ."

"You don't have to say anything else, Danny, not for my sake anyway."

Suddenly, Daniel laughed. "Good," he said. "Because I've said more about my state of mind and my feelings in the past two or three days than I probably have in my entire life! I'm exhausted."

"Identifying and then expressing your emotions gets easier the more you practice. Trust me, Danny."

"I do." Daniel glanced down at his watch—once his father's watch. "I should be going," he said. "I asked the produce manager at the grocery store to set aside some good Hass avocados for me, but if there's an unexpected run on avocados, all bets are off."

Andie smiled. "A client in the mood for guacamole?"

"No, actually. Anna Maria's been craving avocados for some reason these past two weeks." Daniel got up from the table. "Look," he said, "I was wondering if we could all get together soon to sort through Mom's jewelry. It will be fun. I promise. No drama, no throwing paintings."

"Sure," Andie said. "How about this evening? I'm certainly free and I'm sure Emma will make herself available."

"Good. I know the kids will have fun. Well, at least Sophia will." Daniel hesitated a moment before saying, "Will you ask Rumi? Or do you want me to invite her?"

ĠĠĠ

"I'll let her know. About seven?"

"Great," he said. "I'll bring ingredients for ice-cream sodas. You like coffee ice cream in yours, don't you?"

"You remember that, after all these years?"

Daniel shrugged. "Who knows how memory works? I can't remember what day of the week it is sometimes, but I can remember that you like coffee ice cream and that Emma was obsessed with playing dominoes when she was ten."

With a laugh, Andie let him out of the house. And as Daniel walked down the driveway to his car he felt a sense of relief he hadn't felt in a very long time. He and his oldest sister were two very different people and he wasn't naive enough to think that they would never again clash or view a particular situation from two very different and maybe even incompatible perspectives. Still, he believed—he had to believe—that from this point on their relationship would be one of mutual respect. And that, he thought, getting behind the wheel, was a very good thing.

"Emma's got the auction house lined up, but we still have to settle on a real estate agent if we're going to get this house sold," Daniel was saying to his wife as he and his family approached the front door of number 32 at just before seven o'clock that evening.

"That's true, but let's just have fun tonight," Anna Maria suggested gently. "Let's keep all talk about anything other than necklaces and bracelets out of the conversation. All right?"

Daniel squeezed his wife's hand. "All right," he said. And he thought, *I should listen to my wife more often. Really listen.*

Before Marco could ring the doorbell Emma opened the door and welcomed them all inside the house.

"And here comes Rumi," she said. Daniel turned to see that his niece had just parked her car along the curb. A moment later she joined the family in the living room; Andie, too, was there.

"I can only stay a minute," Rumi told them. "But I wanted to say hello to everyone."

Daniel was disappointed. "Please stay, Rumi. I was hoping we all could be together this evening."

"I'm sorry, Uncle Daniel. My friend Marina's boyfriend just dumped her by text, if you can believe it, and she feels awful. I need to be there for her."

Andie nodded. "Being a good friend is always important."

Rumi smiled. "Thanks, Mom. Have fun, everyone." And then she was gone, hurrying back to her car and her friend in distress.

Daniel looked to his oldest sister. "Did you two talk?" he asked. "She seems . . . She seems better."

Andie nodded. "Bob got us together last night. We three talked openly and honestly with each other. I think it was helpful. At least, when I called her earlier about coming over this evening she took my call and was pleasant."

"Good," Daniel said. "I'm glad."

"So am I," Emma added. "Now, let's get this party started. Into the dining room, everybody."

Daniel first went to the kitchen to deposit the ingredients for the ice-cream sodas and then joined his sisters in the dining room, where they had laid out Caro's jewelry on the long dining table. "Wow," he said. "I never knew Mom had this much bling."

"Me, neither," Andie admitted. "She never wore much jewelry at any given time. I guess I thought she didn't care all that much for baubles."

"Mom!" Sophia cried. "Look at these earrings!"

"Let me see them," Daniel said. He took the teardrop-shaped danglers from his daughter and clipped them to his earlobes.

"Dad!" Sophia screamed a little, and Marco pointed at his father and howled with laughter. "I so have to have a picture of this!" he gasped. "Aunt Emma! Aunt Andie! Someone take a picture!"

Emma obliged her nephew.

"If you send it to your friends, Marco, you're grounded. Ow, these things really pinch." Daniel removed the earrings and put them back onto the table.

"Anything for the sake of fashion, darling," Anna Maria joked.

Emma picked up a pearl-studded piece about the size of a fifty-cent coin. "Look at this brooch," she said. "It's really exquisite.

The mark says it's a Dior. Obviously their costume line, but how lovely."

Daniel picked up another brooch, this one made with blue and green crystals in a spiral pattern. "Remember when Mom wore that turban for a while to parties?" he said. "Back when it was fashionable to wear turbans, I suppose. She used to pin a different brooch on it depending on what color dress she wore."

"I do remember. Was she channeling Elizabeth Taylor?" Andie wondered.

"Elizabeth Taylor wasn't classy enough for Mom to emulate," Emma said. "No insult to Liz; I think she was fantastic. Grace Kelly was more Mom's fashion icon, though I don't know if she ever wore a turban."

Anna Maria sighed as she examined a marquise-shaped brooch studded with rhinestones. "People don't wear brooches and stickpins like they used to. It's a shame, really. They can be so pretty."

"Like a silk scarf, a brooch elevates an outfit," Emma said. "Though I can't see most of these pieces working with anything I own."

"Me, neither." Andie smiled. "Though this crystal snowflake brooch might be nice on my fleece-lined hoodie."

Daniel looked down at all of the precious objects that had once meant so much to his mother, objects that now had no owner, no one to cherish them. He felt sad and nostalgic for what had once been, but he also realized that for the first time since his mother's passing he felt just a little bit free of the raw emotions that had been dogging him. His mother, he thought, had had every right to her secrets, to a friend named Susan, to a man not his father. The healing, he thought, seemed finally to be taking place.

"So, if you guys can't wear a lot of this, what do we do with it?" he asked. "Certainly we can't throw anything out. That wouldn't be right."

"We could include it in the general auction of furniture and crystal and china," Anna Maria suggested.

"As a separate lot, of course. Or two lots, the real and the faux?" Emma asked.

Daniel nodded. "First we should each choose something special, something we remember Mom wearing."

"There are some valuable pieces here," Emma pointed out. "Like the Schlumberger blue enamel bangle. How did Dad afford this? It's not a knock-off. It's the real deal."

"I'd forgotten about that bracelet. It was a gift from Mom's parents," Daniel told her. "They gave it to her for her twenty-first birthday."

"So, do we keep the bracelet and anything else we can identify as important in the family? Or do we sell the important pieces and split the profit? Of course I don't mean Dad's watch and Mom's pearls and her wedding set, the items they gave us specifically."

Andie shrugged. "Whatever seems fair."

"Some pieces have more financial value than others," Emma went on, almost as if to herself. "To replace them if they were stolen might be too expensive for whichever of us has chosen the piece."

Daniel felt a sudden surge of annoyance. "So? What are you saying?"

"I'm just thinking aloud," Emma said. "Let's say we don't sell the important pieces. We should all be aware that whoever chooses the bracelet, for example, will be getting a far more expensive item than whoever chooses, say, this stickpin with the single pearl. We all need to be okay about those disparities. Of course, before we each make a choice we might bring in a jewelry appraiser, which we'd have to do anyway if we decide to auction off the lot. And to make things really fair we might decide that we each have to choose an item of similar value."

"Do you think I care if you or Andie winds up with more money than I do?" Daniel snapped.

Anna Maria put her hand on his arm. "Daniel, that's not what Emma is saying."

"It's not, Danny," Emma said quickly. "Really. I'm not making any accusations. I'm just being practical. It's my job. Where money's concerned, people can become unusually sensitive or irrational."

"Well, not me!" Daniel protested. And then he became painfully aware that every one in the room was watching him. Emma's expression was tense with anticipation; Andie's was guarded and wary. Marco looked puzzled, Sophia, a bit worried. And his wife . . . Well, "stern" wasn't quite the word to describe the look on Anna Maria's face. Maybe the word was "disappointed."

Daniel burst out laughing. "You're right. Sorry, Emma. Sorry, everyone. I was the one pushing for us to get this whole lot settled. Money does come into it—it has to. I can't pretend that it doesn't."

"That's okay, Danny." Emma smiled. "You know what? I say we just choose what pieces we like and to heck with the financial value."

"I agree," Andie said. "Danny?"

Daniel nodded. "It's done."

After a moment's hesitation Emma opted for the Schlumberger blue enamel bangle and a strand of carved jet beads. "Grandma Martha used to wear these," she told the others. "They had once belonged to her mother. I'm pretty sure the necklace dates back to the Victorian period when jet was all the rage in mourning jewelry, thanks to the queen's favoring it when Prince Albert died." Anna Maria chose a gold and jade ring Caro had bought on her trip to China with Cliff—"Green is my color," she said—and Andie gathered a few paste and semiprecious stone pieces to give to Rumi. "Maybe she can repurpose the stones," she said. "Incorporate them into her jewelry designs."

Sophia was allowed the pair of clip-on dangly earrings her father had so bravely modeled. "We can have the clip removed and posts put on so you can comfortably wear them when you're older," Anna Maria told her. Marco huffed when he was asked if he wanted a keepsake.

"Jewelry is for girls. I'm not ever going to wear jewelry," he said stoutly.

Daniel grinned. "Not even a wedding ring?"

Marco made a face. "Ick. I'm not getting married. Girls are gross."

"I'm not gross!" Sophia protested.

Marco shrugged. "Yeah, you're okay."

"Hey," Daniel said, "don't forget those cuff links of Grandpa's he left you when he died. The gold and onyx ones he bought when I was a kid and we all went to Italy. You'll wear those someday, won't you?"

"Yeah," Marco said. "I forgot about the cuff links. They're cool. Like the tie bar thing that Grandpa left you, Dad. Man stuff."

Daniel smiled and finally decided that he would keep a small gold ring set with an Australian opal. "I remember being so fascinated with this ring," he told his family. "I loved how the blues and greens and oranges shifted and flared when Mom moved her hand. It was magical." He shook his head. "For some reason she stopped wearing it a long time ago. I never asked her why." *And now*, he thought, *I'll never know. But that's okay. I have the memories.*

Anna Maria slipped her arm through her husband's. "It's a lovely piece, Danny."

"Did someone mention ice-cream sodas?" Andie asked. "I'm simply dying of thirst! Or would it be hunger?"

"I'm on it! Marco, want to help me?"

The two men went off to the kitchen; within fifteen minutes they were back in the dining room, Daniel bearing a tray of ice-cream sodas in genuine old-fashioned soda fountain glasses. The long-handled spoons, too, were of the good old-fashioned variety.

"You always go all out, Danny," Emma said with a smile. "Even a cherry on top!"

"Don't forget the whipped cream!" Sophia said. "Dad always uses real whipped cream."

Daniel felt pleased and yes, proud. "I found the glasses and the spoons at a flea market last year and I couldn't resist. Sorry the straws are nothing special." He distributed the ice-cream sodas to each member of his family and then raised his glass. "To Mom," he said.

"To Grandma!" Marco added. He took a long sip of his ice-ceam soda and winced.

"Brain freeze?" Daniel asked sympathetically. His son nodded.

"What time did you say your reading was tomorrow?" Daniel asked his oldest sister, who was already halfway through her dessert.

"Three-thirty. Why? Do you think you can make it after all?"

"I'm going to give it my best try."

"Thanks. Tonight was a good idea, Danny." Andie grinned. "Especially the coffee-ice-cream soda."

Sophia shuddered. "I hate anything coffee flavored, especially ice cream."

"Good," Daniel said with a smile for his sister. "That means there's more for your aunt."

CHAPTER 70

"Again, Ms. Reynolds, it's so good of you to do this for the community."

Andie smiled at Chris Owens, one of the most earnest and dedicated young men she had ever met. "It really is my pleasure," she said. "And please, call me Andie."

Chris had provided a table and chair from which she could read or, he said, if she preferred, he could bring out a podium he kept in the back of the store. She told him a table and chair would be fine. On the table was a pitcher of water and a glass or, he said, if she preferred, he could make her a cup of tea or coffee. She told him that water would be fine. It occurred to Andie that Chris was more nervous than she was, and she *was* nervous, and excited, too. Andie had never spoken professionally with members of her family in the audience, and she realized that she wished her parents could be there to see and support her. *Am I still then a child, needing my parents' approval? Of course I am. We all are.* What was it that Shakespeare had written somewhere? "The voice of parents is the voice of gods, for to their children they are heaven's lieutenants."

Daniel made good on his promise to try to attend by showing up five minutes before the reading was scheduled to start. "Anna Maria sends her apologies," he told her. "Both kids woke with a bit of a cold this morning, and she's worried things might get worse and ruin their Christmas."

Andie thanked him for joining the crowd, and Daniel went to take the seat Emma had saved for him next to her in the front row; Rumi was sitting on Emma's other side.

Though Andie recognized a few familiar faces—Morgan Shelby, Maureen Kline, and Alexis Fitzgibbon, the wife of Mary Bernadette's grandson PJ, were all there, as were Bob and Ralph, the young man she had met in the Eclectic Gourmet—many other faces were new to her. And many of the audience were young, certainly no older than thirty, too young for Andie to remember them as anything other than toddlers in their strollers. *In so many ways*, she thought, *I'm no longer part of Oliver's Well. And yet at this very moment, and for this moment only, I* am *a part of my hometown. And that matters.*

Chris Owens introduced Andie—"Oliver's Well's very own Andie Reynolds!"—to enthusiastic applause, and after thanking her audience for being there with her, Andie began to read from her latest book, *The Root of the Root of Love.*

She looked at the faces before her with frequency as she read; it helped, of course, that she was very familiar with the passages she had chosen and didn't need to keep her eyes glued to the page. And unless her brother was a good actor, and Andie didn't think that he was, Daniel was truly paying attention, sitting forward in his seat, his expression one of concentration.

About halfway through the twenty-minute reading Andie was aware that Rumi was quietly slipping out, but not without giving her mother a small wave. Her leaving caused Andie a twinge of worry, but she carried on smoothly. "Remember," she said, "life is a beautiful gift from God." Before the applause could begin, Andie added, "And thank you all for coming. I hope you all enjoy a blessed holiday season."

When the applause had died down Chris Owens announced that Andie would be available to sign copies of her books. "Just give her a moment to speak with her family," he requested with a smile.

Andie joined her siblings, who were standing aside with Morgan Shelby and Bob.

Morgan offered Andie his hand. "Thank you for this gift to Oliver's Well," he said. "I bought your latest book just this morning."

Andie shook his hand and smiled. "Thank you for coming today. And for helping my family settle our mother's estate."

Morgan smiled at Andie and then at Emma. "It's been my pleasure," he told them. "But now I must run. I'm off to my family's place in Baltimore. I hope you all have a happy Christmas."

When Morgan had gone off, Bob kissed Andie on the cheek. "Well done, Andie," he said. "As always. But I've got to run, too." He nodded at his brother-in-law. "Daniel's got me covering for him at a party this evening."

"Just until I get there," Daniel explained. "With Anna Maria home with the kids, we're a bit short-staffed tonight."

Bob left to prepare for the catering gig, and Daniel went back to his house to check on his family.

"Where did Rumi take off to?" Andie asked her sister when the men had gone.

"She got a last minute call to take a shift at the Angry Squire. She asked me to apologize for having to slip out."

Andie nodded. "I'm just glad she was here at all. Now, to sign some books! Will you wait for me?"

"Of course," Emma said. "I'll chat with Maureen while you're busy. She's over in the romance aisle at the moment."

Andie found that the people who had come to the reading were without exception enthusiastic seekers of peace and understanding. None of them were present to toss an ill-considered insult or criticism her way, and for that she was very grateful. The signing took about twenty minutes, and when the last appreciative reader had gone off with Andie's latest book in tow, she rejoined her sister and Maureen.

"I love when I get to meet and talk with the people who read my books," she told them.

"You looked so at ease chatting with everyone," Emma said. "You really are connected with your readers, aren't you?"

Andie nodded. "It's a wonderful thing, though sometimes it can be difficult to keep boundaries in place." She smiled. "I do value my private life."

"Then it's probably a good thing you live where and in the way that you do," Maureen commented. "Not out in constant view of the public."

"Life in my quiet little community definitely has its benefits. Hey, how about a drink at the Angry Squire?" Andie suggested. "I feel like celebrating."

"The successful reading?" Maureen asked.

Andie smiled. "More like a renewed state of peace and tolerance."

CHAPTER 71

"To Andie!" Emma and Maureen chorused.

"To all three of us," Andie amended.

Because it wasn't quite five o'clock, the bar at the Angry Squire was quiet. The women had been able to secure what Maureen told them was her favorite table in the corner. "See? There's a perfect view of the front hall so you can keep an eye on who's coming and going. It's the busybody in me," she explained.

"At least you're not a gossip," Emma pointed out, remembering Maureen's particular ability to keep a person's secrets.

"Gossip is foul," Andie said with a shudder, taking a sip of the mulled wine she had ordered. "Sociologists say it serves a purpose, but I've never understood its value myself."

"How's the eggnog?" Emma asked her friend. She herself had ordered her favorite Beaujolais.

"Excellent. Richard makes his eggnog from scratch. And it packs quite a punch if you're not careful. Hey, it was nice of Morgan Shelby to show up at the reading."

Emma took a sip of her wine before answering. "Yes," she said. "It was."

"He's an attractive man," Andie said, "and I don't only mean physically. There's something good about him, something solid and real. I can sense it."

Emma was aware that Maureen was giving her a look of disarmingly mild curiosity. "Yes, he's a nice man," Emma said in as neutral a tone as she could manage. "He went with me to the auction house in Winchester, and it wasn't something he was obliged to do."

"So things are all patched up with Danny?" Maureen asked the sisters. "He certainly seemed to be enjoying the reading."

"Yes," Andie said. "Things seem to be better all around. Peace and tolerance."

Emma smiled at her sister. "All we had to do was believe that things would change for the better."

"It was a bit more work than that," Andie corrected with a laugh. "You know, there's a Buddhist teaching that goes like this: 'Know well what leads you forward and what holds you back and choose the path that leads to wisdom.' I think that Danny has started to understand what it is he's been allowing to hold him back."

"I'm glad." Maureen turned to Emma. "On another note entirely, has Ian given up pestering you?"

The question took Emma by surprise; she realized that she hadn't given Ian a thought in what seemed like an age. "As a matter of fact," she said, "I haven't heard from him in two days. Not one electronic peep."

"Good," Maureen said. "Maybe he finally got the message. Or he's changed his strategy."

Emma frowned. "What do you mean?"

"Even the most mild-mannered of men don't like to be thwarted in achieving their goals. All I'm saying is that you might not have seen the last of him."

The thought unsettled Emma; she hoped that when she got back to Annapolis she didn't find Ian waiting on her doorstep.

"Where will Ian spend Christmas?" Andie asked.

"I haven't a clue," Emma admitted. "But he has some very good old friends. He won't be on his own unless he chooses to be. And what about you and Jim?" she asked Maureen. "Will you spend the day together?"

"He'll come to my parents' house for dinner. My sisters will be there, too, with their husbands and at least a few of their kids."

Andie grinned. "Baptism by fire for poor Jim."

"Oh, I think he can handle it. I'm more worried about what to get him for Christmas. It's been so long since I've given a man a gift—I mean, a man not my father—I'm still at a loss and the clock is ticking. Tomorrow is Christmas Eve, for cripes' sake!"

"There are always socks," Emma suggested with a smile.

"I'm not trying to send the man running!"

"Any clue as to what he's giving you?" Emma asked.

Maureen laughed. "As long as it's not an engagement ring! But no, not a clue."

Emma's attention was suddenly caught by a family of four standing in the front hall of the restaurant. "Cute kid alert," she said. "My gosh, could those children be any more adorable? Fur-trimmed red coats, no less! And ringlets. When was the last time you saw a little girl in ringlets?"

"Those are the Welsh girls," Maureen told the sisters. "Identical twins. Tara and Claire. I believe they just turned three."

"That's refreshing," Andie commented, peering at the sisters. "Two distinct-sounding names. There must be confusion enough with the matching outfits, not to mention the matching faces!"

Maureen sighed. "You know," she confided, "every once in a while, like when I'm with my goddaughter or I see little kids like the Welsh twins, I feel a pang of loss, if you can feel the loss of something you've never had. Still, I'm eternally thankful to whatever God there is that I didn't have a child with Barry. That would have been a disaster. He's completely irresponsible, and I would have been entirely on my own." Maureen looked at her watch. "Oops, I'd better get going. I promised my parents I'd have dinner at their house this evening and I'm on mashed potato duty."

"We'll go, too, okay, Andie?" Emma asked. "If you're in the mood, I was thinking we could watch *Chocolat* after dinner."

Andie smiled "Sounds like a plan. What will this be, our fourth or fifth time?"

"More like ninth or tenth!"

"Rats," Maureen said with a pout. "I wish I could join you. Johnny Depp? Swoon."

"Next time," Emma told her friend. Then she thought, *And there will be many a next time if I decide to come home.*

CHAPTER 72

Christmas Eve day dawned gray and gloomy, but the weather didn't dampen Emma's spirits. She was up early and spent a pleasant morning puttering around the house and taking in the enticing aromas coming from the kitchen—Andie was baking *pfeffernüsse* cookies. All was finally calm in the Reynolds home. What was it Andie had said they were celebrating last night with Maureen? Peace and tolerance. And to that Emma would add excellent meals, thanks to her brother.

Carefully Emma placed the gifts she had gotten for Sophia and Marco under the tree. For Sophia she had chosen a massively comprehensive book on the history of clothing in the Western world; recently Sophia had taken to teaching herself how to sew on her Grandma Spinelli's old machine. For Marco, Emma had gotten a video camera he could attach to his helmet for taking films while riding his bike. For Rumi, she had purchased a gift certificate to her favorite online shopping source. It felt like a bit of a cop-out, but it was better than no gift at all.

Emma and Andie shared a quick lunch of leftovers before Daniel, Anna Maria, and the kids—who had both thankfully recovered from their brief colds—came over to begin preparations for the celebratory dinner.

At about one-thirty in the afternoon, as Andie and the children were in the backyard playing a game of catch, and Emma was helping her brother and Anna Maria in the kitchen, the doorbell rang. "I'll get it," Emma said with a smile. "You guys are elbow deep in fish bones!"

She hurried out to the front hall and opened the door. For a moment she thought she was having a hallucination, because standing on the doorstep, wearing his camel-colored wool overcoat and carrying his familiar leather weekend bag, was Ian Hayes. *So much for calm*, Emma thought. *This is now officially a tempest!*

"Emma," Ian said, giving her a big smile. "I've missed you."

Emma stood frozen, her hand still on the doorknob. She couldn't find the voice to ask the question that was burning a hole in her head. *What are you doing here!?*

Ian gestured toward the living room behind her. "Aren't you going to ask me inside? It's kind of nasty out there today."

Good manners kicked in and Emma stepped back, allowing Ian to enter the house.

"It looks beautiful in here," he said. "The tree is massive! Let me guess—Danny picked it out."

Daniel came out of the kitchen, wiping his hands on a dish towel. "Who was th—?" he began, and then froze in midstride as well as word.

Ian came forward, hand extended. "Danny, good to see you."

Daniel took the hand offered—the Reynolds children were so well trained, Emma thought, almost laughing at the absurdity of the situation—and then managed a greeting that was also a question. "Ian?" he said.

Ian put his bag on the floor. "I'll be right back," he told them. "I must visit the gentleman's."

When he had gone off to the powder room, Daniel leaned in to his sister. "What's he doing here?" he whispered. "Do you want me to tell him to leave?"

"First, I have no idea why he's here. And no, Danny, but thanks. I'll take care of Ian. Somehow."

Daniel looked dubious, but he practically dashed back into the kitchen, no doubt to share the odd news with Anna Maria.

And when Ian returned to the living room, Emma wasted no more time being shocked.

"We need to talk," she said. "But there's no privacy here. Let's go for a drive."

"We'll take my car," Ian said.

"No." The word came out quickly and left no room for argument. "We'll take my car." Emma grabbed her coat from the hall closet and, neglecting gloves or a scarf, she strode out the front door and to her car in the driveway. Ian dutifully followed.

"You look well, Emma," he said as she pulled onto the street. "Being away from the office these past weeks has done you good."

If he only knew what I've been through, she thought. *What we've all been through.* But she said nothing.

Without much forethought Emma drove to Oliver's Grove, parked along the curb, and climbed out. Ian followed and they stood side by side looking out at the bare ginkgo trees and the lacebark pines decorated with tiny white lights.

"I noticed the portrait of your parents wasn't over the fireplace," Ian said.

"Yes. We took it down."

"Why?"

"A personal reason."

If Emma had hoped Ian would be put off by her terse replies, she was disappointed. "I've always liked the Grove," Ian said brightly "Well, the park as well as the town. It's such a nice change from Annapolis. I—"

"Why are you here, Ian?" Emma blurted.

"We're friends, Emma," Ian said promptly. "We've known each other so long we have no choice but to be friends. Why can't friends spend Christmas together?"

"Because we broke up," Emma said carefully. "I didn't want you here with me in Oliver's Well this Christmas. I *don't* want you here."

"Oh, Emma," Ian replied without missing a beat, his face a mask of—what was it?—mild amusement tinged with pity, like an adult fondly setting a silly child straight on some vital point. "You don't mean that."

Emma looked away from Ian, her mind racing. She remembered what Andie had tried to explain to her, that Ian was reluctant to let go of Emma and the rest of her family because they had become *his* family over the years. Ian was a man in pain. She had to remain kind in her dealings with him, no matter how final and disappointing her ultimate message.

But at that moment, standing at the edge of the Grove, hands shoved in her pockets and shivering in the cold damp air, Emma just couldn't muster the sort of strength she knew it would take to finally extricate herself from this barely existing—and now, slightly ludicrous—relationship. Kind now, she decided, firm later. For the sake of her sanity and in an effort to keep yet more drama at bay, she would play along with Ian's fantasy or delusion or whatever it was. For a little while.

"All right, Ian," she said, looking out at the trees strung with delicate white lights against the gloom of the day. "You can stay. But we're not sleeping together. That's over."

Before she could step away, Ian put his arm around her shoulder. She allowed it to stay for a short moment before moving out of his touch. "I should get back to the house," she said. "Danny needs me." Ian followed wordlessly as she walked back to the car.

CHAPTER 73

Daniel was preparing the stuffing for the calamari, a combination of rice, ground pork and lamb, minced herbs, and mushrooms. Anna Maria was putting together the clam sauce for the linguini. Their children had come in from the cold and were currently poking at the wrapped presents under the tree, trying to guess what was inside each. If it weren't for the bizarre appearance of Ian Hayes, Daniel would have said that it was a perfect day before Christmas.

"I can't believe Ian just showed up," Daniel said for about the twentieth time. "What do we say to the guy? Emma broke up with him. We can't pretend we don't know."

"Just be polite," Anna Maria advised. "He's a nice enough man. And if Emma says he can stay, she must be able to handle the situation herself."

"If he upsets my sister . . ."

Anna Maria sighed. "Daniel, there's no need to be macho. Look, Ian's been a part of this family for a long time. I feel bad for him, really. He probably couldn't face spending Christmas alone. What it must have taken for him to show up unannounced . . . Either courage or desperation, maybe a bit of both."

"He could have some self-respect," Daniel argued. "Doesn't he realize he's making a fool of himself showing up like he did?"

"Daniel, be nice. If not for Ian's sake, then for Emma's."

"I'll be nice. Heck, I like the guy. Or rather, I used to like him. Now I'm just confused by him."

Anna Maria yawned hugely.

"That's the third big yawn in the past half hour," Daniel said worriedly. "Didn't you sleep well last night? Was I tossing and turning again? You know you should wake me if I disturb you. I can easily sleep on the couch."

"I slept just fine," Anna Maria assured him. "And you were as quiet as a mouse. I just feel tired lately. It must be the fact that we've been working nonstop for the past six weeks, first with the Thanksgiving parties, then with the demands of the Christmas season."

Daniel reached out and drew his wife into his arms, where he hugged her tightly. "I'm sorry it has to be like this," he said, resting his cheek against her hair. "Once we sell this house we can afford more help with the business and you can take it easy."

"Don't ever apologize for our life, Daniel," she whispered. "It's exactly the life I want. Exactly."

And at that moment Daniel felt gratitude flow through him as it never had before. *This*, he thought, *is exactly the life I want, too.*

CHAPTER 74

Rumi and Bob arrived together at the house on Honeysuckle Lane that afternoon. Andie was at the door to greet them.

"A bit nippy out there today, isn't it?" she said.

Rumi shivered. "I totally should have worn my heavier jacket."

"We had a bit of excitement here earlier," Andie went on, lowering her voice. "Ian showed up unannounced. It was quite a shock for Emma."

"I'll say." Bob frowned. "Is she okay? What did she do?"

Andie shrugged. "She didn't send him packing, but I don't know what's going to happen."

Bob took his coat and Rumi's jacket to the hall closet. "Well, it's Emma's business," he said, "not ours, but if she needs our support, we're here."

"Dad's right." Rumi shook her head. "I hope he's not here to start a fight with her. That would be awful."

"Let's not imagine the worst," Bob said. "Well, I was told that my chopping skills are required, so I'm off to the kitchen."

Andie and Rumi sat on either end of the living room couch. The aroma of freshly baked gingerbread filled the house, along with sudden waves of a more savory smell Andie couldn't quite identify.

"Hey," Rumi said, pointing to the fireplace. "Where's the painting of Grandma and Grandpa?"

Andie thought quickly. She hated to lie, but she didn't want her daughter to know the truth, either. "It's being reevaluated," she said carefully. "We thought we should redetermine its worth."

The explanation seemed to satisfy Rumi. "You were pretty good yesterday at the reading, Mom," she said. "I'd be so nervous standing up in front of a lot of people like that. I'd be afraid of hecklers."

"You learn over time how to handle the pressure and the nerves," Andie told her. "And how to defuse hecklers. It took practice. I wasn't a natural. And I still get upset when a hater sends me an e-mail or text. It happened again just the other day, in fact. It feels like such a violation."

"That's so not right," Rumi said stoutly. "You shouldn't have to put up with that sort of abusive treatment. I'm sorry, Mom."

Andie shrugged. "Comes with the territory, I'm afraid. And with the relative anonymity electronic communication allows, some people feel they have a right to bully and attack without repercussion."

"Cowards."

"Yes. But enough of that." Andie went to the breakfront and removed a velvet pouch from the top drawer under the display shelves. "I set aside some of Grandma's jewelry for you," she said. "I was thinking that you might want to use some of these stones in your work. They're not valuable money-wise, but . . ."

Rumi opened the pouch and smiled. "They have sentimental value, as much as the expensive stuff that Grandma gave me over the years. The gold bangle she got for her sixteenth birthday, and the signet ring once belonged to her aunt."

"Exactly," Andie said, sitting by her daughter's side. "Your grandmother really enjoyed wearing her jewelry. It seems a shame that it sits around unworn."

Rumi nodded. "Unloved. I know, I know. It's an inanimate object. But I can't help thinking that personal belongings become infused with a person's spirit. I know little kids do it all the time; their teddy bear, or whatever, is totally real and alive to them. But I still do it, and I don't mean just with things from the natural world like stones. *Of course* they have an energy and a personality! Who couldn't understand that? What I mean is, stuff like that little Native American doll you sent me a few years ago from Arizona. She's got a soul, Mom. I love her."

Andie smiled. She was so very glad that Rumi was once again sharing her thoughts and her feelings with her. *This* was their relationship, this was the easy and natural give and take they had always enjoyed. "I'm glad you love the doll," she said. And then she gathered more of her courage. "I was thinking that you might want to visit me in Woodville Junction next summer," she said, "when school's out. You don't have to make a commitment now, and I know you'll need to work, too. Just think about it."

"That might be fun," Rumi said. "I could finally meet some of your friends, the ones you've told me about."

"And they could finally meet you." Andie laughed. "I talk about you so often I'm sure they feel they already know you."

"You talk about me?"

Andie put her hand over her daughter's hand and gave it a brief squeeze. "Of course. You're my daughter. I might be an . . . an unusual mother, but I'm still a mother."

Rumi laughed. "Well, at least you're not boring! Most of my friends' mothers are deadly dull. Some of them have never been farther away than DC. Can you imagine?"

"No," Andie said. "I can't. Look, Rumi, I can't make up for the time we've lost over the years—and for missing your twentieth birthday—but I can promise not to waste the future."

"Thanks, Mom. And I promise not to be so childish."

"Grief and longing aren't childish emotions."

"But acting like a jerk to someone you love because you're upset is childish behavior."

"Well, yes. Can I quote my poet?"

Rumi smiled. "Sure, Mom."

" 'Yesterday I was clever, so I wanted to change the world. Today I am wise, so I am changing myself.' "

"I'll keep that in mind. Oh, Mom, I forgot to tell you! The Artful Soul sold all of my jewelry. I must have gotten the creative gene from you." She laughed. "Dad can't even draw a straight line."

"That's wonderful, Rumi. So, do you still think your making jewelry is just an unimportant hobby?"

"I guess not," she admitted. "But I'm not giving up on being a dental hygienist just yet."

"There's no reason why you can't pursue both paths. Life is long, if you're lucky. At the very least there's room for more than one adventure. Now I'm quoting the Buddha: 'It is better to travel well than to arrive.' Enjoy the journey, Rumi."

Rumi laughed. "So, I can have it all?"

"No," Andie said. "No one can have it all, and why would they want to? But you can enjoy what you do have and let go of what might have been."

Rumi pulled one of her grandmother's pieces from the velvet pouch and looked down at it lying in her palm. It was a cocktail ring featuring a cabochon lapis. After a moment she said, without looking up, "Dad always talks about how you've helped so many people with your work."

"It's what I try to do. Help people."

Rumi raised her eyes and looked directly at her mother. "Maybe you should have stayed home and tried to help me. I'm not being a jerk again, Mom," she added quickly. "What I mean is, sometimes when you try to be there for everyone, you wind up not noticing the person right in front of your nose. I guess since Grandma died I've been feeling a bit—ignored. Lost."

Andie sighed and brushed a lock of her daughter's hair away from her face. "Oh, Rumi," she said. "I'm sorry I couldn't be what or who you wanted me to be. I am. And you're right. Sometimes people do lose sight of the needs of the individual when they focus on the greater good. I'm more than sure I have! But hey, your dad was here and he didn't do such a bad job on his own after I left Oliver's Well, did he?"

"No. Dad's great."

"He is," Andie agreed. "I have a lot of love for your father, and a lot of respect."

"Hey, did I ever tell you that not long before Grandma died I read *Pride and Prejudice* to her? We got through the entire book in about two weeks. You know it was one of her all-time favorites."

"I do. But wasn't she able to read on her own?" Andie asked. "Was she too weak to hold a book?"

"She said that reading hurt her eyes too much," Rumi explained, "but I think she just enjoyed the company of someone else's voice. Anyway, she told me that every time she was in a bookstore or a library and she saw someone with one of your books, she felt really proud of you. She used to think, 'My own daughter, on the shelves with Jane Austen!' And she also said she liked to listen to your interviews on the radio because she thought you had a very good speaking voice." Rumi smiled. "You know how she had to take elocution lessons when she was young. She was always commenting on people's lazy speech."

"Thank you for telling me," Andie said, unabashedly wiping away her tears. She wished that her mother could have told her how she felt about her directly, but Andie finally truly believed Caro Reynolds had done all that she was capable of doing. Like Andie had told Rumi, it was vital to appreciate and enjoy what you had and let go of what might have been.

"I'm so glad you had Grandma and Grandpa for as long as you did," she said. "They will always be in your heart. And you still have your father and Danny and Anna Maria and your cousins. And Emma, of course."

"And you?"

Andie smiled. "And me. If you'll have me."

"Duh, Mom," Rumi said, rolling her eyes. "Just remember that I want to feel necessary to you. I want to really matter to you. And sometimes, though I'm not a kid anymore, even though I can act like one, I need to hear you say that to me. That I mean something *necessary* to you."

Andie took her daughter's hand again and held it tight. "I won't ever forget to tell you," she promised, "and in my own words."

At that moment Bob came back into the living room bearing a plate. "Snacks, anyone? An *amuse-bouche*? An appetizer?" Bob laughed as he offered the plate to his daughter and his former wife. "Whatever you call them, nothing beats stuffed mushrooms hot out of the oven!"

CHAPTER 75

Anna Maria and Daniel traditionally spent Christmas Eve with her family, but this year, because Emma and Andie had come home to Oliver's Well, they were very kindly holding the traditional Italian Christmas Eve Feast of the Seven Fishes at the Reynolds house. There would be plenty of time, Anna Maria had told Emma, for celebration with the Spinellis in the days to come.

At six-thirty, the family—with the addition of Ian, who took a seat next to Emma—gathered around the table. Emma and Andie had set it with Caro's best linens and china and crystal stemware. In the center a beautiful floral arrangement held pride of place. It was a gift to Daniel and Anna Maria from a grateful client. "Red roses like velvet," Emma commented. "This must have cost your client quite a bit of money."

Daniel grinned. "She has quite a bit of money."

Daniel identified each dish he had laid out on warming trays atop the sideboard. "First," he said, "we're having the traditional *baccalà*, salted codfish in tomato sauce."

"It's like soup," Marco added helpfully, "with chunks of fish in it."

"And these are fried smelts, for those of us who need something fried whenever possible." Daniel winked at Emma when he said that, and she winked back, remembering, of course, the wonderfully greasy onion rings they had shared.

"What was that about?" Ian whispered, leaning into Emma's shoulder.

Emma pulled away. "Something between Danny and me," she replied tersely.

"Next, for the carb lovers we have linguine with a creamy crab sauce."

Anna Maria laughed. "That's my addiction!"

"Then," Daniel went on, "there's stuffed calamari, and clams casino—Mom's favorite. And Dad's favorite, shrimp cocktail. And finally, *insalata di mare*, cold seafood salad." Daniel pointed to the table. "And, of course, lots of bread to mop up all the good stuff."

"Thank you, Danny and Anna Maria," Emma said, "for your generosity."

Ian lifted his glass. "Yes," he said, "thank you. And I'd like to make a toast."

Emma could barely refrain from a grimace as everyone dutifully raised his or her glass.

"To dear friends and family," Ian said. "May we always share the important moments together."

There were murmurs of agreement. *He's delusional*, Emma thought, wondering if she could already have another glass of wine. This meal was going to be a trial and she needed some fortification, but the last thing she wanted was to get tipsy, not when there was a confrontation looming.

Andie had made herself a delicious-smelling casserole with peppers, onions, and eggplant, and Daniel had also prepared a bowl of linguine with a sauce minus the crab, as well as a warm salad of winter vegetables.

"Don't you ever crave a hamburger?" Rumi asked, snagging a chunk of parsnip from her mother's plate.

"Bacon." Andie sighed. "I crave bacon."

"Did you ever make a mistake and eat something you shouldn't have?" Marco asked.

Bob laughed. "It doesn't really work that way," he said. "Vegetarianism is a firmly held belief that outweighs mere physical craving and temptation."

"Except," Andie said, "when it comes to bacon."

"Maybe I'll become a vegetarian," Sophia announced.

"No," Anna Maria said firmly.

"What your mother said," Daniel said, equally as firmly.

Sophia looked genuinely puzzled. "But why not? If Aunt Andie can be one, why can't I?"

Andie smiled. "I think what your parents mean, Sophia, is that it's a decision a person should make when she's older than you are. And I agree."

Daniel grinned. "Besides, are you really ready to give up my famous pigs-in-a-blanket?"

"No!" Sophia cried.

"I tried to be a vegetarian once," Ian said. "It didn't work out so well, I'm afraid. I literally dreamt of the foods I wasn't supposed to be eating. I was haunted by visions of beef Wellington and lobster thermidor."

No one laughed. Emma supposed that Ian had been hoping for a jolly reaction, and for a moment she dared to hope that he had finally become aware of the discomfort his presence was causing. She glanced at his face and there still sat the same bland smile. *No such luck*, she thought.

When the silence started to become too loud, Andie piped up. "Vegetarianism is not for everyone," she said. Her tone was kind.

"I certainly couldn't handle it," Bob said, spearing a piece of calamari. "You're in good company, Ian."

Emma was grateful for her sister's graciousness and for Bob's bonhomie, because as the meal wore on, increasingly she felt as if she were trapped in some bizarre comedy; she just hoped she wouldn't suddenly laugh out loud at the absurdity of it all.

"I thought we might use Caro's Wedgwood vase this holiday season," Anna Maria was saying. "But when I took it out the other day I noticed a hairline crack along one side. I'm not sure it would be watertight. I wonder if it can be mended."

"I could take a look at it if you like," Ian offered.

This is insane, Emma thought, gripping her fork. *Ian can't even straighten a crooked picture on the wall, let alone mend a cracked vase.* "You don't want to be bothered about an old bit of crockery, Ian," she said tersely.

Ian shrugged. "Sure I do. If it's important to your family, then it's important to me."

"Oh, it's really not a big crack," Anna Maria said hurriedly. "I shouldn't even have bothered to mention it. Would someone please pass the salt? Daniel, these fried smelts are really wonderful."

Finally, after what seemed an age, the meal was over. "I'll help you clean up, Danny," Emma said. "Ian, why don't you go into the den with the others and help the kids set up the Monopoly board."

"Sure," he said enthusiastically. "Come on, kids."

Anna Maria, Andie, Bob, and Rumi each shot Emma a glance of concern and sympathy before following Ian, Sophia, and Marco into the den. Emma joined her brother in the kitchen where they set about putting away what few leftovers there were and loading the dishwasher.

"That was one of strangest things I've ever experienced," Daniel said to Emma, his voice low. "The man is oblivious! I've never seen him act so . . . so oblivious!"

Emma sighed as she ran hot water into a pot to soak. "I've got to talk to him again tonight. I should have stood my ground this afternoon. Damn. I don't know what I've got myself into. And I hope I didn't ruin dinner for everyone."

"I don't mean to brag," Daniel said, "but I think the food took at least some of the attention away from Ian Hayes."

Emma smiled weakly. "Good."

"Are you sure you don't need help dealing with Ian?" Daniel asked, his tone genuinely worried. "I could be with you when you confront him, if you like. I could even show him the door, forcibly if I need to."

"Stop being so protective," Emma told him. "I'll be fine. But you *can* wish me luck. I'm afraid I'm going to have to force Ian out of denial, and I don't think it's going to be pretty. For either of us."

"Well, you know where you can find me. Right here. Anna Maria and I aren't leaving this house until we know you're okay."

"Thanks, Danny." Emma gave her brother a kiss on the cheek. "I mean it."

"Where's your stuff?" Ian asked, glancing around the room in which Emma had slept for the first seventeen years of her life. "The room looks unoccupied."

It was a little before nine o'clock in the evening. After helping Daniel in the kitchen Emma had briefly looked in on the others in the den and then gone quietly upstairs, assuming that Ian would soon follow. He had.

"I've been staying in my parents' room," she told him. And before Ian could start another ridiculously banal conversation as if nothing momentous had happened between them only a few weeks earlier, Emma said, "Why did you come here, Ian? And don't start again about how we have to be friends. We *don't* have to be friends."

To Emma's surprise, Ian, no longer acting the obtuse, rejected lover, took two strides toward her and gripped her by the arms. His tone when he spoke was intense; his eyes were intent upon her face. "I came here," he said, "because there's something I need to know, once and for all. Emma, I don't believe that you want things between us to be over."

Before Emma could react in any way at all, Ian let go of her and reached into the pocket of his tweed jacket. There was no need for him to open the black velvet box he extracted for Emma to know what was inside. But he did open it and held it out to her. A substantial cushion-cut diamond winked at Emma from a rich and mellow yellow gold setting.

"Emma," Ian went on, "for the sake of all we've built in the past ten years, for the sake of all that we've shared, will you marry me?"

This can't be happening, Emma thought. *It just can't be.* She suddenly recalled Maureen's words at the Angry Squire the night before—"As long as it's not an engagement ring!"—and she wondered if Ian was playing a practical joke on her. But Ian had never been the sort for jokes of any kind.

She felt anger surge through her, and with some difficulty she managed to keep her voice low. It wouldn't do to have her brother come barging into the room, harsh words at the ready. "Ian," she said, "what don't you understand? Our relationship is over. Your proposing to me now is an insult. It's a complete refusal to believe that I meant what I said when we last saw each other. It's a refusal to take me seriously. It's totally disrespectful. The relationship is *over.*"

Ian's face tensed. "Is there another man?" he asked. "Is that what this is all about?"

"You asked me that back in Annapolis," Emma whispered fiercely, "and I told you no! There's no other man! There's no one. I made this decision on my own, for my own sake. For my own happiness."

Emma watched as Ian tried to process this last bit of information. Assuming, of course, he had even heard it. "Are you telling me that our relationship meant nothing to you?" he said finally.

"Of course the relationship meant something to me," she replied. "Just . . . just not the *right* sort of something." Emma sighed and put a hand to her suddenly aching head. "Look, Ian, why are you refusing to hear me? How can I be any more clear?"

At this Ian seemed to gather himself, to grow in stature. For a moment Emma thought he was going to take hold of her again and she took a step back. She realized that she was beginning to feel afraid. How long would it take her brother to get upstairs? she thought. If she screamed very loudly or risked a dash to the door . . .

When Ian spoke his voice held a note of mockery she had never heard in it before, not once in all the years they had known each other.

"Is this going to be a repeat of the time you decided you were done with me only to call me less than two weeks later and beg me to take you back?" he asked.

Emma cringed. She had not begged, of that she was sure, but maybe Ian needed to see it that way now. "Things were different then, Ian," she said. "I wasn't ready to end our relationship and I'm sorry for acting without proper thought. But now, I'm sure I've done the right thing. Absolutely sure." And as she said those last words, she felt her courage return. There was nothing to fear, she realized. Nothing. "I don't love you, Ian," she told him. "I just don't."

Ian grew so still it was almost as if he wasn't there; it was almost as if he had gone away someplace safe and dark. His eyes seemed to be seeing nothing; his lips were held tightly together. When he didn't respond after yet another moment, Emma went on. "Ian," she said, "you can stay here tonight—I doubt you'd get a hotel room anywhere with its being Christmas Eve—but you'll have to leave first thing in the morning. I'm sorry."

Suddenly, Ian came back to life. He shut the black velvet box with a loud snap and shoved it back into his pocket. "I'm leaving now," he said. "I'm driving back to Annapolis. Oh, and here." He reached into his travel bag and took out two small packages wrapped in bright red and green paper. "I brought these for Sophia and Marco. They might as well have them."

Emma took the packages without meeting his eye. "Thanks," she said.

"You won't be bothered by me again. Good night, Emma."

Emma stood very still as Ian picked up his bag and without another word opened the door and left the room. She heard his feet thundering down the stairs and then the front door slam.

Only then did she leave her old room, holding the two brightly wrapped packages against her chest, and join her family, all of whom but for Sophia and Marco were gathered in the living room, expressions full of expectation and concern.

"Are you all right?" Andie asked, putting a hand gently on her shoulder.

Emma laughed a bit wildly. "I will be. He proposed. I told him again that I wanted nothing to do with him and he proposed."

"He actually asked you to marry him?" Rumi asked, eyes wide.

"With a ring, and a pretty nice one at that."

"Poor man," Andie murmured. "Poor deluded man."

"I'm finished feeling sorry for him, Andie," Emma said firmly. "It was a scene I could have done without. I just hope he gets some help in moving on."

"I should have thrown him out when he first showed up!" Daniel said.

"He looked so angry when he left," Rumi said, folding her arms across her chest. "I'm glad he's gone. There would be too much negative energy if he spent even one more minute in this house."

"What are those?" Anna Maria asked, pointing to the packages Emma still held.

"Oh." Emma had almost forgotten that she was holding them. "Presents from Ian for the kids. I guess I should put them under the tree."

Andie took the packages from her sister. "I'll do it," she said.

"Thanks, Andie," Emma said as she gladly relinquished the presents.

"I hope he's going right back to Annapolis," Daniel said, still frowning with concern. "I don't like the idea of him hanging around Oliver's Well."

"He said he's driving back tonight," Emma told him. "I'm sure we won't be troubled by him again." And then she stifled a yawn. "Gosh, suddenly I feel utterly exhausted. That scene upstairs—this whole day!—really took it out of me." *The fear,* Emma thought. *The fear and the frustration are what exhausted me.*

"Don't forget a seven-course meal!" Anna Maria added. "That could make anyone tired."

"Eight courses," Emma corrected, putting a hand to her stomach. "You forgot about dessert. I had two servings of the gingerbread with Danny's whipped cream and a few of Andie's *pfeffernüsse.* Well,

good night, everyone. I'm toddling off to bed. And thanks for
being here as my support team."

"It's what family is about," Daniel said, "being there to support each other."

Emma knew just how much her brother meant those words.
To a chorus of "good night," Emma went upstairs to her parents'
bedroom and stripped off the clothes she had been wearing since
morning. All she wanted was to climb into her flannel nightgown,
slip under the covers, and wipe from her mind the bizarre en-
counter with Ian Hayes. Just as she was plugging her phone into
its charger for the night, there came a text from Morgan Shelby.

Emma felt a smile rise instantly to her lips. **Surviving the aunt,**
he wrote. **But stories to tell when I see you.**

And Emma wrote: **Can't wait to hear them when you're home.**

Home, she thought, turning out the light on the bedside table.
It could be a pretty amazing thing.

CHAPTER 76

At a little after eleven o'clock Andie looked up from the book she was reading—a new exploration of Mahayana Buddhism, from which Zen Buddhism, so popular in the Western world, had grown—to see her sister descending the stairs. "You okay?" she asked, putting the book onto the cushion next to her.

"I couldn't stay asleep," Emma explained. "Too much on my mind, I guess."

"Care to share?" Andie asked. She supposed that the confrontation with Ian was still preying on Emma.

Emma flopped into the armchair that had been their mother's. "Ian left his slippers here."

"Oh. And?"

"And nothing, I guess. Should I mail them back to him?"

"No. I'm sure Ian will be fine without them."

Emma suddenly looked sheepish. "Andie? You believe me when I say that my ending things with Ian had nothing at all to do with another man?"

"Of course I believe you."

"The thing is, now I think there just might be another man. Morgan Shelby. I have feelings for him. It's all very tentative at the moment. Honestly, I don't really know what he feels about me, if anything other than mere friendliness. Though he did kiss me the night we went to the theater to see *A Christmas Carol*. I'm sorry I didn't tell you that I was meeting him that evening. I've just been so . . . It was a sweet kiss. It was very nice."

Andie smiled. "I've always believed that true lovers have known each other from the very start, long before they finally meet."

"Like with Mom and Dad?" Emma said. "You mean they didn't actually meet on that city bus? They simply recognized each other across the aisle?" And then she laughed. "Maybe someday I'll be telling Danny's kids how I fell in love with the great love of my life when he came into the bakery for a corn muffin!"

"Now, that's what I call romance! Great things can grow from humble beginnings, Emma. You know, I'd begun to suspect something was up with you and Morgan," Andie admitted. "When we were at the Angry Squire with Maureen. The look on your face when his name was mentioned. And I stand by what I said then. He seems like a good man."

"I think he is, and Maureen says he's honorable. But, Andie, it's completely unlike me to fall for someone in a matter of days!"

"There's always a first time! And remember, you and Morgan might have known each other all along. It's yet to be seen. But a long distance relationship is never easy, you know."

"I know," Emma said, plucking at the belt on her robe.

Andie had the distinct feeling there was something her sister wasn't telling her, but it would wait. Emma would share all in good time; it was never wise to force a confidence. "Well," she said, "whatever happens with you two, I'm happy for you."

Emma smiled. "Thanks, Andie. You and Rumi seemed much more relaxed with each other this evening."

"Yes. Rumi and I have arrived at a good place. Bob was wonderful, of course, bringing us together at his house for dinner. As you said, being brave enough to force the moment to its crisis."

"I'm so glad things are on the mend. I think she's sensitive in the way that you are, Andie. I think she's very easily affected by other people's energies, if that's the right term."

"Though I've learned how to detach." Andie smiled. "Well, at least to some extent some of the time. Healthy detachment is a work always in progress."

"Maybe Rumi can learn more from you," Emma suggested.

"Maybe. You know, only a few days ago I was viewing this visit home as something to be endured and survived. But now I believe this visit is an occasion for celebration and rejoicing."

Emma smiled. "I'm so glad," she said. "Really."

Just then Caro Carlyle Reynolds's antique grandfather clock struck midnight, and both sisters jumped.

"That's something I *never* want to have in my house!" Andie said, putting her hand to her heart. "Sometimes I think it's worse than that old alarm clock!"

Emma lowered her voice to a mock whisper. "Don't tell Danny," she said, "but I tossed the alarm clock."

Andie laughed. "Your secret is safe with me. Merry Christmas, Emma."

"Merry Christmas, Andie."

And, Andie thought, *it did indeed feel like a truly merry Christmas.*

CHAPTER 77

Daniel was sitting next to Anna Maria on the couch, sipping his second cup of coffee. They'd had breakfast at home before coming to Honeysuckle Lane to open yet more gifts with his sisters. He had gotten each of them something special—the packages were sitting by his side—in spite of the fact that the siblings hadn't been in the habit of exchanging gifts in years.

Andie and Emma had been generous with his children and there was nothing unusual there. Emma had given Sophia that massive tome on clothing or costumes or something, and Sophia had been oohing and ahhing loudly since she opened the book. To Marco she had given that video camera he'd been going on about, and already he had announced plans to begin filming as soon as they got home.

And Andie's gifts were also a hit. To Sophia she had given a length of fabric in a paisley print of bright blues and purples. "Your mom told me you'd been learning to sew, and I thought, why not some fabric?" she'd told her niece. "There's enough there for you to really play around with. Plenty to make a skirt or a dress or just something funky."

Sophia had thanked her aunt with a big hug. "Maybe," she'd said, "I'll get good enough and make something for you!"

To Marco Andie had gifted another thing he'd specifically

asked for—a thesaurus. "Words are cool," he'd told his father, after thanking his aunt. "There's so many of them, and people are inventing new ones all the time!"

Maybe he'll be a writer after all, Daniel thought.

"This package says it's from Ian." Marco, kneeling by the tree, looked to his father. "Why did he just come for dinner and not stay over?" he asked.

Sophia frowned at her brother. "That's Aunt Emma's personal business, Marco."

Daniel hid a smile. Sophia enjoyed lording her exalted status as a twelve-year-old—"almost a teenager"—over her ten-year-old brother. But Marco could hold his own. He frowned back at his sister and then turned to Andie.

"You know, Aunt Andie," he said, "I don't believe in Santa Claus anymore."

"Really?"

"Yeah. I was such a kid last year, but now I know better. Santa Claus is just Mom and Dad."

Andie sighed. "I kind of wish I still believed in Santa Claus. I think it's a good thing to embrace a little magic."

Marco shrugged and turned his attention back to tearing the paper off his package. Ian had done nicely, Daniel saw. To Marco he had given a new light for his bike (lights were always getting lost), and for Sophia, he had chosen a selection of the wide hair bands she loved to wear.

"It was nice of Ian to bring gifts for the children," Anna Maria said diplomatically.

"If a bit manipulative," Emma, sitting on the floor with her back against the couch, added softly. Andie, sitting cross-legged not far from Emma, grunted.

Daniel smiled. "You think? But here," he said, handing each of his sisters a wrapped package about the size of a shoe box. "This is from me. Merry Christmas."

"But, Danny," Emma said, "we haven't given each other Christmas gifts in years. I have nothing for you."

"Giving gifts isn't about accounting. I'm not asking for anything in return." *Except gratitude,* he thought, smiling at his wife. *And now I know without a doubt that I have my sisters' gratitude and their respect.*

Emma and Andie each opened their packages to find a beautiful wooden box decorated with inlay.

"This is gorgeous, Danny!" Emma exclaimed.

"Truly lovely," Andie added. "Thank you."

"I'm glad you like them. They were made by a craftsman in Somerstown," Daniel explained. "I met him at one of the parties we catered last year. He shows his work at the Foss Gallery and at a gallery in Lawrenceville as well." What Daniel didn't tell his sisters was that he had decided only the day before to give them each a gift this year. He had managed to catch Harry Peters just moments before he was leaving his studio for the holiday; as luck would have it, Harry had a few finished pieces ready at hand. "Emma," Daniel went on, "your box is made of mahogany and the inlay is done in ash. Andie, yours is walnut and the inlay is maple. Look inside. There's a small treasure for each of you."

Emma opened the lid of her box first and extracted a sheet of paper. "It's a copy of Dad's love note to Mom," she said in surprise. "The one we found in the photo album."

"Thank you, Danny," Andie said, smiling at her copy. "This is a treasure indeed."

Daniel cleared his throat. "It's like Emma said. They were our parents, not just mine. I've put the original back where Emma found it, just so you know."

While his sisters admired and compared their presents, Daniel thought about the one great *big* treasure his wife had presented him with just that morning. He was dying to share his good fortune with his family, but he had promised Anna Maria they would wait until dinner to make their happy announcement. Still, he was afraid the smile that kept coming to his face would give him away. And they had made the possible mistake of already telling Sophia and Marco. If they all could keep the secret until dinner it would be a miracle.

"Hey." Marco suddenly got to his feet and pointed to the fire-place. "Where's the picture of Grandma and Grandpa?"

Daniel felt his face flush. Neither of his sisters nor his wife offered an explanation, but studiously kept their eyes from him. "It was dirty," Daniel blurted. "It's gone to be cleaned."

"When's it coming back?" Sophia asked.

"I don't know exactly," Daniel went on. "Soon?"

Marco snorted. "I hope it never comes back. That thing is weird."

And at once, Anna Maria, Emma, and Andie broke out in splut-terings of laughter. Daniel tried to control his own laughter, but it was a wasted effort. When he had recovered enough to speak, he said, "Okay, time to get ready to leave for church. Andie? Emma? Are you coming with us?" He would like it if his sisters came along, but he would not criticize them if they did not. Emma and Andie might not share his every opinion and belief, but they were his sisters and deserving of as much respect as he wanted and needed from them in return.

"Sure, I'll go," Emma said. "Just give me a moment to tidy myself up. I can't show up for Christmas services in sweatpants, even though it is the Unitarian Universalist Church!"

"Count me in." Andie got up from the floor, where she had been surrounded by crumpled wrapping paper. "Prayer never hurt anyone. And I think what I'm wearing is just fine. Harem pants are *universally* approved of, aren't they?"

Daniel laughed again. He had so much for which to be thank-ful this Christmas, including his sister's goofy attempt at a joke.

Bob and Rumi came over to the house midafternoon after hav-ing had breakfast with Bob's cousins in Smithstown. They came bearing several jars of homemade raspberry jam—"My friend Sally makes it," Rumi told them—and two loaves of blackberry-zucchini bread, baked just that morning by Bob himself. "Not that we need more food," he said, handing the loaves to Daniel. "But I just couldn't help myself."

At five o'clock the family gathered around the dining room table, once again set with one of Caro's fine linen tablecloths and napkins (carefully pressed by Emma that morning), silverware, plates, and glasses. Daniel had made a traditional roast goose dinner but, as he had the night before, he had also prepared a few interesting vegetarian dishes for Andie.

"I'm learning," he told her. "It's a challenge and a challenge is always good. Besides, so many people are vegetarians these days, I really should be offering creative meat-free options at parties."

"Smart idea," his sister told him. "I'll send you some of my favorite recipes to try out."

Bob asked if he could be the one to offer a toast, and the idea met with no opposition. "To our family," he said. "May we all continue to thrive in our love for one another."

Then the food was passed, and after the initial exclamations of praise and approval of the meal had died down, Daniel felt that the moment had come. So far the day had been one of quiet celebration. But as he cleared his throat and looked to his wife, sitting at his right hand, for her go ahead, he suspected things were about to get exciting.

"Anna Maria and I have an announcement to make," he said. And then he felt his throat choke with tears and he simply couldn't go on.

Anna Maria took his hand. "We're having another baby," she told the family.

"Marco and I knew already!" Sophia cried before anyone else could react. "I was so afraid I wouldn't be able to keep it a secret."

Anna Maria's announcement was met by a chorus of congratulations and exclamations of surprise and happiness. When it had died down, Marco shrugged. "I don't know what the big deal is. Babies are boring. They just sleep."

"Ha!" Sophia said. "That's what you know!"

Daniel, his voice recovered, said, "I wish Mom and Dad were with us to share this moment."

"One of my teachers says that when people die and go to heaven they can look down on you to see if you're okay." Marco turned to his father. "So Grandma and Grandpa are kind of here, Dad."

Andie smiled at her brother, and Emma asked, "When are you due?"

"Next August," Anna Maria told them. "A Virgo baby, just like Daniel."

"Oh, no," Emma said teasingly. "Another Virgo!"

"Do you want to know the sex of the baby?" Rumi asked.

Anna Maria shook her head. "Nope. I love a surprise!"

Marco frowned. "I hope it's a boy. I already *have* a sister."

"You'll love the baby no matter what sex he or she is," Daniel assured his son. But Marco only frowned more deeply.

The meal proceeded with much laughter and general good feeling. When the main course had been cleared, Anna Maria lowered the lights in the dining room, and to great applause Daniel brought the Christmas pudding to the table. It had been made months earlier and had been waiting in the pantry in a rum-soaked piece of muslin to make its grand entrance.

"You did Mom proud," Emma told him. "She said she never really felt like it was Christmas until the pudding came out!"

"And you even got Christmas crackers! How did you manage to find them?" Andie asked, holding up one of the tubes of paper wrapped in brightly colored foil. "Mom often had trouble tracking them down. I think one year she even ordered a box straight from England."

Daniel shrugged. "The Internet, where else?"

"I'll pull the other end of your cracker, Aunt Andie," Sophia said eagerly. Together Daniel's daughter and sister pulled on either twisted end of the tube, and with a loud *crack!* the cracker opened to reveal its paper crown, a bit of paper with a joke printed on it, and a trinket. "You got a little dog!" Sophia announced. "Now read your joke."

Andie cleared her throat. "Okay," she said, "here goes. 'Where does a general keep his armies?'"

Daniel and the others shrugged.

"Give up?" Andie laughed. "'In his sleevies!'"

There was a collective groan and then a series of small explosions as the others opened their crackers. Daniel sliced the pudding, and when everyone had been served, Marco suddenly stood up.

"I want to say something," he announced. "I want to say, 'God bless us, everyone!' It's what Tiny Tim says in the story."

Daniel felt himself beaming with pleasure and with pride. "I'll echo that sentiment," he said, raising his glass. "God bless us, everyone."

CHAPTER 78

As she was getting dressed the next morning, Emma found herself fondly remembering how her mother had insisted on referring to the day after Christmas as Boxing Day, as indeed it had been known in her family for generations, first in England and then the United States. The fact that Caro had no servants to whom she could give a Christmas box didn't matter. What did matter was that she make the day a special one for her family. Caro had inherited two very special family recipes, one for roasted chestnuts—not as easy to prepare, Emma knew, as one might think—and a rich baked fruitcake drizzled with marzipan icing. She served each of these delicacies at dinner on the twenty-sixth, and she also gave her husband and each of her children a small handcrafted gift—a bookmark made with pressed wildflowers, an embroidered handkerchief, a needlework eyeglass case, a brightly painted toy soldier ornament made with empty spools of thread.

"Thanks for all you did for us, Mom," Emma whispered to the room, looking once again at Caro's wedding portrait. "I'm sorry if I didn't say that often enough when you were here."

And now I'm *here*, Emma thought, *and for good this time.*

That very morning Emma had woken from a refreshing, almost dreamless sleep, with the decision finally and firmly made.

She would once and for all give up her life in Annapolis and move back to Oliver's Well. She would buy the house in which she had grown up and she would move steadily and bravely into the next phase of her life.

Emma felt a huge sense of freedom with having made the decision. At moments since getting out of bed she had felt almost giddy with excitement. She looked over to her mother's vanity table, on which sat the lovely wooden box Daniel had given her for Christmas. She would keep the key to her new home in that box, she thought, along with other small treasures, those she already possessed and those that might be to come.

Finally dressed for the day in a pair of gray slacks and a pale blue sweater, Emma headed downstairs to join her family. She found Andie, Daniel, and Anna Maria at the kitchen table. Bob and Rumi, she knew, had taken Sophia and Marco to an indoor ice-skating rink in Smithstown.

"Coffee?" Anna Maria gestured at the full press pot. "It's our second round."

Emma gratefully poured herself a cup and sat. Even after what had seemed like an endless meal the night before, she felt her stomach growl with hunger. But before she indulged in breakfast, there was something she needed to share with her family.

"Everyone?" she began, looking from Daniel to Andie and then to Anna Maria. "I've come to a big decision. I'd like to buy Danny and Andie out of their shares of this house. I've decided to move back to Oliver's Well."

Andie only smiled; Emma suspected her sister had already intuited her intentions. Daniel looked from his wife to his two sisters in turn. "I'm stunned," he said. "Absolutely floored."

"I think it sounds wonderful," Anna Maria said. "But . . . are you sure this is what you want?"

Emma nodded. "I'm sure. This decision hasn't come out of the blue, though I know it must look that way."

"Wait a minute. Is that why you were dragging your feet about choosing a real estate agent and getting the house on the market?" Daniel asked, a smile dawning on his face.

"Yeah," Emma admitted. "Sorry. I just wasn't ready to say anything. I'll have an official offer to you and Andie this week and get started on lining up the financing. Assuming neither of you has any objections to my buying the place."

"Of course not!" Daniel said, smiling broadly. "I think it's fantastic."

"Me, too," Andie said. "Really, Emma."

"I still think we should go ahead with the general auction of the contents of the house," Emma said. "That is, after we each choose a few things we want for our own, which I think we all pretty much agreed to do. And I want to bring in my own furnishings, maybe do a few renovations. I want to make the house my own, not keep it as a shrine to Mom and Dad."

Anna Maria nodded. "That sounds very smart."

"It's a big house for one person," Andie pointed out, eyes all innocent.

Emma shrugged. "Who says I'll always be living here alone?" To which her sister only smiled again.

"So, what are you going to do back here in Oliver's Well?" Daniel asked.

"The same as I do in Annapolis," Emma told him, "but on a smaller and more personal scale. Actually, I plan to ask Joe Herbert if he's interested in a partner. If he's not, well, I'll think on my feet."

"If you want to build a career in a small town like Oliver's Well," Daniel said, "especially for someone whose family is relatively well known, like we are, you'll need to get involved in the community. You can't just go to the office, see clients, and go home. If you do, you won't have many clients at all after a time. You'll have to get yourself on a committee or join the Chamber of Commerce or even the OWHA."

"I've thought about all that, Danny," Emma told her brother, "and I'll admit I'm a bit cowed by the challenges I'm facing. But I've never been the sort to back away from a challenge. Almost everything about my life will change. But it's what I want. A new direction."

"You know you won't make the sort of money in Oliver's Well you're making in Annapolis."

Emma laughed. "Are you trying to get me to change my mind, Danny?"

"No," he said hastily. "Honestly, I'm really glad you'll be around. I've missed you. I know the kids will be thrilled to have you here. We all will."

"And just think, I'll be here to watch the new baby for you when you need a night out."

"A night out?" Anna Maria laughed. "What's that?"

Andie cleared her throat. "Could we get back to the contents of the house for a moment? If it's okay with everyone I'd like to pass to Rumi my privilege of choosing a few items from the estate before it goes to auction. She'll be setting up on her own before long, and it costs money to furnish a home, even with just the basics. Besides, I really don't need anything. Well, other than my family. Well, okay, one more thing. I really would like to have Mom's Lenox tea set, the Buchanan. It brings back such good memories of when I was little, when life was so simple and happy."

"Of course, Andie," Daniel said, looking to Emma for affirmation. "I'm so happy you feel a strong attachment to something of Mom's."

"I know you'll give it a good home," Emma said. Then she turned to her brother. "And now for a really important topic. Are there going to be roasted chestnuts, Danny?"

"And Caro's famous Boxing Day cake?" Andie added.

"Would I ever let my family down?" Daniel asked, eyes wide.

"No," Emma said roundly. "You wouldn't."

That afternoon Morgan sent Emma a text letting her know that he was back in town. They arranged to meet at the Angry Squire for a late lunch.

Emma arrived before Morgan and was able to procure "their" table in the bar. And while she couldn't wait to tell him the news about her moving back to Oliver's Well, she also felt some trepidation. What if he greeted her news with a distinct lack of enthu-siasm? What if he thought that she was coming home for him, that she was rushing their relationship to a place he might not want it to go? That would be a disaster. Morgan Shelby might be a serious attraction to life in Oliver's Well, but she wanted him to know that she had made the decision for herself and by herself. That was essential.

But the moment Emma saw him walk into the room her wor-ries evaporated. Whatever his reaction to her news would be, there was one thing she was sure it *wouldn't* be—and that was negative.

"So, how was Aunt Agatha?" she asked with a smile as Morgan slipped into his seat.

"Aunt Agatha-like. Stern. Foreboding. And the cat was worse."

"And your parents?"

"Good, thank you. They're very pleasant people, my parents. And my grandmother was only mildly curmudgeonly. How was your Christmas?"

Emma considered for a moment. "Eventful," she said, "but in the end quite nice. My brother and his wife announced they're having another baby. And I've probably gained about six pounds, but it was worth it. Daniel's food is amazing."

Morgan laughed. "First, congratulations on the new member of the family. And I wish I could say the same about the food back home. No one in my family has ever been known as a good cook. In fact, I'm not sure anyone in the Shelby family has ever been introduced to salt. Except for me, but then again, I'm the family oddball. I'm the only one who's ever left the state of Maryland to make a life elsewhere."

Before Emma could reflect on that bit of information, their waiter came to the table. Morgan ordered a bowl of the Angry Squire's famous chicken soup and Emma ordered a salad. Once the waiter had gone off, Emma realized that she couldn't wait an-other moment to speak. "I have some big news to share," she said.

Morgan folded his hands on the table. "I'm all ears."

"I've decided to move back to Oliver's Well. I'm buying my brother and sister out of our parents' house. I've been thinking about it for some time. . . ."

Morgan's instant smile, the way his eyes lit up, made Emma feel weak at the knees, and very, very happy. "That's fantastic news!" he said, reaching for her hand. "Wow." With his free hand Morgan raised his glass. "The new year is looking brighter already."

Emma touched her glass to his. Morgan still held her hand, and she felt so happy right then she was afraid she would begin to cry.

"You said you've been thinking about this move for some time," Morgan went on. "Tell me."

Their waiter returned with their meals, and though Morgan was forced to let go of her hand, Emma still felt the warmth of his touch.

Her lunch ignored, Emma told him about her father's long ago offer of a partnership, of her rejection of his offer, and of her mother's anger. "She thought," she said, "that I was being ungrateful." She told him about her early determination to build a life of her own on her own, away from her home—"like you did," she added. "I don't regret leaving Oliver's Well all those years ago," she said finally. "I know I disappointed my parents and I'm sorry for that. But now . . . it's time to come home."

"Why now?" Morgan asked. "Is it just a gut feeling that's telling you the time is right?"

"More than that," Emma said, finally picking at her salad. "I don't know if I can explain it aloud so that it makes sense but . . . But it's as if now that my parents are gone, Oliver's Well is available to me again. The question is, why was it necessary for me to wait until they were gone before I could come home? Why was it that a healthy detachment from my parents' expectations could only come about after their deaths? Does that make me a monster? Was I in some way waiting for them to die?" Emma shook her head. "What an awful thought."

"I'm sure you weren't waiting for them to die, Emma," Morgan said, his voice low but strong.

Emma sighed. "No, of course I wasn't. Still, it's only since my mother passed last year that I started to realize there was something lacking in my life, something not right. You know, Andie's always quoting the poet Rumi, so I don't see why I shouldn't, too. 'There is a void in your soul, ready to be filled. You feel it, don't you?' I guess I began to feel the void." Silently, Emma added, "And there is a candle in my heart, ready to be kindled."

"Thank you for telling me all this, Emma," Morgan said solemnly. "I'm honored by your trust."

Emma smiled. She felt relieved, as if she had finally been able to put down a heavy burden she had been carrying for a very long time. There was just one more bit of her story to be told. "Before you hear it on the grapevine," she said, "my ex showed up at the house on Christmas Eve. It seems he didn't quite believe me when I ended our relationship."

Morgan frowned. "That must have been—unpleasant."

"It was seriously unpleasant," Emma admitted. "That's why I said that Christmas on Honeysuckle Lane was eventful. But he finally got the message. I don't think he'll be a bother anymore. Especially not once I've moved back to Oliver's Well."

Emma paid their check this time and together they left the restaurant. The moment they reached the sidewalk, Morgan put his hands on her shoulders and drew her toward him for a kiss. This time, he kissed her with more intensity, an intensity that Emma returned. It was a bold move, a sign of affection offered in full view of anyone who might be passing.

"I hope that was all right to do," Morgan said when he had pulled away, but only after delicately tracing the line of her cheek with his finger. "I couldn't help myself."

"Nor could I," Emma told him truthfully.

Morgan smiled. "I've got to get back to the gallery. There's an online auction in about a half hour—yes, even on the day after Christmas we antique types are hunting for treasures—and I want to bid on a pair of late eighteenth-century candlesticks."

"To sell at the gallery?" Emma asked.

"Nope. Just for me!"

"Good luck," Emma told him.

"Emma," Morgan said, his tone quite serious. "When will I see you again?"

"Soon," she said. "Very soon. That's a promise."

She watched him go—at one point he turned and waved—and then, when Morgan had gone into the gallery, she sent a text to Maureen. **Say hi to your new neighbor. Me.**

Her phone rang a moment later. It was Maureen. "Oh, my God," she cried. "I can't believe it. I'm so happy! But what if you come back to Oliver's Well and realize it's not what you want after all? Sorry. You know me, Ms. Practical."

"Then I figure out where it is I should be," Emma told her, "and move on. But I don't think that will happen. I really don't. I believe that coming home at this point in my life is what I'm meant to do. I feel as if . . ." Emma thought of Morgan. "I feel," she said, "as if I'm welcomed here. As if I've been expected."

"Good. Want to meet for a celebratory drink?"

"Yes," Emma said, "but after I see Joe Herbert. I'll meet you at the Angry Squire in about half an hour." *At this rate,* Emma thought, *I really will be getting a nameplate on a chair!*

Emma walked the few blocks to Joe Herbert's office. She assumed he would be at his desk, if he really was as busy as he'd told her he was. And he *was* there, red bow tie printed with sprigs of holly firmly in place.

"Emma," he said, rising from his chair to shake her hand. "What brings you in today?"

So she told him that she was relocating permanently to Oliver's Well and she wondered—"no pressure," she assured him—if he might be interested in taking on a partner. Joe's grin was answer enough, but she was glad when he said, "You've been reading my mind, Emma Reynolds. I've been considering the idea quite seriously."

"I'd love to explore the possibility then, Joe," Emma told him.

Then she smiled. "I wonder what Dad would think if he knew I was coming back. That you and I might be working together."

"I think," Joe said, "that he'd be thrilled."

Emma got up from the guest chair and put out her hand. Joe shook it warmly. When she left his office—with the promise of a more formal meeting in a few days' time—she turned back toward the Angry Squire. The restaurant was busier now than it had been when she'd had lunch with Morgan, and as she passed into the bar she heard a pleasant voice call out to her, "Hi, neighbor." Word certainly traveled fast in Oliver's Well, Emma thought as she smiled and waved to the woman she recognized from the Christmas concert a few days earlier and, she realized, also from behind the counter at the Pink Rose Café.

Maureen was waiting at her favorite table, a bottle of champagne in an iced bucket. "To coming home," Maureen said as Emma joined her. She handed Emma a glass of the bubbly.

Emma clinked her glass against Maureen's. "To coming home," she said. "At long last."

EPILOGUE

It was the middle of October, just about two years since Caro Reynolds had passed, less than a year since her daughter Emma had bought the house at number 32 Honeysuckle Lane. So, so much had happened to Emma and her family in the past months, and in Emma's opinion, it was all for the best.

For one, her sister-in-law Anna Maria's third child, another healthy boy, had been born at six o'clock in the morning on August the twenty-fifth. Emma had given the baby an antique silver rattle she'd had engraved with the initials ACR—Andrew Clifford Reynolds. The baby would be called Andy for short, which, Emma thought, would probably cause confusion in later years whenever he and his aunt Andie were in the same room. But that mattered little.

Along with Emma's new nephew and new home, she could add her new job as a partner at Reynolds Herbert Accountants. Emma and Joe made a good team, as Emma had suspected they would, each contributing their own strengths to a firm that had won a sure place in Oliver's Well so many years earlier. And now, with a partner to carry half of the workload, Joe was able to be home by six o'clock each evening, something that made him very happy.

Another wonderful thing that had happened for Emma—the best, actually—was that she and Morgan Shelby had gotten engaged in the spring. Morgan had given Emma a Georgian era rose-cut diamond ring, so perfectly suited for her she had cried buckets when he presented it to her. Emma had found that she liked to receive gifts from Morgan. It was a totally new experience for her, enjoying the enjoyment it gave a loved one to spoil her. Especially, she thought, when everything the loved one gave her was so . . . perfect. So . . . *Emma*, like the complete DVD set of one of her all time favorite TV shows, *The Avengers*, and the pasta maker she had been secretly eyeing online. Andie was right about the danger of possessions owning the owner, but Emma didn't feel any particular worry about her own newfound delight in both giving and receiving.

"You look wonderful."

Emma turned to see Morgan in the doorway of what had once been her parents' bedroom, a room that was now theirs. "You don't look so bad yourself," she said, admiring his well-cut suit and his crisp white shirt. "I don't think we'll disgrace anyone at the dedication ceremony."

"I certainly hope not!" Morgan came into the bedroom and with a glance at the mirror, straightened his already perfectly straight tie.

At the start of the summer, Morgan had rented his apartment above the gallery to a young couple recently returned to Oliver's Well after four years at college and had moved in with Emma at 32 Honeysuckle Lane. When Morgan and Emma were married the following January, his name would go on the mortgage. Together they had stripped off old wallpaper and redecorated with their own belongings once the auction of the house's contents had gone through. They had changed the paint colors in every room but for Emma's childhood bedroom (she was sentimental about the sunny yellow walls), and with the help of a contractor they had extended the kitchen further into the backyard, still leaving plenty of lawn and flower beds. In only a few months time the house had come to feel truly theirs, and not, as Emma had sworn it would not be, a shrine to Cliff and Caro Reynolds.

"How are you enjoying the books Andie recommended?" Morgan asked, picking up a paperback from her bedside table and flipping through it slowly.

"I'm enjoying them very much," Emma said, putting an earring in place and looking at Morgan through the mirror. "Hafiz's writing is really beautiful."

Morgan smiled and returned the book to the table. "Why don't you quote me something?"

Emma turned away from the mirror. "Well, I haven't got any of the poetry by heart," she admitted, "but something I read just last night seems to have lodged in my brain. Here goes. 'When all your desires are distilled; you will cast just two votes: To love more, And be happy.'"

"Words of wisdom indeed." Morgan raised an eyebrow. "But I'm not sure I could love you more than I already do."

"Try," Emma teased.

"Gladly." In two strides he had enveloped her in his arms and kissed her.

"Mmmmm," Emma said after a moment. "This is very nice, but we'll be late if we don't hurry. You know how Danny can be about ceremonies!"

Morgan released her. "At least he can laugh at himself now."

"But I'm one of the godmothers," Emma pointed out. "I *can't* be late!"

"Are you nervous, Mom?" Rumi asked. "You keep checking your watch. You never care much about what time it is."

Andie laughed a bit. They were sitting side by side on chairs that had been placed in a circle in the main meeting room of the Unitarian Universalist Church—the room where the Reynolds siblings had lit candles in memory of their parents the Christmas before—waiting for Daniel and his family to arrive. Members of the Spinelli family, most notably, Anna Maria's parents and siblings, had arrived a bit earlier, and after greeting Andie and Rumi, had taken their own seats in the circle.

"As a matter of fact," Andie said, "yes. I am nervous. And yet, this is probably the most thoroughly receptive audience I've ever had to stand up in front of."

"Well, you've never been a godparent before. I mean, even though it's not the same as being, say, a Catholic type of godparent, it's still a big responsibility. I guess it's normal you'd feel a bit anxious."

Andie took her daughter's hand. She had been deeply touched when Daniel had asked her to stand up with Emma at little Andy's child dedication ceremony. She loved her younger nephew with a strength she hadn't felt when Daniel's other children had been born. She didn't question this attachment to the child; she simply acknowledged and respected it. And if it brought her back to Oliver's Well more often, her daughter's home, so much the better.

It had been an exciting year for mother and daughter. Early that summer Rumi had visited Andie's home in Woodville Junction. Andie had introduced her daughter to her friends and colleagues. They had "taken tea" using Caro's Lenox tea service and had shared meals they prepared together. They had enjoyed long walks and periods of meditation. They had shared memories of Cliff and Caro, new vegetarian recipes, and laughter. They had talked about everything under the sun, from the past to the present to the future, from the spiritual to the mundane.

At one point during Rumi's visit, Andie had given her Caro's wedding set. "You can do with it what you will," she told her daughter. "You can sell it and use the money to help pay back your student loans or to save up for a house of your own one day.

You can keep the rings in a safe deposit box at the bank and forget about them. Or you can wear the rings now. You don't have to wait until you marry."

"I think I will save them to wear when I marry someday," Rumi had replied. "I think Grandma would like that."

Rumi was still pursuing her studies in dental hygiene—as she pointed out, bills had to be paid somehow!—but with Andie's and Bob's encouragement she had also decided to study jewelry design at the GIA—the Gem Institute of America—at its New York City location, right in the heart of the Diamond District. "What if I can't cut it?" she had worried. "The GIA is the big time." Bob had replied that she would never know what she could achieve unless she tried. "Maybe I should just do the e-course and stay here in Oliver's Well," Rumi had suggested. To which Andie had replied that being in the company of teachers and other students, people who shared her growing passion for stones and creation, was bound to be infinitely more nourishing than sitting alone at home. In the end, Rumi had found the courage to make the commitment and as soon as she finished her dental studies she was off to the Big Apple.

The sound of a door opening caused Andie to look over her shoulder to see Emma, Morgan, and Bob entering. She waved and whispered to Rumi, "Have you met the woman your father is seeing?"

"Not yet. They've only been out a few times. I don't think Dad wants to bother introducing me to someone who might be gone before long."

"Probably not," Andie agreed. "But from what he's told me, she sounds very nice. I guess we'll just wait and hope for the best between them."

Emma, Morgan, and Bob greeted the Spinelli family, and then Bob slipped into the seat next to his daughter; Emma and Morgan sat to Bob's right. A moment later, Daniel and his family arrived, and a few minutes after that the dedication ceremony began.

After Reverend Fox had welcomed the Spinelli and the Reynolds families—"most especially, Andrew"—he spoke a few words about what it meant to belong to the community of those who shared and lived by the seven principles of the church. "Perhaps most important," he said, "is our first principle, that of the inherent worth and dignity of every person." And then he offered a blessing. After this, Daniel and Anna Maria expressed their hopes for their child's life, including that he learn to embrace the virtues of justice, equality, and compassion, and then everyone gathered promised to support and to nurture Andrew as he grew.

Finally, Andie was invited to offer a benediction from her beloved poet and prophet.

"You were born with potential.

You were born with goodness and trust. You were born with ideals and dreams.

You were born with greatness.

You were born with wings.

You are not meant for crawling, so don't.

You have wings.

Learn to use them and fly."

When she had finished reciting the lines she knew so well by heart, she glanced at the others gathered around the baby who had brought them all together. She noted their smiles and their tears. She noted the joy that shone on their faces. And in that moment she felt such bliss as she thought she had never felt before.

"It was a lovely ceremony, wasn't it, Daniel?"

Daniel smiled at his wife, who was holding their youngest child in her arms.

"It was," he said. "And thanks again for agreeing to our naming my sisters Andy's godparents."

Anna Maria smiled. "It was only fair, what with my siblings being godparents to Sophia and Marco. Oh, look!" she said. "There's Richard Armstrong. He promised he'd come by."

Anna Maria went off to welcome the most recent guest to the celebration at number 32 Honeysuckle Lane. The Herberts were already there, as was Maureen Kline and her beau Jim, the elder Klines, as well as various locals and members of Anna Maria's extended family. Reverend Fox and his partner had stopped by on their way to a family event of their own. The house was bursting with people and brimming with good feeling.

Daniel smiled at the sight of his sister and her fiancée sharing a brief hug. Emma and Morgan had insisted on making all the food for the party. "Just this once, Danny," Emma had said. "You need to take a break every now and again. And the day of your new baby's dedication ceremony is the perfect time!" If certain dishes weren't exactly as Daniel himself would have presented them—he would have served the duck sliders with chutney instead of blackberry jam—they were no less good for that.

No doubt about it, Daniel thought, stepping aside to let two of the young Spinelli cousins dash through to the kitchen, this was a real celebration. At this time the year before he had been in a very dark place. Now, life was so much brighter, and he credited his wife as well as his sisters for helping him to cast away the demons—the regrets and haunting memories of the past—and focus on what mattered most, the present and the future.

And that future could be anything Daniel chose it to be. Earlier that year he had been scouted by Le Petit Versailles in Lawrenceville. It was an honor, but especially with a third child on the way, he had been and still was determined to stay in catering. It was a challenging business—made a bit easier by the kitchen upgrade the sale of his parents' house has afforded—but it allowed a more flexible schedule than what could be found in restaurant work. And to be with his wife and children was the most important thing, hands down. That said, Daniel had taken on a few more private cooking students; the money was good, but more importantly, the work was becoming increasingly meaningful to him.

Daniel noted that the elder Fitzgibbons hadn't yet come by, though he was sure they would make an appearance at some point, if only to thank the Reynoldses yet again for the five-year loan of the George Bullock desk to the OWHA. At the end of the five years the Reynolds family would decide either to renew the loan or to bring the desk back to the house on Honeysuckle Lane. The plaque identifying the Regency piece thanked Caroline Carlyle Reynolds for her generosity; Daniel had come to see that the gift was a fitting tribute to his mother, after all. And if Mary Bernadette Fitzgibbon thought it odd that the offer of the desk had been once made, then retracted, then made again in an altered version, she was far too well bred to say anything.

Daniel looked around at the guests once again. His mother- and father-in-law were comfortably settled on the couch—Emma's couch—chatting with Jenna Herbert. His sister-in-law Gabriella was laughing with Emma. Richard Armstrong was deep in conversation with Daniel's brother-in-law Carlo, also the owner of a restaurant. Daniel decided it was the time for a toast.

"May I have everybody's attention!" he cried. The living room quickly quieted, and following Daniel's lead, the guests raised their glasses. "To Andrew Clifford Reynolds," he said, "and his very bright future!"

Before the guests could reply, Andy, in his mother's arms, let roar, just once, but it was enough to silence everyone in the room—for a moment. Emma flinched and Rumi put her hands to her ears. Over laughter and the clinking of glasses, Bob turned to Daniel. "He wanted to add his voice to his father's!" he said.

"My, gosh, that child has lungs!" Andie declared.

Anna Maria grinned at Daniel. "Just like his daddy."

"I'll take him for a while, Mom," Sophia offered.

"No, I want him," Marco protested. "You held him last time."

"Marco's turn," Daniel said with a smile. "There's plenty of baby to go around."

"He is adorably chubby," Rumi said. "I love chubby babies!"

Once Marco was settled in a chair with his little brother firmly in his arms, Daniel went over to the food table to grab another of Morgan's now famous steak tartar appetizers. Emma joined him there and took one of her own.

"So," Emma said, "I guess Marco doesn't think babies are boring anymore."

"He and Sophia never stop arguing over who's going to hold him or feed him or help with his bath." Daniel shook his head. "Would I be jinxing things to say I have the perfect family?"

"No," Emma told him, linking her arm in his. "You wouldn't."